INTRODUCING
KATIE MAGUIRE

KATIE MAGUIRE was one of seven sisters born to a police Inspector in Cork, but the only sister who decided to follow her father into An Garda Siochana.

With her bright green eyes and short red hair, she looks like an Irish pixie, but she is no soft touch. To the dismay of some of her male subordinates, she rose quickly through the ranks, gaining a reputation for catching Cork's killers, often at great personal cost.

Katie spent seven years in a turbulent marriage in which she bore, and lost, a son – an event that continues to haunt her. Despite facing turmoil at home and prejudice at work she is one of the most fearless detectives in Ireland.

THE KATIE MAGUIRE SERIES

GRAHAM MASTERTON

BURIED

First published in the UK in 2016 by Head of Zeus Ltd

9 7 5 3 1 2 4 6 8

A CIP catalogue record for this book is available
from the British Library

ISBN (HB) 9781784081379
ISBN (TPB) 9781784081386
ISBN (E) 9781784081362

Typeset by Ben Cracknell Studios, Norwich.

Printed and bound in Germany by GGP Media
GmbH, Pössneck

Head of Zeus Ltd
Clerkenwell House
45–47 Clerkenwell Green
London EC1R 0HT

WWW.HEADOFZEUS.COM

In memory of my friend Andrzej Kuryłowicz
10 April 1954 – 21 March 2014
You left us on the first day of Spring

'*Chan eil saoi air nach laigh leòn*'
Irish saying: Even a hero can be hurt

One

'Are you coming inside or not, you useless collop?' Declan demanded.

It was obvious, though, that Christy wasn't going to come any nearer. He stood on the front doorstep, his black and tan fur bedraggled by the rain, and Declan had never seen him look so apprehensive. His eyes were wide, and his nostrils were twitching, and every now and then he tilted his head sideways as if he were trying to peer inside the hallway and in through the living-room door, because he was sure that there was something frightening in there.

Colm called out, 'Declan, for feck's sake, will you stop discussing the weather with that mutt of yours and give me a hand with this fecking fireplace?'

'I'll tell you something, Christy, you're some jibber,' Declan told him. 'If you want to stay out there getting yourself soaked, that's your lookout. But if you die of pneumonia, don't come blaming me for it.'

He left Christy and went into the living room where Colm had knocked the brown-tiled fire surround loose from the wall and was now trying to lever it further away with a crowbar. The air in the tiny room was filled with dust and the floorboards were gritty underfoot so that the soles of his boots made a scrunching sound.

'Never known him act like that before,' said Declan, picking up a shovel and wedging it into the opposite side of the fireplace. 'It's almost like he's scared of something, do you know what I mean? Maybe there's a ghost in here, like.'

'That wouldn't fecking surprise me at all,' said Colm, violently wrenching the crowbar from side to side. 'The old feller who used to own this place, they discovered him dead down the bottom of the stairs, that's what that girl from Sherry Fitzgerald's told me. Tripped over his cat, so she reckoned. Broke his neck like a fecking stick of celery and they didn't find him for a month.'

Colm had reckoned that it would take them at least two weeks to renovate the whole house. It was a small two-bedroom property in Millstream Row, Blarney, in a terrace of eleven cottages that had been built sometime in the 1860s to house woollen workers from Mahony's mill.

Although the previous owners had lived in it since 1952, they had decorated it only once during the whole of their years there, with dingy brown floral wallpaper. In 1964 they had built a single-storey lean-to extension in the backyard to accommodate a bath and a twin-tub washing machine, but that had been their only concession to modernization.

Now that the widowed owner had died, the house had been sold to a young professional couple for 123,000 euros as their starter home.

Together, grunting like two prize hogs being prodded to market, Declan and Colm manhandled the fire surround out of the house and into the rain. Christy was still sitting there, soaking wet, and when he stepped back to allow them to shuffle out of the front door he shook himself furiously.

'You're a lunatic, do you know that?' said Declan, after he and Colm had heaved the fire surround, with a deafening crash, into the empty skip that was parked in the narrow road outside. 'Why don't you go in and get yourself dry?'

He bent down and took hold of Christy's collar, but when he tried to drag him into the house Christy stiffened his legs and growled. When Declan pulled harder he scrabbled his claws against the wet pavement and barked, refusing to step over the threshold.

'Sure look at him,' grinned Colm. 'I bet you're right about a ghost. How about it, Christy? Can you see a ghost in there, boy? *Woooooo*!'

'Maybe there's just a smell he doesn't like, dead rat or something,' said Declan. 'Most people don't know it, but your Kerry beagle has an even more sensitive nose than a bloodhound.'

'Yeah, but come on, Dec. How much of him is Kerry beagle and how much is some stray mongrel that gave his mother the lad when her owner wasn't looking?'

'It's all very well you skittin', boy,' Declan retorted. 'This feller can smell if somebody's farted in Limerick, I swear to God. He can smell tripe boiling even before you've lit the gas.'

He yanked at Christy's collar one more time, but Christy snarled and bared his teeth, and Declan gave up. 'Okay, have it your way. You need a bath any road.'

Declan and Colm went back into the house. Now they needed to pull up all the floorboards in the living room because the new owners were going to replace them with hand-scraped Victorian oak.

Colm lit a Johnnie Blue and took three deep drags before pinching it out and tucking the butt behind his ear. Then he picked up his crowbar and used it to jemmy the skirting board away from the wall underneath the window. While he lifted the skirting board over his shoulder and toted it outside to the skip, Declan bent over and gripped the exposed end of the central floorboard, tugging at it again and again until he dislodged the nails out of the joists underneath. He tilted it up and dropped it to one side with a clatter.

Declan was used to finding builder's rubble underneath the floorboards of these old houses, as well as the skeletons of rats and mice. Once he had discovered a black tin box containing thirty-five pounds in Saorstát, the banknotes issued by the Irish Free State, a tarnished harmonica, and a Valentine's card for 'my own dearest Muirgheal'.

In this house, however, it looked as if several bundles of old clothing had been stuffed between the joists – a man's suit, a woman's maroon dress, a girl's yellow pinafore, and a baby's pink nightgown. They were all faded until they were almost colourless and covered thickly in fine grey dust, so it was anybody's guess how long they had been hidden there.

Declan pulled up another floorboard, and then another, the nails screeching in protest, and he was just about to start pulling up a third when he saw that a hand was protruding from the cuff of the man's green coat.

He stared at it for a long time, feeling as if his scalp was shrinking. The hand looked papery and dry, and it was almost completely flat, but he could tell that it was a real human hand all right. Some of the knuckle bones had broken through the desiccated skin and it still had all of its fingernails, even though they had turned amber with age.

He knelt down to examine it more closely, but he didn't have the nerve to touch it. Instead, he reached out and gently squeezed the sleeve from which it was protruding. There was no question about it: there were two stick-like arm bones inside it.

'Lord lantern of Jesus,' he whispered.

He was breathing hard through his nostrils now and his heart was thumping. He let go of the sleeve and cautiously patted the back of the coat, as if he were frisking it. Underneath the fabric he could feel the hard curved bones of a ribcage.

He sat back on his heels. *Holy Mary, Mother of God, if there's a mummified feller inside of this coat, what's inside of the woman's dress? And the children's clothes, too?*

Still kneeling, he shuffled himself sideways to the space between the next two joists where the woman's maroon dress was lying crumpled up, with buttons all down the back. He hesitated for a moment, because it didn't seem right to be touching a woman without her consent, even if she was long dead. Then he reached out and gently pressed against the bodice. Beneath the coarse dyed linen he could again feel ribs, although these ribs were looser, as if they had become detached from the spine.

These weren't bundles of old clothes at all, these were bodies. Years and years ago somebody must have laid them face-down beneath the floor and then nailed the boards down over them. Declan still hadn't pulled up enough boards to be able to see their shoulders or their heads, but it looked to him as if a

4

small family had been hidden there – father, mother, daughter and baby.

He stood up, wiping his hands on his black denim jacket. As he did so, Colm came back from outside, relighting his cigarette.

'Jesus, it's lashing,' he said, his head half hidden in smoke. Then he glanced down at the gap in the floorboards and frowned. 'What the feck's all them old clothes doing down there?'

'They're not just old clothes, boy, they're bodies,' said Declan. 'Man and a woman and their two wains, too, by the looks of it.'

'You're codding,' said Colm, but Declan pointed to the man's dried-out hand. Colm leaned forward and squinted at it short-sightedly, and then he said, 'Feck.'

'I'd say they was probably murdered,' said Declan.

Colm stepped over the gap and crouched down to see if he could make out what the bodies' heads looked like. 'You don't know that for certain,' he said. 'They could have died of the flu or something. People used to die like flies in them days, of all sorts. My old man's youngest sister died of the chickenpox when she was only three years old.'

He stood up straight again and nodded at the bodies. 'Maybe their relatives couldn't afford a funeral.'

'Oh go 'way. Even if you can't afford a funeral you don't bury your nearest and dearest face-downwards underneath the fecking floorboards.'

'I don't know. My Uncle Patrick was buried lying on his left side. That was the way he specified it in his will. Serious. He said that when my Auntie Saoirse was buried next to him he wanted to be looking at her.'

'What, he had X-ray vision did he?' asked Declan. 'He could see through coffins?'

'Don't be soft – he was dead, wasn't he?' said Colm. 'He was just being romantic, do you know what I mean, like?'

'Romantic? Stone-hatchet mad, more like. Anyway, give me a hand to take up the rest of these floorboards.'

Between them, Declan and Colm lifted up all of the floorboards in the living room and carried them outside to the skip. When they had finished they stood and looked in silence at the four bodies lying between the joists. It had stopped raining outside and a silvery sun had appeared behind the clouds, so that the living room was filled with colourless light like an over-exposed photograph.

The man was lying furthest away from the window, with his left arm by his side. His right arm was crooked up, with his forehead resting on it. His hair was thick with dust but it was still brown and curly. The woman had long black hair, very straight, fastened with a simple brown horn slide. The little girl had brown curly hair, too, tied with ribbons into bunches. The baby had a single dark tuft, like a leprechaun.

'Ah, the pity of it,' said Declan.

With a succession of hideous screeches, they prised up the last two floorboards. Underneath they discovered that the space between the joists was crammed with a tangle of thick grey hairs, which at first looked as if it could have been a coat or a shaggy blanket of some kind. Colm took his shovel and prodded at it, and then tried to pick it up. As he lifted it up, however, the blanket tore softly apart and one half of it dropped with a dull thump back into the floor space. Colm immediately dropped the other half, too, because now they could see that what they had uncovered was not a coat or a blanket but the dried-up bodies of two young Glen terriers.

'The family pets, I'll bet you,' said Declan. 'Whoever did this, Jesus, they didn't leave nothing alive, did they? Surprised there's no fecking goldfish down here.'

Because the adults' hair was so thick and so dusty it was not immediately obvious what had happened to them, but Declan and Colm could tell from the baby and the little girl how this family had died. They had all been shot once in the back of the head, including the puppies.

Declan crossed himself. 'You'd best ring the guards,' he told Colm.

Colm nodded and took his mobile phone out of his shirt pocket. Both of them had been deeply sobered by what they had discovered.

They could have been sleeping, this dust-covered family, like characters in a fairy tale. Declan was surprised that he wasn't frightened or horrified by them, only saddened. He almost felt as if he had known them, despite the probability that they had been nailed down under the floorboards long before he was born. They didn't smell – not as far as he could tell, anyway – although Christy must have picked up the scent of human decay, even if it was decades old, and that was why he had refused to come inside. Either that, or he was psychic and Colm had been right about a ghost. Or *ghosts*, plural.

Colm had got through to 112. 'That's right,' he was saying. 'Millstream Row, Blarney. You have it, just past the factory. You'll find it easy, there's one of O'Brien's green midi skips directly outside. No, we won't touch nothing. No. Well, if they are, they must be about a hundred and ten years old by now, so I don't reckon they will be. No. Thanks a million.'

Once he had finished his call they went outside. Colm took out his pack of Johnnie Blues and handed one to Declan. They lit up and stood beside the skip, smoking.

'Did the guards tell you how long they'd be?' asked Declan.

'Fifteen minutes at least. The Garda station on The Square isn't manned at the moment.'

'What was that you was saying to them about somebody being a hundred and ten years old?'

'The feller on the switchboard asked me if there was any chance that the person who hid the bodies could still be lurking around, like. You know, in case you and me was in any kind of danger because we'd discovered what he'd done.'

'Holy St Joseph, and they say that criminals are thick.'

'No, fair play to him, I hadn't told him how old the bodies were, like. Well, we don't *know* how old they are, do we? All I told him was, we'd found some people who looked like they'd been shot.'

'Then you're three times thicker than he was. These people must have been shot practically before guns were invented.'

Normally, the two of them would have carried on bantering, but now they lapsed into silence, smoking and stamping their feet to keep warm. Although he was shivering, Christy stayed by the open front door, still looking inside with his head tilted inquisitively, almost as if he was expecting to hear somebody calling out to him.

After a few minutes, a white Garda patrol car came speeding round the curve in front of the woollen mills, its blue lights flashing. It was followed closely by a second patrol car, and then an unmarked blue Focus. There was a chorus of slamming doors.

'You realize we'll be in all the papers,' said Declan, as the uniformed gardaí came towards them.

'So long as they don't print my fecking address,' Colm told him. 'I don't want that Big-Arsed Blathnaid coming after me for child support.'

Two

Detectives Aislin O'Connell and Gerry Barry had been sitting at their stall in Mother Jones Flea Market since it had opened and so far they had made 67 euros from selling two mismatched table lamps, three party dresses and a pink lace-up corset, as well as a stack of old copies of *Ireland's Own*.

It was 3.15 in the afternoon now, but there was still no sign of Denny Quinn, the young suspect they were waiting for. Detective O'Connell had found the time to paint her nails turquoise and Detective Barry had stepped outside five times on to York Street for a smoke, and they were both beginning to think that their informant had either been mistaken or else had been stringing them along. They had been given false tip-offs with increasing frequency lately, almost as if somebody was deliberately trying to waste their time.

A Garda patrol car with two uniformed officers was parked further up the steep slope of York Street, just out of sight in the cul-de-sac of Little William Street, and Detective Barry had been keeping in touch with them via an earpiece and r/t microphone. They had started by regularly keeping in contact with each other, but as the day wore on almost all he heard from them was yawning and complaining that they were busting for a piss.

Detective Barry checked his watch and said, 'I feel like a right gom sitting here. I'll bet money your man never shows.'

He looked almost too young to be a detective, with an upswept quiff of blondish hair like Tintin and a button of a nose. Not that Detective O'Connell looked much older – she was dark-haired, petite but plump, with a pretty, heart-shaped face and lips that could have been the bright red satin bow on a birthday present.

But their appearance was the reason why Detective Super-intendent Maguire had picked them for this stake-out. They were supposed to look like typical stallholders at Mother Jones indoor market – youthful and slightly hippy-ish – so that they could watch their target without arousing suspicion that they were gardaí and then approach without him feeling immediately threatened. That was, if he ever put in an appearance.

Detective O'Connell spread out her fingers to admire her nails. 'Maybe the shipment never arrived,' she suggested. 'Or maybe somebody else stroked them.'

'Sure, well, that's always a possibility,' said Detective Barry. 'I know we told the customs to turn a blind eye, but if Billy Duffy knew the fags were coming, and *when*, don't tell me that a whole crowd of other skangers didn't know as well. Maybe Óglaigh na hÉireann got their hands on them before Quilty could pick them up. Or maybe they straight out robbed him.'

'Go away, they'd have to be mental to do that,' said Detective O'Connell. 'Cross Bobby Quilty, Jesus! You might as well say, "Excuse me, boy, would you mind putting a bullet between me eyes?"'

'I don't know. That Brendan Ó Marcaigh, I don't think he's freaked by nothing or nobody. A pit bull went after him once and he got hold of its tail and bashed its brains out on a lamp post.'

'Charming.'

They waited another half-hour. The Flea Market began to fill up with even more customers, wandering in between its yellow-, pink-, green- and blue-painted iron pillars and browsing around the stalls. Detective Barry raised one eyebrow at Detective O'Connell, but he didn't have to say anything because it was clear to both of them that although these new customers were picking up vases and dolls and old Wolfe Tones LPs and making a show of examining them, none of them was actually making a purchase.

Just a few seconds after 4 o'clock a voice in Detective Barry's earpiece said, 'Quinn's arrived. He's just been dropped off outside.'

A few seconds later Denny Quinn entered the Flea Market from the street, carrying two black vinyl rubbish bags, both of them bulging. He was skinny as a rail and pasty-faced, with a spattering of scarlet acne spots across his forehead. Since his last police photograph was taken his gingery hair had been shaved up the sides to give him a cockatoo crest, and he was sporting gold stud earrings in both of his ears as well as several gold chains and a heavy gold identity bracelet. He was wearing a red Cork GAA T-shirt, sagging grey tracksuit bottoms, and white Nike tackies.

'Enter the schwaa,' said Detective Barry.

'At last,' said Detective O'Connell. 'Billy Duffy might have told us what time he was coming. He must have *known*, like. All of these people here do. Eejit.'

'Oh, come on, Billy Duffy can't think and speak simultaneous, you know that.'

Without hesitation, Denny weaved his way between the pillars to the back of the market where there was a vacant alcove with a plywood table and chair. He dropped his black bags on the floor, pushed them under the table with his foot, and then sat down, wiping his nose with the back of his hand.

Almost at once, the six or seven browsing customers began to gravitate towards him. They were all different types: a middle-aged woman with jet-black dyed hair and a tight green satin top; a thirtyish man with a brown beard wearing a grey Marks & Spencer's business suit; an older man with fraying white hair and thick-rimmed glasses and a purple nose; and a girl who couldn't have been much more than school age, with long brunette hair, black eye make-up and tight black leggings. There was also a woman still wearing her blue Dunne's Stores overall, and a thick-set man with a paint-spotted denim jacket and no front teeth who looked like a Polish builder.

The middle-aged woman said something to Denny and then took out her purse and handed him fifty euros in folded notes. He leaned back to stuff the money into his tracksuit pocket before he reached into one of the black bags and lifted out two yellow bricks of two hundred cigarettes. As he passed the cartons across the table, Detective O'Connell had her iPhone held up high in front of her, frowning and prodding at it as if she were texting, although she was actually recording the transaction on video.

The girl with the black eye make-up paid Denny twenty-five euros – one crumpled ten-euro note and the rest in assorted loose change. He gave her one yellow carton which she pushed into a duffel bag and hurried out of the Flea Market with it slung over her shoulder.

Detective Barry leaned close to Detective O'Connell. 'One more sale should do it,' he said, speaking very quietly and looking in the opposite direction as he did so, so that Denny wouldn't guess he was talking about him. 'He might be able to tell the court that one sale was a favour. He might even be able to explain away two. But three – that's a pattern.'

Detective O'Connell said nothing but continued to video the young man as the thirtyish man with the brown beard gave him what looked like at least 200 euros in twenty-euro notes.

'I'm sure I reck that feller,' said Detective Barry. 'I think he works for that estate agents on Marlborough Street, what are they called, Callaghan Screws or something like that? He looks like an estate agent, any road.'

The young man took out four yellow cartons and set them on the table. Detective O'Connell started to stand up, but Detective Barry said, 'Stall it a second, Aislin. Wait till your man actually lays his hand on one.'

The thirtyish man with the brown beard pulled a folded Tesco shopping bag out of his coat pocket and opened it up. As soon as he picked up the first yellow carton, Detective Barry said, 'Right, that's it. Let's go. But real easy, like.' Into his r/t microphone, he said, 'We're hauling him in now, okay?'

The two of them stood up and ambled slowly towards the alcove at the back of the Flea Market, pretending as they went that they were having a conversation. Denny took no notice of them at all as they approached. He had half-turned away from them to serve the elderly man with the wild white hair and thick-rimmed glasses.

Detective Barry reached under his jacket at the back and felt for the handcuffs that were fastened to his belt. 'Okay, then, just as we rehearsed it,' he told Detective O'Connell, nodding his head and smiling as if he were talking about a joke that somebody had told him last night. 'I'll grab him and put the cuffs on him, and you can caution him while we're heading for the door. We need to get him out of here so quick that nobody decks what's happened until we're off and away.'

Detective O'Connell smiled and said, 'I have you, Gerry, don't you worry.'

They had almost reached the alcove now, where Denny was rummaging in one of his black bags for more cartons. The thirtyish estate agent with the brown beard had stepped away and was struggling to push the last of his four cartons into his shopping bag. When he had managed it, however, he looked up and saw Detective Barry, and his face lit up with recognition.

'Well, the dead arose!' He grinned, showing his teeth. 'What are *you* doing here, Detective Barry? Looking for stolen property, is it?'

Instantly, Denny turned around. He saw Detectives Barry and O'Connell making their way between the jumble stalls towards him and he jumped up as if he had been sitting on a powerful spring.

'Tell me, detective, did you ever nick that feller who was robbing those house deposits?' asked the estate agent blithely, still grinning. Detective Barry ignored him and made a dash towards Denny, but Denny pushed the estate agent in the chest so that he stumbled sideways into a display of books and records and second-hand handbags.

'Hey, what the feck?' he exclaimed, but as he regained his balance Detective Barry pushed him, too, to get him out of the way, and this time he fell over backwards on to the floor, knocking a vase and a six-piece tea set off a shelf in a shower of shattered china and purple potpourri.

Denny feinted and weaved between the pillars, trying to obstruct Detective Barry by tipping over antique chairs behind him and kicking over cardboard boxes so that religious figurines and ashtrays and other bric-a-brac scattered all across the floor. There were shouts of '*Hoi!* What do you think you're doing there?' from the stallholders, but none of them seemed to understand what was happening and none of them made any attempt to stop him.

Instead of chasing after Denny, Detective O'Connell made her way directly back to the street door so that she could cut him off. As he neared the entrance, Denny pushed over a coat stand that was heavily laden with second-hand overcoats and hats, which fell across the floor in front of Detective Barry, but then he turned around to find Detective O'Connell standing between him and the street outside, her arms outstretched like a goalkeeper.

By now Detective Barry was climbing over the heap of fallen overcoats. 'Stall the ball right there, boy!' he ordered him, 'You're lifted!'

The young man stopped, both hands raised, although he kept his head down and his back to Detective Barry.

'Turn around,' Detective Barry told him. 'Hold out both of your hands.'

'What for, like?' said the young man. 'I ain't done nothing. Selling a few fags to some friends, that's all.'

'I said turn around and hold out both of your hands.'

Denny started to turn around, but as Detective Barry approached him with his handcuffs raised, he swung back to face Detective O'Connell. With no hesitation at all, he seized her hair with his left hand and swept his right hand diagonally across her face. Detective O'Connell didn't realize what had happened to her at first, but then bright red blood spurted out of her cheek, all the way from the side of her left eye to her chin. She gasped and lifted up her hand, and blood flooded down her wrist and soaked the sleeve of her pale blue blouse. She staggered back and then dropped to her knees.

Detective Barry tried to snatch Denny's arm, but he twisted it away and was bounding through the open door and out on to York Street before Detective Barry could catch him.

Detective Barry crouched down beside Detective O'Connell

and put his arm around her shoulders. She was pressing her hand against her cheek and blood was dripping between her fingers, but she managed to wave her other hand and blurt out, 'Go after him, Gerry, for Christ's sake!'

Two women were hurrying over from the Flea Market cafe to help, so Detective Barry left her where she was and ran outside. He looked left, up York Street, but there was no sign of Denny running up towards Wellington Road, and in any case the hill was so steep that he wouldn't have been able to make it all the way to the top. He must have turned right and run off along MacCurtain Street instead.

Detective Barry went to the corner and again he looked right and left. Between the pedestrians on MacCurtain Street he caught a glimpse of Denny's red GAA T-shirt as he sprinted flat-out past Dan Lowery's Tavern, in the direction of Brian Boru Street. That would lead him to the Brian Boru Bridge across the River Lee, and if he managed to reach the city centre before Detective Barry could catch him he could easily mingle with the Friday afternoon shoppers and get away. Detective Barry started after him, calling up the two gardaí who were waiting in Little William Street as he did so.

'Quinn assaulted Detective O'Connell and gave us the slip,' he told them. 'He's done a legger down MacCurtain Street, heading east.'

He had run only a few more paces before he heard the whooping sound of the patrol car's siren start up. *Got you now, Denny*, he thought. By the time he had reached the blue-painted LeisurePlex building on the corner with Brian Boru Street, however, the siren didn't seem to be coming any closer. He turned his head to see that a mustard-coloured Volvo had turned the corner into York Street and stopped. Since York Street was only one-way, uphill, it was obviously preventing the patrol car from coming down the hill and turning into MacCurtain Street.

He looked ahead and saw that Denny was already crossing the road at St Patrick's Quay towards the Brian Boru Bridge.

'What's the hold-up?' he asked over his radio. 'Denny's crossing the river already. I don't want to lose him in the bus station or the shopping centre.'

'Some gowl's blocking the street and he won't fecking budge. Mulliken's got out to tell him to shift but it looks like he's arguing the toss about it.'

'Jesus. Arrest him. Or push him out of the way. And check if there's any uniforms on Pana who can give me some backup. Come on, *urgent*, like! You saw Denny yourself. Rebel County T-shirt. Grey tracksuit bottoms. Hair sticking up like a fecking red rooster.'

Although the traffic was so busy, and the pedestrian light was red, Detective Barry stepped off the kerb and zig-zagged his way across St Patrick's Quay. A bus and two cars honked their horns at him and one of the drivers shouted out, 'Looking to get yourself killed, you nickey?'

Denny was almost halfway across the bridge now, but he had slowed down so that he was half jogging and half walking and he was clearly out of breath. Detective Barry was in better shape now than he had ever been: he still played Gaelic football for St Finbarr's whenever he could and he regularly worked out at the RB Fitness Centre. Even if the patrol car didn't turn up for another three or four minutes, he reckoned he still had a good chance of catching up with Denny before he reached the bus station and Merchants Quay shopping centre – and holding him, too. *And* smashing him on the gonk for cutting Aislin. He could always plead reasonable force while the suspect was resisting arrest.

Denny had reached the far side of the bridge, but there was so much traffic on Merchants Quay that he was teetering on his Nikes on the edge of the kerb, unable to cross. Detective Barry had to dodge his way past two women with baby buggies and a hugely obese man in a mobility scooter festooned with shopping bags, but he was sure that he had Denny now. Because he had his eyes fixed ahead, though, he hadn't become aware of the silver-grey Land Rover that was burbling slowly across the bridge, keeping pace with him, so that it was holding up all the cars behind it.

For most of the bridge's 200-foot width, cars and pedestrians were separated from each other by steel railings and by the massive cast-iron structure of the bridge itself, which originally used to lift up to allow boats to pass through. The steel railings, however, didn't reach all the way across. As Detective Barry neared the far side, where they came to an end, the Land Rover's engine suddenly roared. With a loud bang from its front suspension, it mounted the pavement, swerved sideways and collided with him, crushing him against the bridge's balustrade.

Detective Barry felt as if a bomb had exploded right behind him and that he had been blown apart. The Land Rover had smashed his legs and snapped his pelvis in half. Even at only 5 mph it had rammed him against the balustrade so hard that his stomach had burst open and his intestines were sliding out between the blue-and-white cast-iron uprights and dangling in loops over the river.

He was so stunned that he felt almost nothing, but as the Land Rover backed away from him and jolted back on to the road he grimly gripped the top of the balustrade to keep himself upright. *I mustn't fall over*, he thought. *If I fall over, I'll die for sure.* He could see the river and the buildings alongside it, and St Patrick's Bridge, and the blue summer sky, and the clouds. He heard the sound of traffic and a woman screaming. *What do I do now?* he thought. But then he heard somebody talking to him and when he managed to turn his head he saw that standing beside him there was a grey-haired man with a reddish face. He smelled strongly of stale Murphy's.

'You just take it easy, boy,' the man was saying, although his voice sounded very muffled. 'You're going to be grand altogether, so long as you don't move. Somebody's called for a white van, okay? Don't move, though.'

Unexpectedly, the sky began to darken. 'Is it night?' whispered Detective Barry. 'I'm killed out, like. I think I need to lie down.'

The reddish-faced man gripped him under his left armpit to help him stay on his feet. 'You're going to be grand altogether so long as you don't move. You're all intertwangled with the railings, like, do you know what I mean? If you move at all you'll just pull yourself apart.'

Detective Barry closed his eyes. He didn't know if he was dead or simply sleeping, but he could still hear voices and traffic so he assumed that he couldn't be dead.

Most of the voices sounded very distant, but then he heard somebody speaking so close to his ear that he could feel their breath.

'My son, my name is Father O'Flynn, from the Holy Trinity Church.'

'Don't let him get away, father,' said Detective Barry, and as he did so blood slid out of both sides of his mouth.

He felt slippery fingertips touching his forehead. He heard Father O'Flynn saying, 'With this anointing, may the Lord in His love and mercy help you with the grace of the Holy Spirit. May the Lord who frees you from sin save you and raise you up.'

He heard sirens. Fantastic. His backup had caught up with him at last.

'Don't let him get away,' he repeated. 'He'll have made it across the road by now. Denny Quinn. Rebel County T-shirt. Don't let him get away.'

Three

Katie was gathering up the papers she needed for her meeting with the County Council Joint Policing Committee when Detective O'Donovan knocked quickly at her half-open door and came straight in. He looked flushed and sweaty and his pink stomach was bulging out of his shirt.

'Garda Brophy just called in,' he told her. 'Gerry Barry's been hit by a car on the Brian Boru Bridge.'

'Oh God,' said Katie, immediately dropping the folder back on to her desk. 'Is it serious?'

'Brophy's still at the scene,' said Detective O'Donovan. 'He says a hit-and-run driver mounted the pavement and smashed him into the railings at the side of the bridge. The paramedics are working on him now but it's not looking hopeful.'

'Right, let's get there now,' said Katie. She crossed her office and took down her pale green linen jacket. 'What about Aislin? Was she hurt at all?'

'She wasn't with him, so far as I know. It seems like Denny Quinn was making a run for it and Gerry was in pursuit of him on foot.'

'Why was he chasing him on foot? We had a car there, backing him up, didn't we?'

'I'm not sure exactly why, like. Brophy said something about them being boxed in, but I don't know the details.'

'What about the vehicle that hit him?'

'A Land Rover. He has a description, although nobody got its number.'

Katie walked briskly along the corridor just as Chief Superintendent Denis MacCostagáin was coming out of his office in his shirtsleeves and braces, looking, as usual, like somebody's miserable uncle.

'Ah, Kathleen, you're on the way to Merchants Quay, then. Michael Pearse has sent out backup already and called Bill Phinner for a technical team. Terrible thing to happen. Terrible. Let's pray to God that young Barry survives.'

'I'll keep you in touch,' said Katie.

Detective O'Donovan had already pressed the button for the lift and was holding the door open. They went down to the ground floor in silence and out to the car park. The morning's heavy showers had passed over and although the streets were still shiny and wet the afternoon was cloudless, with a warm breeze blowing from the south-west. Katie could hear two small children laughing as they ran down the street.

As they sped up Eglinton Street, Katie said, 'A hundred to one it was one of Quilty's thugs. If not Quilty himself. I've said right from the beginning that the only way we're ever going to stop him is if we nail him in person.'

'Sure, I agree with you totally,' said Detective O'Donovan. 'The only trouble with that, like, is getting a conviction. None of his dealers is going to give evidence against him, are they? It's a choice between getting your kneecaps shot off and making six hundred yoyos a week, and I know which of those I'd be going for.'

Clontarf Street, which led to the Brian Boru Bridge, was one-way in the opposite direction, but it had been closed to traffic and Katie and Detective O'Donovan reached Merchants Quay in just three minutes. Five Garda patrol cars were parked at different angles, as well as an ambulance and a Ford Ranger rapid response vehicle from the fire brigade. The pavements were crowded with onlookers and further along the quay, by the bus station, Katie could see an RTÉ television van arriving.

She crossed the road. Detective Barry was lying on a stretcher, with two paramedics kneeling beside him. His face was covered by an oxygen mask and one of the paramedics was holding up an IV drip. Three gardaí and a fire officer were gripping a blue plastic screen between them to shield him from the wind and from public view. The screen made a monotonous flapping sound, but apart from that there was almost complete silence.

'Detective Superintendent Maguire,' said Katie, as one of the paramedics stood up. He was a middle-aged man with flat triangular bags under his eyes, as if his skin were tissue paper, and very pale green irises. 'What are his chances?'

'Somewhere between zero and nil, I'd say,' said the paramedic. 'He's suffered massive crushing injuries to both his legs and pelvis, and his abdomen was split open by the impact. We've done everything we can to replace his intestines and hold him together, but I can't see him surviving this. I'm amazed he's still with us, to be honest with you. The father over there gave him the last rites, so that side of it's been taken care of.'

'He's not conscious at all? If I speak to him, will he hear me?'

The paramedic shook his head. 'We gave him fifteen milligrams of morphine while the firemen were cutting him free from the railings. It'll wear off, of course, and he'll be able to speak to you when it does, but he'll most likely be dead by then.'

Katie looked over towards the blue-and-white balustrade. Three of the uprights had been cut through at stomach height and there was rusty-coloured blood on the surrounding bars. Two firemen were packing away the Holmatro hydraulic cutters which they usually used for extricating dead and injured victims from car crashes.

'We'll be taking him to CUH now,' said the paramedic. 'We've already alerted them that we're bringing him in, and what kind of state he's in, so there'll be surgeons there waiting for him. You never know. We've taken people in before who were knocking on heaven's door and they've come out a couple of weeks later as fit as a butcher's dog.'

Katie bent over Detective Barry. His blonde hair was sticky with blood, but even under the oxygen mask he looked as if he had a smile on his face. She knew that a strong dose of morphine often gives people pleasant dreams, even when they're dying.

'God bless you, Gerry,' she said quietly, and crossed herself.

The paramedics lifted up the stretcher and carried Detective Barry to the ambulance. As they did so, Garda Brophy came over to Katie. He was broad-shouldered and bulky in his yellow hi-viz jacket, with a Neanderthal forehead and an S-shaped nose like a boxer. All the same, he looked grey and strained, and Katie thought he could be very close to tears.

'Quilty's wide to what we're doing, ma'am, no doubt about it,' he told her. 'He definitely has his people hovering around to keep an eye on his dealers. Denny Quinn made a run for it, but as soon as me and Mulliken went after him a car turned into the bottom of York Street and boxed us in.'

'How did Quinn get away? Was somebody keeping sketch for him?'

'It's possible, of course, but Detective O'Connell said that one of the customers in the Flea Market recognized Detective Barry just as they were about to put the cuffs on Quinn and blew the whole thing. She tried to stop Quinn but he slashed her face with a blade of some kind and took flight. That's about all she could manage to tell us. Mulliken's taken her to the Mercy.'

'What about the car that boxed you in?'

'It was a Volvo. We have all its details and Mulliken took the driver's name and address. He may have been working for Quilty or maybe he was just being bold.'

'All right, Brophy, thanks,' said Katie. A white Technical Bureau van was approaching over the bridge, followed by an unmarked green Toyota. Bill Phinner, the chief technical officer, climbed out of the Toyota and came across to join them. He was thin and hollow-cheeked and sharp-nosed, and he always reminded Katie of Dr Van Helsing in Dracula, as if he knew all of the science necessary to catch vampires but found it a constant irritation.

'How's Detective Barry?' he asked, his attention fixed on the gap the firemen had cut in the railings.

'Bad,' said Katie. 'I don't think he's going to live.'

Bill Phinner looked down. The Land Rover's black tyre tracks were clearly visible where it had swerved off the road and mounted the kerb.

'How old is he?'

'Just had his twenty-fifth birthday. One of my brightest.'

'It's always the brightest, isn't it?'

Three technicians in white Tyvek suits were waddling across the road now, carrying cameras and metal cases of sampling equipment.

Katie said, 'There's some bits of orange plastic over there. They may have come from the vehicle that hit him.'

'Well, we'll collect them anyway. If it actually hit the railings, it could well have left some paint on them, too. What type of vehicle was it? Do you know?'

'A Land Rover. Garda Brophy has a full eyewitness description. They didn't get its number, though.'

'Pity. Do you know how many Land Rovers are registered in Ireland? Six thousand three hundred and ninety. And that's if they haven't sold any more since April.'

Detective O'Donovan came over to join them. He had been interviewing eyewitnesses and talking to the firefighter who had been in charge of cutting Detective Barry free.

'No question that it was deliberate, like, do you know what I mean? Five different witnesses say that the Land Rover was driving dead slow across the bridge like it was following him. Then it sped up and went straight for him. The firefighters reckon there was no attempt to brake. Three witnesses said the Land Rover was a silver-grey colour, two said it was goldy. One said there was only two fellers in it, the others were sure there was a third feller sitting in the back.'

'Well, that's a remarkable consensus of opinion, considering,' said Bill Phinner. 'Usually they swear it was a red, green, blue and white Nissan Ford Opel saloon estate car driven by three black Chinese fellers with freckles and red brown hair.'

'They meant to kill him, though,' said Katie. 'That's what worries me. It's only cigarette smuggling, but this takes it to a totally different level altogether.'

Detective Barry had already been taken into the operating theatre when Katie arrived at Cork University Hospital. She had sent Detective Pádraigin Scanlan to the Mercy to talk to Detective O'Connell about exactly what had happened, in case she had noticed some critical details but had forgotten them in her shock at having her face slashed. At the same time, she had sent Detective Sergeant Begley and Detective Dooley to Mother Jones Flea Market to interview any witnesses they could find there, and to confiscate whatever remained of Denny Quinn's bags of contraband cigarettes.

Detective O'Donovan had returned to Anglesea Street to see if the hit-and-run had been caught on CCTV and to help in organizing the search for the Land Rover and for Denny Quinn. Katie had also told him to check on Bobby Quilty's whereabouts at the time, but to be careful not to alert him that he might be under suspicion. Although Detective Barry had been deliberately knocked down while pursuing one of Quilty's dealers, she had no evidence yet that Quilty was responsible, either directly or indirectly, and she didn't want to make him any more wary than he already was.

Katie was prepared to wait at the hospital for as long as it took the surgeons to save Detective Barry's life. He was special to her – one of a crop of five young detectives that she had been working hard to recruit. Some of the older officers called them 'Katie's Kids' and mocked them for their lack of street experience. But they were not only energetic and open-minded, they were highly computer-literate and they had already solved several serious cases of hacking and online fraud, including a complex attempt to divert over two million euros from Permanent TSB.

Katie sat down on a beige-coloured couch in the waiting room, opposite a woman with dyed gingery hair who was continually letting out mewling noises like a cat that wanted to be let in from the garden, and blowing her nose on an increasingly diminishing ball of tissue.

'How are you doing?' Katie asked her. 'Here, look, I have some fresh Kleenex.'

The woman gratefully took the small packet of tissues that Katie offered her. 'It's my daughter, Sháuna,' she said with a sniff. 'She took an overdose this morning and they're doing everything they can to save her. I'm just waiting on news.'

'That's tragic,' said Katie. 'Was she very depressed?'

'She was bullied, that's what it was, and I never even knew the half of it. She was being bullied at school because she's taller than all the rest of the girls, and she was being trollied on the interweb, too, or whatever you call it. She'd been cutting herself and everything, like, and how she managed to hide it from me I just don't understand. I mean, what kind of a mother doesn't know when her own daughter's cutting her arms and thinking of killing herself?'

'Come on, it wasn't your fault,' Katie told her. 'I'm a Garda officer and I've seen this happen again and again. Girls of that age often feel they're worthless and ugly, especially when their so-called friends start to pick on them.'

The woman shook her head and said, 'Holy Mary, Mother of God, if she dies, what will I do then? Her father passed on only two years ago and Sháuna was his bar-of-gold. If she arrives in heaven and she's only fifteen, what's he going to think of me?'

'What's your name, sweetheart?' Katie asked her.

'Brenda. Brenda Molony.'

'Well, give me your address, Brenda, and when Sháuna's recovered I'll send a detective around to call on you and check her computer. We'll be able to identify those bullies and stop them.'

'That's if Sháuna recovers. They said she swallowed a whole bottle of the paracetamol.'

Katie said, 'She'll recover, Brenda. I'll say a prayer to St Benedict for her.'

Brenda's eyes overflowed with tears. 'Ah, you're a good woman, thank you. Here – take your tissues back.'

Katie smiled and shook her head. 'Keep them. I think you need them more than I do.'

Just then, a nurse came into the waiting room and said, softly, 'Mrs Molony? Your daughter's conscious now. Would you like to come up and see her?'

'Good luck,' said Katie, as Brenda followed the nurse out of the room. She couldn't speak, but gave her a complicated wave which expressed her thanks and her despair and her trepidation more than any words could have done. Katie knew exactly how she felt.

She opened her laptop and started to go through the figures she had been intending to present to the County Council Policing Committee. She was concentrating so intently that she didn't notice the young woman with cropped blonde hair who came into the waiting room and sat down very close to her. It was only when she smelled her perfume that she looked up from her computer screen. There was only one person she knew who wore Miracle by Lancôme.

'*Kyna*.' She smiled and put aside her laptop. 'What are you doing here?'

Detective Sergeant Ni Nuallán had lost nearly twelve kilos after she had been shot five months ago, and her face was still gaunt. She had sooty smudges under her eyes and her cheekbones were sharper, but that made her look even more elfin than before. Katie thought she could have been one of the *Aes Sidhe*, the Fairy Folk.

'I've just been for a scan and a check-up with Doctor Kashani,' she said. 'The nurse told me you were here. She said that a detective was seriously hurt, but she didn't know who.'

'Gerry Barry. He was hit by a Land Rover on the Brian Boru Bridge. Crushed against the railings.'

'Mother of God. Was it deliberate?'

'We're almost sure of it. I'm praying that he's going to make it, but the doctors are not holding out a lot of hope. His family's on their way here from Tip.'

'Any notion who did it?'

'I can't say for sure, but it wouldn't surprise me if Bobby Quilty had something to do with it.'

'Quilty. That scummer. He'd run over his own mother if he thought she had a couple of euros in her purse.'

Katie took hold of Kyna's hands. Her wrists were as thin as kindling sticks, so that her large watch and her hospital identity tag were hanging loose. 'So are you okay?' Katie asked her. 'I'm so sorry I couldn't meet you last week. I was up the walls with all those Irish Water lorries getting burned and that Cronin case. It seemed like everybody was setting fire to anything that annoyed them.'

'Oh, I'm grand altogether. Doctor Kashani was worried because my blood sugar was low and I was having difficulty breathing, but he says my stomach's almost completely healed up now and I don't have to worry.'

'You haven't changed your mind, though?' Katie asked her.

'About coming back? No. I've thought about it, like you asked me to, but it wasn't just my body that got shot, Katie.' She tapped her forehead and said, 'It's gone. All my confidence. I'm even scared when I go out for the messages. I was waiting at the checkout in Dunne's the other day and I saw this feen staring at me real narrow-eyed, do you know what I mean, like? I couldn't help thinking, oh Jesus, what if he's a member of a crime gang and recognizes me and shoots me?'

'I could arrange for counselling for you, Kyna. I'm sure you can get over it, in time.'

Kyna shrugged and smiled. 'There's too many other complications, Katie. Losing my confidence is only part of it. There's my feelings for you, too. I'm better off looking for something else to do with my life. I can sing, too, did you know that?'

'No, I didn't. Serious?'

'Oh, yes. I used to sing at The Foggy Dew in Temple Bar. They were always telling me I ought to go professional. I'll sing for you one day. "One Morning in Autumn", just for you.'

'I think you know how much I'll miss you if you *do* decide to quit for good,' said Katie. 'Apart from anything else, I've never known anybody get confessions out of offenders the way you do. They're always so busy fancying you that they'll tell you they robbed a bank just to impress you, even if they didn't.'

She paused, and then she said, 'Will you go back to Dublin?'

Kyna nodded. Katie could understand how she was feeling. She looked haunted. If she was ever going to recover fully, both physically and psychologically, she needed the comfort of her family around her and to forget the grey pavements of Cork City for a while, and the grey waters of the River Lee, and guns, and men who were only too ready to use them.

Kyna lowered her head. Katie, still holding her hands, leaned forward and kissed her parting.

It was then that a surgeon came into the waiting room, still wearing his theatre cap and gown and surgical clogs. He pulled off his cap and approached them with a grave look on his face. His eyes were bulging and sad, like a Boston terrier, and Katie wondered if he had been born with eyes like that or if they had become like that because of all the tragedy he had witnessed. He was dark-skinned and unshaven.

'Detective Superintendent Maguire?' he said, and then he had to stop to clear his throat. Katie started to stand up, but then sat down again. She knew it was bad news and she hadn't eaten all day and didn't want to feel faint.

The surgeon sat down next to her. 'I am Dr Walid. My team and I did everything we possibly could to try and save the life of Detective Barry. Regrettably he died five minutes ago. The trauma he had suffered was too great for him to survive.'

'I see,' said Katie.

There was a long silence between them, and then Doctor Walid said, 'I am sorry. If you would like to see him, he is in the recovery room at the moment. Yes, I know. Not a very appropriate name under the circumstances. Then he will be taken down to the mortuary. I presume that you will be asking for his remains to be examined by a state pathologist.'

'I will be, yes. His family's on the way here and they should arrive soon. Is he fit for them to see him?'

'We will do our best to make his appearance acceptable, of course.'

Once Dr Walid had left, Katie turned to Kyna and said, 'I'll wait here for Gerry's next of kin. Will you be free later this evening? I think I'm going to need a shoulder to cry on, even if you're one of the reasons I'm going to need it.'

Kyna gently twisted her fingers free from Katie's and then took her face in both hands and kissed her on the lips.

'Just call me,' she said. 'You know what they say. A shoulder to cry on is better than money found in a sycamore tree.'

'What does that mean?'

'I don't know, Katie. Not really. I'm beginning to wonder what anything means.'

Five

It was nearly half past nine before Katie returned to Anglesea Street. Detective Barry's mother and two brothers had arrived at the hospital at six from Tipperary and she had tried to explain to them as gently as possible how he had died, and that the shock would have meant that he suffered very little.

His mother was unable to speak. All she could do was wring her handkerchief between her hands and stare at Katie as if she were pleading with her to tell her that she was lying and that her darling son wasn't dead at all, but simply sleeping. His older brother stood behind his mother with his hands on her shoulders and tears running freely down his face, so that they dripped into her hair.

Katie hung up her jacket and sat down at her desk. She was so exhausted she thought she would probably stay at the station overnight and call her new neighbours, the Tierneys, to feed her Irish setter, Barney, for her. She didn't feel hungry any more, but she knew she ought to eat something, so she would probably go down to the canteen and see if they could make her a bowl of lentil soup and a ham sandwich to go with it.

She was leafing through the files that had been left for her to look at when Inspector O'Rourke appeared at her door, carrying a tablet. He was short and blocky and red-faced, and with his shirt sleeves rolled halfway up his biceps he looked as if he were ready to claim anybody who annoyed him.

'Francis, are you still here?' said Katie. 'I thought you were getting up early tomorrow to go to Kinsale.'

'I was, ma'am. I am. But something's come up and I thought I'd wait for you to come back before I briefed you about it. I didn't want to disturb you at the hospital, like.'

'Well, thanks for that,' said Katie. 'Gerry's family turned up and it wasn't the happiest of occasions, as you can imagine. So, what's happened?'

'We've kept this totally under wraps at the moment because we think there could be political ramifications, do you know what I mean, like?'

'Go on.'

'Two fellers were renovating a cottage just behind the Blarney woollen mills this morning and when they lifted up the floorboards in the living room they found the remains of a whole family – father, mother, two kids and even two dogs. Not recently deceased, though. They were practically mummified.'

'Mother of God. Do we know how they died?'

'All of them were killed by a single shot to the back of the head. All of them – even the baby and the dogs. That's what made me think that it could well have been political. I mean, it could have been a gang killing, but I think that's unlikely considering the whole family was executed.'

'Who did you send out there?'

'Two of your Kids, Markey and Ó Doibhilin. They've interviewed the two fellers who discovered the remains and all of the neighbours, and they've sealed the cottage off. The technical experts will be going up there first thing tomorrow morning, but I don't think there's any real need to make a bust. Ó Doibhilin sent me a few pictures and I'd say that by the style of the clothes they're wearing and the dried-up look of them, that family's been lying under those floorboards for a good fifty years, or even longer.'

'That doesn't make it any less tragic,' said Katie. 'A whole family murdered – name of Jesus, children, too. You would have thought that somebody would have missed them, especially in a small community like Blarney.'

'Sure, that's one of the first questions we'll have to be asking,' said Inspector O'Rourke. 'But if the bodies have been lying there for all that length of time, that solves one problem, doesn't it? For us, at least. Whoever killed them has almost certainly passed away themselves by now.'

'You're probably right, Francis. But we still have to find out who they are and how they died. I'll tell you one thing for certain, Dr Reidy isn't going to be pleased. You know how much historical pathology costs, and I gather he's overspent this year's budget already. He threw a sevener last summer when they dug up that bog woman in Mayfield. It cost a rake of money to carry out a post-mortem, even though she'd been lying there since the Iron Age.'

'Still and all, I don't think identification is going to be all that difficult,' Inspector O'Rourke told her. 'That row of houses was built specifically for workers at the Martin Mahony mill, so the odds are that the father was employed there, and maybe the mother, too.'

'But the mill went out of business in the seventies, didn't it? Does anybody still have any records of who worked there?'

'It went into receivership in 1973 and it seems like when it closed down the last employee was told to burn all the company records in the furnace. However, he decided to keep them for posterity's sake, along with some sample cards of wool, and when he died he donated them to the Blarney Historical Society and they still have them. We've already been in touch with them and they've said that they'll be more than happy to cooperate. They're in a bit of a mess, apparently, but they'll search through them for us and see if they can find what we're looking for.'

'Do you have the pictures that Ó Doibhilin sent you?' Katie asked him.

'Oh, sure, yes,' said Inspector O'Rourke. He prodded at his tablet, frowned, prodded again, then handed it across. Detective Ó Doibhilin had taken at least a dozen photographs from different angles of the bodies lying between the joists, including close-ups of the father's desiccated hand and the backs of the heads of all four victims, clearly showing bullet entry wounds.

Katie examined the pictures closely. 'I don't know,' she said after a while. 'It's not easy to tell for certain when they were killed – not from what they're wearing, anyway, because their clothes are so plain. From the style of the children's smocks, though, I'd guess early to mid-1920s. Maybe a little earlier, looking at the baby's little lace-up boots.'

'Myself, I reckon 1910 or thereabouts,' said Inspector O'Rourke. 'But like you say, they're dressed very plain because they were most likely millworkers and they wouldn't have been able to afford the latest fashion, even if they knew what it was. They probably wore the same clothes for years until they wore out, so I could be a decade adrift either way. My old feller wore the same pair of green corduroy trousers for thirty years. After he died my mother swore that she could still hear them walking around the house at night, all on their own.'

Katie said, 'I'll go up to Blarney tomorrow morning and take a sconce at those bodies for myself. You were totally right to keep it quiet, though. I don't want this getting out until we know a whole lot more about the circumstances. You know what people in Cork are like – far more touchy about the past than they are about the present.'

'Tell me about it,' said Inspector O'Rourke. 'The mother-in-law still goes on about the old Opera House catching fire in 1955 and how she stood for hours in the lashing rain with her da watching it burn right down to the ground. Not too many people had TV in those days of course.'

'Well, my father's the same,' said Katie. 'He can't stop talking about Coal Quay in the old days. But let's get back to Gerry Barry. Has O'Donovan played back the CCTV?'

'He did, yes. I watched it myself, too. You can see Denny Quinn come running around the corner from MacCurtain Street and Barry running after him. Then almost immediately the Land Rover appears around the corner, very slow, like it's been following him. Quinn crosses the bridge, but halfway across he's slowing down and Barry's beginning to catch up to him. The Land Rover is creeping along just behind Barry. You can make out two fellers in it, but they're both wearing dark glasses and the sun's reflecting off the windscreen so you can't clearly see their faces. You can just make out that the driver's wearing a black Cork Hurling T-shirt, but that's all.'

'Number plate?'

Inspector O'Rourke shook his head. 'Stolen. It was taken about six months ago from a Honda Civic registered to some music teacher in Carrigaline.'

'How about the hit-and-run itself?'

Inspector O'Rourke shook his head again. 'As bad luck would have it, this huge great container lorry from John O'Donovan's Haulage goes past just at the moment when Barry was hit. By the time the lorry's balled on you can only see the Land Rover reversing off the pavement and then shooting off down Clontarf Street as fast as you like. Then you can see some old feller coming to help Barry, but that's about it.'

'Have you managed to identify what model of Land Rover it was?'

'It's a Discovery TDV6 5E, probably dating from 2004 or maybe 2005. The colour doesn't tally but it's probably been resprayed. We've been checking with the NVDF of course, and our own records of stolen vehicles, but so far nothing at all.'

'You've checked with the DVA in Coleraine? And the DVLA in Cardiff?'

'Of course, yes, but still nothing. I contacted Knock Road, too, Quilty being an Armagh man. Don't worry, though, I didn't mention Quilty by name or give any indication that we suspect him of being involved.'

'Good man yourself,' said Katie. She stood up and said, 'I think I'll get myself down to the canteen now. Are you finished for today?'

'I'd be better be, otherwise the old doll will kill me. Her sister was coming around this evening for dinner, with her husband, and she's not exactly buzzing that I had to cry off. Mind you, to be honest with you, I'd rather be here than there. That brother-in-law, he works for the county council and all he ever talks about is the never-ending battle against fly-tipping. He'd break your melt.'

Katie smiled. Francis O'Rourke was a hard-bitten, uncompromising officer with twenty-three years of experience, but she had seen who enforced the law in the O'Rourke family and it was definitely Maeve.

* * *

Because it was so late, there was only one cook on duty in the canteen and all she had to offer was leek and potato soup and Cooleeney cheese rolls, but Katie was too tired to leave the station and go to a restaurant, and not hungry enough, either. As she sat alone at a table by the window, eating her roll, she couldn't stop herself from seeing Detective Barry smiling under his oxygen mask, fatally crushed but dreaming optimistic dreams.

The soup was thick with plenty of pepper, the way she made it herself, but she had only taken three or four spoonfuls when her iPhone pinged and she saw that she had a text message.

Are you coming home tonight? I'm here outside waiting for you. I love you and need to talk. J.

Katie slowly lowered her spoon. She could hardly believe what she was reading. She had been sure that she would never hear from John again, ever. When he had discovered that her fling with her former neighbour had left her pregnant he had reacted with such fury that he had ripped in half the portrait of her that he had been painting, and stormed out of the house. That had happened before Christmas and since then he had answered none of her texts or emails. She hadn't even known if he was still in the country.

She felt as if the floor were sliding away beneath her, like in an earthquake. She didn't know if she ought to reply to him or not. She had been deeply in love with him, which was one of the reasons she had left it so late to tell him she was expecting another man's baby. After all, he had already left her once before, to go and work in America, and that was when her brief entanglement with her neighbour had taken place. The man was dead now, and she had miscarried, but had John found out about that?

The cook came out from behind the counter and approached her.

'Your soup all right, ma'am?' she asked her, with a worried frown.

'Yes, yes, it's very tasty,' said Katie. She held up her iPhone and said, 'Something critical's come up, that's all. It goes with the job.'

The cook was a young, plump girl, no more than nineteen. She had a pink plastic hair slide to pin up her floppy fringe and unplucked eyebrows and a smooth puppy-fat face that was still untouched by disappointment or grief or betrayal – or by love that unexpectedly turned to bitter resentment, if she had ever been in love at all. How could Katie explain to a girl who looked like that why she was suddenly unable to finish her soup?

She read John's message again. She was tempted simply to trash it, but then she thought that would be petty. She thought for a few moments, and then she wrote: *Not at home tonight. Up the walls tomorrow. But could meet you at Hayfield Manor bar maybe 6-ish.*

She stared at her text for a long time before she sent it. She had chosen the five-star Hayfield Manor because the bar was dark and discreet and she was less likely to be seen there by any of her fellow officers or Cork's resident skangers. But was she also trying to remind John of what he had walked out on? Last year they had spent a very expensive and romantic night there to celebrate her birthday.

She took a deep breath and pressed Send.

Six

When she arrived in Blarney the following morning, she found that two white Technical Bureau vans were already parked on Millstream Row, nose to tail behind the green builder's skip, as well as three Garda patrol cars and two unmarked Ford Mondeos. She had to park right at the end of the row, next to the grey stone wall that surrounded the Blarney Woollen Mills Hotel. After Mahony's mill had closed down in 1973 the factory had become derelict, but two years later a former employee called Christy Kelleher had raised enough investment capital to reinvent the site as the largest Irish shop in the country and, eventually, as a hotel, too.

A light drizzle was falling, but every now and then the sun gleamed silver behind the clouds, so there was hope for a brighter afternoon. All the same, Katie had put on her black waterproof jacket with the pointed hood that John had always said made her look like Fuamnach, the witch goddess. She had reminded him that Fuamnach had turned her husband's second wife into a pool of water, and then a worm, and finally into a beautiful butterfly that had fluttered away out of his grasp.

Detective Ó Doibhilin had seen her arriving and was waiting for her by the front door. He was a tall, serious, good-looking young man, even though his face was very long, which had led to his fellow officers giving him the nickname 'Horse'. They would rib him when he walked down the corridor by singing the Rubberbandits' song 'Horse Outside'.

Even before she reached the house Katie could see intermittent flashes from the technical experts' cameras coming from inside, like summer lightning. Two technicians were dragging a dark green tarpaulin over the top of the skip and tying it down with cords.

'How's it going?' she asked Detective Ó Doibhilin.

'Slow,' he told her. 'Bill Phinner says the bodies are so fragile it's going to take days to get them out of there without breaking them all into bits. He says the pathologist ought to study them *in situ* before they're moved, in case they do damage that destroys any evidence – like breaking their skin, like, or dislocating their bones.'

'Well, I called the State Pathologist's Office first thing this morning and they're sending down the acting deputy, Dr Kelley.'

'Come on anyway, I'll show you,' said Detective Ó Doibhilin, and led Katie through the front door and into the narrow hallway, which was already crowded with two gardaí, one male and one female, both of them bulked out in their hi-viz jackets, and a technical expert in a white Tyvek suit.

Katie had known what to expect, but when she entered the living room and saw the bodies lying face-down between the joists, their clothes and hair covered in a fine layer of dust, she felt a sense of sorrow that she rarely experienced when she confronted the bodies of recent murder victims. She had seen entire families killed before: in head-on crashes on the N20, or asphyxiated by carbon monoxide fumes in holiday homes in West Cork. But even before she knew who this family were, she strongly suspected that Inspector O'Rourke had been right and that their killing had been political. It had been not only a tragedy for this father, and this mother, and these two small children, but part of the ongoing sadness of Irish history.

She balanced her way over the joists and the few remaining floorboards to the opposite side of the room where Bill Phinner was showing one of his newer assistants how to take a fibre sample from the woman's faded maroon dress. He didn't look at Katie as she joined him, but said, 'Bring tears to a stone, wouldn't it? Doesn't matter how long ago it happened, somebody came into this house one day and shot every one of them, and we can't even tell in what order. I pray to God they shot the parents first. The last thing you'd ever want to see is your own children murdered in front of you.'

From the doorway, Detective Ó Doibhilin said, 'The fellow from the Blarney Historical Society is going through the records for us, but he says they're in no kind of order at all, so he's still trawling through them and we don't have a name for this family yet. But an auld wan two doors down thinks they were called Langtry, because her mother used to talk about them.'

'Langtry. I see. Did her mother say anything about them disappearing all of a sudden?'

'She did, yeah. She said she used to play with the little Langtry girl but one day she called for her and she wasn't there any more. That was about all she could remember, though she heard somebody say that the family had all headed off to America.'

'It's biggus ovus that they didn't,' said Bill Phinner, glumly surveying the bodies that lay at their feet. 'Did this auld wan give you any idea when it was, that the Langtrys went missing?'

'No, she couldn't tell me exactly.'

'Well, how old is she?'

'Mid- to late seventies, I'd say.'

'That would mean she was born in the 1940s. This little girl here is probably seven or maybe eight years old, taking into account that children were less well nourished in those days, and so they didn't grow nothing like as big as they do now. Let's suppose that when your auld wan's mother was playing with this little girl they were roughly the same age, and then let's suppose that she was around nineteen or twenty when she brought your auld wan into this world. That means we're talking about 1920 for these killings, or thereabouts.'

Katie knelt down so that she could examine the bodies more closely. 'I think you're right. Francis O'Rourke showed me the pictures you took yesterday and I thought their clothes had a 1920s look about them. Of course we'll be able to pin down the date exactly if the Historical Society can find them in their records.

She gently stroked the little girl's dress. 'Provided these *are* the Langtrys, that is. For all we know at the moment, the Langtrys murdered another family and hid them under their floorboards and that's why they took off to America.'

'You have a very imaginative mind, detective Superintendent' said Bill Phinner. 'You ought to be writing them mystery novels.'

'Until I have all of the facts, Bill, I have to think about all of the possibilities.'

'Listen, we're taking the floorboards back to the lab. They have some dark marks on them which could be bloodstains, and we can test those for DNA.'

'I read that report you produced last year on historical DNA testing. But after more than ninety years? Is that possible?'

'It should be. You remember that case in Togher, when that feller who ran the bicycle shop was accused of stabbing his wife to death?'

'Of course. You found bloodstains on the legs of the bed, and you proved that they were hers. But they weren't more than fifteen years old, were they?'

'No, but if we do find any bloodstains on these floorboards, I have pretty high hopes that we can still get full DNA profiles, even if they're a whole lot older. DNA is a fierce stable molecule, do you know what I mean? In every one of those tests we ran last year the bloodstains came from cold cases that were more than twenty-five years old, and we got positive results from 82 per cent of them. We'll be running the same kind of tests on these floorboards.'

'Well, good luck with it. We need to know for certain who this family were, even if we never find out who killed them, or why.'

'We'll start by using crossover electrophoresis. That's the same method they used to identify bloodstains in Kosovo. It was more than a year and a half after an ambush and the blood was soaked right into the soil, but they still managed to put a name to most of the victims. And they identified the body of that young mountain climber in New Zealand, didn't they, even though he'd been missing for forty-two years?'

Katie said, 'My father used to say "if bloodstains could only talk". Now it seems like they can.'

'Oh, not just bloodstains. Semen and vaginal fluid – they're fierce talkative, too.'

Tell me about it, thought Katie, thinking of John, and of David Kane who had made her pregnant even though he had sworn he had had a vasectomy. *We think we pass through this world without leaving any trace that we were here, but all of us leave lasting evidence behind us, every day, wherever we go. Blood, skin, sweat and fingerprints, hair and saliva. Even our breathing tells where we've been.*

'All right, Bill,' she said. 'I'll let you crack on. I think I'll go and have a chat with this auld wan two doors along.' She turned to Detective Ó Doibhilin and said, 'Would you care to introduce me to her? Sometimes a woman will say things to another woman that she wouldn't think of saying to a man.'

'You can say that again, like,' said Detective Ó Doibhilin, more to himself than to Katie.

They walked to the house two doors down and rang the bell. The door was opened by a small boy with his hair sticking up at the back and a half-eaten jam sandwich in his hand.

'How's it going, sham?' asked Detective Ó Doibhilin. 'Okay if I have another word with your granny?'

'Granny!' the boy called out, with his mouth full. 'Granny, it's the shades again!'

After a few moments a diminutive woman appeared, wearing a long pond-green cardigan. She was almost as small as the boy, with curly grey hair stained orange from nicotine at the front and a face that was puckered up from years of heavy smoking. She was clutching tightly at the large glass beads around her neck, as if Katie and Detective Ó Doibhilin were vampires, and her necklace was a crucifix.

'I told you all that I can remember,' she said, and coughed, and coughed again.

'I know you did, girl,' said Detective Ó Doibhilin. 'I'm pure grateful for it, too. But this is Detective Superintendent Maguire and she wanted to come and see you personal-like, so

that she could show her appreciation for the assistance you've
given us.'

'Oh?' said the woman expectantly, as if she thought that Katie
might have come to give her some kind of reward.

'Is it all right if I come inside and talk to you?' Katie asked her.

'I told this feen all that I can remember.'

'I know. But I'd appreciate it if you could go over it again.
Maybe there's some little detail that you thought you'd forgotten.'

The woman shrugged and said, 'All right.' She dug into the
drooping pocket of her cardigan and brought out a crumpled
ten-euro note. 'Run down to the SuperValu would you, Micky,
and bring me twenty Carroll's? And make sure you're back before
you get there. You can keep the cobbage.'

'There won't be no cobbage, Gran, they've gone up.'

The woman tutted and dug into her pocket again and gave
him fifty cents. 'The price of fags these days, it's enough to make
you weep.'

Katie gave her a tight smile, but said nothing. The price of
cigarettes was the reason why Detective Barry had been killed.

The boy ran off, still holding his jam sandwich, while the woman
opened the front door wider and shuffled into the living room.
Katie said to Detective Ó Doibhilin, 'It's okay. I'll take it from here.'

'You're sure?' he said, although he didn't try to hide his relief.

'Go on,' said Katie, and followed the woman inside.

The living room was gloomy and wallpapered with faded
brown roses. The Artex ceiling was brown, too, but that had
been stained by cigarette smoke. The carpet was slime-green,
almost the same colour as the woman's cardigan, with smaller
off-cuts of carpet on top of it to keep it from wearing out. A
picture of the pope hung over the fireplace and there was a 3-D
picture of Jesus over a display cabinet crowded with china dogs
and tarnished silver teapots.

Katie sat down opposite the woman in a large armchair uphol-
stered with slippery brown plastic. 'I don't know your name,' she
said.

The woman was poking about in a crowded glass ashtray until she found a half-smoked cigarette. She lit it, took a deep drag, and then breathed out twin tusks of smoke from her nostrils. 'Nora,' she said. 'Nora O'Neill.'

'So you've lived here all your life, Nora?'

Nora had swallowed smoke, so to begin with she could only shake her head. Then she said in a strangulated voice, 'I only moved back here when my husband Bryan passed away. Ah, I tell you, it was shocking, how quick he went. The panchromatic cancer, that's what it was. One minute he was eating pork sausages, the next minute he was knocking on heaven's door. That was in 1989. Then my ma passed away, so I'm here on my own now.'

'Who's the boy?'

'Oh, Micky. I take care of him while his ma goes to work. She's a waitress at the Muskerry Arms and that's only across The Square, like. He's a bit of a cheeky scheltawn but he'd do anything for me. I'm not really his gran, but that's what he calls me.'

Katie said, 'Your mother used to play with the little Langtry girl.'

'That's right. Aideen, her name was. My ma often used to wonder why the Langtrys disappeared like that, without so much as saying goodbye to no one. There one day, vanished the next. Well, now we know why, God have mercy on their souls. It wasn't only my ma who was playmates with Aideen of course. My granny was best friends with Aideen's mother, Radha.'

Nora sucked the butt end of her cigarette down to the filter and then crushed it out. 'Do you have children yourself?' she asked Katie. 'Must be fierce difficult, with your job, having children.'

'Yes it is, but no, I haven't,' said Katie. 'I had a little boy, Seamus, but he passed away when he was only a year old. Cot death.'

'I'm sorry to hear that. Will you be trying again? You're still young enough, aren't you? I think that children bring such a light to your life. You see your kids, do you know what I mean? – you see your kids and you think to yourself, at least I've done something with all these years that God gave me, apart from smoking fags and playing bingo and watching the telly.'

'Sure I'd like to have another child,' Katie told her. 'It's just that I don't have a partner at the moment.'

'You're wearing a ring, though.'

Katie held up her left hand. 'I *was* married. Not any more. I think I wear this just as a souvenir. You know, a reminder to myself not to do it again, or to be very careful if I do.'

Nora was poking around in the ashtray again, but then she stopped poking and said, 'Talking of souvenirs, my ma left me one that my granny passed on to her. She said that Radha Langtry had given it to her, not as a present, like, but to keep it safe. Of course when the Langtrys disappeared like that, my granny kept it because she didn't know what else to do with it. Radha had made her promise that she wouldn't let anybody know that she had it, ever, and she kept her word right until the day she died.'

'Do you still have it?' Katie asked her.

'It's upstairs, at the bottom of the press. I haven't thought about it in years.'

'What exactly is it?'

Nora stood up, brushing ash from her skirt. 'I'll show you so, if you wait there for a minute.'

She left Katie in the living room while she climbed the stairs, coughing all the way. Katie heard her footsteps creaking across the bedroom floor above her and then the press door banging. She prayed that Nora wouldn't take too long. The smoke in the room left her feeling as if she couldn't breathe, and she wondered how she had ever smoked herself when she was in her teens.

After a while, though, she heard Nora coughing her way back down the stairs. She paused in the hallway and said, 'What's taking that Micky? He's as slow as a spa's appetite that boy.' Then she came back into the living room and handed Katie a small cardboard box with the lid fastened with withered elastic bands. The box was no more than ten centimetres square. It was yellowed and its edges worn through with age.

'Open it,' said Nora. 'See for yourself. It doesn't mean nothing to me. I only held on to it because my granny promised Radha

Langtry she'd keep it safe.'

Katie snapped off the elastic bands and carefully opened the lid. Inside, wrapped in tissue paper, she found a bronze metal badge with a shield on it. On the top of the shield there was a terrestrial globe, covered with bees, and on the shield itself there was a ship under sail. On the left side stood a heraldic antelope, with a chain around it, and on the right side a lion, guardant. There was a motto beneath the shield, *Concilio et Labore*, and beneath that the name *Manchester*.

Underneath the badge there was a small folded sheet of paper. Katie opened it and saw that there was a message on it, written in faded blue ink.

My Darling, this protected me through every battle. May it always protect you. Yours for all eternity, Gerald.

'What do you make of it?' asked Nora. 'It looks like Radha may have had a fancy-man, don't you think? A British soldier, too.'

Katie carefully replaced the sheet of paper and the badge. 'That's a possibility, yes. But we'll have to do a lot more research into it first. The note doesn't mention Radha by name, so it may not even have been hers, but something she was keeping for a friend. Would you mind if I borrowed it? I'll give you a receipt and we'll take very good care of it.'

Nora flapped her hand and said, 'Keep it if you like. It'll only go back in the press until I die, and then what?'

'I'll still give you a receipt for it,' Katie told her. 'I'll also need your written acknowledgement that it's yours and that you inherited it from your mother.'

The front door opened and Micky appeared with a lollipop stick protruding from his mouth. He tugged a packet of Carroll's cigarettes out of his trouser pocket and handed them over. Nora had peeled the cellophane off the packet with her claw-like fingernails and taken out a cigarette and lit it before Katie had even had time to compliment Micky on how quickly he had run to The Square and back.

Katie took out her notebook and pen and wrote Nora a receipt, as well as a short note for Nora to sign to confirm that the badge was hers and how she had come by it.

As she opened the door to leave, Nora said, 'This isn't going to cause trouble, is it? I suddenly have this feeling in my water that this is going to cause trouble.'

'Don't worry,' said Katie. 'And thank you for your help. It could prove very valuable.'

As she walked back to the house where the dead family had been discovered, however, and where the technicians' cameras were still flashing, she had the strongest feeling that Nora was right and that it might have been better if the badge had remained at the bottom of her press, unopened until all of Cork's old enmities were long forgotten – or forever, whichever came the sooner.

Seven

As she drove back to Anglesea Street, Detective O'Donovan called her to say that the Land Rover had been found at the end of a small track off the road between Frenchfurze and Boycestown, south-east of Carrigaline.

'It was totally burned out, like, so it probably won't be much use for forensics, but the goms left the number plates on it so we know for sure it was the same vehicle that hit Gerry Barry. We've checked the VIN and it seems like it went missing six weeks ago from a farm in Tassagh, just south of Armagh. The owner reported it stolen at Newtownhamilton and the peelers there are scanning the incident sheet for me and sending it down as a PDF.'

'Mother of God, this smells more and more like Bobby Quilty by the minute,' said Katie.

When she arrived back at her office she rang Eithne O'Neill, one of Bill Phinner's technical experts. Eithne specialized in identifying bodies that were decomposed or crushed or mangled beyond all recognition, and one of the ways she did that was by tracing and dating the jewellery they had been wearing.

Katie was prising the lid off her cappuccino when Eithne came in, looking scarlet-cheeked and flustered. She was a very pretty girl, but this morning she was wearing no make-up at all and her hair was tousled.

'Eithne, you're looking kind of shook there,' said Katie. 'Are you all right?'

Eithe took a balled-up tissue out of her pocket and wiped her nose. 'I'm not, as it happens. I've got one of my summer colds and they're always worse than the winter ones. I'm as sick as a small hospital, to tell you the truth.'

'You should go home, make yourself a goody and go to bed.'

'I can't. I'm too busy. I've more than a dozen DNA tests to get through.'

'Don't worry. I'll talk to Bill and make sure he gives you a couple of days off. If you're up to it, though, I'd appreciate it if you'd to take a look at this for me.'

She handed Eithne the box with the badge in it. Eithne opened it up and peered at it closely.

'It's a British Army cap badge,' she said. 'I mean, that's obvious of course, because it has "Manchester" on it.'

'Any ideas how old it might be?'

'Not offhand. It's oldish, of course, but I couldn't give you a precise date until I look it up. It might be easier than you think, though, because quite a few British regiments changed their badges or amalgamated or got disbanded, especially after the First World War.'

'So early 1920s would be a fair guess?'

'I'll check it for you. It shouldn't take long. I've a record of just about every military badge that ever was.'

'There's a letter in there, too. Perhaps you could test that for age. I'm pretty sure it's contemporary with the cap badge, but I just want to be certain, especially after that Yeats business.'

Katie was referring to a case they had dealt with in March, when a Cork art dealer had sold a smeary-looking seascape as a genuine Jack Butler Yeats. The buyer had paid nearly 50,000 euros for it but had later become suspicious and made a complaint to the Garda. The dealer had produced a letter allegedly written by Yeats and specifically mentioning the seascape, but Eithne had used a video spectral comparator to prove that the signature was a good, but not perfect, copy.

'Sure I can do that for you,' said Eithne. 'I'll check it out with the spectrometer.'

'Thanks,' said Katie. 'But make sure you get yourself well.'

When Eithne had gone she started to leaf through all the notes and folders that had been left on her desk. After a while, though, she sat back, staring at nothing at all. She still couldn't stop visualizing Gerry Barry's smile, and she still couldn't stop herself feeling responsible for his death.

She had insisted all along that trying to cripple Bobby Quilty's tobacco-smuggling business by arresting his dealers was a waste of their time and resources. Most of the dealers were so young they couldn't be prosecuted anyway, even if they were caught, and Quilty was smuggling in so many cigarettes that the loss of a few hundred cartons was hardly any inconvenience to him at all. Two months ago, he had abandoned five lorryloads when he discovered that Revenue had attached tracking devices to them.

She flicked through most of her paperwork, folding down the corners of the reports she wanted to read more thoroughly. Then she finished her coffee and went along the corridor to see Chief Superintendent MacCostagáin. She knocked and he called out, 'Yes, what is it?' He sounded impatient, as if he were busy, but when she entered his office she found him standing by the window staring out at the rain.

'Oh, Katie, it's you,' he said.

'Patrick O'Donovan's just called me. They've found the Land Rover that knocked down Gerry Barry, near Boycestown. It was totally burned out, but the number plates match. It was stolen from a farm in Armagh about six weeks ago.'

'Well, that's a start, I suppose,' said Chief Superintendent Mac-Costágain, turning away from the window. 'Are you going to put out a press release?'

'No, not yet,' Katie told him. 'I want to keep this under wraps at least until the PSNI send us their crime sheet on it and we have more evidence as to who might have taken it.'

'It'll be Bobby Quilty or one of his scummers, I'll bet you money on it.'

'Of course. But we can't prove that there's a link, not yet, and if I put out a press release, then Quilty will know that we know. Right at this moment I want to keep him in the dark about what we're doing, as much as we possibly can. I want him to believe that he's clear got away with it.'

'That Quilty. I swear to God, sometimes I wish I could send half a dozen uniforms to drag him into a back alley and kick the tripes out of him. Mind you, I've said nothing.'

'So what's our plan of action now?' asked Katie. 'I don't want to see any more of my team getting themselves killed, not for any amount of smuggled cigarettes.'

'Assistant Commissioner O'Reilly's just been on the blower. He wants to hold a general conference tomorrow morning about how we're going to tackle this whole tobacco-smuggling trade.'

'He'd better have some pure brilliant ideas, then,' said Katie. 'The way we're going about it at the moment is having no effect at all. In fact, it's making the situation worse. Bobby Quilty must be laughing his head off at us.'

'Well, it isn't easy, Katie. Smoking cigarettes isn't illegal, not like shooting up drugs.'

'Of course not, but the government isn't helping either. Every time they hike up the price of tobacco, more and more smokers start buying smuggled cigarettes and Quilty gets richer. Did you see those figures that came in this morning from the tobacco manufacturers?'

Chief Superintendent MacCostagáin nodded towards the folders on his desk and said, in an oddly sad voice, 'No, I haven't. Well, I haven't had the time yet.'

'I've only just read them myself,' said Katie. 'But they reckon that since the last budget the proportion of illegal cigarettes smoked in Ireland has gone up to 32 per cent. I don't exactly know how they've worked that out, but that means that nearly one in three cigarettes is NIDP.' By that she meant Non-Irish Duty Paid.

'I totally agree with you,' said Chief Superintendent Mac-Costagáin. 'But the government have the cancer pressure groups to contend with, don't they? And they might not openly admit it, but they need the money. It's going to be fierce difficult, though, trying to go for Quilty himself. As you know well enough, Katie, he has a crowd of politicians in his pocket, both north and south, as well as plenty of local sympathizers.'

Katie was well aware how difficult it was going to be to break up Bobby Quilty's tobacco empire. She knew he was using the huge profits he made from cigarette smuggling to finance a new republican splinter group who called themselves the Authentic IRA. Like the Real IRA and the New IRA and the OnH, they were bitterly opposed to the Good Friday Agreement and believed that the Provisional IRA were not nearly aggressive enough in their continuing fight for Irish independence. Quilty had been described by the media as chief of staff of the Authentic IRA, but he had always denied it, saying that he simply believed in 'Ireland as one country, as God had created it, and had always meant it to be, and who the feck are we to argue with God?'

That was his political justification for cigarette smuggling, anyway, although he wasn't doing too badly out of it himself. Katie had recently been sent a report by the Police Service of Northern Ireland that estimated that in the last eighteen months alone Quilty had enriched himself by close to 30 million euros. He had so much cash he was burying it in barrels.

'Well, I do believe that Jimmy O'Reilly has some kind of a new strategy in mind,' said Chief Superintendent MacCostagáin. 'Myself, I think it's like pissing in the wind, if you'll excuse me.'

Katie said, 'I also wanted to update you on those remains that were found in Blarney.'

'All right, the family under the floorboards. I understand they've been there quite a while.'

'My best estimate so far is the early 1920s. But Dr Reidy's sending Mary Kelley down to examine them, and she's like second to none when it comes to historical pathology. Remember that little boy's body they found stuffed up a chimney in Macroom? That was one of her cases.'

'That's right. He was so well preserved, wasn't he, they thought he'd only been up there a couple of months, but how long was it? Eighty years, if I remember rightly.'

Katie was about to tell Chief Superintendent MacCostagáin about the Manchester cap badge, but he suddenly turned back towards the window and pressed his finger and thumb against his eyelids, as if he had a sudden headache. She hesitated, and then she said, 'Is something wrong, sir, if you don't mind my asking?'

Chief Superintendent MacCostagáin shook his head, but he didn't answer.

'Should I come back later?' asked Katie. She could clearly see that something was distressing him.

He gave a snort and took a deep breath and dragged a hand-kerchief out of his pocket. He dabbed at his eyes and then turned back to Katie with a sad, puckered-up smile.

'I'm sorry. It's an anniversary, that's all. They say it takes four years to get over your grief but it's five now and it's still just as painful. I apologize. I shouldn't be burdening you with my sorrows, should I? Or anybody else, for that matter. It's not very professional, is it?'

'Your wife,' said Katie, and Chief Superintendent MacCostagáin nodded.

'I know how you feel, sir. I've lost people, too. And you're right, I'm afraid. You don't get over it in four years, or even in forty, I suspect, or ever. It's a pain that never goes away.'

Chief Superintendent MacCostagáin stood silent for a few moments, and then he sniffed again and briskly chafed his hands together and said, 'Listen, tell me more about these bodies in Blarney. Francis says that you're reluctant to tell the media about them, in case they were murdered for some kind of sectarian motive.'

'We have to consider it,' said Katie, and told him about the cap badge and the letter. 'I don't want the press to start making wild speculations, that's all – not before we know for sure who the family were and before we have at least some idea of why they were executed like that. They may very well have been killed for some personal grudge, or some falling out over business, we don't know yet. Sure, they were murdered nearly a hundred years ago, but if they were killed for political reasons then you know yourself it could be like prodding a hornets' nest.'

'Well, you're right about that,' said Chief Superintendent MacCostagáin. 'A hundred years ago is like yesterday afternoon to some of your rebels.'

He paused, and then he said, 'How about Detective Barry's funeral? Have you had the chance to talk to his family yet?'

'They want it private,' said Katie. 'I told them that we could arrange for him to have a state funeral, but they'd prefer it very quiet. They'd like it if his fellow officers attended, but they don't want a show.'

'All right,' said Chief Superintendent MacCostagáin. He sat down at his desk, looking more mournful than ever. 'I can understand that. The way you feel when you lose somebody, it's fierce strange, it's almost the same as when you have your first child. You'd think you'd want to go shouting out to everybody about it, but you don't, not to begin with at least. You want to keep it to yourself.'

'I know,' said Katie. She waited for a moment, but he said nothing more and didn't even look up at her, so she left his office, closing the door quietly behind her.

* * *

When she returned to her own office, she found Inspector O'Rourke waiting for her, although he was talking to his wife on his iPhone.

'Yes, Maeve. I have you. Yes. No, I won't forget. I'll do it. I have to go now. Yes.'

He ended the call and then he said, 'Sorry. Just taking orders from the petticoat government.'

Katie raised her hand to tell him not to worry. But then he said, 'Guess who we just hauled in, literally five minutes ago? Only Denny Quinn. Two guards spotted him crossing the Shaky Bridge on his way back to Blackpool. He's downstairs now in the interview room with DS Begley and Detective Dooley.'

'Has he been arrested?'

'Yes, on a charge of assault, and cautioned. He's said nothing so far, though, except effing and blinding.'

Katie and Inspector O'Rourke went down to the interview room. Denny Quinn was slouching back in a beige plastic chair, his eyes darting in every direction around the room except towards Detective Sergeant Begley and Detective Dooley, who were facing him across the table. His cockerel's-crest hair had been tilted to one side and he had the crimson swelling of a bruise on his left cheek.

Detective Dooley stood up so that Katie could have his chair and brought over another one for Inspector O'Rourke. Denny briefly glanced at Katie and then continued to look up at the ceiling, and then at the opposite wall, and then at his shoes.

'Denny,' said Katie.

Denny didn't answer, but drummed his fingers on the table.

'Denny, I'm talking to you,' Katie told him. 'You understand why you're here, don't you?'

Denny frowned and said, 'I'm sure there's a fecking mouse in this room. I can hear something squeaking, any road.'

Katie thought: *You can talk*. Denny's voice still had the uncontrolled pitches of late adolescence, deep and growly one second and almost falsetto the next.

'Denny, you're in serious trouble,' said Katie. 'You were caught at the Flea Market selling illegal cigarettes – cigarettes that had been smuggled into the country without paying the appropriate tax. When you were challenged you resisted arrest, you assaulted a detective garda, and we can also charge you with being an accessory to the murder of a second detective garda.'

Denny suddenly blinked at Katie and said, 'Oh, sorry. Were you talking to me, like?'

'There's nobody else in this room who's under arrest.'

'Oh, then you *were* talking to me.'

'Yes.'

'You think I give a shite?' asked Denny. 'There's no law against selling fags.'

'There's a law against assaulting a detective garda and causing her harm.'

'How the feck was I supposed to know she was a shade? She didn't show me no badge, she didn't tell me who the feck she was. I just thought she was some cracked old whore who was trying to rob me gold chains off of me.'

'You'd already been told that you were under arrest.'

'I didn't hear nobody say that.'

'Why did you run away then?'

'I was late for my tea. My ma would have given me all kinds of grief if I'd let it go cold.'

'You seriously expect me to believe that you were totally unaware that you were being arrested for selling illegal cigarettes?'

'I didn't know they was illegal. They was just fags.'

'Jin Ling brand? You know where they come from, don't you?' put in Detective Sergeant Begley.

'No fecking idea. I don't smoke, as it happens, so I don't know one fecking fag from another.'

'Russia, they come from, for your information. They're made specially for smugglers. Most of the time they have industrial chemicals and asbestos in them, and human faeces, as well as tobacco.'

'I wasn't going to smoke them so why the feck should I care? There's no fags that's good for your health, any road.'

Katie said, 'On top of that, you want me to believe that you had no idea that the detective garda who arrested you was chasing after you? He was only a few metres behind you all the way along MacCurtain Street and over the Brian Boru Bridge.'

Denny slowly shook his head. 'No idea at all, missus. You can believe whatever you fecking like, but that's the God's honest truth. I never knew that I was arrested and I never knew that there was nobody running after me.'

'Where do you live?'

'You fecking well know where I live. The law comes round so often my ma's thinking of charging them rent.'

'Just for the record, Denny. Tell me where you live.'

'O'Connell Street, Watercourse Road, Blackpool. Just along from Galvin's Carry-Out.'

'So if you were late for your tea, why were you running in the opposite direction to Blackpool?'

'I was going the long way round, that's all. I had to work up an appetite, like, because me ma's not that good a cook. You have to be starving to eat the shite that she dishes up.'

Katie took a deep breath and then she said, 'Who gave you the cigarettes that you were selling?'

'Nobody give them me. Some feen sold them me in a pub. But like I say, I don't smoke, you know, and so I thought I'd flog them.'

'What feen? What was his name?'

'How the feck should I know? Just some feen.'

'What pub?'

Denny shook his head. 'I don't fecking remember, do I? I was langered at the time.'

'Why did you buy the cigarettes from him if you don't smoke?'

'I don't know. Just to help the feller out. He said he needed the grade, like.'

'So it wasn't Bobby Quilty who gave you the cigarettes?'

'Who?'

'Bobby Quilty.'

'I never heard of nobody of that name, never.'

Katie questioned Denny for another twenty minutes, but the questioning just went round and around, with the same denials and the same pointless answers. In the end she stood up, beckoned to Inspector O'Rourke to follow her and walked out of the interview room.

'Goodbye, then, missus!' called out Denny as she left. 'Nice to talk to you! G'luck to you so!'

Katie said to Inspector O'Rourke. 'We have him for assaulting Aislin, but I can't see that we can make any of the other charges stick. It's not like he was selling heroin or crack.'

'Crack?' said Inspector O'Rourke. 'I'd like to give the little gobdaw a crack round the head.'

Eight

Katie was over half an hour late for her meeting with John at the Hayfield Manor. She had tried ringing and texting him to say she was going to be delayed, but he hadn't picked up his phone or responded to her text messages. When she parked outside the front of the hotel she couldn't see his car there, either.

She went inside, crossed the lobby and went into the bar. There was a party of local businessmen in there, who had obviously lunched rather well and spent the rest of the afternoon drinking. She also recognized a county councillor sharing a bottle of Prosecco with a bosomy young brunette in a red dress who, to Katie's certain knowledge, wasn't his wife. He glanced up and saw Katie and immediately half shielded his face with his hand, as if that was going to make him unrecognizable. But there was no sign of John.

She sat down at a table by the window. One of the bar staff came over and asked her what she wanted to drink, but she smiled and said not just yet, she was waiting for someone. Five minutes passed and she texted John again, telling him that she had arrived, but he still didn't reply. The businessmen were shouting and bellowing with laughter so raucously that she couldn't hear herself think. She waited five minutes more, then she stood up and walked out. It was clear that John wasn't coming. Maybe he had never had any intention of coming. Maybe he had contacted her simply to punish her. *You let me down, Katie. Now I'm going to let you down.* If that was the reason, though, it was ridiculously petty and all that he had managed to do was waste her time.

* * *

It was almost ten to eight when she arrived home at Carrig View. The river estuary was the colour of tarnished steel and the sky was piling up with bruised-looking clouds. Rain was forecast overnight, but clearing by the morning. She hoped so. She hadn't taken Barney for a really long walk for weeks, and she felt as if she really needed some fresh air and exercise herself, and a chance to think about nothing at all.

When she reached her house she saw that a huge black Nissan Navara pickup was parked with two wheels on the pavement outside. She guessed it must be somebody visiting the Tierneys. She should have gone next door and told them that their guest had left hardly any room for anybody trying to walk past, especially old Mr O'Halloran in his mobility scooter, but it was late and she was tired and she didn't want to upset them, especially since they had volunteered to feed and walk Barney whenever she was late back home from the city.

When she turned into her driveway, however, she was surprised to see a heavily built man in a pale green linen suit standing in her porch, smoking a cigarette. She climbed out of her car and walked up the steps, and as she did so he took a last deep drag at his cigarette and then flicked it across her front lawn.

'Well, this is unexpected,' she told him, trying to sound calm and unimpressed.

The man blew smoke out of the side of his mouth. He looked as if he had no neck and his globe of a head could roll off his shoulders at any moment. His hair was cropped very short at the sides, Kim Jong-un style, and his eyes were tiny pinpricks. Underneath his jacket he was wearing a pink and blue floral shirt, with the three top buttons undone so that his grey chest hairs curled out of the top of it like traveller's joy.

Katie reached the top step. She had her keys in her hand, but she made no attempt to open the front door.

'What about you, DS Maguire?' said the man, in a croaky voice.

'Surviving, Mister Quilty,' replied Katie. 'And may I ask what you think you're doing here at my house?'

'Just came to pay you a sociable visit, that's all,' said Bobby Quilty. 'If Maguire won't come to the mountain, and all that.'

'The only time I'll ever come to see you is to haul you in,' said Katie.

'Ach, come on, you don't have to give out like that. Live and let live, that's what I always say.'

'Tell that to Detective Barry's parents. See if they agree with you.'

Bobby Quilty grimaced and scratched the back of his neck. 'I heard about that. Well, who couldn't? But don't you go accusing me of nothing. I didn't have nothing at all to do with it.'

'Sure you didn't. And pigs have wings. But I think you need to be getting away, don't you? I don't know what you're doing here, but you're not at all welcome.'

Bobby Quilty took out another cigarette and lit it, which made it obvious that he wasn't thinking of leaving just yet. This was one of those times when Katie was glad to feel her Smith & Wesson Airweight revolver against her hip.

'Well, DS Maguire, since it's plain you're not going to invite me inside for a wee drop, I'll tell you here and now what I drove all the way out here to tell you. The thing of it is, I'm running a business that is much in the public demand, as you know fine rightly, and at the end of the day I'm doing nobody no harm at all. In fact, I'd say that I'm providing a brave good public service and they ought to be awarding me a medal rather than setting the polls on me.'

Apart from feeling tired, Katie was growing impatient. 'I'm not going to argue with you about the popularity of cheap cigarettes, Mister Quilty. But every country needs its taxes and the fact remains that importing and selling tobacco without paying the duty on it is against the law.'

She said nothing about him using a large proportion of his profits to fund acts of terrorism. Working closely with G2, the Directorate of Intelligence in Naas, her team had already gathered a mass of incriminating evidence against the Authentic IRA, phone-taps and videos and witness statements, but she wasn't ready yet to give Bobby Quilty even an inkling of how much she knew.

All she said was, 'What you're doing is illegal and as soon as I'm ready I'll arrest you and charge you, and believe me, you won't see it coming, so you won't have the chance to nip over the border.'

Bobby Quilty blew out a long stream of smoke. 'Aye, I know that's what you get paid for, and it isn't yourself that makes the laws. So there's nothing personal in it, by any means at all. But I'm asking you to be reasonable, DS Maguire. You and me, I'm sure we can rub along together quite happy, without any need for getting up each other's noses.'

'Detective Barry was deliberately crushed to death, Mister Quilty. You may be surprised to hear it, but that got right up my nose.'

'Ach, I'm sure that must have been an accident. And it needn't have happened at all. Like, why was he bothering to chase after a jaunty like Denny Quinn?'

Katie said, 'Why exactly are you here, Mister Quilty? You know that I won't stop coming after you, you and all your dealers, too.'

'What – what if we made kind of a treaty between us?' said Bobby Quilty. 'You know, like the Good Friday Agreement, only the Quilty–Maguire Agreement.' There was a thick whispery quality in the way he said it that made Katie's wrists prickle. It was like, *Let's keep this to ourselves, shall we?* It almost had the feeling of an indecent proposition.

'I'm sorry,' said Katie. 'I'm not open to making any kind of treaties, especially with you.'

'I know you're a woman who doesn't scare easy,' Bobby Quilty told her. 'I read in the paper about you and them nuns. It takes some hard neck to stand up to the church, I'll tell you. Those priests, they scare me more than the O'Flynns ever did. So that's why I knew I had to have a trump card when I came to talk to you.'

Katie said nothing, but stayed where she was, watching Bobby Quilty smoke. Inside the house, Barney must have heard her and smelled her by now, because he was scratching and whining behind the front door. He probably couldn't understand why she wasn't coming in. She was tempted to call out to him, to reassure him, but she thought that could make her sound anxious and vulnerable and in front of Bobby Quilty she needed to appear utterly unyielding.

'I'll tell you what my trump card is,' said Bobby Quilty. 'It's not actually a card at all, it's a feller – a fine sham-feen by the name of John Meagher. A good friend of yours, as I understand it, or was once.'

Katie actually shivered, as if somebody had poured ice-water down the back of her blouse. *'John?'* she said.

'That's your man. The thing of it is, we have him. Kind of like a guest, you might say.'

'You've abducted him, is that what you're saying? You haven't hurt him, have you?'

'Ach no, catch yourself on, he's in grand condition. But we have him, yes, and we have him in a location where you couldn't find him in a month of Sundays. So this is where you and me, we're already in agreement. You wouldn't like to see nothing appalling happen to him, would you? And nor neither would I.'

'Do you know how many years they're going to give you in Rathmore Road for doing this?' Katie retorted, although she was so angry and afraid that she couldn't stop her voice from shaking. 'Kidnap, and threatening to cause physical harm? Even if you don't touch a hair on his head, you'll get ten years minimum. If you hurt him, I'll kill you myself.'

'You don't frighten me one iota, DS Maguire,' Bobby Quilty told her. 'Like I said to you, I'm only running a public service, and if you let me carry on with it without any more of your inter-ference, your John will be laid and lifted. We'll only keep him for a wee while, just to be sure that you're cooperating. But if you start coming after my dealers again, or sticking trackers on to my trucks, I can't guarantee that he's going to stay in one piece, do you know what I mean?'

'How do I know you really have him?'

'I thought of that,' said Bobby Quilty. He reached into the top pocket of his jacket and took out a silver bracelet. He held it out to her, but at first she made no move to take it.

'Go on, you know what it is. The inscription inside will prove it for sure.'

Katie reluctantly held out her hand and Bobby Quilty laid the bracelet in her palm. She didn't need to look at it to know what it was: the silver Ardagh bracelet she had given to John when he came back from America to live with her. It was engraved with beastly faces copied from the Ardagh Chalice and inside it was inscribed with the words *Grá agus dea-fhortún, K.*

'All right,' said Katie. 'But this doesn't prove he's alive and unharmed.'

'Aye, dead on, but you'll just have to take my word for it. Like, there'd be no point in my harming him if I wanted to make a deal with you, would there?'

'I could arrest you here and now,' said Katie.

'Come on then, scoop me if you want to. But whatever you say I've said, I'd flat out deny it and this garden isn't exactly black with witnesses, is it? There's something else you need to think on, too. What time are we on? My associates know where I am, and if I don't come back by eleven, your one-time fancy man will pay a very painful price for every minute that I'm late. Did you ever have a jag with a blind feller before?'

Katie didn't answer. Bobby Quilty was right – even if she arrested and charged him, she wouldn't be able to prove in court that he had threatened her. Apart from that, she had no doubt at all that he would hurt John, and hurt him severely, if she didn't agree to comply with his demands. Late last year a seventeen-year-old boy from Gurranabraher had given Detective Dooley a tip-off about one of Bobby Quilty's cigarette consignments and two days later he had been found with his ribcage impaled on the railings outside the Holy Trinity Church on Father Mathew Quay, still alive, with the word 'tout' burned into the skin of his forehead.

'Just go, Mr Quilty,' said Katie. 'If you think I'm going to stand here a moment longer and listen to you blowing, then you have another thing coming.'

'Don't panic, I'm out the gap,' Bobby Quilty told her. 'One more thing I'll say to you, though. If I get to hear that you've told anyone at all about this wee treaty of ours – even your da – then your John's going to suffer, I swear to God.'

'You leave my father out of this,' Katie warned him.

'No, DS Maguire, *you* leave your father out of this. And your fellow polls. This is just between you and me, you get it? And – oh, yes – I'll be wanting to see Denny Quinn back on the street by midnight.'

With that, he went up to Katie's front door, lifted the flap of the letter box and puffed smoke into it.

'There you are, Fido!' he said. 'Don't let nobody say that I never gave you a suck off my fag! You make sure your mistress keeps her bake shut, okay? Wouldn't want anything unpleasant to happen to your Uncle John, would we?'

Barney growled, but Bobby Quilty let the flap drop and lifted his fingertips to his lips to blow Katie an extravagant kiss. 'Grand to talk to you, DS Maguire. And grand to be able to come to such a mutually agreeable understanding. You're a princess among women, no mistake about that!'

He shuffled his way past her with a grin on his face, holding in his belly so that he didn't bump her. Katie didn't turn around as he went down the steps and crunched out of her shingle driveway, and didn't move at all until she had heard him start up the engine of his pickup and drive away. Only then did she open the front door and go inside. Barney clearly sensed that something was wrong because he snuffled and whuffled and circled around her, his tail beating against the radiator.

'It's all right, boy, don't stress yourself,' said Katie, tugging at his ears to calm him down. She could smell Bobby Quilty's cigarette smoke in the hallway and it made her feel sick. 'It was only some scummer, not worth you getting all stooky about.'

* * *

She went into the living room and switched on the lights, although she didn't switch on the TV as she normally did. She felt shaken right down to the core, and completely defenceless, which she had never experienced before. In the past two years she had dealt with several serious cases of kidnapping, where the perpetrators had threatened to maim or kill the people they had abducted, but she had always been able to handle them with professional detachment. Bobby Quilty, however, had taken John, and even though John had walked out on her, she still loved him, and the thought of him being blinded or mutilated or murdered made her tremble.

She looked at the small square clock on top of the bookcase. It was only five past eight, although it felt as if she had been talking to Bobby Quilty for nearly half an hour. She stood in the middle of the living room, gripping John's Ardagh bracelet tightly in her hand, sick with indecision. She knew exactly what procedure she had to follow. She should immediately contact Inspector O'Rourke and the rest of her team and send them out to discover when and where John had been abducted and where he was being held. But that would be critically risky. If Bobby Quilty caught wind that she had broken their 'treaty', she didn't doubt for a moment that he would order John to be mutilated or murdered, just to prove how much of a hold he had over her and that he wasn't a man to be messed with.

She trusted her detectives implicitly but it wasn't beyond the bounds of possibility that Bobby Quilty had one or two officers at the station in his pocket. Even gardaí who had served for five years took home less than 30,000 euros a year and she knew that any number of them had serious debt problems.

Barney stood looking up at her and made that creaking noise in the back of his throat. He needed to be fed and then taken for a walk. But how could she take him for a walk knowing that John was being held hostage and doing nothing to initiate his rescue?

She went to the mirror that hung over the fireplace and stared at herself, as if her mirror image were another, calmer Katie, who could give her an answer. Her dark red hair was looking messy and chopped-about, and her eyes were puffy, as if she had just woken up.

You have to handle this one very, very carefully, she told herself. *You're angry. You're afraid. But don't be rushed into taking some course of action you might regret. Bobby Quilty isn't going to hurt John so long as he thinks you're playing ball, because he knows that if anything happens to John, you'll set the dogs on him.*

For the first time, she held up the Ardagh bracelet and examined it closely. It was slightly bent out of shape, as if it had been forcibly pulled from John's wrist without opening the clasp. She wondered why he had still been wearing it. Did he still love her, in spite of having left her?

She placed the bracelet carefully on the shelf over the fireplace, next to the silver-framed photograph of John which she should have taken down, but hadn't. He standing next to a tractor at the Meagher family farm, stripped to the waist, one eye closed against the sunlight. He was tall, with dark curly hair and a crucifix of hair on his chest. She had always told him that he looked like a Greek god, but like a Greek god he had been jealous and controlling. In the end, that was why their relationship had broken down, because Katie refused to be controlled by any man, even a man she loved.

In spite of that, the Katie that she could see in the mirror was already beginning to work out a way of saving him from Bobby Quilty. It wasn't orthodox, and it was far from accepted procedure. It was probably illegal. But it could be the best way to protect John from coming to any harm and at the same time to bring down Bobby Quilty's cigarette-smuggling empire.

She sat down on the end of the leather couch and picked up the phone. It took the operator at Anglesea Street a few minutes to find Inspector O'Rourke for her, but eventually he picked up, sounding as if he had his mouth full.

'Sorry, ma'am. I was just getting myself a sandwich.'

'That's okay. We all have to eat. How are things going?'

'We're making some progress with the bodies in Blarney. Just after you left, the Blarney Historical Society came back to us. There was definitely a family called Langtry lived in that house, up until February 1921. The father's name was Stephen, so we should be able to trace him through public records.'

'Grand. I think Dr Kelley should be coming down tomorrow afternoon, so maybe we'll be able to make a positive ID within the next few days. I'd still like to keep this under wraps until we do. You haven't had the media sniffing around, have you?'

'Nothing. I reckon they're too busy with this gay marriage vote and this water meter fracas.'

'All right. Listen, the reason I'm ringing you is Denny Quinn. I want you to release him.'

There was a moment's silence and then Inspector O'Rourke said, '*Release* him? Did I hear that right? He's up in the district court tomorrow afternoon. What if he does a runner?'

'Just let him go. We're dropping the charges.'

'What? With all due respect, ma'am, he was flogging illegal fags and he cut Detective O'Connell's cheek wide open. Not forgetting that Gerry Barry was killed when he was trying to arrest him.'

'I know, Francis. But believe me, I have a very good reason for letting him go.'

'Am I allowed to know what it is, this very good reason?'

'Not yet, no. But I'll tell you as soon as I can, and when I *can* tell you I think you'll agree that it was the right thing to do.'

Another silence, longer this time, and before Inspector O'Rourke could answer her Katie said, 'Please don't discuss this with anybody else. If anybody wants to know why we're letting him go, all you have to say is "insufficient evidence". I'll be talking tomorrow to Chief Superintendent MacCostagáin, but it's very important that we keep this as quiet as possible. Let's just say it's a matter of life and death.'

'Okay,' said Inspector O'Rourke, although he still sounded troubled. 'I have you.'

Nine

A broken-down car transporter had caused a three-kilometre tailback on the N25 the following morning and it was raining hard so Katie had to keep her windscreen wipers flapping at full speed just to see the car in front of her. She didn't arrive at the station until 8.35, by which time she was already feeling anxious and irritable.

Detective 'Horse' Ó Doibhilin was waiting for her. He stood smiling expectantly while she took off her dripping-wet witch-goddess jacket, sat down at her desk and had a cursory look through all the folders and messages and letters that were piled up for her attention.

Then, 'Yes, Michael?' she said, as if she had only just realized he was there.

'The fellow from the Blarney Historical Society finally got in touch with me. Douglas Pike.'

'I know, yes. Inspector O'Rourke rang me yesterday evening.'

'He's found copies of the old staff records from Mahony's mill, going right back to nineteen-oh-something. All of their names, how much they got paid and where they all lived. He said that the Langtry family took up residence on Millstream Row in April 1916. They'd moved there from Dripsey. Stephen Langtry had been a machinist at the Dripsey woollen mills but for some reason he gave up his job there and moved to Blarney. Better money, more than likely, that was Douglas Pike's guess. The Langtry family lived in Blarney until the second week of February 1921.'

'But this Historical Society fellow didn't know what happened to them?'

'He had no idea they were all shot dead and buried under the floorboards, no.'

'You didn't tell him that?'

'Oh, no, of course not. But if he had known, he would have told me, for sure. He knows everything about Blarney right down to who drowned whose dog in 1937 for barking and keeping them awake all night, and who won the best barmbrack competition in 1951. He wasn't backward about telling me, either. I thought I was going to be stuck on the blower all afternoon. But—'

Detective Ó Doibhilin held up his notebook. 'I think I have a result. He told me that some of the Langtry family still live in Dripsey, in the Model Village. I've traced two people of that name there, and I've tried ringing them, but neither of them answered, so I'll go out there this morning and see if I can locate them. Tyrone from the Technical Bureau will be coming along with me, to take DNA swabs.'

'Good work, Michael,' said Katie. 'If we can positively confirm who *they* are, then it might help us find out who killed them. Grand. Thank you.'

She turned her attention back to her paperwork, but then she was aware that Detective Ó Doibhilin was still standing there. She looked up again and said, 'Yes, Michael? Was there something else?'

'No, not really, ma'am. It's just that I've never worked on a case like this before – you know, when the crime was committed such a long time ago. It's almost ninety-five years, like.'

'Well, I haven't either,' said Katie. 'Not unless you count that bog woman who was dug up in Mayfield.'

'I was only wondering why we're carrying on this inquiry at all. Like, whoever the offenders were, they must have passed away years ago. And, you know, I would have thought that we'd more than enough on our plates just at the moment.'

Katie said, 'You're right of course, Michael, and believe me, I'm not giving it a very high priority. But justice has to be done, even if it's long overdue, do you know what I mean? You might manage to hide whatever crime it is that you've committed, and nobody might discover what you've done until you're dead and buried, but you still ought to know that one day you could be found out and your name shamed for it.'

'Well, I suppose,' said Detective Ó Doibhilin.

'Look at Sonny O'Neill, for instance. He was the fellow who shot Michael Collins at Béal na Bláth in 1922, but that wasn't known for certain until they opened the files in the 1980s. O'Neill was long gone, but it was still important for us to know that he actually fired the fatal shot, do you know what I mean, whether you think he was a hero or a villain? What happened in the 1920s, it's still resonating, isn't it, even today?'

Detective Ó Doibhilin nodded, and nodded again, and said, 'All right. Yes, I deck that,' and left Katie's office. After he had gone she sat at her desk for a few minutes, thinking about what she had just said to him and hoping it hadn't made her sound too much like her old history mistress, Miss Mulvaney, whose grandfather had been shot dead at Croke Park on Bloody Sunday in 1920, and never let anybody forget it.

She felt frayed and exhausted. She hadn't been able to sleep all night, worrying about John and how she could rescue him from Bobby Quilty. She had also been trying to work out what she was going to say at this morning's operational meeting about cigarette smuggling, and how they were going to change their strategy after the murder of Detective Barry. Up until now – in open and sometimes angry disagreement with Assistant Commissioner Jimmy O'Reilly – Katie had repeatedly argued that they should go after Bobby Quilty in person and not spend valuable time and budget chasing after his small-time dealers and mules. This morning's meeting wasn't going to be easy. Now that John was being held hostage, under threat of his life, she would have to find a way of backtracking without losing authority or credibility or, most of all, face.

* * *

The meeting started fifteen minutes late and everybody in the conference room was growing restless and checking their watches even though there was a large clock on the wall. Superintendent Pearse was having a furious finger-jabbing argument with somebody on his tablet, and Chief Superintendent MacCostagáin was looking deeply disgruntled. In the hoarsely whispered words of Detective Markey, who was sitting close enough for Katie to be able to hear him, he had the face of a bulldog sucking piss from a stinging nettle.

At last, Assistant Commissioner Jimmy O'Reilly walked into the conference room, skull-like and ill-tempered, his thinning silver hair greased back, his eyes as dead as ever. He was still wearing his blue full-dress uniform and Katie remembered that he had attended a formal reception earlier that morning for the new minister for justice and equality, Mary Brennan. Jimmy O'Reilly never enjoyed being reminded that there was somebody up the ladder higher than him, especially when that somebody was a woman.

Behind Jimmy O'Reilly, holding a bulging folder of notes under his arm, came his senior personal assistant, James Elvin. He was a very good-looking young man, with fashionably brushed-up blonde hair and a smart grey suit, and despite Jimmy O'Reilly's permanent scowl James always seemed to be having a secret smirk to himself. Katie had found herself wishing when she first met him that she was ten years younger.

Chief Superintendent MacCostagáin stood up, cleared his throat, and said, 'Before we start, I'd appreciate it if you'd all stand for two minutes in silence to pay our respects to Detective Garda Gerald Barry, who gave his life in the line of duty.'

They all stood. Some crossed themselves and almost all of them closed their eyes or stared down at the floor. Katie kept her eyes open because she knew that if she closed them she would see Detective Barry's smile again and wonder what he had been dreaming as he died.

When they had all sat down, Jimmy O'Reilly rose stiffly to his feet. He was addressing more than sixty detectives and gardaí and technical specialists, but he fixed his eyes on the clock at the very back of the conference room and spoke in a barely audible

monotone, as if he were reluctantly reading out a restaurant menu
to somebody who had forgotten their glasses.

'Good morning. Tobacco smuggling. Point number one.
Strategy. I think we have to accept that it was the way in which
we conceptualized our role in dealing with tobacco smuggling that
led partly if not almost entirely to the tragic loss of Detective Barry.'

He paused for so long that Katie began to think that he had
forgotten what he was going to say next, or that he had even
forgotten where he was and that he was supposed to be talking
to them. The lengthy silence was punctuated by coughing and
shuffling, and one distinctive sneeze.

Eventually, though, he carried on in the same indistinct monotone. 'Point number two. Of course we acknowledge that the
smuggling and selling of NIDP tobacco is organized by criminal
gangs and our intelligence has clearly shown that some of those
criminal gangs are channelling their profits into illegal political
activities – such as, for instance, the Authentic IRA. However, the
offence of evading duty on tobacco is not of itself a direct threat
to public order.'

He paused again, licking his lips with the tip of his tongue,
like a lizard that had just swallowed a fly. 'Point number three.
Detective Barry is the first and so far the only fatal casualty of
tobacco smuggling in Cork, but that is one fatality too many. I,
for one, want to see no more lives lost, either gardaí or civilians,
not for an offence that is essentially financial. I'm not pretending
for a moment that smoking is harmless, or that health care for
smokers isn't a serious drain on government resources, but smoking
in designated areas is not in itself a crime. I accept that evading
duty on tobacco deprives the government of much-needed revenue,
but I think we have to ask ourselves how much responsibility the
government itself has to bear for bowing to pressure from the
cancer lobby and setting the retail price of cigarettes so high, the
highest in Europe.

'In my view, An Garda Síochána should be leaving the investigation into tobacco smuggling and the enforcement of duty entirely to

Revenue, except when violence or threats of violence are involved, or when illegal cigarette factories are set up in this country for the purposes of avoiding duty. Furthermore, we should leave the tracing and confiscation of any profits made from contraband tobacco to the Criminal Assets Bureau.'

Again he paused and licked his lips, and then he said, 'I've had detailed consultations with the deputy commissioner and with Chief Superintendent MacCostagáin, and we're broadly in agreement. Since the recent budget cuts, this division has burdened with an increasingly onerous caseload but has fewer officers and less money to cope with that caseload. It's patently clear that our efforts to break up cigarette-smuggling gangs by the piecemeal arrest of their dealers is not proving at all effective. Almost as soon as we arrest one dealer, another one appears on the same spot within minutes, and if we confiscate their stock, the gang simply resupplies them with a whole load more. It's like trying to cut the head off a hydrant.'

'Hydra,' Katie quietly corrected him, though she wasn't sure that he heard her.

Jimmy O'Reilly at last looked down at the faces of his audience, although his emotionless expression showed that he had made up his mind and that he wasn't expecting anyone there to challenge him. 'To sum up, I'm proposing that we curtail our strategy of arresting dealers and in future act only in support of Revenue and the CAB when called upon to do so. Does anybody have any views on that? Detective Superintendent Maguire, you've always been very vociferous when it comes to cigarette smuggling.'

Katie hardly knew what to say, although she was feeling a deep sense of relief. *Thank you, St Raphael*, she thought. St Raphael was the patron saint of lovers and she had said a prayer to him in the darkness of the night, pleading with him to keep John safe.

She hadn't expected for a moment that Jimmy O'Reilly intended to cut back Garda operations against cigarette smugglers. He had given an interview to the *Irish Times* only three weeks ago claiming that his pursuit of tobacco gangs would continue to be 'relentless'. But now she wouldn't have to come up with some fictitious justification for releasing Denny Quinn and suspending her inquiry into Bobby Quilty.

Even though she was relieved, she knew that it would arouse suspicion if she welcomed Jimmy O'Reilly's change of strategy with too much enthusiasm. It was common knowledge in Anglesea Street that there was no love lost between the two of them, either personally or operationally.

'Well, sir, I can't say that I totally go along with what you're suggesting,' she told him. 'In particular, I'm concerned that young people are being tempted by the smugglers to take part in organized crime and that that's going to lead them into much more serious offending as they grow older.'

Jimmy O'Reilly didn't look at her but kept his eyes on the audience, to see what their reaction was. 'Fair play to you, detective Superintendent I can see where you're coming from. But on the whole I think that we can rely on our social services to manage that particular problem – as we mostly do already, to be fair. If the courts won't convict fifteen-year-olds for selling illegal cigarettes, why are we bothering with arresting them and going through all the committal procedure? It needlessly ties up officers who could be going after car thieves and pimps and drug-dealers, and worse.'

Katie lifted both of her hands, as if she couldn't argue with what he was saying. 'All right, then. My team are up the walls at the moment with some very serious inquiries, no question about it, and it would certainly free up some of their time. So, yes, let's break off our surveillance of the dealers for a few weeks and see how things work out.'

'You *agree* with me, then?' Jimmy O'Reilly's lips twisted themselves into something that was almost a smile. 'That's a first. What about Detective Barry? You'll still be pursuing *that* investigation, I imagine?'

'Of course, although it's not going as well as I'd hoped. There's no forensic or CCTV evidence to identify the driver who knocked him down, and no witnesses have come forward yet, although that doesn't surprise me.'

She saw Detective Sergeant Begley shift around in his seat and frown at her. Only yesterday afternoon she had vehemently told him that she would find out who had killed Gerry Barry if it took the rest of her life. But Bobby Quilty or one of his gang were by far the most likely suspects and she wanted to give the impression that she didn't hold out much hope of arresting any of them.

Maybe I'm being more than a little paranoid, she thought. *Maybe there's nobody in this room who's going to contact Bobby Quilty as soon as this conference is over and tell him what I've just said. But how had Bobby Quilty managed to react so quickly to their attempted arrest of Denny Quinn at Mother Jones Flea Market, unless he had known in advance that Denny was under surveillance?*

Katie had little doubt that it would reach his ears somehow, and the less threatened Bobby Quilty felt, the better John's chances of survival.

* * *

She was buttoning up her jacket ready to go out when Detective Ó Doibhilin knocked at her door. He was carrying an old green Governey's shoebox.

'Oh, you're back,' she said. 'How did you get on? I'm in a bit of a rush, I'm afraid. I'm meeting somebody and I'm ten minutes late already.'

'To be honest with you, ma'am, I'm not too sure *what* I got.'

'What do you mean? Did you manage to find any of the Langtry family?'

Detective Ó Doibhilin put down the shoebox on the corner of Katie's desk and took out his notebook. 'I did, yes. Two in fact. The most direct descendant was Dermot Langtry, thirty-nine years old, lives with his wife and three children at O'Mahoney Terrace in the Model Village. He has his own painting and decorating business.'

'All right,' said Katie, trying not to sound impatient. 'So what's his connection to Stephen Langtry?'

'His great-grandfather, Colm Langtry, was Stephen Langtry's

younger brother. That, er, that would make him Stephen Langtry's great-grand-nephew.'

'That's correct. Who was the other one?'

'Dermot Langtry's second cousin, Ronan Fitzgerald. Forty-two years old, married with no children. He's an accountant for Crowley and McCarthy in Macroom. Lives only round the corner in Radharc Na Chroisigin.'

'So, did either of them know anything about the Langtrys' sudden disappearance?'

'Not Ronan Fitzgerald. All he was good for was triangulating our DNA sample. But Dermot Langtry did, yes, and that's why I'm so puggalized.'

'Go on.'

'Well, it seems like the Langtrys took off one day without inform-ing a soul that they were going – the same as that auld wan told us. They didn't tell their family, they didn't tell any of their friends. Stephen Langtry didn't even tell his boss at the mill that he was leaving. The house was cleared, too, all of the furniture gone. After about four months, though, Dermot's great-grandfather received a postcard from Stephen from America. Stephen wrote that the family had settled in New York State and he was working for a company called Glenside Woollen Mills there and that everything was grand.'

'Did he explain why they upped sticks like that, without telling anybody?'

'The postcard's right here in the box, ma'am. There's some letters, too, but I haven't had the time to read them yet. There's five letters and eleven postcards altogether. The last of them is dated Christmas 1923. After that, the Langtrys in Dripsey never heard from Stephen again. They couldn't write back to him and ask him where he was because he never them gave his full address. The letters just say "New York", with the date.'

'But they were definitely sent from America?'

'Take a sconce at them yourself, ma'am,' said Detective Ó Doibhilin. He snapped on a black latex glove, lifted the lid of the shoebox and picked out an envelope. Its address was scrawled in faded purple ink and a cluster of pale green 10 cent stamps were stuck on to it, each with a portrait of President Hayes, as well as two brown 4 cent stamps with a smiling Martha Washington.

Katie could also see a few of the postcards inside the box. Some of them were hand-coloured but most were sepia photographs of tall buildings and streets crowded with men in straw skimmers and women in ankle-length skirts.

'You're right, Michael, this *is* confusing, isn't it? If the Langtrys were shot dead and lying under the floorboards in Blarney, how could they be sending mail from America? These letters and post-cards – they certainly *look* genuine, don't they?'

'I'll be taking them down to the lab now to have them tested,' said Detective Ó Doibhilin. 'Unfortunately we don't have any authenticated samples of Stephen Langtry's handwriting to compare them with. Still and all, Tyrone took a DNA sample from Dermot Langtry and he should be able to give us the result of that later today or tomorrow.'

'Good. Dr Kelley will be arriving here about three and she'll be going directly up to Blarney, so we may be able to move the bodies sometime tomorrow. She didn't want them touched until she'd had the chance to examine them *in situ*, in case they fell to pieces. Now, I'm sorry to cut this short, but I really must go.'

As she hurried along the corridor, zipping up her jacket as she went, Detective Ó Doibhilin followed close behind her, carrying the shoebox under his arm.

'I'll tell you the truth, ma'am,' he said, as she pressed the button for the lift. 'You know what I was asking you earlier, why are we are trying to identify this family and find out who killed them even though it happened so long ago? I understand now what you were talking about. Like, I *really* understand. We *do* need to know, don't we? Like, *I* want to know myself. Whoever he is, there's a feller lying in a cemetery somewhere who shot them, the father, the mother, the two little kiddies and their dogs. I want to stand over his grave and tell him that he hasn't got away with it, even if he's dead.'

Ten

John was woken up by a man and a woman arguing with each other. Then he heard a dull thump and a complicated clatter, like furniture being knocked over.

'You're a fecking dirty clart, that's what you are!' the man shouted out in a strong Armagh accent. 'You're a fecking *hoo*-ah! I should clean your clock, so I should! I should kick your fecking teeth right down your fecking throat, you *hoo*-ah!'

The woman screamed something back at him, although John couldn't understand what it was. There was another thump and then she started wailing.

'Stop your gurning or I'll give you something to gurn about!' the man told her, but she carried on mewling and sobbing.

John slowly and painfully sat up. He felt bruised all over and his head was throbbing. His left eye was so swollen that he could barely see out of it and his cheekbone ached.

He looked around the room. It was small and stuffy, with a purple cotton blind pulled down over the window so that he couldn't see out, although he could hear rain pattering sporadically against the glass. It must have been a child's room because the walls were papered with space rockets and flying saucers and planets, and there was a white chest of drawers with stickers of smiling cars and aeroplanes on it. The narrow single bed had a pine headboard covered with more stickers and a stained mattress that smelled of dried urine. The purple carpet was spotted and moth-eaten, and one of the door panels was split as if somebody had once tried to kick it open from outside.

At last the woman stopped crying. John heard the man say something to her which sounded conciliatory, but then she shrilled, 'Away to feck, you frigger!'

He could clearly remember leaving his friend Peter Doody's house in Knocknadeenly, where he had been lodging since he had walked out on Katie before Christmas, and driving down Summerhill into the city. He could remember turning from Western Road into Donovan's Road on his way to the Hayfield Manor Hotel. A young woman had stepped out into the road in front of him with a baby buggy and when she had tried to jump back out of the way the buggy had tipped over. He had stopped and climbed out of his car to make sure that the child hadn't been hurt, but after that everything was a blank.

Very cautiously, he touched the back of his head. His black curly hair was stuck together and he could feel a large lump. He could only assume that he had been hit very hard and knocked unconscious. Not only that, he had a strange, bitter taste in his mouth, as if he been drinking some kind of medicine.

He tried to stand up. He managed to take two staggering steps forwards and then the floor tilted and he had to sit back down on the bed. His head was banging even harder and he felt as if he could hardly breathe.

He was about to try again when he heard a key being turned in the lock and the door opened. Two men crowded into the room. One of them had a huge belly that hung over his belt, a piggy-looking face, and his hair shaved up the sides of his head in what the Northern Irish called a scaldy. The other was scrawny, with tufty grey hair and brown crowded teeth and tattoos of a woman's hands around his neck, as if he were being choked. Both of them were smoking. Behind them, in the next room, John could see the same young woman who had crossed the road in front of him with her baby buggy. She had bleached-blonde hair and enormous breasts that were straining under a tight green T-shirt with a picture of Bono on it, and a dark maroon bruise next to her mouth.

'All right, big lad?' said the huge-bellied man. 'How's it cutting?'

'Who the hell are you?' John demanded. 'What the hell did you do to me? And where am I?'

'Bobby Quilty's the name, and this is my valet, Chisel. My apologies, like, if you've been inconvenienced. But, you know, that's the price you pay for cosying up to the polls.'

'*What?* What in the name of Jesus are you talking about?'

'You and that tasty Detective Superintendent Maguire, that's what I'm talking about.'

'What about her?'

'You and she are a bit of an item, right?'

'What the hell has it got to do with you? Who the hell are you?'

'I told you, big lad. Bobby Quilty. Did your old doll never mention me? Let's just say that I'm one of Cork's most successful entre-pren-hoo-hahs.'

'I still have no idea what you're talking about.'

Bobby Quilty took a deep drag on his cigarette and then blew a long stream of smoke directly into John's face, so that he had to close his eyes and his mouth tightly and turn his head away.

'Calm your knickers, big lad, I'll tell you what I'm talking about. For fecking *months* now, your Detective Superintendent Maguire has been sticking her neb into my entre-pren-hoo-ring something desperate. In fact, she's been doing my fecking head in. So in order to persuade her to leave me in peace, I decided to acquire myself something to negotiate with, like a trump card, like – and that trump card is you. The long and the short of it is, she and me have come to an agreement.'

'What kind of agreement?'

'Catch yourself on, will you, what do you think? If she lets me carry on my business undisturbed, you'll stay sound. But if she keeps on after me, John, and keeps on scooping the people who work for me, well, I can't guarantee that God will preserve you. Not in one piece, any road.'

John said, 'You're out of your mind. You don't seriously think that she's going to leave you alone just because you're holding me hostage?'

'It had crossed my mind,' said Bobby Quilty, taking another drag, but this time blowing it out sharply upwards and sideways.

'Detective Superintendent Maguire and me, we're not even an item any more,' John told him. 'We split up just before Christmas.'

'You were going to meet her last night, though?'

'How the hell did you know that?'

'Ach, that's for me to know and you to find out. But let's just say there's nothing that happens in Cork that Bobby Quilty isn't wise to.'

'So, how long do you intend to keep me here?' John asked him.

Bobby Quilty shrugged. 'I hadn't really given it a whole lot of consideration, to tell you the truth. But I'd say long enough to make sure that your old doll sticks to what she promised.'

'I think you're underestimating her badly,' said John. 'She's far more dedicated to the law than she is to me. She broke up with me because I wanted her to leave the Garda. Whatever you do to me, she'll still come after you. That's what she's like.'

'We'll just have to wait and see, won't we?' grinned Bobby Quilty. 'Well, *I'll* be able to see, but if she chooses not to honour our agreement, it's very possible that *you* won't be able to. But don't worry. I still have my da's old walking stick and a tin of white Dulux.'

Chisel grinned, too, exposing his crowd of mahogany-coloured teeth.

'Just settle yourself down, John,' said Bobby Quilty. 'Sorcia will fetch you some tea later. You're okay with a Bigfoot sausage, are you, from the chippie?'

Eleven

Kyna Ni Nuallán was waiting for Katie in the small alcove just inside the front door of Henchy's Bar, up in St Luke's Cross. She was sitting in the corner with her back to the stained-glass window and even though the alcove was so gloomy she was wearing large black Chanel sunglasses. She had also tied a black silk scarf around her head, pirate-style, and the collar of her black nylon jacket was turned up.

'If I hadn't known who you were, I wouldn't have recognized you,' said Katie, taking off her jacket and sitting down beside her.

'Well, you said to be discreet,' said Kyna. 'Do you want a drink of anything?'

'I could murder a double vodka, but a cup of coffee would be grand.'

Kyna lifted her hand and called out to the bearded young barman, 'Declan, would you do me a favour there and fetch my friend a cup of coffee?'

Katie said, 'You know him? I thought you'd never been in here before.'

'I haven't. But he was coming on to me as soon as I walked in. He said I was the first beour to set foot in the place since Paddy's Day.'

Katie couldn't help smiling. Kyna was very pretty, in a blonde, elfin way. Even her fellow detectives used to come on to her. What they usually failed to realize was that she had no interest in men whatsoever – not sexually, anyway. Katie couldn't stay smiling for long, though. She had asked Kyna to meet her here because she needed to ask for her help. She hadn't been able to think of anybody else who could not only do what she wanted but could be trusted to do it. The trouble was, what she wanted could turn out to be hazardous in the extreme. Kyna had almost sacrificed her life for Katie once already, by stopping the bullet that had been meant for her, and Katie was beginning to wonder if it was too much to ask her to do it again.

It was because of the dangers involved that Katie had arranged to meet her here, at Henchy's. It was less than five minutes north of the city centre, up at the top of Summerhill, but it was not a bar frequented by any of Bobby Quilty's gang, or any other city scobes, or anybody at all who was likely to recognize Katie. Even so, she was wearing a purple beret into which she had tucked most of her dark red hair.

'So what's this about?' asked Kyna. 'I was planning to go back to Dublin tomorrow to see if I can find myself a flat. There's still nearly six months left on my current lease here, but I met a girl from the university last week and she's desperate for somewhere to live so I may be able to sublet to her.'

The barman brought over Katie's cup of coffee with two ginger biscuits in the saucer, so she waited until he was out of earshot.

'It's Bobby Quilty,' she said. 'He's kidnapped John and he says he's going to do him serious harm if I carry on interfering in his tobacco-smuggling business.'

Kyna looked both shocked and baffled. '*John?* You mean *your* John? I thought he was totally out of the picture. Didn't he go back to the States?'

'He might have done. In fact, he probably did. But he's here in Cork now,' said Katie. She took the silver Ardagh bracelet out of her pocket and passed it across the table. 'This was my present to him when he came back last year. Bobby Quilty gave it to me as proof that he really has him.'

'Oh, Jesus,' said Kyna. She handed the bracelet back and squeezed Katie's hand. 'You must be so worried. Have you told anybody at the station?'

Katie shook her head. 'Not yet. They'd want to take immediate action. Or at least, Denis MacCostagáin would. He won't tolerate anybody trying to intimidate individual guards. But Quilty only has to pick up the slightest sniff that we're still after him and God alone knows what he might do to John. I'm sure that Quilty killed Gerry Barry, or one of his henchmen did it on his instructions, and that was over what? A few dozen boxes of Russian cigarettes. I don't think he'd have the slightest compunction about killing John and dumping his body where I'm never going to find him.'

Kyna stared at Katie for a long time without speaking. Eventually, though, she said, 'Do you still love him?'

'John? Love doesn't come into it. He's a human being and Quilty's threatening to mutilate or murder him.'

'But come on, that happens almost daily, doesn't it? Abduction, like, do you know what I mean, and blackmail? I've never known you to pull the plug on any inquiry, *ever*, just because somebody was being held hostage. Completely the opposite, in fact. You've gone after them tooth and claw.'

'Of course,' said Katie. 'But most of the time it's one scummer kidnapping another scummer because he's been horning in on whatever racket he's running. But John isn't a rival tobacco smuggler, or a drug-pusher, or a pimp who's been grooming another pimp's prostitutes. John is totally innocent, Kyna. His only crime was to have a relationship with me.'

Kyna kept hold of Katie's hand for a while, but then let it go. 'You should drink your coffee before it gets cold.'

Katie said, 'It'd be different if I had any idea at all where Quilty's holding him. I could set up a raid, which might be risky but at least we'd have a chance of getting him out of there in one piece.'

'Don't we know anybody who's prepared to grass on Quilty?' asked Kyna. 'What about that Barty McGee? If it wasn't for him, we wouldn't have known half of what Quilty was up to.'

'I don't think Barty's going to be talking to us again, Kyna. Quilty gave him the choice of leaving the country and never coming back or eating his own mebs fried in Kerrygold – or that's what he told Dooley.'

'So what are you going to do?'

'Well, I've had one heaven-sent stroke of luck. Jimmy O'Reilly has decided that after Gerry Barry being killed we should suspend our inquiry into Quilty and instead leave it to Revenue to go after him. He says he doesn't want the lives of any more officers put in jeopardy for such a low-level crime, but I suspect that he's run way over budget this year and this is how he's going to save himself money. Anyway, I said a novena to St Raphael and he must have answered me because at least I didn't have to stand up in front of half the station and come up with some lame excuse why I thought we should lay off Quilty.'

'St Raphael?'

'The patron saint of lovers.'

'So you *do* still love him? John, I mean. You do know that St Raphael is also the patron saint of insanity and nightmares? And short-sightedness, too.'

'Mother of God, you must have been paying attention in catechism.'

Kyna gave her a small, regretful smile. 'No. But I looked him up not long ago to see if he could help me win my ideal partner.'

Katie sipped at her coffee and snapped one of her ginger biscuits in half, though she didn't eat it.

'Officially, you're still on sick leave,' she said. 'You don't have to do what I'm going to ask you, not if you don't want to. It won't be insubordination. And I won't think badly of you, either.'

'I can guess what it is,' said Kyna.

'I'm sure that you can, but believe me, Kyna, if there was any other way, I wouldn't ask. It's no use my pretending that it won't be fierce dangerous, especially if anybody recks you. But you haven't been in Cork all that long, and you haven't been involved in any cases of smuggling or evading tobacco or alcohol duty – nor the Authentic IRA, either.'

'Listen, there's lots of ways I can disguise myself,' Kyna told her. 'I can dye my hair. I've had it all kinds of colours over the years – shamrock green, once! But black looks good on me. And

I can wear clothes that make me look a whole lot younger. Really skinny jeans, loads of bangles and necklaces, and I have a tattoo on my shoulder already, which I can show off.'

'You have a tattoo? What of?'

'A lyre, as a matter of fact. L-y-r-e, not l-i-a-r, although I like the double meaning, too. Sappho the poet used to play the lyre, that's why I had it done.'

'All right,' said Katie. This wasn't the time to go into the implications of that any further. 'If you can do this for me, I'll contact you tomorrow, probably, and tell you where you can find one of Quilty's dealers. They're growing more and more brazen about selling their cigarettes out in the open so it shouldn't be hard to locate one. But, like I say, you don't have to do it. I don't want you getting hurt again.'

'Detective Superintendent Maguire, I'm a police officer. I know what the risks are. I'm not one hundred per cent sure that this is the right way to go about rescuing John, but if this is what you want to do, I'll do it.'

'So how would you handle it? We can't lift Quilty because we don't have any evidence to bring charges against him, and even if we brought him in for questioning his lawyers would have him out again in five minutes flat. In the meantime he'd make sure that something horrible happened to John. He threatened to blind him.'

Kyna took hold of her hand again. 'I've said I'll do it, Katie, and I'll do it.'

Katie reached into her pocket again and took out a pink iPhone in a pink sparkly case. 'Here, take this. It belonged to one of the girls we picked up when we raided that BTB massage parlour on Princes Street. If Quilty asks to check your phone, this one has the numbers of enough pimps and pushers and generally dubious characters to fill Páirc Uí Chaoimh twice over. I've also changed the number marked 'Ma' to my own mobile number, so if he asks you to call your mother just to make sure that you are who you're pretending to be, you'll be able to do it.'

'And who am I pretending to be?'

'Sheelagh Danehy, of Mount Nebo Avenue in Gurra. Late of the support centre for troubled teenage girls at North Pres Secondary School. You went through the copping on course but didn't really cop on, and when they gave you art therapy you got yourself thrown out for emptying your paint water over another girl's head. I'm sure you can improvise the rest.'

'I'll try my best. I was always a goodie two-shoes at school, and of course I never fancied any of the boys. Whenever I walked down the corridor, some of them used to sing out "Kyna, Kyna, with the Untouched Vagina".'

Katie smiled again. 'I'm sure you can act like a slutbag if you try.'

She spent another twenty minutes briefing Kyna on how she could inveigle herself into Bobby Quilty's cigarette-smuggling operation. Soon after she had been appointed a detective garda herself, Katie had been planted undercover into a drug-dealing gang in Togher and she knew how difficult and dangerous it was to repel the sexual advances of some of the men involved.

Expressionless behind her sunglasses, Kyna said, 'I have done it with men, you know. Sometimes because I was langered. Usually out of pity.'

'Don't bother about the cigarette-smuggling itself,' Katie told her. 'I'm not interested in that, nor in Quilty's connections to the A-IRA, or that he was probably responsible for Gerry Barry being killed. Not yet, anyway. All I want to know is where John is.'

'I know,' said Kyna, almost sadly.

Katie didn't embrace Kyna as they parted on the pavement outside, although she would have liked to. It was still raining and there was nobody around, but she didn't want to risk anybody seeing them. As it turned out, there was a white-faced young man watching her from the window of Ladbroke's betting office as she returned to her car. She wondered what he would say if she went in and asked him to give her the odds on John surviving.

Twelve

Katie headed directly to Blarney. Dr Kelley had arranged to meet her at Millstream Row rather than going into the city centre first and then having to come all the way out again. Because she had needed to bring so much specialist equipment with her, she had driven from Dublin with one of her assistants instead of taking the train. That would have taken her nearly three hours, especially in this weather, and she had told Katie that she was anxious to get started as soon as possible.

When she arrived, Katie found that Millstream Row been completely cordoned off and a diversion had been set up around Sunberry Heights for what little traffic there was. A wet and miserable-looking garda unhooked the crime-scene tape for her so that she could park behind the two patrol cars that were already there, as well as two vans and an estate car from the Technical Bureau and a large blue Transit van which was probably Dr Kelley's.

She found Dr Kelley inside the living room, which was lit so brightly with forensic lamps that she had to raise her hand to shield her eyes. Dr Kelley was kneeling on the floor on the opposite side of the room, cutting samples of hair from the head of the mummified man. She was a small, tubby woman, who looked even tubbier in her Tyvek suit. She had a round face with a double chin and round glasses and bushy, mannish eyebrows. In spite of that, Katie thought that if she had plucked her eyebrows and applied a little blusher and lipstick, she could have made herself looked quite sweet and appealing, like a child's doll that had unexpectedly grown to adulthood.

'How's it going?' she asked. Bill Phinner was there, too, standing next to Dr Kelley, and he patted Dr Kelley on the shoulder so that she looked up and saw Katie standing by the door.

'I'll be with you in – *two* seconds,' said Dr Kelley, carefully dropping the hair sample into a clear plastic envelope. Then she stood up and edged her way around the room, tugging off her latex glove and shaking Katie's hand.

'Mary Kelley,' she said, in a brisk, enthusiastic voice. 'I saw you last April, at that forensic symposium at Dublin University. I *so* much wanted to talk to you about the bog woman in Mayfield, but I'd been buttonholed by some *terminally* boring Nigerian biochemist and by the time he'd finished regaling me with his anecdotes about Ebola you'd disappeared.'

'You could have called me any time.'

'Well, time is what I never have. It would be a *blessing*, I can tell you, if so many people in Ireland would stop dying in unusual or unexplained circumstances and give my head some peace once in a while. And now we have this unfortunate family and they passed away before anybody in this room was even born.'

'My guess is the early 1920s,' said Katie. 'The problem is, we have some uncertainty about who they actually are. The records show that in 1921 a family called the Langtrys were living here and that they suddenly vanished without telling anyone they were leaving. A few months later, though, they started sending letters and postcards from America, somewhere in New York State, so maybe they'd just done a moonlight flit. If that was the case, though, who are *these* people, and who shot them, and why?'

Bill Phinner said, 'We should have the results of the DNA tests sometime tomorrow morning, so at least we'll be able to see if they were related to the Langtrys in Dripsey.'

'We'll be moving the bodies, too, first thing tomorrow morning,' said Dr Kelley. 'Once I have them in the morgue I'll be able to carry out comprehensive tests to find out exactly how old they actually are, and how they became desiccated like this, as well as what diseases they might have been suffering from and what their last meal was.'

'Once Mary has retrieved them we'll be testing the bullets, too,' Bill Phinner put in. 'That may give us an idea of what kind of gun was used to kill them – but of course the chances of finding that weapon today are infinitesimal.'

Dr Kelley turned to her assistant, who was a slight young woman who looked as if she were half-Chinese. 'Have you all the photographs you need, Annie? Then we can start on the X-rays.'

Annie went outside to the van and came back after a few minutes carrying a grey handheld MINI Z X-ray machine and the tablet viewing screen that went with it. Katie had seen one of these handheld scanners being demonstrated but had never seen it in use at a real crime scene. It used backscatter technology to detect not only metal and bone but organic material such as drugs and explosives, or even plastic guns that had been made with 3-D printers.

'It's X-ray, all right, but the radiation level is so low we don't have to shield it,' said Dr Kelley. 'I have to tell you, I've been finding it a *boon*, an absolute boon, but it wasn't cheap. Fifty thousand euros, which is why Dr Reidy wouldn't let me take it on the train. He knows me and trains, and what I leave on them. I left a fifteen-hundred-year-old skull on the ten past three from Ballinasloe and it went all the way to Tullamore on its own.'

Katie said, 'What will you do once you've finished the X-rays?'

'We'll be wrapping each of the bodies in polythene and constructing a frame around it to keep it in position so that we do as little damage as possible. Once we have them in the morgue and properly laid out we'll be able to undress them and do full CGI scans and radiocarbon testing.'

'I'll let you crack on, then,' said Katie. 'You have my number, so call me if you need anything at all. You're staying at the Clarion tonight, aren't you? Their restaurant's good, if you like Asian. I'd join you for dinner, but I'm afraid I've a rake of paperwork to catch up on.'

'That's all right,' said Dr Kelley. 'Annie's very good company. I chose the Clarion specially because I knew she'd like the food.'

In reality, Katie had almost finished her paperwork, but she and John had eaten in the Kudos restaurant at the Clarion several times and she knew she wouldn't have the appetite for it, or for any other restaurant.

She stayed for a while to watch Annie carefully scanning the body of the little girl, then she gave a salute to Bill Phinner and walked out of the house into the rain. She was only halfway back to her car, however, when she saw an RTÉ outside broadcast van parked further along the terrace, and then she saw Fionnuala Sweeney from the *Nine o'Clock News* standing by the crime-scene tape, holding up her microphone as if she were carrying the Olympic torch.

'Detective superintendent!' she called out. 'Detective Superintendent Maguire! Can you spare me a minute?'

Katie waved her hand from side to side to indicate that she was too busy and opened the door of her car. Before she could climb in, however, Fionnuala shouted out, '*Langtrys!*'

Katie closed her car door and walked over to the tape. Fionnuala was gingery and white-skinned, but she would have been attractive to men who liked mermaids, especially with the rain sparkling in her hair. Her cameraman was standing close behind her left shoulder and as Katie approached he pinched out his cigarette and tucked it behind his ear.

'I hear that some bodies have been found underneath the floorboards of that house they're doing up.'

'I can't comment at the moment, Fionnuala.'

'I'm given to understand that they're a family called the Langtrys, who disappeared in 1921. Father, mother, two small children and even the family dogs.'

'Who told you that?'

'I'm sorry, detective Superintendent I can't reveal my sources. But it *is* the Langtrys, isn't it, and they've all been shot?'

'Did that Mrs O'Neill tell you that?'

'I'm sorry. Like I say, I can't reveal my sources.'

Katie took a deep breath and looked away. She didn't want to antagonize Fionnuala because she needed RTÉ's support so often in broadcasting appeals for information about robberies or news of missing children, or eyewitness accounts of fatal traffic accidents. On the other hand, she had felt right from the very beginning that the discovery of these bodies needed to be handled with extreme sensitivity. An entire family wouldn't have been shot for no reason at all, especially in 1921, and before she made a media announcement she really wanted to know what that reason had been.

Maybe she was being over-cautious, but she knew from experience that historic grudges could very quickly get out of hand, even if they were nothing more than old family feuds. She had dealt with a case only three weeks ago when a farmer in Curraheen had come close to being killed by his neighbour over a sixty-year-old argument about fifteen and a half metres of scrubby turf.

She turned back to Fionnuala and said, 'All I can tell you now is that several human bodies were discovered during the renovation of one of the houses here on Millstream Row. Currently, they're being examined by the Acting Deputy Pathologist, Dr Mary Kelley, who specializes in historic forensics. That is because our immediate impression was that the bodies had been hidden on the property for some considerable period of time.'

'A family called the Langtrys suddenly disappeared from Millstream Row in 1921. Is it them?'

'We've taken DNA samples, but so far we haven't made a positive identification. We can't yet be sure who they are or when they died or how. As soon as I have more information I will, of course, let you know.'

'It *could* be the Langtrys, though?' Fionnuala persisted.

'As I've just told you, Fionnuala, we can't yet be sure.'

'But they were shot?'

'I can't comment until Dr Kelley has completed her full examination of the bodies.'

'And how long will that take?'

'It will take as long as it takes. That's all I have to say at the moment.'

'Was Radha Langtry having an affair with a British soldier? Do you think that the family might have been shot because of that?'

Katie could have stalked straight to Nora O'Neill's house and taken hold of her by her withered neck and shaken her until she was sick. Instead she said, 'I have absolutely nothing to say about that, Fionnuala. This family have not yet been identified and I am certainly not going to start inventing wild theories about how and why they died until I have all the facts. It's going to be a long and painstaking business, and we may never know the whole truth, but I can promise you that as soon as I know any more, so will you.'

Thirteen

Hours went by, although John could only guess how many because his abductors had pulled off his wristwatch, as well as the Ardagh bracelet that Katie had given him. Eventually he eased himself over on to his side, wincing with pain, and then stood up. He swayed for a moment before taking a single lurching step towards the window. First he held on to the footboard at the end of the bed, and next he reached out for the knobs on the chest of drawers. The top drawer unexpectedly slid open and he almost fell backwards, but there was something inside the drawer that jammed it halfway. He paused, breathing with quick little sniffs, then managed to stagger to the window and hold on to the sill.

When he had first woken up it had already been gloomy outside because of the rain, but now he lifted up the cheap purple blind and saw that it was dark and the street lights were shining. He was in a first-floor room overlooking a small walled yard with green wheelie bins and a bicycle in it. The window handle was stiff, but he managed to wrench it upwards and push the window open, though it had a safety cable fixed to it and would only open about twenty centimetres.

Up on the skyline, only about half a kilometre away, John could make out the spires of St Mary and St Anne's Cathedral. He craned his neck sideways and pressed his head against the glass, even though the lump was still so tender that he gritted his teeth and whispered, 'Ow, *shit*. Ow!' When he did this, he could just see Shandon Bells Tower with its clock faces and pepperpot dome, and its salmon-shaped weathervane. That meant this house was somewhere in Blackpool, on the north-east side of the city centre – maybe on Leitrim Street or Pine Street. If he could get out of here, it wouldn't be difficult for him to find help. He might even be able to walk to Anglesea Street – or hobble there, anyway – and find Katie.

He peered down into the yard. Although the bedroom was on the first floor, there was a lean-to roof directly below the window, probably a toilet or wash-house. Whatever it was, John reckoned that if he could remove the safety cable from the window he would probably be able to clamber down to the yard below. He was badly bruised and his head was pounding with every beat of his heart, but he was still strong and reasonably fit. After he had given up working on his late father's farm he had accompanied Katie to her kick-boxing sessions whenever he could, and after he had walked out on her and moved back to Knocknadeenly he had kept up his running. It was while he was out running last week, under a low grey sky, with only the crows on the telephone wires for company, that he had suddenly realized how much he missed Katie. He knew that he had hurt her. That had been the whole point of his walking out. But standing between the hedgerows on that empty road, panting and sweaty, he saw that he had probably suffered much more pain from his jealousy than she had. She wasn't as tough as most people thought she was, but she knew how to put the past behind her.

He let the blind drop and made his way back to the bed. He sat there for a while, listening. He could hear the muffled sound of a television downstairs, but couldn't hear any voices. With any luck, he could climb out of the window without making too much noise and be out and away before Bobby Quilty and Chisel realized he had gone.

He stood up again, crossed the room, and pressed his ear against the door. He could hear the closing music of *Fair City*, so it must be 8.30. He thought he heard Bobby Quilty barking something and then letting out a harsh, abrasive laugh, but all he could hear after that was the blurting of one TV channel after another as if somebody was using the remote to see if there was anything they wanted to watch.

Okay, he told himself, *if you don't go now, you may never get another chance, especially if Katie doesn't give a damn what happens to you – and who could blame her?*

He crept back towards the window, steadying himself on the end of the bed again and then holding on to the chest of drawers. Looking into the half-open drawer he could see now what had caused it to jam. It was filled with a whole heap of assorted junk – ballpoint pens, Christmas-tree lights, suitcase keys and rolls of Sellotape, as well as a pair of sunglasses with only one lens and a diary for 1996. But what had caused it to stick was a red-handled screwdriver that had tilted upwards and dug its point into the underside of the frame.

John jiggled the drawer and forced it back in. Then he slid his hand in and lifted out the screwdriver. *Exactly what I need to open this window. There is a God. Or at least a patron saint of those whose lives are in danger because they don't have the right tools on them.*

He raised the blind, opened the window as far as it would go and started to unscrew one end of the safety cable. The screws were crossheads and the screwdriver was slightly too large for them, so he had to hold it at an angle. Eventually, though, he managed to loosen both screws to the point where he could twist them out between finger and thumb. With the safety cable hanging loose, he could open the window as far as it would go. It was still raining, but John could smell fresh air, and river, and traffic fumes, and freedom.

He took hold of the window frame and heaved himself up, but as he did so he whinnied in pain and almost bit off the tip of his tongue. When his chest was pressed against the edge of the sill, he realized that Bobby Quilty's men must have broken at least two of his ribs, and he was in agony. He hung there, unable to breathe because the pain was so intense, his mouth filling up with saliva and blood, and for a moment he was tempted to let himself drop back to the floor and give up any attempt to escape.

I can't do it. I can't take it. It hurts too much. But then he thought: *If this is what they've done to you already, John, what do you think they're going to do to you if Katie keeps after them? You heard what Bobby Quilty threatened to do, he threatened to blind you. And that was just for beginners.*

He didn't know how long he stayed there, with his head and shoulders sticking halfway out of the window, blinking at the rain that was spitting into his eyes. At last, however, he summoned up the will to pull himself up even further. The pain in his chest was unbearable, greater than any pain he had ever experienced before, and he could feel his ribs crunching. He began to weep like a small boy and he couldn't help thinking of his mother and the way she used to comfort him when he was little and he had tripped over and scraped his knees on the cinder path. He could almost hear her soft voice cooing at him and smell her perfume as she hugged him better. But his mother was in a home now, with dementia, and he was here, halfway out of this window, and nothing could turn time back.

You're not giving up. Pain is imaginary. Pain is only your body's way of protecting itself, but your body doesn't know what Bobby Quilty is going to do to you, and that will cause you infinitely more pain than the pain you're suffering now.

He tried to lift up his right leg so that he could perch his knee on the windowsill. That would give him the leverage he needed to lift up his left leg, too, and then he would be able to climb or tumble out of the window – tumble, more likely. If he fell, though, he fell. At least he would have escaped.

The first time he tried to lift his leg he simply couldn't summon up sufficient strength for his knee to reach the edge of the sill. He gripped both sides of the frame even tighter and heaved himself a few more inches out of the window.

Oh God, I can't do it. Yes, you can. Oh God, please, I can't do it. Yes, you can. You have to.

He rested for a few seconds, blood pounding in his ears, and then raised his leg again, more slowly. He still couldn't lift it as high as the sill and he had to let it sink back down.

You can. You have to. You have to get out of here.

He tried a third time, whinnying through his nostrils with pain and effort, and at last succeeded in pulling himself up on to the sill, first with his right knee and then, immediately afterwards, with his left.

Holy Mary, Mother of God, please let me survive this. If this was my punishment for abandoning Katie when she needed me, I accept it. But please, Holy Mother, enough is enough.

He clung on to the window frame with both hands, leaning out as far as he could. He had done almost the same thing when he was a young boy, kneeling on his bedroom windowsill at his parents' farmhouse, staring up at the sky at night, trying to see angels – though he had never seen angels. He couldn't see any tonight, either.

This window was too small and he was in too much pain to be able to turn himself around and climb down backwards on to the slates. He would have to climb out head-first and then try to slide and scrabble down the lean-to roof like a body-surfer and hope that when he reached the gutter there wasn't too much of a drop down into the yard below.

Right, he thought, although he was in so much agony that he could hardly think at all. *Count down from five, and then dive, and hope the Lord spares you.*

He bent forward as far as he could, until his fingertips touched the wet lead flashing where the lean-to's slates joined the wall of the house. He was just about to launch himself off the sill when he heard the bedroom door open and almost at once Sorcia's voice screeching out, '*Chisel! For feck's sake, Chisel, your man's only climbing right out the feckin' windie! Chisel!*'

John see-sawed himself out of the window and on to the slates. He might have imagined he was going to surf down the roof on his stomach, but he pitched head over heels on to his back, cracking and splintering the slates as he fell, and then slid down the rest of the way at a forty-five degree angle, still on his back, frantically scrabbling for any kind of a hand-hold. Before he knew it he had reached the gutter. He made a grab for it, but it was rusty and sharp-edged and all he managed to do was rip the skin of his hand and tear the gutter away from its soffit. Together, both he and the length of rusty metal dropped down into the yard.

It wasn't a long drop, no more than two and a half metres, but there was a rabbit hutch directly underneath and a stack of old sash-window frames, with the glass still in them. John fell face-down, smashing one of the windows with his forehead and almost flattening the rabbit hutch, so that the rabbit had to scrabble to the other end. He lay on top of the hutch and the window frames, still conscious but unable to move. He was far too badly bruised and, besides, the wire netting from the hutch had snagged in his sweater. His nostrils were filled with the rancid smell of damp straw and rabbit droppings.

He tried to lift up his head, but when he did so blood dripped down into his eyes and he had to blink furiously before he could see. He felt shattered, smashed to pieces. Every bone in his body felt dislocated from every other bone, and every tendon had been ripped. He didn't care whether he stayed there or not, even though the rain was gradually soaking through his clothes and mucus was dripping from his nose and he was beginning to shiver.

* * *

He heard a door unlocking, and footsteps. He managed to raise his head far enough to see Bobby Quilty and Chisel standing in the yard, the tips of their cigarettes glowing.

'This is pure wick, this is,' said Bobby Quilty. He crouched down close to John and shook his head in exasperation. 'Are you wired to the moon with a faulty plug or something? Look at the fecking state of you.'

John said nothing, but closed his eyes.

'You're not dead, are you?' Bobby Quilty asked him. 'Jesus, you're some quare gaunch, you are. I'm supposed to keep you in one fecking piece. Like that was the fecking agreement. If your old doll could see the condition of you now, she'd scoop me without a second thought. I mean, what in the name of feck did you think you were doing, climbing out the fecking windie?'

'I just hope he hasn't squished De Valera,' said Chisel, shading his eyes so that he could peer into the broken remains of the rabbit hutch.

'As if you give a tinker's shite for that fecking rabbit,' Bobby Quilty retorted. 'When do you ever clean him out? The last time I looked there was so much bobbly shite in that hutch the poor creature was almost crushed to death against the ceiling.'

Chisel had managed to open the hutch door. The rabbit was crouched on its sodden straw, its ears folded back, its pink eyes wide with terror, but it was still alive and it appeared to be unhurt.

'Joseph and Mary, are you going to you help me lift up this looper and get him back upstairs?' Bobby Quilty protested. Chisel reluctantly closed the hutch door again and came round to help.

It wasn't easy, picking John up off the hutch and the window frames, because he had now lost consciousness. Apart from that, the wire netting was hopelessly snarled in his sweater. After two or three minutes of struggling to get it free, Bobby Quilty wrenched all of it away from the front of the hutch and said, 'I can't believe this. This is totally fecking hectic. And what are you doing, Chisel, for feck's sake, wandering around like a fart in a trance? Get ahold of him under the oxters and let's hoick him up.'

'Look at the state of this fecking hutch now,' said Chisel. 'What if De Valera gets out?'

'If he has any luck at all, wee lad, he'll run straight out into the road and get himself flattened by a bus. Better than being flattened by his own shite. Now start lifting, will you?'

'Jesus, he weighs a fecking ton,' Chisel complained as they hoisted John up and shuffled with him over to the open back door.

'Oh, so what do you want to do, leave him out here all night? It's lashing. He'll catch cold, won't he, if we do that, and he'll die of the fecking pneumonics, and then where's our trump card, eh?'

With Chisel holding John under the armpits, and Bobby Quilty holding his legs on either side of him as if he were pushing a wheelbarrow, they carried John into the house and struggled up the stairs with him. Sorcia stood on the landing smoking as they puffed and grunted and swore and eventually managed to wrestle him back into his bedroom and drop him with a crunch of springs on to the mattress. John opened his eyes for a moment but then closed them again. He had regained consciousness but he was in such pain that he could hardly think.

'Don't you say a word,' Bobby Quilty told Sorcia.

'I wouldn't dream of it,' she said. 'I was only going to ask how you're going to stop him from getting away again. Like, what's going to happen when we all go to sleep? If you think that I'm going to stay awake all night watching him, like, you've got yourself another think coming.'

'And if you don't shut your bake, you've got yourself another slap in the kite coming, so you have.'

Sorcia shrugged and blew out smoke, and said, 'Just asking, like. You don't have to go schizo.'

Bobby Quilty turned back to look at John lying on the bed. 'Well,' he said, 'maybe you're not totally away in the head.' He thought for a moment, slowly rubbing his belly as if had eaten something that disagreed with him, and then he said, 'Chisel? Do you still have them nuts and bolts, the ones you used for fixing the trailer?'

'What do you want them for?' asked Chisel.

'I said, do you still have them?'

'Yeah, I'd say so. Somewhere in the bottom of my toolbox, most likely. Why?'

'And you still have your drill here, right?'

'Chalk it down, right. What do you have in mind?'

'Do you know something, Chisel, my life would run a whole lot smoother if you didn't ask so many fecking stupid questions. Go downstairs, will you, and bring up them nuts and bolts, and your drill, too, with a drill bit.'

'What size of a drill bit?'

'A drill bit big enough to make holes for the bolts, you clampit. What else?'

John heard Chisel clomping downstairs. A few more minutes went past during which he could hear Bobby Quilty and Sorcia murmuring to each other. They didn't sound like affectionate murmurs – more like a bitter under-the-breath argument that they didn't want him or Chisel to hear. As Chisel came clomping back upstairs again, Bobby Quilty distinctly said, 'You do that again, you dirty clart, I'll fecking kill you, so I will.'

As Chisel came back into the bedroom John lay still and kept his eyes closed. It was the only way that he could bear the pain and at the same time hide from Bobby Quilty how frightened he was. He had never been frightened like this before, ever, in the whole of his life, even when he had first met Katie and he and his mother had been attacked on their own farm and almost killed. When that had happened he had been surging with adrenaline, but lying here at the mercy of Bobby Quilty he felt helpless. All he could feel was the sickening conviction that Bobby Quilty and Chisel were going to hurt him badly.

Without warning, he felt his left ankle being seized and his shoe tugged off. His sock was pulled off next. Immediately afterwards, his right shoe and sock were taken off, too. While this was happening neither Bobby Quilty nor Chisel said a word, although Sorcia said, 'I can't fecking watch this,' and he heard her clattering erratically downstairs.

Now both legs of John's jeans were dragged halfway up his calves. His ankles were gripped tight and the sole of his bare left foot pressed flat against the bed's footboard. He knew that it was Bobby Quilty who was holding him because he could feel his heavy patterned signet rings pressing into his skin.

There was a *chukk* noise, like a plug being pushed into a wall socket, and then the sudden high-pitched whine of an electric drill. The next thing he knew, John felt a pain in his left foot so intense that he jolted up and down on the mattress and shrieked out loud.

'Jesus!' said Bobby Quilty. 'Shut the feck up, will you, you sound like a woman giving birth to a full-grown pig!'

Almost hysterical, John tried to twist his leg away, but Bobby Quilty's grip was far too strong for him. When he looked down to the end of the bed he saw that Chisel was drilling a bloody hole into the top of his foot. He could feel the bit separating his bones and then biting through the skin of his sole and into the pine footboard.

'Aaaaahhhhhh!' he screamed. 'No! *Stop it! No! Don't – don't! No-no-no-no-no-gaaaaahhhh!*'

Bobby Quilty and Chisel looked at each other and both of them shrugged. Chisel drilled right through the footboard and then took the drill out. The tip of the bit was still hot from cutting into the wood and John jumped as it touched his flesh.

In a matter of fact way, as if he had been doing this every day of his working life, Chisel took a fifteen-centimetre stainless-steel bolt out of the pocket of his dirty denim waistcoat. He slid a wide penny washer on to the bolt so that John wouldn't be able to tear his foot free from it. Then he inserted it into the hole he had drilled in John's foot and right through the hole in the footboard. John lay back on the mattress, his eyes closed again, shaking, as Chisel took out a nut, spat on it, and twisted it on to the end of the bolt. He tightened the nut by hand, then picked up a spanner from the floor and gave it three or four extra turns so that nobody could loosen it unless they had a spanner, too.

John was rising and falling in and out of consciousness, as if he were struggling to stop himself drowning in the sea at night. The shock of Chisel drilling through his foot was so overwhelming that his brain wanted to drag him down into darkness where he wouldn't feel anything, but the pain kept bringing him up to the surface again. He kept seeing his mother's face again and hearing her voice. *There, there, it's only a scrape, like! Nothing that a poke with sprinkles won't heal!*

But then Bobby Quilty held his right ankle even harder and Chisel started to drill through his right foot, too. There was a brief ripping sound as the drill bit tore through skin and muscle, and then an odd *sqyerkk!* as it glanced off one of his bones. He wanted to pray as the drill bit went through his sole and into the footboard, but his mind couldn't assemble any sensible words. All he could smell was burning wood and flesh, and he was in far too much agony even to scream, let alone pray.

When Chisel had finished drilling through his right foot, he fastened a second bolt through it and tightened that up, too. Now both of John's feet were bolted to the bed.

'There, that's grand altogether,' said Bobby Quilty. 'Now you won't be able to go climbing out the windie again, not unless you take the whole fecking bed along with you.'

'What if he needs a shite?' asked Chisel.

'You've a wee want, Chisel, what do you think? We unscrew the bolts and then he can walk to the jacks on his own. When he's finished dropping the kids off, all we have to do is bolt him back up again.' He mimed the act of twisting the spanner.

'Oh, I have you now, I have you!' said Chisel in admiration. 'I've got to hand it to you, Bobby, that's fierce crabbit, that is. It's exactly like what the Romans did to Jesus when they nailed Him on the cross, except it's more crabbiter than that because the Romans used nails, like, didn't they? So Jesus couldn't come down from the cross to take a shite and then climb back up again. Not that the Romans probably would have let Him, do you know what I mean, like?'

Bobby Quilty said nothing for a moment, but stood over John, breathing in and out through nostrils clogged with catarrh. John opened his eyes and looked up at him, but then closed them again as unconsciousness dragged him down. He couldn't be sure if he was dreaming or not, and that round-faced man with his Kim Jong-un haircut wasn't simply some nursery-rhyme character from his childhood. *The Man in the Moon came down too soon.*

At last Bobby Quilty said, 'Do you know something, Chisel? If I'd been given ten euros for every time you'd ever said anything that made any sense, I'd be flat fecking broke by now.'

Fourteen

The next morning was warm and summery, with huge white clouds that billowed over Cobh like the Spanish Armada under full sail. Katie had slept badly again, so she got out of bed early and took Barney for a walk all the way up to the Rushbrooke Tennis and Croquet Club.

Barney knew this walk well and normally he would trot fifty or sixty metres ahead of her, only waiting at the street corners with his tongue hanging out for her to catch up. Today, he must have sensed that she was anxious, because he stayed very close to her and every now and then turned his head around and looked up at her as if to reassure her that he wasn't going to leave her far behind.

As she reached Grove Garden, her iPhone played *'Buile Mo Chroí'* – 'The Beat of My Heart' – which her mother had loved and which had always set her off dancing around the kitchen.

'Good morning, ma'am. It's Detective O'Mara here.'

'Good morning to you, Bryan. How's it going?'

'We've located one of Quilty's fag-peddlers for you. He's sitting in the doorway of that linen shop in the Savoy Centre, the one that closed down, so that you can't see him on the CCTV. I don't know how long he's going to be there, but he has three or four bags of fags with him. He's even got himself a folding chair like he's on his holliers or something.'

'Thank you, Bryan. Just make a note of that, would you, and put it in the case log.'

'You don't want him lifted?'

'No. You know how we're dealing with this now.'

'You don't want me to tip off Revenue or nothing?'

'No. Just leave him be. How old would you say he was?'

'He has a bit of a scobe tash but it wouldn't surprise me if he's hopped off school.'

'Well, there you are. If he's underage that's one good reason not to pick him up. Thanks, Bryan. I'll be into the station by eleven so I'll talk to you after.'

Immediately, she called Kyna. Barney stood patiently beside her while she waited for an answer. She was beginning to think that Kyna wasn't going to pick up when she heard her say, 'Katie – yes, what? Sorry, I've just woken up. What time are we on?'

'Half past eight. Sorry. Did you have a late night?'

'Didn't sleep very well, that's all. I keep having this nightmare.'

'What's it about? Getting shot?'

'I suppose it must be something to do with that. I keep hearing people talking about me in other rooms but when I go to find out what they're saying about me all these doors start slamming – upstairs, downstairs, everywhere.'

'Detective O'Mara just rang me,' said Katie. Although she was concerned about Kyna, because she knew that she was still suffering from post-traumatic stress, she didn't want to start trying to interpret her dreams, not this early in the day. Most of all, she didn't want to hear anything that would put her off sending Kyna to find John for her. Stress could be treated by therapy. Blindness or amputation or death was irreversible.

'One of Quilty's dealers has set up shop in the Savoy Centre. He's probably catering for the early crowd, people on their way into work. O'Mara couldn't say how long he's going to be there, but he says he has a heap of cigarettes.'

'All right. It'll take me a while to squeeze into my leggings and stick up my hair and put my face paint on, but I'll get down there as quick as I can. I'll ring you if he's gone by the time I get there. I'll ring you anyway.'

'Thanks, Kyna. But for the love of God be careful.'

'You know me.'

'Exactly. That's what I'm worried about.'

* * *

Katie had just poured boiling water into her coffee mug when she received a text from Dr Kelley. The four mummified bodies had now been lifted from underneath the floor at Millstream Row and they were being transported to the mortuary at Cork University Hospital. The remains of the two dogs had been sent to VLSI, a specialist veterinary pathologist in Vicar's Road.

Katie tipped her coffee into the sink and went into the bedroom to fetch her purple linen jacket out of the wardrobe. Barney followed her, hopefully expecting another walk, but when she went into the room that had been Seamus's nursery and took her revolver out of the chest of drawers he realized that she was off to work and simply stood in the living-room doorway patiently waiting for her to leave.

'It's all right, Barns,' she told him, tugging at his ears. 'I won't be back too late, with any luck, and I'll bring you something special for your supper.'

When she walked in through the swing doors at the mortuary, Detective 'Horse' Ó Doibhilin was already waiting for her. 'Morning, ma'am,' he greeted her. His voice was oddly watery, and he kept on swallowing, as if his mouth was flooded with saliva. 'They're all here now, the bodies, and Dr Kelley's started work on them already.'

When she saw the man's body lying on the stainless-steel autopsy table, Katie could understand why Horse might be feeling nauseous. All of his clothes had been removed and sent to the Technical Bureau laboratory for testing. Dr Kelley was leaning over him, wearing a lab coat and clear plastic goggles, cutting his breastbone apart with a battery-powered sternal saw. The saw was making a high-pitched screaming sound that set Katie's teeth on edge.

As she made her way across the morgue, Dr Kelley switched off the saw, lowered her surgical mask and gave her a smile. 'Ah, Detective Superintendent! I thought I'd make an early start.

Fascinating, wouldn't you say? I haven't come across a cadaver in this condition for years. Totally *dried out*, like bresaola. It must have been the constant draft under the floorboards and the house being constantly warm.'

The man's skin was so stretched that it looked as if his skeleton had been shrink-wrapped in translucent yellow vinyl, and some of his ribs and finger bones had pierced through it in places. Dr Kelley had combed most of the dust out of his curly brown hair, but his face was grotesque. On the left side it had become flattened, with his eye half-closed, but on the right side his forehead bulged out and his lips were turned down in what looked like a sneer.

'He was shot in the back of the head, about seven centimetres behind his left ear, and slightly upwards,' said Dr Kelley. 'It wasn't a high-velocity bullet. It ricocheted around inside his skull and there isn't an exit wound, so I'll be able to retrieve it once I've opened his cranium. It also appears that he was badly beaten, because his collarbone and several ribs are broken. Of course it isn't possible to say whether this was done before or after he was shot, but logically there wouldn't have been much point in giving him a thrashing once he was dead.'

The bodies of the woman and the two children were lying on trolleys beside the wall, with green sheets draped over them. Katie went over and lifted the sheet that was covering the woman. She had probably been quite pretty when she was alive, but the shot to the back of her head had distorted her face, too. It looked as if she might have been kneeling when she was shot, because the bullet had entered the top of her skull and penetrated her sinus cavity, lodging in the upper side of her hard palate. Her nostrils were tilted upward like a pig's snout and her lips were curled, as if she were singing a very lewd song, or trying to show that she was thoroughly disgusted by what had happened to her.

After she had looked at the girl and the baby boy, Katie was sure that she was going to have bad dreams tonight. Both of their faces had been blown apart by the bullets that had been fired into the back of their heads, so that they looked more like huge dried white chrysanthemums than faces. Only the tiny jawbones among the petals gave away the fact that they were human children.

Dr Kelley came up to Katie and stood beside her as she was staring down at the baby boy.

'Makes you wonder what kind of a person could do that to a defenceless child, doesn't it? Poor mite. He didn't even get to live for a single year.'

Katie lowered the sheet and crossed herself. She couldn't help thinking of her own little Seamus, dead in his cot, although Seamus had simply stopped breathing. 'I almost wish they hadn't been killed such a long time ago,' she told Dr Kelley. 'I would dearly love to find out who did this and make sure they were punished for it.'

'Time stops for nothing at all, I'm afraid, not even us,' said Dr Kelley. 'So you'll excuse me if I get back to my dissection. I have an autopsy scheduled at the Mid-West in Limerick the day after tomorrow and I'd like to get all of these completed.'

'You'll be able to give me some idea of how long they've been dead?' Katie asked her.

'Within a few years either way. Of course I'll be able to tell you if they were born before nuclear testing started in 1945 because of the carbon-fourteen level in their teeth – that's if there is any. I expect the stomach contents will help me a fair bit, too. But their complete desiccation isn't going to help. If anything, I think your best indicators are going to come from their clothing – the style and the fibres and dyes. And any records or photographs that you can find.'

'Well, as you know, we've been given plenty of documentary evidence of who they *might* have been, but it's very contradictory. What you're doing here should at least tell us if these are the Langtrys or not.'

Dr Kelley pulled up her mask and returned to her high-pitched sternum sawing. Katie watched her for a moment and then checked the time. She wondered if Kyna had managed to make contact with Bobby Quilty's cigarette-seller at the Savoy Centre. 'Come on, Michael,' she said to Detective Ó Doibhilin. 'I think we could both use some fresh air, don't you?'

* * *

Before she returned to her office, Katie paid a visit to the Technical Bureau laboratory. There had been a major traffic accident on the N20 to Mallow, so she found that Eithne and Bill Phinner's new assistant were the only ones there. The white cotton blinds were pulled down because the sunlight outside was so bright, and there was a strong smell of hydrochloric acid in the air. Eithne was sitting at her bench under the window, filling an array of test tubes with pale green liquid out of a beaker, while the new assistant was frowning at a tangle of chemical formulae on her computer screen.

Katie went up to Eithne and stood watching her for a moment.

'I thought you were going to call in sick,' she said.

Eithne shook her head and took out a tissue to wipe her nose. 'I'm not too bad today, thanks, ma'am. I've too much to do, any road. I was going to come up and see you after.'

'What are you doing there?' Katie asked her, nodding at the test tubes.

'This is one of the things I was going to come and see you about.'

She reached across and picked up a glass retort that was half-filled with liquid. There were several saturated wool fibres floating in it, like weeds.

'This is a sample from the man's trousers. They were dyed with a water-soluble anionic dye, which was used for almost all garments before 1920. After that, though, there was much wider use of dispersal dyes. That was because more and more manufacturers were using acetates to make clothing and acetates, of course, are hydrophobic.'

'So what does that tell us?'

'In terms of precise dating, not very much. People keep their clothes for years, if not decades, especially if they're less well off. But it does indicate that these trousers were probably made before 1921, and if that's the case, it's likely that your man could either be Stephen Langtry himself or some other fellow who was killed in the Langtrys' house before the Langtrys disappeared. Of course I'm testing the woman's dress and the children's clothing, too. In any case, we're expecting the results of the DNA tests sometime this afternoon, so that should pretty much confirm their identity one way or the other.'

'Did you get anywhere with the cap badge and the letter?' Katie asked her.

Eithne slid off her stool and went across to the opposite side of the laboratory. She came back with the Manchester cap badge that Nora O'Neill had given to Katie, and a clear plastic folder containing the note from *Gerald*.

'I checked this coat-of-arms cap badge against my records. It was worn by soldiers of the Manchester Regiment until 1922, when their commanding officer made an application to the Army Council to change it to a fleur-de-lys.'

'Why did he do that?'

'The troops didn't feel that this badge was very military, especially the ones who came from Manchester. What they didn't like was that the exact same badge was worn by every worker for the City of Manchester Corporation. Like, you know, dustmen and rent collectors and road-menders.'

'So at least we know when it dates from.'

'That's right. And in 1921, C Company of the Manchester Regiment were based at barracks in Ballincollig, only ten kilometres away from Blarney. Even in those days, it would have taken less than fifteen minutes to drive from one to the other. Maybe half an hour by horse and buggy.'

Katie was beginning to feel uneasy again about the political implications of this investigation. She had known ever since she was at school that C Company of the Manchester Regiment was a black name in the history of Cork's struggle for independence in the 1920s. During the war against the British, the IRA had planned to ambush an army patrol as it passed through Dripsey. However, the army had been warned of the intended ambush by a wealthy local woman, Mrs Mary Lindsay, of Leemount House, who had strong loyalist views.

In the late afternoon of Friday, 28 January 1921, seventy men of C Company of the Manchester Regiment outflanked the IRA ambush party and captured eight of them. At the subsequent trial, five were found guilty and sentenced to death.

In retaliation, the IRA abducted Mrs Lindsay and her chauffeur, James Clark, and threatened that if the death sentences were carried out, they would die, too. The authorities ignored their threat and the five IRA men were executed by firing squad and their bodies interred at Cork Gaol. Twelve days later, Mrs Lindsay and her chauffeur were shot, their bodies burned and buried deep in the mountains. The day after, Leemount House was burned down.

Katie's history teacher at school, Mr O'Sullivan, had been passionate about Irish independence. He had even taken the class to see the memorial that had been erected for the IRA men at Godfrey's Cross. She remembered that day clearly, although less for the story of the ambush and more for the fact that it had been raining hard and her mother had made her cheese sandwiches which she had dropped in a puddle.

'What about the letter?' she asked Eithne.

'Genuine, no question at all. I've tested the paper and the ink and it's authentic. And there's indentations in the paper which indicate that the cap badge was wrapped in the letter for a very long time.'

'Okay, Eithne. Thanks for that. All we have to do now is find out who Gerald was. The Manchester Regiment should have records. I'll have Ó Diobhilin get in touch with them.'

Eithne wiped her nose again and then she said, 'If you don't mind my saying so, ma'am, this seems to be bothering you more than a bit, this inquiry.'

'It is, yes,' Katie admitted. 'I'm sure we'll find out what happened to that family eventually, but I'm worried that won't be the end of it. I always have a bad feeling when we start poking around in the past – not because we *shouldn't* poke around in the past, because I think we should. The trouble is, no matter what it is we discover, it's going to upset somebody, even today. I guarantee it. It always does.'

* * *

Walking along the corridor back to her office, she checked her iPhone but there was still no word from Kyna. She told herself not to worry, Kyna was level-headed and highly professional and wouldn't make any careless mistakes that would give her away. In spite of that, though, John's life depended on her. Katie couldn't imagine how she would feel if John were blinded, or maimed, or murdered.

She couldn't imagine how she would deal with her emotions if anything happened to Kyna, either. She felt guilty enough already about asking her to do this, but she hadn't been able to think of any other way of finding out where John was being held. It was far too dangerous to start raiding Bobby Quilty's houses and flats and business premises in the slim hope that they might find John in one of them. They suspected that he owned or rented numerous properties that they didn't know about. After the Dripsey ambush, the British army had set up a huge search in the Inniscarra area for Mrs Lindsay and her chauffeur, but they never discovered where they were because the IRA kept moving them from house to house.

Almost as soon as she had sat down at her desk, Detective Sergeant Begley knocked on her door. He looked flustered. His tight blue shirt had semicircular sweat stains under the armpits and his scarlet braces had slipped off his shoulders and were hanging down behind him like a toddler's reins.

'What's the story, Sean?' Katie asked him, popping open the can of Diet Coke she had brought up with her.

'Look at the state of me,' said Detective Sergeant Begley. 'I saw you out of my window in the car park and I went running down after you but by the time I caught up with you, you'd gone. Jesus and Mary, I'm sweating like a priest in a playground.'

He paused to catch his breath and then he said, 'You saw the *One o'Clock News*, did you?'

'No, I didn't. I was down in the lab to see how what progress Eithne's been making with all the evidence we took from Blarney. That British army cap badge, that definitely dates from the early 1920s, and the love letter that went with it. The dead man's clothing was probably 1920s, too.'

'Listen, it seems like your friend Fionnuala Sweeney from RTÉ News knows just as much about those bodies as we do, if not considerably more. She's sure that they belong to the Langtry family, that's what she said, no question about it, and she even gave out their first names – Stephen, Rahda, and the wains' names, too.'

'Holy Mary, Mother of God,' said Katie. 'It was that Nora O'Neill woman told her all of that, it must have been. It's highly probable that they *are* the Langtry family, though we don't have any idea how Stephen Langtry managed to send postcards from America after he was supposed to be dead, and of course we're still waiting on the DNA results.'

'Oh, there's more,' said Detective Sergeant Begley. 'You're going to love this, I tell you.'

'Go on,' Katie told him.

'According to local legend, Mrs Langtry had been having an affair with a British army officer.'

'Well . . . that's conceivable, considering the cap badge and the letter, and what the letter said. But it's only speculation at the moment. We don't even know for certain that they were hers.'

'Ah, no, but this local legend has it that Stephen Langtry belonged to the IRA and that he actively encouraged his wife to have an affair with a British army officer so that she could tap him for secret information, especially about the movements of army patrols. But the officer found out that she was what you might call a honeytrap, and British soldiers came around one night and shot the whole family.'

Katie sat down, shaking her head in exasperation. 'I don't suppose Fionnuala said who told her this so-called local legend? And if she'd checked to find out if there was any truth in it?'

'No, that's about all she said. After that there was a clip of you looking more than a little fried and saying "no comment", and Mathew McElvey from the press office trotting out his usual excuse that "our investigation is still ongoing and so I can't say anything conclusive". After that they went on to a report about Irish Water warning folks with the lead pipes still in their houses that they could be poisoned.'

'Jesus, I hope that Nora O'Neill has lead pipes in her house. Do you realize what trouble this is going to stir up?'

'I can't say that I do,' said Detective Sergeant Begley. 'But my old grandpa always used to say that there's no treachery worse than the one that you never knew was being done to you.'

Fifteen

It was pay day, so St Patrick's Street was already crowded with shoppers. Kyna had parked her car on the north side of St Patrick's Bridge and walked across the river. Because it was such a warm morning the river smelled even stronger than usual and under the surface she could see a shoal of grey mullet greedily feeding around the effluent pipe. She couldn't help thinking of the song 'The Boys of Fair Hill' – 'the smell on Patrick's Bridge is wicked, how does Father Mathew stick it?'

Kyna was whistled at three times as she made her way past the statue of Father Mathew down to the Savoy Centre. She had gelled up her short blonde hair and she was wearing a low-cut pink T-shirt with TROUBLE printed across her breasts, skintight black jeans and wedge-heeled black patent shoes. She had completed the look with red make-up around her eyes, huge hoop earrings and at least six bangles on each wrist, and she had sprayed herself with too much Obsession.

The Savoy Centre had once been a cinema, but after it had closed in 1975 it had been turned into an indoor shopping mall with stores like Champion Sports and Hickey's Fabrics and a coffee shop. Standing in the entrance was a podgy tousle-haired boy of about nine years old who should have been in school. He kept looking up and down the street as if he were waiting for somebody and Kyna guessed that he was keeping sketch for the law.

She had no difficulty in finding Bobby Quilty's cigarette-dealer. He was sitting in the doorway of a shop called Erin Linens which had sheets of last week's *Echo* stuck all over the windows and a large sign saying *Closing Down Sale*.

Detective O'Mara had told Katie that he was young, and in spite of a wispy black moustache on his upper lip he looked as if he hadn't even taken his Junior Cert yet. He had short black hair with two parallel lines shaved into the side of it, and a milky-white, pimple-spattered face. He was wearing a coral-pink T-shirt from Penney's, a pair of super-skinny blue jeans and Nike runners.

Around his feet were three large black refuse bags, two of them crumpled up and empty, the third half full with red and white cartons of West cigarettes.

Kyna went directly up to him and said, in a high Mayfield whine, 'What's the craic, boy?'

'Twenty-five yo-yos for two hundred,' he told her. 'Buy four and you can have them for eighty.'

'So how much are they paying you?'

The boy blinked at her as if he hadn't understood what she meant. 'I told you, twenty-five yo-yos the box. How many do you want?'

He held up a carton of two hundred cigarettes. On the side Kyna noticed the warning *Rauchen kann tödlich sein*. She knew that West were made in Germany, where they cost 54 euros per carton. They weren't sold in Ireland, but they would have cost 100 euros.

'I didn't say I wanted to buy any,' she told him. 'I want to know how much you get paid for selling them.'

'You what?' the boy retorted. 'What the feck's it got to do with you? Do you want any fecking fags or don't you?'

'I told you, *no*, you gom,' said Kyna, just as aggressively. 'I'm looking to make some grade for myself and I saw you there and thought, that looks like child's play. Better than gobbling manky old scummers in the bus station jacks, I'll tell you.'

The boy glanced left and right. 'I don't know, like. I'm not supposed to talk about nothing to nobody, like, do you know what I mean?'

117

'Aw, come on,' said Kyna, leaning against the door frame and batting her eyelashes at him. 'Don't tell me they're not looking for gorgeous-looking girls to flog their fags for them. I bet you I could sell twice as many as you any day. Three times more if I was wearing a really short skirt. Four if I didn't wear knickers.'

'Well . . .' said the boy. Kyna could read his mind almost as clearly as if his thoughts were running across his forehead as a text message. Bobby Quilty was always looking for young recruits to sell his smuggled cigarettes on the streets, especially if they weren't already known to the Garda, and Kyna knew from other school-age dealers they had picked up that he would probably drop this boy at least fifty euros for introducing her.

The boy took his mobile phone out of his pocket and tapped in a number. After a few seconds, he said, 'Ger? It's Benny. No, no bother, everything's grand. I reckon another half-hour or so. Listen, there's a beour here who's interested in selling fags. Yeah. That's right, yeah. No. No. She's well fit, like. Yeah. Okay, then. Right. I will.'

Once he had put his phone down, he said to Kyna, 'He's in the Long Valley, sitting at the bar on the left as you walk in. You'll recognize him easy. He'll be wearing a white hat with a black band around it and shades and he has a grey ponytail. His name's Ger.'

'Okay, thanks a million, Benny,' said Kyna. She winked at him and lasciviously licked her lips and said, 'I'll have to think of some way of repaying you, won't I?'

The boy's pimply face flared even redder and he seemed relieved when a young woman came up to them, pushing a buggy with two baby girls in it and a small boy standing precariously on the footrest.

'Give us two boxes, love, would you?' she asked him, opening up her purse. 'No, best make that three.'

Benny rummaged around in his black plastic bag while Kyna walked back to the St Patrick's Street entrance. The boy who was keeping sketch was still there. He was looking bored and assiduously picking his nose.

'Digging for gold?' she asked him.

'Ah, get away to fuck,' said the boy, but all the same he took out his finger and flicked his rolled-up gullier across the pavement.

* * *

Ger was exactly as Benny had described him. When she walked into the Long Valley, the traditional old-style pub at the end of Winthrop Street, she found him perched on one of the barstools like a huge elderly vulture that had dropped directly out of the sky.

He was wearing the white hat that Benny had told her about, although it was grubby and stained. He was also wearing a drooping black jacket with wide shoulders and pockets that were weighed down with loose change and Kyna could only guess what else, as well as raspberry-coloured chinos that were several centimetres too short, so that his bruised white calves were exposed.

Kyna went up to the bar and stood close behind him without saying a word. One of the barmen approached her in his white butcher's apron and said, 'Over eighteen, are you, flower?'

Without turning around, Ger said in a deep, whispery voice, 'You're all right, Séan, she's with me.'

'Oh, no bother at all,' said the barman. 'In that case, what'll it be?'

'Kopparberg Mixed Fruit, if this gentleman's treating me,' said Kyna. She was trying to think what Sheelagh Danehy might consider to be a sophisticated drink to order.

Still without turning around, Ger said, 'How old are you really?'

'Nineteen,' Kyna told him. She doubted that Ger would believe her if she said she was any younger.

* * *

He shifted around on his stool, so that his chinos made a farting noise on the leather. It was difficult to tell what he looked like facially because of his huge dark glasses, but he had a hooked Fagin nose and deeply lined cheeks and a turned-down mouth, as if he wasn't prepared to believe anything anyone told him. His chin was covered in sharp white prickles and his breath smelled of stale beer and garlic and something else rancid.

'What's your name, then?' he asked her.

'Sheelagh. Sheelagh with a "g".'

'A "g" like in "slag", you mean?'

Kyna was hard put to think how the real Sheelagh would have responded to that, but then she decided that the real Sheelagh was probably used to being called names that were a lot worse than 'slag' and would have ignored it.

'My friends call me Sidhe. Or Pixie sometimes.'

'All right, Sidhe. And why are you so interested in selling fags for us?'

'It's only for some spare grade. That's all I want. I lost my job at Coqbull because they said I wasn't being respectful to the customers. Like, you know, it's only a fecking burger bar, what do they expect? Bowing and scraping? I told this one woman that we'd have to charge her for an overnight stay, because if she ate any more we wouldn't be able to get her out the door. I mean, like, scorpy, or what?'

'There's plenty of other work around,' said Ger.

'Oh, for sure, especially for a girl who got herself kicked out of school, with no leaving cert? Like washing-up dishes at O'Brien's, I suppose, or giving the happy-ending massage to stinky old men? I've tried both of them, like, and they was both enough to make a maggot gag.'

Ger took a measured sip of his Murphy's and wiped his mouth with the back of his hand. 'You won't be able to work for us if you don't learn to keep your bake shut. I'll tell you that, girl, for nothing.'

'I'm not stupid,' said Kyna. 'I know you're selling the economy fags. I sold dance biscuits for some feller once and he was so delighted with how quick I sold them and how much profit I made that he wanted me to work for him full-time, and I would have done if he hadn't gone and got himself killed in a car smash.'

'What was his name, this feller?'

'Well, he's dead now, so I don't mind telling you, but I would never have done if he was still alive, not until I was dead myself. So I don't need you telling me to keep my bake shut, thank you very much. His name was Kenny O'Flynn.'

Ger was silent for a moment. Then he patted his left forearm and said, 'Kenny had a tattoo, right here. Can you remember what it was?'

'Of course. It was one of them Celtic knots, like, with *Níl mícheart dearmad riamh* written around it.' Kyna thought: *I certainly* should *remember.* She had interrogated Kenny O'Flynn on three separate occasions after he was arrested for dealing D2PM and Bubble in Cork's nightclubs and dance venues, and even outside the gates of the Presentation College on the Western Road.

'So, well, you did know him, then,' said Ger. 'In that case, okay, I reckon we might be able to find you a pitch. All we have to do now is see if the Big Feller takes a fancy to you.'

'Who's the Big Feller?'

'You'll find out soon enough. He's the one who runs the whole business. So take it from me, you want to stay on his good side, like.'

They spent another twenty minutes in the Long Valley, finishing their drinks. Ger seemed to believe that Kyna was who she claimed to be, but all the same he kept asking her questions about her family, and her home life, and where she had said she was living on Mount Nebo Avenue, and why she had got herself into so much trouble at school. Kyna had been trained in interrogation techniques at Templemore and Katie had always been impressed by her ability to persuade suspects to incriminate themselves. But Kayna had to admit that Ger was adept at setting traps in his questions.

'Oh, yes,' he said, 'I used to have a regular scoop with some good old pals of mine who lived on Mount Nebo Avenue. We used to go to that boozer on Gurra Avenue, what's its name?'

'Top of the Hill Bar,' said Kyna. 'I used to go in there when I was only sixteen, hoping they'd serve me a bottle of cider.'

'Top of the Hill Bar, that's right,' said Ger. 'And what was the name of that baldy barman, the one who always looked at you like he wasn't looking at you but whoever it was standing next to you?'

'I don't know,' said Kyna. 'I don't remember no baldy barman.'

Ger lifted one finger. 'You're right there, girl. My mistake. That was Kevin at The Flying Bottle in Knocka. Swivel, they called him, on account of his eyes. Swivel, that was your man.'

Sixteen

Eventually they left the Long Valley and Ger led Kyna across the road to Pembroke Street, beside the main Post Office, where his mustard-coloured Volvo was parked in a disabled bay. There was no blue disabled card displayed behind his windscreen, but the parking attendant who was checking the cars parked along the street simply turned his back when he saw Ger approaching and slowly walked off in the opposite direction.

'Get in,' said Ger, opening up the passenger door. Kyna obediently climbed in and fastened her seat belt. The inside of the Volvo was littered with empty plastic bottles and crumpled copies of the *Irish Racing Post*, and the ashtray was crammed.

'We'll go round and pick up Benny first, then we'll head off to see the Big Feller,' Ger told her. 'I'm presuming you don't have any other engagements, like.'

'I need the grade, don't I?' said Kyna, turning her head away and staring out of the window with a sulky pout. As they drove up Parnell Place, however, she had to turn her head back and half-shield her face with her hand because Detective Dooley was standing on the corner talking to two gardaí and he would have recognized her immediately. How could she explain why she was driving around the city with one of the biggest scumbags in Cork, dressed like a brasser?

They stopped outside the Savoy Centre and the nose-picking lookout went inside to bring Benny out. Benny dropped his black plastic bags into the Volvo's boot and then climbed into the back.

'What's the story, then, Benny?' Ger asked him, shaking out a cigarette and lighting it before he drove off.

'Only two boxes left and they was them Afri Rot fags which nobody wanted.'

'They're so fecking thick, some people! You told them that "rot" is Kraut language for "red"?'

'Well, no, I didn't. I didn't know myself, like. I thought it meant they was humming a bit, like, and that was why they was going so cheap.'

'Jesus, you'd break my melt, you would,' said Ger. 'Didn't I fecking tell you what it meant only this morning when I dropped you off?'

'Yeah, but I thought you were taking the piss, like, do you know what I mean?'

Ger drove up the steep incline of Summerhill and then east beside the high stone walls of the Middle Glanmire Road. Eventually he turned into cul-de-sac of six large brand new houses. Outside the house at the end of the cul-de-sac, three vehicles were parked – a black Nissan Navara pickup, a shiny red Jaguar XF R and an Audi A3.

Ger parked behind the Jaguar, then climbed out and opened the door for Kyna. 'Just remember what I said, girl. You need to keep the the Big Feller smiling, all right, so none of your cheek. And if he wants you to do something for him, no matter what, just fecking do it and no getting uppity.'

Kyna gave Ger a contemptuous Gurra look but said nothing. She and Benny followed him between the cars parked in the driveway and up to the mock-Palladian porch. He rang the door chimes and almost immediately the front door was opened by a tall, gaunt woman with her hair pinned up in a messy brown bun. She was wearing a short summer dress that was splashed all over with huge red poppies.

'Holy Mother of God, Margot,' said Ger. 'You look like you got run over by the 208!'

'Get away, would you?' the woman snapped back. 'I bought this down Opera Lane only yesterday, and if you knew what it cost.'

'Don't tell me. I'm not in the mood for feeling pity for anybody, not today. Besides, it'll probably look massive once you've washed the blood off.'

The woman took them through the house and into the back garden where Bobby Quilty was pacing up and down on the patio, dressed in a jazzy yellow shirt with palm trees and hula girls on it and a pair of flappy khaki cargo trousers. He was giving somebody a dressing-down on his iPhone, barking at them in his strong Armagh accent. He was wearing red flip-flops and Kyna noticed that his toenails were so long that they curled over the ends of his toes. Perhaps his belly was too big for him to bend over and cut them, she thought, although it was obvious from the size of his house and all the cars parked outside that he could have easily afforded a pedicure.

'Don't you be giving me that slabber, wee lad!' he was shouting. 'So far as I'm concerned you nuck that money and I want it back in my hand by Monday morning at the latest. You'll regret it else, so you will, and so will all the family you leave behind you. What do you want it to say on your headstone?'

He wedged his iPhone back into the pocket of his shorts and then looked Kyna up and down and said, ''Bout you, Ger? Who's this? I thought I told you not to fetch any of your slappers back here with you.' He pronounced 'with you' as 'whichew', like a hay-fever sneeze.

'She's all right, Bobby. Her name's Sheelagh. She's looking for a bit of work flogging fags, that's all.'

Bobby Quilty took a pack of cigarettes out of his shirt pocket and lit one with a gold flip-top lighter. He blew out smoke and then he said, 'You know we don't pay good money, sweetheart. You sell two hundred fags for twenty-five euros, you get to keep two euros and fifty cents, that's all. You're a cracking-looking girl, so you are. There's plenty of ways you could be making yourself a shiteload more money than that for a whole lot less effort.'

'I know that, Mister Big Feller,' said Kyna. 'I've tried them. They gave me the gawks, to be honest with you.'

'Call me "Bobby" for feck's sake,' Bobby Quilty told her. His iPhone beeped and he tugged it out and frowned at it, but when he saw who was calling he stuffed it back into his pocket. Then he looked at Kyna more narrowly, with his cigarette dangling between his lips, one eye closed against the smoke, and it was obvious that he liked what he saw.

'Ger, Benny,' he said, 'why don't you go and load up some more fags? A pet day like this, the Peace Park's going to be rammed this dinnertime.'

'Maybe I should go with them, see how it's done,' said Kyna.

'No, no. You come inside with me, girl. I need to give you a briefing before you go out flogging fags. There's a whole lot of ins and outs you have to be familiar with, if you follow me.'

Ger made a strange snorting noise as if he were laughing, and shook his head.

'You all right, there, Ger?' Bobby Quilty asked him. 'I'll see you after, okay?'

'Okay, Bobby,' said Ger, laying his hand across Benny's shoulders and almost pushing him back into the house. Kyna could see them in the hallway talking to Margot and then all three of them disappeared from view.

'Come on, then, sweetheart, come inside, and I'll show you the ropes,' said Bobby Quilty.

'What's to learn?' asked Kyna. 'All you have to do is sit there and sell fags.'

Bobby Quilty grasped her right elbow like a clamp and steered her in through the patio doors. 'Oh no, my darling, there's a whole lot more to it than that. You have to have your regular customers on your phone so that you can tip them the wink when a new shipment of fags has come in, and where and when you'll be selling them. You'll get plenty of casual sales of course, but more than half of your stock will be pre-ordered.'

'But you sell them in shops, too, don't you?' said Kyna. 'Why don't your regular customers just go to the shops?'

'Ach, the polls keep busting the fecking shops, that's the problem. Your shops are an easy target, see, because the polls can fetch in the dogs to sniff out any fags that a shopkeeper might have stashed away in the back or in the ceiling or wherever. Not only that, the shopkeepers are old enough to be hauled up in front of the court. How old did you say you was, sweetheart?'

'Nineteen,' said Kyna. 'Well, nearly nineteen.'

Bobby Quilty propelled her by her elbow along the white-carpeted hallway until they reached the foot of the stairs. There were Jack Vettriano prints hanging all the way up the staircase, couples dancing on a rainy beach, nudes standing in front of mirrors, men in evening wear staring lecherously at women in corsets.

'Away up with you,' said Bobby Quilty and gave a thick, phlegmy cough.

'What do you mean?'

'I mean, away up the stairs with you.'

'What for?'

'Do you want to work for me, or don't you?'

'Chalk it down. I told you.'

'Well, if you want to work for me, you'll do what I tell you, and if I tell you "away up the stairs with you", you'll be away up the stairs.'

Kyna glanced upstairs and then at Bobby Quilty. He jerked his head in an upward direction to emphasize what he had just told her.

She hesitated for a few seconds. She knew that whatever was going to happen upstairs, it wasn't going to be good. She had a choice now. She wasn't on official Garda duty. She was only doing this because Katie had begged her for help, although Katie had made it clear that she wouldn't blame her if she decided that she didn't want to go through with it. But what if she didn't go through with it and John was blinded, or mutilated, or murdered? How could she ever face Katie again?

She took a step up the stairs, and then another. As she climbed, she could still feel the tightness of the stitches where the surgeons had sewn up her stomach after she had been shot. Bobby Quilty watched her, smoking, but it was only when she was halfway up that he began to haul himself up after her.

She reached the landing. The upstairs rooms were furnished in the same soulless modern style as the reception rooms downstairs. They were carpeted in pale grey throughout and every bedroom had white fitted wardrobes with mirrored doors and beds covered with black-and-white diamond-patterned throws. On the walls hung more Jack Vettriano prints and on some of the windowsills stood white earthenware vases of dried chrysanthemums. There was a strong smell of jasmine carpet freshener, which was probably intended to mask the eye-watering reek of Bobby Quilty's cigarette smoke.

Bobby Quilty pointed to what looked like the master bedroom, obviously indicating that Kyna should lead the way inside. Kyna walked in and went across to the window. Through the tall, ivy-covered trees at the end of the garden she could see the dull silvery shine of the River Lee and an orange oil tanker making its way towards the Shell depot.

'Grand view you get from here,' she said.

Bobby Quilty came up and stood close behind her. 'You could make it ten times better. You know that, don't you?'

'Oh, yes?' she said, without turning round. She dreaded to hear what he was going to say next.

'Why don't you pull down your breeks?' he suggested. His smoke was drifting over her shoulder and she could hear the phlegm rattling in his lungs. She started to turn around but he seized her right shoulder, hard, and forced her to remain facing the window. 'You just enjoy the scenery, sweetheart. Pull down your breeks and watch the boats go by.'

'They're too tight,' she said, trying not to sound panicky. 'It took me all the morning just to get them on.'

Bobby Quilty reached around her waist and unfastened her mock-crocodile belt. As he did so, she could feel his belly pressing up against her back.

'What do you think you're doing?' she protested.

'I'm showing you why they call me the Big Feller. I'm also testing you out, just to make sure you're always going to do what I tell you to do, no matter what it is, no questions asked.'

'And what if I tell *you* to take your grubby maulers off me, you fat stinky bastard?'

The instant Kyna said that, Bobby Quilty slapped her around the back of the head so hard that she felt as if her skull had cracked. She staggered forward, her knees giving way, so that she had to grab at the windowsill with both hands to keep herself upright. For a split second, every muscle in her body was tensed up to hit him back. Even though she was still convalescing, she was still fit and she was still highly trained in tae kwon do, and she could have spun around and almost kicked his football-like head clear off his shoulders.

But no, she stayed where she was, her eyes tight shut, her teeth clenched, holding on to the windowsill. *He's not worth it*, she thought, even though her head was ringing. Bobby Quilty was wearing several heavy signet rings and she could already feel where they had bruised her. *Think of John. Most of all, think of Katie.*

'You ever fecking speak to me like that again, sweetheart, and by Joseph and Mary I swear that I'll smack your kite a hundred times harder than that, so I will!' snapped Bobby Quilty. He gripped the back of her neck so hard that she felt as if she were going to black out and for a few seconds she could feel him fumbling around behind her. Then, suddenly, she felt a sharp cold pocket-knife blade pressing against the small of her back and he was sawing roughly through the waistband of her jeans. She heard the stitches tear and then he released his grip on her neck so that he could use both hands to wrench the seat of her jeans apart, and then down. As tight as they were, he managed to pull them nearly down to her knees.

'Keep your bake shut and don't move a muscle!' he told her. His words were indistinct because he still had a cigarette waggling between his lips. 'Don't you even *think* about it, not for a second!'

Kyna was conscious of more fumbling behind her, and more wheezing. Then Bobby Quilty gripped the cheeks of her bottom and spread them wide open, as if he were opening up a book. His fingernails dug into her skin so hard that she couldn't stop herself from sucking in her breath, and then she felt him push his penis in between her thighs, and she sucked in her breath a second time and let out an '*aaaahhhh*' of sheer discomfort. His penis was stiff and he had been right to boast, it was enormous. But it was very dry, like a wooden rolling pin, and Kyna was dry, too, and he had to force it into her vagina a centimetre at a time. He grunted with every thrust, blowing out ash and cigarette smoke. Kyna kept her teeth gritted and clung on to the windowsill, but he was hurting her now, more and more, and she didn't know how much longer she was going to be able to stand it.

'Jesus, doll, you've a flange like the fecking Sahara Desert!' Bobby Quilty protested.

He tried three or four more thrusts, but all he managed to do was push Kyna's hips repeatedly up against the wall.

'I can't fecking believe this,' he said. He withdrew his penis, took his cigarette out of his mouth, and spat on his fingers so that he could lubricate himself. By the time he managed to jostle himself back into position, however, his erection had begun to subside. He squashed it up against the lips of Kyna's vulva, but it was far too soft now and no matter how hard he squashed he couldn't penetrate her.

'Ach, that's me,' he said and stepped away from her. Kyna turned around to see him bending over so that he could pull up his trousers. 'I never knew any floozy as dry as you, I swear to God. It wouldn't surprise me if you had camels up your cunt.'

Kyna managed to tug up her ripped-apart jeans and buckle her belt. 'I suppose you're going to pay for a new pair,' she said. 'River Island, these are.'

'I'll tell you what I'm going to do with you, you fridge-did bitch,' Bobby Quilty told her. He snatched hold of her wrist, twisting it hard, and when she tried to pull away from him he lifted his other hand as if he were going to slap her again.

'You want another one? You're welcome, so you are.'

With that, he tugged Kyna across the master bedroom and opened the door to the en suite bathroom.

'Fridge-did bitch,' he repeated, as he pushed her inside.

The bathroom was tiled floor to ceiling with mottled grey ceramic tiles with pink flamingos on them and there was a vast jacuzzi and a corner shower with a curved glass door. He pulled her over to the shower and opened it.

'There, get in.'

'What?' said Kyna.

'This is your last chance, sweetheart. Do you want to work for me or not? If you do, then by God you do whatever I tell you. And since you're too fridge-did even to flah, you'll just have to show me in another way, won't you? Now, get in.'

Even though she still had her wedge-heeled shoes on, Kyna stepped into the shower and stood there with her arms crossed defensively over her breasts.

'Kneel down,' said Bobby Quilty. His cigarette had burned down right to the filter now but he gave it a last suck before he lifted the lid of the toilet and flicked it in.

Awkwardly, Kyna knelt down. She couldn't think what he was going to do next. Turn on the shower and soak her in freezing water? But when she looked up at him she saw that he was pulling down his cargo trousers again. He took out his flaccid penis and held it in front of her face. It looked now like a crumpled, grumpy worm.

'Look up,' he said. His voice was strange now – still harsh, but unsteady with excitement. 'Look up, and open your mouth, and keep it open.'

Mother of God, no, thought Kyna. But then Bobby Quilty shivered and started to urinate. He aimed it directly into Kyna's face, stinging her eyes and flooding her mouth with acrid liquid. She spat, and spat again, and shook her head, but he continued to relieve himself all over her. It streamed from her chin and dripped from her earlobes and she could feel it running down warm inside her pink TROUBLE T-shirt.

When he had finished, she stayed where she was, dripping, her eyes closed, trying not to breathe in the alcoholic smell of his urine.

'There, good girl. I think we can say that you've passed the test with flying colours,' said Bobby Quilty as he tucked himself away. 'You stay there, sweetheart, and I'll have Margot come up with some dry clothes for you.'

He walked out of the bathroom, leaving the door open. As soon as he had gone, Kyna clambered to her feet, pulled off her shoes and threw them out of the shower cubicle, followed by her jeans. She was whimpering with disgust as she did so and when she had to drag off her wet T-shirt she retched and would have vomited if she had eaten any breakfast.

Naked, she turned on the shower full, as hot as she could bear it, and soaped herself all over with the shower gel that was hanging from the taps. It smelled of lavender and she knew that she would never be able to smell lavender again without feeling sick.

She was still standing under the shower when Margot came in, carrying a pair of jeans and a top. She stood patiently outside the shower door while Kyna washed her hair again and again. Through the steamy glass she looked like a sympathetic ghost.

Seventeen

At lunchtime, Katie drove to the three-storey building on Lavitt's Quay that housed the Walnut Tree shelter for battered women, which she had helped to set up. It was a run-down nineteenth-century property, which had once been a music shop, and it was still in need of rewiring and some redecorating, but donations had fixed the leaky roof and five of the seven bedsitting rooms were now wallpapered and carpeted.

She was feeling so anxious about John and Kyna that she had almost put off this visit. However, the house manager, Blathnaid O'Keeffe, had called her this morning and told her that they had taken in a new family late yesterday evening and that the mother, Neala Murphy, was very keen to meet her, and thank her.

Katie rang the doorbell outside the dark red-painted facade and Blathnaid opened it so quickly that Katie thought she must have been waiting in the hallway for her.

Inside the house, there was a smell of takeaway pizza and Katie could hear children running about upstairs and laughing. There was always a family atmosphere at Walnut Tree. Katie had insisted from the beginning that it should feel more like a friend's house than a refuge from violence and bullying. There was no lack of crying or arguing, but the women who came here always had a sympathetic counsellor to calm them down and wipe their eyes.

Katie went into the day room, where three young women and their children were watching television. She knew all of them by name. She knew their partners, too, only too well. A fair-haired mother of twin girls was called Moira, and the bruises that still encircled her eyes like yellowish racing-goggles had been inflicted by her boyfriend, Flynn. Fiona was only thirty-six years old but her hair had turned completely white. Her husband, Michael, had burned her with cigarettes all around her genitals and upper thighs and had broken one of her arms so badly that she held it like a pigeon's wing.

Aoife smiled at Katie briefly but didn't speak. As a punishment for cooking meals that he didn't like, her husband, Michael, had kept her locked in a cupboard under the stairs, sometimes for days on end.

'Saw you on the box, Katie,' said Fiona. 'You looked like you was fair odd with that news reporter woman.'

'Oh, you know me,' Katie told her. 'Never happy unless I'm giving somebody a hard time.'

One of Moira's twin girls came up to Katie and held up her a floppy pink bear for her to look at. The girl was only about four years old, with tangled blonde hair and a faded Peppa Pig T-shirt.

'Pink Bear was crying,' she said, very seriously.

'Oh, dear,' said Katie. 'Why was that?'

'She got pushed down the stairs and she bumped her head really, really hard.'

'That's terrible. Who pushed her down the stairs?'

The little girl shook her head so that her hair covered her face. 'She's not allowed to tell.'

'Well, I hope she's feeling better now,' said Katie, touching the little girl gently on the shoulder. She wasn't trained as a child psychiatrist and she knew better than to get involved in conversations like this with children from violent homes.

Blathnaid said, 'Neala's upstairs, Katie. Do you want to come up and have a chat with her?'

'Of course,' said Katie, and followed Blathnaid's large brown-trousered behind up to the second floor.

Neala and her two children had been given one of the newly decorated rooms at the front of the house, overlooking Lavitt's Quay and the river. The ceiling was sloping because it was an attic room, but it was sunny and bright. A boy of about three was kneeling in the window bay playing with two toy cars, while a little girl of about six was lying on one of the beds sucking her thumb.

Neala herself was a taut, nervous-looking young woman with her black wiry hair pulled back in a bunch. Her face was pinched and angular with enormous brown eyes and her wrists were as thin as wooden spoon handles. She was wearing a skimpy purple T-shirt and a voluminous black skirt that looked three sizes too big for her. She started to stand up when Katie came into the room, but Katie said, 'You're all right, Neala, relax.'

'I was hoping you'd come,' said Neala, in a voice that was hoarse from stress and smoking. 'Well, to be honest with you, I was hoping you'd come and I was hoping you wouldn't.'

'You've lovely children,' said Katie. 'What are their names?'

'Peter, and that's Donna.'

Katie smiled at Donna, but Donna stared back at her solemnly, still sucking her thumb.

'I don't know what to call you,' said Neala.

'Call me Katie. This isn't the Garda station and you're certainly not under arrest.'

'That's why I wanted to see you, in a way,' said Neala. She kept glancing around the room as if she were terrified that somebody might be hiding behind the curtains, or under the bed, listening to her.

'Are you all right?' Katie asked her. 'I mean, physically all right?'

'She has some contusions,' put in Blathnaid. 'Doctor Mulroney will be round later to examine her, and the children, too.'

'He's always careful not to leave bruises where anybody can see them,' said Neala, looking at Donna as she did so. She obviously thought that it was pointless not to discuss her husband's violence in front of her children because they had already witnessed it, daily, for themselves.

'Do you want to make a formal complaint against him?' asked Katie. 'If you do, I can send a garda around to take a statement. A female garda.'

Neala shook her head vigorously. 'There's no future in that at all. He was up in front of the court before and all that happened was that he was fined and given a warning and after that he slapped me around worse than ever.'

'You still shouldn't let him get away with it,' said Katie. 'Just because he's your husband, that doesn't make his assault any less serious.'

'I know that. And that's why I wanted to talk to you, to put a stop to it for good and all.'

'Go on,' Katie encouraged her. She could tell from Neala's agitation that she had something very important to tell her, but she was afraid of the consequences if she did.

'That detective garda that was killed on the Brian Boru Bridge – you know, the one who was hit by a car.'

'Detective Barry, yes. We're still looking for the driver.'

Neala glanced around again and then placed her hand over her heart as if she were swearing an oath, or feeling the bruises to remind herself of what her husband had done to her, or both.

'It was Darragh. My Darragh.'

'Your husband was driving the vehicle that hit Detective Barry?'

'That's right. He told me. It was on the news on the telly, like, and he said, "That was me," and he was laughing about it. I was like, "You're codding me, aren't you?" but he was like, "No, serious, that was me driving with Bobby in the front seat. Bobby told me to squish the pig and I did."'

'You're sure he wasn't just boasting, or doing his best to scare you?'

'Darragh doesn't have to say things like that to frighten me. He'd been late back home for his tea that day. We live in Parklands, like, and he only works in a garage in Blackpool, but he said he was late because he'd had to drive all the way down to Boycestown to get rid of the car. He said he'd set light to it. He was pure pleased with himself, believe me.'

Now Katie was convinced that Neala was telling the truth and that her husband, Darragh, hadn't simply been trying to intimidate her. On Katie's instructions, the Garda press office had still not announced that they had found the burned-out Land Rover that had killed Detective Barry. Almost every time they were investigating an unsolved murder some header would come forward to confess to it, especially when it involved a police officer, so she always made sure that several critical details were held back from the media.

'He won't find out that it was me who told you, will he?' said Neala. 'If he ever does, I swear to God he'll do for me. Either *he* will, or that Bobby Quilty. He has the Devil standing in him, that Bobby Quilty. He's totally evil, through and through.'

'Don't worry – it doesn't have to come out that you tipped us off about your Darragh,' Katie told her. 'In any case, we wouldn't be able to get him convicted on your say-so alone. We'd need to find some corroborating evidence first. Otherwise, Darragh could simply deny that he ever said it, or make out that he was joking. There's no law against joking, although sometimes I think that there ought to be.'

'What do you mean, like? What's – what is it? – corrugated evidence?'

'It just means proof that we can show to a judge that your Darragh was actually driving the vehicle at the time that Detective Barry was killed. You know, like fingerprints, or shoe prints, or DNA, or eyewitnesses picking him out and saying it was him. But at least we know now who it is we're trying to identify, and that's going to make our job a whole lot easier, I can tell you.'

'I don't know,' said Neala, worriedly. 'Maybe I shouldn't have told you. I have Donna and little Petey to think about and I'm frightened enough as it is that Darragh's going to find out where we are and come after us.'

'You're safe here, I promise you,' Katie reassured her. 'They never let anybody into the house without checking them first and if there's any trouble they have an alarm connected directly to the Garda station.'

Neala started to gnaw at her thumbnail. All Katie could do was lay her hand on her shoulder and say, 'Please don't worry. Neala. We'll protect you, I promise.'

She waited for a few moments, then she smiled at Donna and went back downstairs to talk to some of the other women in the house. She looked through Blathnaid's notes on the families that Walnut Tree had taken in that week, and then, ten minutes later, she left. When she climbed back into her car, however, she didn't drive off immediately. She sat staring at her sea-green eyes in the rear-view mirror, feeling both angry and frustrated.

If she could have put out an arrest warrant for Darragh Murphy immediately, she would have done. But she knew that she would have to handle any inquiry into Detective Barry's murder with extraordinary caution. She couldn't arrest Murphy on suspicion because he would guess where she had got her information, and she had nothing else to back it up. She would only be putting the lives of Neala and her children in extreme peril – and John's life, too. She couldn't even bring him into the station for an identity line-up. As soon as Bobby Quilty got wind that she was still investigating him, God alone knew what revenge he would take. He would believe that he was justified, too – 'You broke the treaty, DS Maguire, not me.'

Even if she could find enough evidence to put Darragh Murphy behind bars for killing Detective Barry, and Bobby Quilty for inciting him to do it, Neala and John would still be in danger of retribution from other members of Quilty's gang, or his so-called Authentic IRA. In the last week of January, the A-IRA had murdered two suspected members of Oglaigh na hEireann who had attempted to hijack a lorryload of Bobby Quilty's cigarettes. In trademark Quilty fashion, they had both suffered shotgun blasts between the legs before being bound and gagged and thrown off Daly Bridge into the River Lee so that they would float through the city centre at the busiest time of the day.

Katie had seen the bodies for herself and the thought of them still made her stomach clench.

She could fully understand that Neala wanted Darragh to be punished for beating her, and to have him locked up so that he could never threaten her again, but she didn't think that she appreciated what this would mean for her and her children. They would have to spend the rest of their lives in witness protection, under assumed names, even if they left the country and were relocated somewhere in England. Bobby Quilty's most lucrative trade came from the cigarettes that he smuggled from Ringaskiddy into Swansea, or from Dundalk into Liverpool, and he had scores of English cronies who would be only too happy to do him a favour and see that Neala was made to suffer for touting on him.

And John – what would they do to John? She might never see him again – or, if they blinded him, he might never see *her* again, even if she managed to rescue him alive.

She had just started her engine when her iPhone pinged to tell her that she had a text message. It was from Kyna and it read simply, *I'm in. GHMOMS.*

Katie knew what *GHMOMS* meant because Kyna had used it before when she was caught up in a situation that was critical or dangerous or deeply unpleasant. *God Have Mercy On My Soul.*

She was tempted to tell Kyna to pull out if there was too much risk, or if her position was becoming untenable, for whatever reason. But now that she knew for certain that Bobby Quilty was behind Detective Barry's murder it was even more urgent that Kyna should infiltrate his empire even further.

She drove back to Anglesea Street. She had intended to go up to the canteen and have a ham and salad roll, but now she felt too nauseated to eat anything.

Eighteen

Bill Phinner and Eithne came up to her office together. Eithne was carrying a large transparent plastic folder, while Bill was sucking at an unlit pipe.

'Bill!' said Katie, looking up from her paperwork. 'I never knew you smoked a pipe!'

'I don't, as matter of fact,' Bill told her. 'Hardly ever, any road. I can't smoke in the lab, and I can't smoke in the pub, and the missus won't let me smoke indoors at home, and most of the time it's raining and believe you me there's fierce little pleasure in standing down the end of the garden trying to keep your pipe alight when it's lashing down. The only good it does me, it stops me from grinding my teeth. My brother says it makes me look halfway intelligent, too. You can point at things with a pipe and look as if you know what you're talking about.'

'So, what have you got for me?' asked Katie.

Eithne held up the folder. 'Final DNA results on the bodies from Millstream Row. There's no question about it. They're the Langtry family all right.'

'I won't bore you with the minutiae,' said Bill. 'But the charts for all four of the family are here and you'll be able to see for yourself that the segments we've tested are well above the threshold for IBD.'

Katie took the folder and opened it up. She had taken the eight-day refresher course in forensics early last year and she knew that IBD meant Identical By Descent. It was sometimes possible that DNA could be IBC, Identical By Chance, but in the case of the Langtrys she could see from a cursory glance at the charts that

140

the samples had been triangulated with Ronan Fitzgerald and that the matches were undeniable.

'All right, thanks,' she said. 'Of course that leaves me with the question of how Stephen Langtry managed to send letters and postcards from America when he was lying dead under the floorboards in Blarney.'

'A ruse, I'd say, so nobody would find out for a while that they'd been murdered,' said Bill, taking his pipe out of his mouth. 'Their bodies would have stunk for a few weeks but sure most people's houses would have stunk in the 1920s, what with the lack of personal hygiene and the peat fires and the smoking indoors, and the same pot of tripe bubbling on the hob for days on end. And, of course, their killers were haunted that their bodies dried out the way they did, what with the atmospheric conditions under those floorboards being the way they were. I don't suppose they envisaged for a moment that they wouldn't be discovered for another ninety-five years.'

'Well, I think it's pure obvious that somebody else apart from Stephen Langtry sent those letters,' said Katie. 'I'd just be interested to know *who*, and exactly *why*. I mean, there was a war going on and people on both sides were getting killed, but usually it was done quite openly. When Michael Collins was shot they didn't hide his body, did they, and send letters from New York to make out that he was simply fed up with politics and had decided to emigrate?'

'Now that would be a grand idea for a film,' said Bill. 'Especially if they could get that Liam Neeson playing Collins again.'

'I'll have Mathew arrange for a media briefing later this afternoon,' Katie told him. 'I expect Fionnuala Sweeney will be crowing, but it can't be helped. Maybe we'll be able to jog somebody's memory and they'll remember something they were told by their grandparents about the Langtrys.'

'You never know,' said Bill. 'My old grandfather was always rattling on about the time his older brother hid guns on his farm at Inniscarra for Captain Frank Busteed and his boys. From what he said, you'd have believed the Phinners won the war of independence single-handed.'

'Like you say, Bill, you never know. I'll also get Detective Ó Doibhilin to contact US Immigration. It's a ten million to one chance, but their historical records are fantastic and they might be able to tell us if somebody calling himself Stephen Langtry was admitted to the USA in 1921, with or without his wife and children. And the New York State police may be able to discover if a Stephen Langtry ever really worked for Glenside Woollen Mills, especially if Glenside Woollen Mills is still in business.'

'So you think some other family could have gone over to America and pretended to be them?'

'I really have no idea, Bill. I don't think it's very likely, but we have to consider every possibility. The Langtrys might have been murdered a long time ago, but they deserve justice and whoever shot them needs to be named and shamed. Grand work with the DNA, by the way.'

Bill looked towards the window. 'It still looks nice and bright out there. I reckon I'll go and have a smoke to celebrate.'

* * *

The media briefing was called for 4.30 p.m. to give RTÉ and the local radio stations plenty of time to include their reports on their six o'clock news bulletins, and the newspapers time to write it up for their morning editions.

Fionnuala Sweeney was there, of course, sitting right at the front, and so was Dan Keane from the *Examiner* with his usual half-smoked cigarette tucked behind his ear, and Branna MacSuibhne from the *Echo* with her blonde hair sprayed into two rigid buffalo horns. Katie could see a new face there, too: a very thin brunette with enormous brown eyes. She had a tapestry bag slung around her shoulders and a Newstalk badge on her lanyard, although she looked almost too young to be a radio reporter.

At the last moment, Chief Superintendent MacCostagáin came into the conference room to join Katie at the top table, looking even more distracted and out of sorts than usual. Although she had already given him the details of the DNA results, and he didn't often make an appearance at routine news briefings, he shared Katie's concern about the political implications of the Langtry case and he obviously wanted to hear what the media's response was going to be.

Katie stood up and said, 'Good afternoon, ladies and gentlemen. Our Technical Bureau have now completed DNA tests on the four bodies discovered beneath the floorboards at Millstream Row in Blarney, and they have established beyond any reasonable doubt that the four were indeed Stephen and Radha Langtry and their two children, Aideen and Clearie.'

She could see Fionnuala Sweeney nodding her head in self-satisfaction, but she ignored her and looked instead at the young woman from Newstalk.

'Based on this evidence, we'll continue to pursue our investigation into how the family were murdered and who might have been responsible, but I have to emphasize that I am not regarding this case as a high priority. My detectives have many more pressing investigations on their hands, particularly in the areas of drug-trafficking, prostitution, property theft and serious fraud, so the public can rest assured that we're giving our full attention to present-day inquiries.'

Fionnuala Sweeney raised her hand and asked, 'Have you found any evidence yet to confirm or deny that Radha Langtry was having an adulterous affair with a British army officer?'

'I'm aware of that so-called "local legend", Fionnuala, but so far we haven't found any conclusive evidence to back it up.'

'But you do have *some* evidence?'

'No.'

'A British army cap badge wrapped in a love letter?'

'Yes, we have those, but as yet we have no conclusive proof that they actually belonged to Radha Langtry.'

The young woman from Newstalk put up her hand. 'If they *were* hers, though, and she'd been having an affair with a British officer, that could have given the British the motive to shoot them, couldn't it?'

'What's your name?' Katie asked her.

'Muireann. Muireann Bourke.'

'Well, let me say this to you, Muireann, whenever somebody's unlawfully killed, it's part of my job to have theories about who might have done it and why. But I test each of those theories to the very limit and make absolutely sure that I have irrefutable evidence before I start making public pronouncements about them.

'Whatever the "local legend" suggests, it's impossible for me to say for certain if Radha Langtry was having a liaison with a British officer or not, and I certainly have no grounds at all to suggest that the British army was responsible for killing the Langtrys because of it.'

'If you found out that they *were*, though, that would be shattering, wouldn't it? Like, think of the repercussions!'

'Muireann, I can comment only on facts, not wild suppositions, and you should know better than to ask me a question like that.'

Muireann Bourke flushed and looked down at the floor in embarrassment. *She'll learn*, thought Katie. She remembered asking similar questions herself when she was a green young garda and being slapped down for it.

Dan Keane said, 'Even if do discover who murdered the Langtrys, though, what earthly use will that be? What about you, Chief Superintendent MacCostagáin? Don't you sometimes think it's wiser to let sleeping dogs lie?'

'Sleeping dogs, maybe,' said Chief Superintendent Mac-Costagáin. 'In this case, though, the dogs weren't sleeping. They were shot dead, as were the Langtrys.'

'Of course, yes, but it was a very long time ago.'

'There's no statute of limitations on homicide, Dan, even if the offenders have passed away themselves. If you take a life, you will always have to answer to the law, even as you always have to explain yourself to God.'

'Sure, I have you,' said Dan Keane. 'But if we're talking about answering to the law, and to God, can you tell us what progress you've been able to make into finding out who it was that murdered Detective Barry – if any, that is? It's his funeral tomorrow.'

Katie turned her head to give Chief Superintendent Mac-Costagáin a sharp, cautionary look. She was all too familiar with Dan Keane and his interview techniques – 'Keane by Name and Keen by Nature' was the way the *Examiner* described him under his byline. He rarely asked a question unless he already had a good idea what the answer was going to be.

Chief Superintendent MacCostagáin was very guarded when he answered. 'We're still in the process of examining the forensic evidence and collating eyewitness statements,' he said. 'Tomorrow morning we'll be making a fresh appeal for information on all news media, and I understand that Assistant Commissioner O'Reilly has been given approval from Phoenix Park to offer a reward for any information that leads to a conviction. The exact amount hasn't been confirmed yet, but I expect it to be in the region of ten thousand euros.'

'You haven't located the Land Rover that ran down Detective Barry, then?'

'I've no comment to make about that, Dan. Not at this time.'

'But you've located at least *one* abandoned Land Rover?'

'I've no comment to make about that, Dan.'

'Well, fair play to you, Chief Superintendent. I fully understand that your inquiry is still ongoing and that you can't be releasing every doonchy little clue that you come across. But if you'd found the Land Rover that killed Detective Barry, I'd say that was quite a substantial clue, wouldn't you? So would it be safe for me to assume that *this* particular Land Rover has nothing at all to do with his murder and that's why you've announced nothing to the media about it?'

Katie didn't like the way this questioning was going at all, and she knew that Chief Superintendent MaCostagáin wasn't going to be able to get away with answering 'no comment' to every question that Dan Keane put to him.

'Which Land Rover exactly are you talking about, Dan?' she asked him.

'Well, it doesn't really matter, does it, if it has nothing at all to do with your investigation into the killing of Detective Barry?'

Dan Keane's left eyebrow was lifted and he had a calm, superior look on his face because he was confident now that he had Katie cornered.

Katie paused for a moment and then she said, 'A Land Rover was found yesterday on a farm track north of Boycestown. It was totally burned out, with the result that it probably won't yield any meaningful forensic evidence, although our technical experts are still going over it. Apart from that, we're continuing to make inquiries into where it came from and who might have been driving it.'

'You're not denying then that it could be the same Land Rover that killed Detective Barry?'

'I'm not denying it and I'm not confirming it, either.'

'But DS Maguire, it still had its number plates attached. So how could you possibly *not* be certain, when you have CCTV footage of the Land Rover following Detective Barry across the Brian Boru Bridge?'

'Excuse me, Dan, but how you can be so sure that it was still carrying its number plates?' Katie retaliated. Although this briefing wasn't going out on live TV or radio, she was becoming seriously worried now. She was counting on Kyna finding out where John was being held before the evidence against Bobby Quilty became so damning that she had no choice but to arrest him. For John, the consequences of her doing that were likely to be disastrous. She had no doubt at all that only minutes after her detectives turned up at Bobby Quilty's door with a warrant John would be dead, or worse, and that she would never see him, or his body, ever again.

Dan Keane held up his iPhone. 'Just as I was leaving the office on my way here today my picture editor caught up with me and said that two Dutch cyclists came in to see him this morning. It seems like they were on a tour of Cork and Kerry and while they were cycling across country on their way to Kinsale they saw a

Land Rover on fire, and there were two fellows standing watching it. They took a few pictures, but being Dutch they never watched the TV news or read a paper, so they had no idea that they might have witnessed anything significant.'

'Why didn't they report it to the Garda anyway?' said Katie.

'Like I say, they didn't think it was anything of any great importance. Just a Land Rover that had caught fire for some reason and two fellows who were helpless to put it out. They only brought the pictures in to us because they were running low on holiday money and thought we might pay them a few euros for them. And so we did, because one or two of them are pure spectacular. In one of them, there's a great ball of fire going up in the air which must have been the Land Rover's petrol tank exploding.'

'Why didn't *you* bring them in to us?'

'I did. I am. I couldn't have done it any sooner. Here they are now, on my phone. I'll share them with you right away.'

'I must say you certainly picked your moment.'

'DS Maguire, I swear to you on the tomb of St Francis de Sales that I haven't even had the time myself to study them in any detail at all. I can tell you, though, that you can see at least one of the two fellows' faces quite distinctly – so if you knew him, like, you'd be able to tell who he was.'

Katie opened the laptop in front of her and said, 'Go on, then. You have me on your list of contacts, don't you?'

There was a rustle of excitement in the conference room. Fionnuala Sweeney stood up and said, 'You'll be releasing those pictures to all of us, I hope?'

'Not yet, Fionnuala,' Katie told her. 'We need to examine them ourselves first and see if we can identify either or both of the two men in them.'

Katie's laptop pinged and an email from Dan Keane appeared with a Dropbox link to seven photographs. They all showed a Land Rover burning in a narrow country track, with dense black smoke billowing out of it and two men standing some distance away, half hidden by the long grass verge. The second to last picture was the most dramatic, with orange flames rolling up into the sky and one of the men turning his face away from the blast so that he could be clearly seen by the camera.

'Thank you, Dan,' said Katie. 'We'll take a look at these immediately and let you know as soon as we're ready to issue a statement. Meanwhile, I'd appreciate it if you didn't publish them yet.'

'I don't know about that,' said Dan Keane. 'We paid for them, after all. Two hundred and fifty euros. Cash.'

'We appreciate that,' put in Chief Superintendent MacCostagáin. 'However, they amount to material evidence in an ongoing Garda inquiry. If you publish them prematurely and the men in the pictures are alerted to the possibility that we're looking for them and flee our jurisdiction, that could amount to obstruction.'

'I think I'll have to talk to our lawyers about that,' said Dan Keane. 'In the meantime, though, can you now verify that this is the Land Rover that killed Detective Barry? Like, the number plates in those pictures *do* match, don't they?'

'You swore that you hadn't had the time to study them,' said Katie.

'I didn't, no. But I couldn't help myself from giving the number plates a quick lamp. They're BXZ plates, from Armagh.'

'Very well,' said Chief Superintendent MacCostagáin, speaking to all of the assembled journalists. 'You can quote me as confirming that we've located an abandoned Land Rover that appears to be the same vehicle that killed Detective Barry. Further than that, I have no more comments to make at this time.'

Katie said, 'The main purpose of this briefing was to inform you that the bodies found in Blarney have been positively identified as Stephen Langtry and his family. If we manage to come up with any information about who might have killed them and what the motive might have been, we will of course let you know. Thank you for coming.'

Dan Keane said, 'Bobby Quilty, he's from Armagh, isn't he? And Detective Barry was trying to arrest one of his dealers when he was killed.'

Katie closed her laptop and stood up. 'If we could convict people on evidence like that, Dan, three quarters of the population of Cork would be in prison.'

'So they would, DS Maguire, and that would be fierce unjust. But think how peaceful it would be, shopping in Paul Street Tesco on a Saturday afternoon.'

Nineteen

When Kyna came downstairs she found Bobby Quilty sitting on a white simulated-leather sofa in the living room, his legs crossed, one flip-flop hanging loose, jabbing at his iPhone. She stood in the doorway waiting for him to acknowledge her. After all, he was supposed to have humiliated her and shown her in the most degrading way possible that he was the boss.

Her hair was still slicked back wet from the shower and she was wearing a faded pair of Margot's jeans that she had rolled up around her ankles because they were much too long for her, and a loose white sleeveless top, without a bra. Without showing even a flicker of surprise at what Bobby Quilty had done to her, Margot had taken away Kyna's own clothes to wash them.

Bobby Quilty didn't look at her, not directly, but beckoned her to come in and pointed with his iPhone towards the armchair next to him. She sat down and waited until he had finished texting, not saying a word. She had been involved in at least half a dozen undercover investigations before, and the secret was not to act *like* the person whose identity she had assumed but to *be* them. It was never easy. Once, when she was gathering evidence against a Dublin brothel-keeper, she had developed such a crush on her that she had been sorely tempted to warn her that she was about to be arrested and give her time to get away.

''Bout you, then?' said Bobby Quilty with a sniff.

Kyna pulled a non-committal face and said nothing.

'Well, wait till I tell you,' Bobby Quilty continued. 'We've a new shipment of fags just arrived last night and a whole heap of

150

orders from our regular customers. Ger will take you to the lock-up to pick them up and then he'll drive you round so that you can deliver them and collect the cash for them.'

'You don't only sell your fags on the street, then?' asked Kyna.

Bobby Quilty shook out a cigarette and lit it and blew out smoke. 'Ach, no, not at all. Most of our trade comes from shops and bars and office workers. The reason I sell them out on the street is mostly to pick up new business. You know, people who never realized that they could buy two hundred fags for a quarter of the price. Once they know where we'll be flogging them, and when, they always come back for more. Well, wouldn't you? Ten euros for a packet of fags, it's fecking inhuman!'

'You don't trust me to go out selling on my own, though? What, in case I run away with your fags and don't come back?'

'Oh, I think I can trust you. I took a squint at your phone, girl, just to make sure. No, I just want Ger to take you around so that he can show you the ropes, like, and you can meet the regular customers face to face. They'll all take to you, believe me. You're very easy on the eye. You'll be good for business, so you will.'

'Can I have my phone back now?'

'Ach, sure.' Bobby Quilty reached around to the table behind the sofa and then threw Kyna's phone across to her. 'I called a couple of your pals from the massage parlour and they were highly complimentary about you, to say the least. One feller said that he only had to hear your name and it got him all chubbed up.'

Ger appeared in the doorway, with Benny close behind him. He took off his hat to wipe his sweaty forehead and when he came into the room Kyna could smell his body odour. It reminded her of a long-dead cat she had once discovered in the kitchen cupboard of an old woman's house she had been searching in Dolphin's Barn.

''Bout you, then?' asked Bobby Quilty. 'Was the park any use?'

Ger reached into his inside pocket and handed Bobby Quilty a thick bundle of crumpled euro notes. 'We sold thirty-seven boxes altogether. We could have sold more, but the shades was beginning to take too much of an interest.'

'Didn't I tell you not to worry about the polls? We're insured, you know that. I have them totally sorted, so I have. They might sniff around, but they won't scoop you.'

'Well, you might say that, Bobby, but you've never spent two years in the slammer. The shades still give me the fecking palpitations.'

Bobby Quilty was counting out the money that Ger had given him, licking his thumb every now and then.

'Nine hundred and thirty euros,' said Ger. 'One fellow didn't have change but he said not to bother.'

'All right, that's magic,' said Bobby Quilty, once he had finished counting and fastidiously turning all the notes around the same way. 'Now you can load up again and take Sidhe here to do the drop-offs round Blackpool and Shandon – oh, and that newsagent on MacCurtain Street. And on the way back, stop off and see Chisel, would you, and check that our friend hasn't managed to unscrew himself?'

Ger said to Kyna, 'Come on, then, girl. Let's get you to work. You might have a tasty arse but we can't have you sitting on it all day.'

* * *

They drove down to Blackpool. Benny sat in the back with his earphones in and Kyna could hear the faint *tish-tish-tish* of his rap music. Ger said almost nothing except to swear at every cyclist who wavered in front of him and any driver who was slow starting off when the traffic lights went to green. His sweat smelled so strongly now that Kyna put down her window and kept her head turned away from him.

They turned through an archway between the run-down shops and houses along Dublin Street and into a row of tatty lock-up garages. Ger said to Kyna, 'You go stand on the corner, Sidhe, and keep sketch, while me and Benny load up the car. If you see any shades coming, don't shout out or nothing, just walk back over here flapping your hand like you've let off a breezer.'

Kyna shrugged and did as she was told. While she stood under the archway, ostensibly watching out for gardaí, Ger unlocked one of the garages, lifting its door with a harsh metallic squeal like a pig being slaughtered. Even from where she was standing, thirty metres away, Kyna could see that it was stacked right up to its asbestos roof with cartons of cigarettes – the distinctive red-and-white packs of Lucky Strike, West and Marlboro, as well as Goal and NZ Gold and Jin Ling and other brands she didn't recognize.

While Ger and Benny filled up black plastic refuse sacks with cigarettes, Kyna surreptitiously slipped out her iPhone and texted Katie with her thumb. She told her that Bobby Quilty had sent her out on a delivery run, but that he had also asked them to check up on 'our friend', whoever that was, to make sure that he hadn't 'managed to unscrew himself', whatever that meant.

She had only just finished texting when a Garda patrol car came slowly towards her along Dublin Street. She backed into the archway in case the officers recognized her or stopped to ask her why she was loitering there.

The patrol car passed by, though, without even slowing down, and a few seconds later Ger gave her a whistle as if he were calling a dog.

Before they started on their rounds, Ger consulted a torn-off sheet of notepaper with a list of all of their customers pencilled on it. 'Right we are, then. First stop, Ali's Corner Store on Thomas Davis Street, then it's O'Grady's, the bookies and The Scissor Shop, the barber's.'

When they reached Thomas Davis Street, Ger pointed to the corner shop and Kyna climbed out of the car. Benny climbed out, too, opened the boot and handed her two bulging black bags. From the driving seat, Ger whistled to her again, and beckoned to her, and said, 'Smile when you give Ali the fags, okay, and make him think that he could take you into the back of the shop and give you one.'

'*Wha*'? But he's a Paki, isn't he?'

'That's not the fecking point, Sidhe. The point is that this is a cut-throat business, the cigarette trade, and we want him to go on buying from us rather than the Duggans or the O'Flynns. So, you know, give him the eye and wiggle your arse when you take his money. You wouldn't have the time to flah him, any road. We have a dozen more drop-offs yet.'

Kyna kept her mouth closed. She took the bags from Benny and pushed her way between the string bags of onions and sponge mops that cluttered the entrance to the grocery store. Inside, it smelled strongly of fenugreek, and the aisles were so crowded with giant boxes of detergent and tins of okra and cut-price washing-up brushes and racks full of Tayto crisps that she had a struggle to reach the counter.

A bearded Asian in a yellow baseball cap was standing behind the counter, intent on mending a mobile phone.

'Are you Ali?' she asked him. 'Here you are then, boy. Here's the fags you ordered from the Big Feller.'

Ali put down his miniature screwdriver and grinned at her, with his two front incisors missing. 'How about you, then?' he said, in a strong Norrie accent. 'First time the Big Feller's sent a good-looking beour like you to deliver his fags.'

'Well, he only wants to make you happy, Ali, do you know what I mean, like?'

'I don't know if the Big Feller could make me happy, but I think you could. What's your name, girl?'

'Sidhe. S-i-d-h-e like in "fairy", like – not "she" like "her over there who looks like a bit of a goer". And that'll be five hundred yo-yos, please.'

'Sure, but how do I know they're all here, all the fags I ordered? Maybe you can stay for a while and help me to count them, Sidhe, just to make sure. What would happen if I was one box short? Where would I find another box?'

Kyna gave him an exaggerated pout. 'Oh, you're such a bad man, Ali. But not today. I'm up the walls, like, with all my deliveries. One day maybe, when I'm not so pushed.'

'I will look forward to it, my darling.'

Ali opened up his till and counted out five hundred euros. He didn't give them to her, though, until he had come out from behind the counter, put his arm around her waist and escorted her to the door. Even then he held the money just out of reach, until he had kissed her on the lips. The peak of his baseball cap bumped against her forehead.

'Christ on a bicycle!' Benny piped up as she climbed back into the car. 'You only shifted him!'

Ger couldn't help grinning behind his huge dark glasses. 'I'll tell you, there's no way he's going to be ordering his fags from Micky Duggan after that! What was it like?'

Kyna was tempted to spit and wipe her mouth but Ali was still watching from the doorway of his shop and giving her a little finger-wave.

'Suppose a badger sat by mistake in a bowl of curry,' she said. 'Then, after the curry was all stiff and dried up, suppose you kissed that badger's arse. That was what it was like.'

Ger laughed – a thin, cracked laugh – and Kyna knew then that she had won his confidence.

* * *

For the next three and a half hours they drove around Blackpool and Shandon and Gurranabraher, delivering black bags full of cigarette cartons to shops and pubs and offices and private houses. Kyna even took a bag to the manager of an old peoples' home in Sunday's Well, and round to the back door of a dental clinic on Commons Road in Farranree.

At every stop she was greeted with smiles of appreciation and thumbs-up gestures and two of her customers asked her out on a date – a spotty young estate agent with protruding ears and a white-bearded pub landlord who was old enough to be her grandfather. The cash was always handed over with no hesitation at all and by the time she delivered the last three sacks to the Golden Shamrock Bar in Blackpool she estimated that she had taken well over eleven thousand euros.

At last Ger parked outside a terracotta-painted house at the junction of Leitrim Street and Pine Street, opposite O'Keefe's pub.

The house had once been a shop but now its large display windows had grimy, fly-spotted blinds drawn down over them.

'What are we stopping here for?' asked Kyna. 'We don't have any more fags left, do we?'

'You just mind your own beeswax girl and wait here for me,' said Ger. He climbed out of the car, but instead of going to the front door of the house he walked around to a side gate, opened it, and disappeared inside.

'What's here, then, Benny?' Kyna asked, but Benny had put in his earphones and couldn't hear her. After they had waited for a few minutes, though, he suddenly took them out and said, 'I'm fecking parched, me. I've a mouth on me like Gandhi's flip-flop. I'm going to get myself a Coke.'

'Fetch me one while you're at it,' said Kyna.

Benny got out of the car and walked two doors down to Brannagan's Bar. Kyna waited a little while, but when he didn't immediately reappear, she got out, too. She looked up at the terracotta-coloured house, but she couldn't see anybody looking back down at her from the upstairs windows, so she went to the side gate, opened it, and quickly went inside. She found herself in a cramped back yard with wheelie bins and a bicycle in it, as well as a stack of broken window frames filled with shattered glass, and a rabbit hutch that looked as if it had been smashed in half and then crudely repaired with a square of hardboard and a length of frayed electrical flex. The rabbit was sitting on a bed of its own buttons and it stared at Kyna bulgy-eyed, as if it were vainly hoping that she had come to set it free.

The back door of the house had been left ajar and Kyna could see a kitchen sink with dirty plates in it and some chipped cupboard doors. She could hear voices, too: a woman complaining loudly and persistently about something and two slurred male voices, one of which she recognized as Ger.

She went up to the door and pushed it open a little more. The voices sounded as if they were coming from somewhere upstairs, so she carefully stepped inside and went through the kitchen into the hallway beyond. The house was in a desperate state of disrepair. The walls were so damp that the floral paper had been bleached of all its colour, and the pale chocolate stair carpet was threadbare and spotted black with mould. Kyna went to the bottom of the staircase and looked up to the first-floor landing. The voices sounded as if they were coming from a room immediately on the left-hand side, and although the door was almost closed, cigarette smoke was curling around it, so she could be fairly sure that Ger was in there with whoever he was talking to – possibly the person whom Bobby Quilty had referred to as 'Chisel'.

Her heart was beating so hard that it hurt because there was every chance that Ger would suddenly open the door and see her standing there. However, there was no point in her going back. Benny would probably have returned with their Cokes by now and he would see her emerging from the side gate and tell Ger anyway.

She had an excuse ready, to explain why she had followed Ger into the house, but that excuse would only work if she kept on going. She grasped the banister rail, hesitated for a few seconds, and then started to climb the stairs. They creaked loudly, but the woman continued to nag, and Ger continued talking back to her, so they obviously hadn't heard her.

When she reached the landing, she tiptoed over to the right-hand side and opened the first door she came to. It was a bathroom, with curled-up green linoleum on the floor and a bath with dripping taps. The inside of the toilet was stained rusty brown, and its wooden seat had come off and was propped up against the wall beside it.

Kyna opened the next door, which she had to do carefully because the knob was loose and rattled as she turned it. This room smelled strongly as if somebody had been sleeping in it. The ill-fitting orange curtains were still drawn and there was a king-sized mattress on the floor with twisted sheets on it, and pillows that were still dented with the impressions of two heads. A single corduroy-covered armchair was heaped with clothes, men's and women's, including a large pair of stained white underpants.

Just as she closed the door of this room, she heard Ger say, 'How's our friend been keeping, then, Sorcia? Has he been giving you any bother?'

The woman said something Kyna couldn't hear, but then she must have turned around because she heard her say, '—shouting out and moaning and groaning, so I give him five paracetamol and that shut him up. I don't care. I don't like to see nobody suffering like that. I remember when my mam was—'

Kyna paused, still on tiptoe, holding her breath. Ger and the woman must be very close to the door for her to be able to hear them so distinctly. The other man spoke, too, but she couldn't make out what he was saying, only that he had a strong Southside accent.

She went to the door at the end of the landing. On the wall next to it was a faded framed print of Pope Paul VI, holding up two fingers in blessing. She tried the handle, only to find that the door was locked, although the key was still in it. She unlocked it and slowly pushed it open.

It was gloomy inside, like the bedroom, because the blind was drawn. The smell was even worse, though – rancid and sour, but with a sickening sweetness to it, too. Several bluebottles were flying around, while others tapped and buzzed at the window.

Kyna didn't recognize John at first, although she had met him six or seven times and seen dozens of pictures of him and Katie when they were together. He was lying asleep on a single bed, completely naked. His face was startlingly white, and shiny with perspiration, so that he could almost have been a marble effigy of himself, except that his mouth was hanging open and he was snoring.

As she approached him, keeping her hand cupped over her nose and mouth, Kyna saw that both of his feet had been fastened to the wooden board at the end of the bed with metal bolts and that shiny green flies were clustered around the stigmata. He had soiled the mattress and the insides of his thighs were smeared with dark yellow faeces.

She laid her hand on his shoulder and gently shook him. 'John?' she whispered. 'John, can you hear me?'

He stirred and groaned like a door creaking, but he didn't open his eyes. Kyna shook him again, harder this time. 'John? Wake up, John! *John!*'

He made a snuffling sound and then he opened his deep blue eyes and stared at her, unfocused.

'John – we're going to get you out of here. So try and be strong, okay? Katie hasn't forgotten you – she loves you. Do you understand me?'

John frowned at her and said, '*Kyna* . . . is that you?' Then he looked around the room and said, 'Where am I?'

'They're keeping you locked up here, but we'll soon get you out, I promise.'

She could hear Ger coughing, and the woman saying something to him, so she tiptoed out of the bedroom and locked the door. She was halfway back across the landing when the door at the top of the staircase suddenly opened and a skinny man in a black T-shirt appeared, with his belt tied tightly into a knot to stop his jeans from falling down. Right behind him came Ger, and a bosomy young woman in a headscarf. All three of them had been smoking so heavily that they came out in a cloud, like characters in a pantomime.

'What in the name of God are you doing here, Sidhe?' Ger demanded. 'I told you to wait outside, didn't I?'

'I'm bursting for a piss,' said Kyna. 'I couldn't hardly do it down the shore, could I?'

'You could have gone over to the pub, for feck's sake.'

'Oh, give the girl a break, would you?' said the bosomy young woman. 'You're so tight, you are, Ger, wouldn't give a starving nun the skin off your skitter!'

'Any more of that, Sorcia, and there'll be less of it!' Ger snapped at her. But then he said, 'You didn't go in *there*, Sidhe, did you?'

'Where?' asked Kyna.

'In there,' he said, pointing towards the room where John was locked up. 'That door there.'

'Why should I? I just need the toilet.'

Ger gave her a ghastly grin and the smoke from his last cigarette came leaking out from between his teeth. 'That's fierce strange, that is. I thought *you* was the toilet!'

The skinny man laughed, honking like a donkey, but Sorcia came over and opened the bathroom door. 'There, love. It's in there. You'll have to forgive the boggin' state of it. Chisel keeps promising to fix the seat but he keeps fixing himself first and then he's too blootered to know one end of a screwdriver from the other.'

'Holy Jesus, Sorcia, I could see you far enough!' Chisel protested.

Kyna went into the bathroom and closed the door. She turned on the tap in the washbasin to make a splashing noise and then took out her phone and texted Katie to tell her the house number, and exactly where John's bedroom was located, and also that his feet were bolted to the bed. She hadn't seen anybody else in the house apart from Chisel and Sorcia, and she hadn't seen any firearms, but that wasn't to say they didn't have any, or that there wasn't another of Bobby Quilty's gang keeping an eye on the house for him.

Ger knocked on the bathroom door and said, 'Get your skates on, will you, we don't have the whole fecking day!'

'Coming!' Kyna called out, and cranked the cistern handle.

'Is that better?' asked Ger as she emerged. In spite of his earlier irritation, she was sure that he really liked her now and that he would do almost anything for her if she asked. What she would really have liked him to do was lie down on the floor in front of her so that she could stamp very hard on his face.

Twenty

Katie was talking to Mathew McElvey in the press office when her iPhone pinged and she saw that Kyna was texting her.

Mathew was saying, 'I agree with you absolutely, DS Maguire. We have to be very diplomatic in the way we handle this Langtry case. On the one hand, we don't want the Garda to be seen to be stirring up old grievances, but on the other hand, like you said at the briefing, we don't want to be seen to be squandering the taxpayers' money trying to find a murderer who's long dead and buried.

'I still think, though, that there's powerful public interest in knowing who it was that murdered the Langtrys, and why – especially if it turns out that Radha Langtry *was* having an affair with a British officer and it was the Brits who shot them. I had a call only this morning from that Stephen Wright fellow from the *Daily Mail* in London and he was very keen to know if—'

'I'm sorry, Mathew,' said Katie. 'I'll have to interrupt you there. I've an urgent case to deal with. I'll get back to you after, if that's okay.'

'Okay, sure,' said Mathew. 'But I have my fingers crossed about what they're going to be saying on the *Six One News*, I can tell you.'

Katie hurried back up to her office and immediately put in calls to Detective Inspector O'Rourke and Detective Sergeant Begley, as well as Detectives O'Donovan, Dooley and Scanlan. Then she switched on her desktop computer, clicked on to a map of Cork City, and brought up a street view of the terracotta-coloured house where John was being held.

For the first time since Bobby Quilty had visited her at home and told her that he had abducted John, she felt that surge of adrenaline that came from being in control again, although she remained deeply anxious about John. *J's feet bolted to bed*, Kyna had texted her. His *feet*, bolted to the bed? She couldn't even begin to imagine what that must look like, or the pain he must be suffering. Maybe Kyna had just meant that his ankles were fastened with leg-cuffs. Pray that she had.

While she was waiting for Inspector O'Rourke and the other three detectives to reach her office she put in a call to Bill Phinner. Bill had already left, but Tyrone Daley answered. He hadn't yet had time to enhance the pictures of the Land Rover at Boycestown and the two men watching it burn, but when Katie told him it had suddenly become urgent he promised to drop everything else and turn his attention to it.

When he arrived, Inspector O'Rourke was carrying a half-finished polystyrene cup of tea, and Detective O'Donovan had obviously been ready to go home because he was holding a large carrier bag from Saville menswear and an empty sandwich box.

Once all the detectives were gathered in her office Katie announced, 'It's Bobby Quilty.' She stood up and swivelled her computer monitor around so that they could all see the screen. 'Things have moved much faster than I thought they would.'

'Like, what things?' asked Inspector O'Rourke. 'We're supposed to be turning a blind eye to Bobby Quilty, aren't we? And *that* diktat came direct from Our Lord and Master Jimmy O'Reilly himself.'

'We *were* turning a blind eye, Francis, until about five minutes ago. But Jimmy O'Reilly's reasons for turning a blind eye were very different from mine. He was trying to save money by not arresting any more of Quilty's street-peddlers, because the courts have only been letting them off, or throwing their cases out altogether. I was trying to save someone from being mutilated, or even killed.'

'Like, who exactly?'

'You know him,' said Katie. 'His name is John Meagher. My ex, if you want to call him that.'

Very briefly – trying not to sound too emotional – she explained how Bobby Quilty had taken John hostage, threatening to blind him or murder him unless she agreed to back away and leave his cigarette-smuggling business unmolested, and stop trying to prove that he had played any part in Detective Barry's death.

'But I couldn't just sit on my hands and let Quilty get away with it,' said Katie, and she told them how she had asked Kyna to infiltrate Bobby Quilty's gang in order to discover the exact location where John was being held.

'I was pure reluctant to ask her, of course I was. But I couldn't think of anybody else I could trust enough to do it – somebody Bobby Quilty wouldn't recognize.'

Detective Sergeant Begley shook his head in admiration. 'That's one fierce brave girl, Kyna. Holy Mary, Mother of God, she's still convalescing from having herself shot.'

None of them questioned what Katie had done, although she knew Detective Sergeant Begley well enough to read from his expression that he would have acted very differently. Regardless of the risk to his career, he would have arrested Bobby Quilty and subjected him to the kind of 'interview' that would have led to him giving away John's location with no hesitation at all. Katie knew very little about his 'interviews' except that sometimes they involved a broom handle and a woodworking clamp.

'There's more, though,' said Katie. 'I'm fairly sure now that I know the identity of the driver who killed Detective Barry.'

'What, somebody grassed?' asked Detective O'Donovan.

'Not exactly. But a woman was taken into the Walnut Tree shelter this morning, a battered wife, and she told me that her husband had boasted to her that it was him. Not only that, he told her that Bobby Quilty was with him at the time, in the passenger seat, and that Quilty had specifically incited him to do it. Her husband's name is Darragh Murphy. Does that name ring a bell for any of you, by any chance? Darragh Murphy?'

'Oh, it does for me, ma'am, for sure,' said Detective Scanlan, raising her hand if she were in class. 'I must have scooped him four or five times when I was working the clubs – mostly for selling coke, although most of the time it was seventy-five per cent baby laxative. His regular customers called him Diarrhoea Darragh. So far as I know he's still living in Parklands.'

'That's right, Parklands,' said Katie. 'His wife told me about him because he's been beating her so badly and she wanted to see him locked up. Her word alone won't be enough for us to charge him with any realistic chance of conviction, but now we have the photographs the Dutch cyclists took of the two men torching the Land Rover. They're very blurred, but Tyrone's working on them now and with any luck we'll be able to identify one of them as Darragh Murphy.'

'What's the plan, then, ma'am?' asked Detective Dooley.

'I'll talk to Chief Superintendent MacCostagáin and Superintendent Pearse now that I've spoken to you. I'm thinking of setting up three simultaneous raids – very early tomorrow morning, if possible. One to pick up Bobby Quilty, one to pick up Darragh Murphy, and one to rescue John Meagher.'

'Holy St Joseph. That's going to take some organizing,' said Inspector O'Rourke. He looked at his watch and said, 'It's almost five-thirty now. We're going to be fierce pushed for time, even if Jimmy O'Reilly agrees to it, and you know him. He's going to umm and ah about the logistics, and the cost of the overtime, and how sound our evidence is, and what's the price of bodice in the English Market.'

Katie said, 'I know. But we can't drag our feet with this one. The longer we put it off, the greater the risk to Kyna and John. You're right, yes, it won't be at all easy to organize because the coordination has to be faultless, but I'm confident that we can do it. Like, when I say "simultaneous", I mean each of the three raids will have to be synchronized right down to the second. I've no doubt at all that if Bobby Quilty picks up even a *sniff* of what we're doing before we can lift him, he'll have John killed to punish me for breaking our agreement, and Darragh Murphy, too, so that he can't give evidence against him.'

'You really think he'd risk doing that?' asked Inspector O'Rourke.

'You know Bobby Quilty better than I do, Francis. Whatever he's involved in, think of the worst possible outcome you can and then double it. Before we enter any of the three premises I need to be sure first of all that Quilty's at home. I also need to know that his landline's cut and that his mobile phone's jammed: (a) we have to him cornered, and (b) he has to be totally incommunicado.'

At that moment, Katie's phone rang. It was Tyrone, telling her that he had sent eleven enhanced versions of the Dutch cyclists' photos to her computer.

'All the pictures had a lot of noise on them,' he told her. 'I tried a Laplacian filter on them and then unsharp masking. In the end, though, I got some really great edge with that new Fuji doodad that Bill just acquired for us – it's amazing.'

'Can you see the men's faces clearly?' asked Katie.

'You can, yes. One of your subjects is seen only in profile, side-on, like, though I reckon you could easy make a positive ID from that, because he has very distinctive features. Like, his beezer's long enough to take your dog for a walk on it. Your other subject is full-face when he turns away from the petrol tank explosion and now that I've sharpened it up it could almost be a mug-shot. A real sham-feen, I can tell you. The sort that doesn't look as if he would take it kindly if you spilled his drink.'

Katie went over to her desk and clicked up the photographs on her monitor screen. She could see the grassy farm track and the burning Land Rover with thick black smoke rolling out of it, and the two men watching it. The man who had turned to face the camera was wearing a black T-shirt with Cork Hurling in white lettering on it, which matched the T-shirt worn by the driver of the Land Rover seen on CCTV. Both men looked as if they were laughing. Tyrone had succeeded in removing most of the motion blur and graininess and made the pictures remarkably sharp – clear enough to be admissible as evidence in court.

Detective Scanlan came over and stood beside her. 'OMG,

that's Darragh Murphy all right! Grown a bit of a scraggly beard since I last saw him, but that's him in the flesh. And I can tell you who the fellow is with him, the one with the schonk. That's Darragh's best friend Murty – Murty Something, I can't remember his surname. I'm not sure I ever knew it. But he would trail along everywhere behind Darragh, whining through that schonk of his – "where are we going now, Darragh?" "what are we going to do next, Darragh?" "give us a drizzle off your can there, Darragh" – and Darragh would smack him around the head, but he never seemed to mind.'

Katie said, 'All we need now is just one member of the public who saw Darragh behind the wheel that day and that will give us all the evidence we need to charge him.'

'You mean if we can find a member of the public who isn't too terrified to stand up in a court and say so,' said Inspector O'Rourke.

'We can cross that bridge when we come to it,' Katie told him – although, even as she said it, she wished that she hadn't, considering where Detective Barry had been killed.

'I'll go and see Denis MacCostagáin now,' she said. 'I'll meet with you after so that we can discuss exactly how we're going to set up this operation.'

'We'll be calling in some armed backup, I imagine?' said Detective Sergeant Begley.

'Of course,' said Katie. 'At least three of Quilty's scummers have served time in the past for carrying guns and I don't have any reason to think they're not still doing it today. We're going to need three Regional Support Units minimum – one at least at each location. Sean – if Padragain brings up the relevant maps and satellite images, can you give me an estimate of how many personnel we're likely to need? We don't want any of Quilty's people sneaking out the back door simply because we didn't deploy enough officers to surround the entire premises.'

Inspector O'Rourke looked at Katie very acutely and said, 'DS Maguire, I pray this all turns out well for you so.'

Katie touched his arm and mouthed, *thank you*. Then she

picked up her laptop and left her office to go and talk to Chief Superintendent MacCostagáin and Superintendent Pearse.

She took several deep breaths to steady herself as she walked along the corridor. This wasn't going to be easy. Chief Superintendent MacCostagáin had been planning on taking three days off, starting tomorrow, to play golf at Fota, while Superintendent Pearse had been invited to speak at a Freemasons' dinner that evening at the Masonic Lodge on Tuckey Street and had been rehearsing his speech for weeks.

Only God knew how they were going to react when Katie told them that she was proposing to launch a major operation not only to rescue John but to arrest Bobby Quilty and Darragh Murphy at the same time. What was more, she was proposing to do it in the early hours of tomorrow morning, before dawn. The sun would come up at 5.27 a.m., which meant they would have to spend the whole night spent in frenzied preparation.

She desperately wished that she could contact Kyna. She knew where 'Sheelagh Danehy's' mobile phone was because she had assigned one of the technicians in communications to track it for her, although she hadn't said whose phone it really was. In spite of that, she had no way of knowing for certain if Kyna still had the phone in her possession, or even if she did, what kind of a situation she might be in. Even sending her a coded message might put her in jeopardy. Bobby Quilty had kept himself out of prison for thirty years by his paranoid mistrust of anybody who came near him, and by quickly and ruthlessly dealing with anybody he suspected of betraying him.

If Kyna was still with Bobby Quilty when they arrested him, they would have to arrest her, too, just for her own safety, and in any case she would never be able to serve in Cork again. *At least that would solve her emotional problems*, Katie thought, sadly.

* * *

'You're codding me,' said Chief Superintendent MacCostagáin. 'Please tell me you're codding me.'

He had already been snapping shut the buckles of his briefcase when Katie knocked at the door of his office and came in to tell him about her plan for Operation Trident, as she had decided to call it on her way along the corridor.

'I only wish I was,' said Katie. 'But I hope you can understand why I didn't tell you that John had been abducted. You would have felt obliged to set up a search for him, especially after that O'Brien business, but in my opinion that would have been far too risky.'

That 'O'Brien business' was a kidnap case three years before, when Chief Superintendent MacCostagáin had agreed to the kidnapper's demands not to try and find out where he was holding his victim, the wife of a prosperous Cork property developer. The ransom had been paid, but the woman had never been returned and her body had never been found. Chief Superintendent MacCostagáin had been severely reprimanded and nearly lost his job.

'I might have set up a search or I might not,' he said. 'I do trust your instincts, Katie, you know that. But you still should have reported it to me as soon as it happened. What you did, keeping it all to yourself like that, and using Detective Sergeant Ni Nuallán to find him, that was all highly irregular. And if this all goes pear-shaped, it'll be me carrying the can again.'

'I know that right enough, sir. But my primary concern was rescuing John alive and unharmed, and still is. And there's not only that – if I can rescue John, Bobby Quilty won't have any leverage against me any longer. But it's essential that we bring Quilty in before he can get a message to whoever is actually keeping John locked up. And we need to bring in Darragh Murphy, too, for his own protection as much as anything else.'

She didn't add that she wasn't at all confident about the security at Anglesea Street and that she still suspected that a very small minority of officers were taking payment from criminals in exchange for useful tip-offs. Even if they could put Operation Trident into action within the next few hours, she was worried that Quilty would get to hear that she had sufficient evidence to arrest him and that she had discovered where John was being held.

'I'm prepared to stand by my decision, sir, one hundred per cent,' she told Chief Superintendent MacCostagáin. 'Under the circumstances I think it was totally the right call to make. Think on it. If tonight's operations go off as planned, we'll have killed three birds with one stone. We'll have saved John, arrested Bobby Quilty and Darragh Murphy for murder, and put a stop to Quilty's tobacco-smuggling.'

Chief Superintendent MacCostagáin sat down at his desk. 'Very well,' he said, in a tone of voice that meant 'there goes my golfing weekend'. 'Show me the pictures. We'd best call Michael in to look at them, too. He's going to throw a sevener, I can assure you of that.'

* * *

As it turned out, Superintendent Pearse wasn't at all upset that he would have to cancel his speech to the Freemasons. He could have delegated Operation Trident to Inspector O'Halloran, especially since Inspector O'Halloran had more than eight years of experience in mounting simultaneous raids on drug-dealing gangs and cross-border car thieves, but he insisted on heading up the arrest of Bobby Quilty himself.

'I won't make any secret of it, Katie,' he told her. 'It's personal. The last time I lifted Bobby Quilty – well, you remember. He walked out of that courthouse sticking two fingers up at me because I couldn't prove a thing. My chief witness against him was found floating in Tivoli Docks with no way of proving that it wasn't suicide and the other two witnesses had vanished off the face of the Earth altogether. That was five years ago and I still don't know what happened to them to this day.'

'Pity to miss your speech, though, Michael,' said Chief Superintendent MacCostagáin dryly.

'Well, that's another reason why I'd like to take over this operation myself. I was dreading it, to be honest with you. It was bad enough when I had to stand up and give a speech at my daughter's wedding. But this was *The Future of Law Enforcement in Cork City and Environs with Special Regard to Immigration and Community Relations.'*

'I'm sure the lodge members will be devastated,' said Chief Superintendent MacCostagáin. 'But you know, Michael, a speech like that doesn't have to go to waste. Next time I can't sleep I'll ring you up and you can read it to me over the phone.'

After that, though, there was no more banter. In spite of their disapproval of the way in which Katie had tracked down John, Chief Superintendent MacCostagáin and Superintendent Pearse both had to acknowledge that this was going to be a rare opportunity to put Bobby Quilty behind bars.

Katie and Superintendent Pearse sat and waited patiently while Chief Superintendent MacCostagáin put in a long phone call to Assistant Commissioner Jimmy O'Reilly, who was in Dublin that day. He explained at length what had happened and what they intended to do, and what the probable costs would be when balanced against the outcome.

Eventually he put down the phone and said, 'We have the go-ahead. He agrees that if we can convict Bobby Quilty for Detective Barry's murder and put a stop to his cigarette-smuggling, too, that will really be a feather in our cap – not just with Phoenix Park but with the government, too. After all, it's no good them putting up the price of fags if it can't be enforced.'

Now they had approval from Assistant Commissioner O'Reilly they had to act quickly. Superintendent Pearse called in the five senior uniformed officers who would be involved in Operation Trident. In less than twenty minutes they had all arrived for a general strategy meeting around the conference table, with Katie chairing it. This was followed by a full briefing of the sixty-three gardaí who would be needed to surround all three target premises – Orange Team, Green Team and White Team. These included eight of Katie's detectives and five armed Regional Support Units, two of which had driven down to give their support from Henry Street Garda station in Limerick. An ambulance would be standing by on Leitrim Street, too, in cased John needed medical treatment.

As she wound up the briefing, Katie said, 'I can't emphasize enough how important the timing of this operation is going to be. We have to enter all three locations at 04.30, on the dot. Speed and surprise are essential. If you have any trouble gaining access, don't stand outside ringing the doorbell, use your door-openers and ferret guns immediately. I would like to think that all three raids will all be over in less than three minutes and that by 05.00 we'll have all of the detainees here, ready for formal charging and questioning.'

'You're not going to let any media in on this?' asked Mathew McElvey. 'It would make for some fantastic TV news footage.'

'Absolutely not, Mathew, sorry. The fewer people know about this in advance, the better. We'll announce it only when Quilty and Murphy are sitting in their cells. You've already been cautioned not to tell your families or your friends why you're on duty tonight. That goes double for anybody you know in the press.'

They returned to Chief Superintendent MacCostagáin's office. His personal assistant had brought in sandwiches and coffee and two bottles of Tanora. Katie stood by the window looking out at the lights of Cork City, sipping coffee. She didn't feel at all hungry.

'Have you decided which team you'll be going with?' asked Chief Superintendent MacCostagáin, sitting behind his desk and taking a bite of a sandwich.

'Orange,' she said. 'I want to arrest Quilty myself. Besides, I've just had an update on the location of Kyna's phone. She's back at Quilty's house on the Middle Glanmire Road, Tivoli Park or whatever it's called. I need to make sure that she's safe and unharmed.'

'So you're not going with the White Team to rescue your John?'

'I can't be in two places at once, sir. I'm not Boyle Roche's bird.'

Chief Superintendent MacCostagáin said nothing for a long moment. Then, 'I know the feeling, Katie. Even though I'm stuck here in the present, I wish I was still in the past.'

Mathew McElvey knocked at the office door and came in. 'For once the Taoiseach has done us a favour!' he announced.

'What kind of a favour?' asked Chief Superintendent Mac-Costagáin. 'I heard that he'd had a mild heart attack.'

'That's right, at a meeting of European finance ministers, as well he might. But it means that the Langtry story was pretty much crowded out of both of tonight's news bulletins.'

'They did mention it, though?' asked Katie. 'I was too tied up at that strategy meeting. I forgot to watch.'

'I have it here,' said Mathew McElvey, holding up his tablet. He switched it on and Katie saw Fionnuala Sweeney standing on Anglesea Street.

'Cork Garda confirmed today that the four bodies found buried under the floorboards in Blarney were in fact those of the Langtry family, who mysteriously disappeared in 1921. Father, mother and two children were all shot in the back of the head. The family dogs were also shot. Gardaí have opened a historical inquiry into who might have been responsible for their murders, but Detective Superintendent Kathleen Maguire emphasized that the case was over ninety years old and was not a high priority.'

'That's a relief,' said Chief Superintendent MacCostagáin. 'No mention of illicit affairs with British officers or other cracked ideas. Tomorrow's going to give us ructions enough without yesterday sneaking up to bite us in the backside.'

Twenty-one

By 4.20 in the morning the three teams taking part in Operation Trident had all been deployed – Orange Team in Tivoli, Green Team in Parklands and White Team on Leitrim Street.

Katie was sitting in a dark blue unmarked Opel with Detective O'Donovan and Detective Scanlan. About two hundred metres further up the Middle Glanmire Road, on the opposite side of the entrance to Tivoli Park, she could see the white Volvo XC70 of the Regional Support Unit with four fully armed gardaí waiting for the signal to move in. Five other uniformed gardaí were already positioned in the woods behind Bobby Quilty's garden to make sure that there was no escape for him that way.

'Hard to work out how many people are in there exactly,' said Detective O'Donovan, leaning over from the back seat. 'Nobody's been seen to leave since we put the house under surveillance, so Detective Sergeant Ni Nuallán's probably still in there, and Quilty's girlfriend, Margot Beeney, but we're not sure if any of his minders are staying overnight.'

'Well, we'll find out soon enough when we get inside,' said Katie. 'Let's hope that whoever's in there, they don't give us any bother.'

Seconds before they entered the house technically trained gardaí would cut the landline and jam all of the occupants' mobile phones. It would have been normal procedure to knock or ring the doorbell first, to give the suspect the opportunity to open the door, but Katie was concerned that Bobby Quilty might have some other means of communication so she had ordered that they break down the door silently to give him no prior warning that they were coming

173

in. They would jam the intruder alarms, too, but if Bobby Quilty had fitted a high-quality alarm system it would almost certainly sense the jam and start ringing. With most alarms, however, there was a polling interval of two minutes and that would give Orange Team more than enough time to force their way inside.

Detective O'Donovan looked up and said, 'Lord, are You listening, Lord? I hope you're not on your cloud asleep at the moment. I think we're going to need a bit of a helping hand here.'

Katie turned round in her seat. 'Just remember, Patrick, your number one concern is finding DS Ni Nuallán and protecting her once you've found her.'

'You can count on me, ma'am,' Detective O'Donovan told her. 'I was just putting in a request for a little divine backup there, that's all.'

Although there was little more than an hour to go before sunrise the sky was still inky black because it was densely clouded over, and the forecast was for low cloud and persistent rain all day. Yesterday had been warm and bright, but Katie found it easy to believe as she waited to arrest Bobby Quilty that summer was over.

She had received no further texts from Kyna, although the latest signal from her iPhone indicated that it was still inside the house. Katie tried to put her to the back of her mind – and John, too. She had prayed to St Leonard to take care of them both, and at the moment that was all she could do.

In her earphone the voice of Inspector O'Rourke blurted, 'Green Team all in position and ready to go in.'

Inspector O'Rourke was on the Parklands housing estate on the far side of Blackpool, outside Darragh Murphy's semi-detached bungalow. As soon as she had received the go-ahead for Operation Trident, Katie had dispatched two plain-clothes gardaí to keep the bungalow under surveillance. They had reported that Darragh Murphy had driven home at 11.17 in the evening, obviously drunk, because his car had struck the low concrete wall around his front garden and then bumped into the garage doors. Once he had managed to climb out and stagger to the front door, it had taken him over three minutes of erratic jabbing to fit the key into the lock.

'White Team ready,' said Detective Sergeant Begley, from Leitrim Street. That house, too, had been watched for most of the previous evening by plain-clothes gardaí. Nobody had been seen entering or leaving, but the officers had heard a man and a woman shouting and arguing until well past midnight.

'There's an alleyway that runs along the back of the houses, past the yard behind Brannagan's Bar,' said Detective Sergeant Begley. 'We have that covered. Unless they land a helicopter on the roof, there's no way anybody's getting out of this place without us catching them.'

'Two minutes and thirty seconds to go, ma'am,' said Detective O' Donovan.

'Right,' said Katie. 'Let's do it.'

As she climbed out of the car five gardaí jogged past her towards Bobby Quilty's house, their all-black combat uniforms rustling, guns clinking and rubber-soled boots pattering on the pavement. All of them were wearing black helmets with protective goggles and black face masks. Two of them were pulling behind them the heavy black case that contained the Holmatro hydraulic door-opener.

One garda ducked his way between the three shiny parked cars in front of the house and headed straight for the side gate, where the telephone junction box was located. Another crouched on the driveway between the cars and took out a mobile phone jammer and a radio signal jammer, both of them not much bigger than a packet of cigarettes, and switched them on.

Detective O'Donovan checked his watch and said, 'Grand stuff. Unless he keeps a carrier-pigeon in his bedroom, that's Quilty totally cut off from the outside world.'

Katie looked up at the bedroom windows of Bobby Quilty's house. The curtains and blinds were drawn in all of them and they were all in darkness, although a single ceiling light was shining on the first-floor landing.

'Do you reckon they're all asleep?' she asked Detective O'Donovan.

'Oh, I'd say so, for sure. They probably only leave that light on in case one of them needs the jakes in the middle of the night. That Bobby Quilty can drink the cape off St Paul.'

Katie was wearing a grade-three protective vest and carrying her Smith & Wesson revolver in a holster on her hip, but all the same she stayed well back in the road. The first few seconds of every forced entry were highly unpredictable. The night was warm, but she shivered. In her experience, the suspects were usually too surprised or drunk or high to retaliate, but occasionally all hell would let loose and there would be wild and indiscriminate gunfire. In only her second week as a detective one of her friends had been killed by a ricochet, and he had been sitting in his patrol car on the opposite side of the road.

'Thirty seconds to go, ma'am. Twenty. Fifteen.'

Now the garda who had jammed the mobile phone signals switched on a software-defined radio to neutralize the burglar alarm. Katie was concerned that this might set off the alarm immediately, but she was relieved when there was total silence. Suddenly, however, an oil tanker on the River Lee below them let out a loud, mournful hoot, like a mother whale that had lost her young.

'Holy Mary!' said Detective Scanlan, close behind Katie. 'That put my heart crossways!'

The two officers operating the Holmatro door-opener carried it quickly and stealthily into the porch and fitted its heavy-duty piston sideways across the door frame. Four armed officers from the Regional Support Unit were lined up next to them, ready to rush into the house as soon as the door fell open.

Detective O'Donovan raised his right hand and said, 'Ten. Five. Zero. Okay – *go!*'

It took only three strokes of the door-opener's pump handle before there was a sharp crack like a pistol shot and the door frame was forced apart. After that it took no more than a single kick for it to drop with a muffled thump into the hallway. At once the four armed officers jostled into the house, screaming, '*Armed Garda!*

Armed Garda!' Still screaming *'Armed Garda!'* they reached the end of the hallway and began to mount the stairs.

Katie would have preferred them to stay completely silent as they entered the house, but there had recently been legal problems when gardaí had failed to identify themselves when they had raided brothels and crack dens in Cork, and she hadn't wanted to give Bobby Quilty the slightest chance to wangle his way out of being convicted. Neither did she want to give him an excuse to shoot at officers if they burst into his bedroom without warning.

She walked over the fallen front door into the hallway, closely followed by Detectives O'Donovan and Scanlan. As she did so, she looked down at the bronze door knocker and saw that it bore the face of a snarling wolf. A knocker to keep out the *Sluagh*, the spirits of dead sinners, since the doorway faced to the west.

Detective O'Donovan immediately turned left into the living room, beckoning a young woman officer, Garda O'Leary, to follow him. Katie had assigned them both to find Kyna and get her clear of the house as quickly as possible. Detective O'Donovan's mobile phone tracker was showing that 'Sheelagh Danehy' had left her phone downstairs somewhere at the back of the house.

Katie carried on to the end of the hallway. She could hear hoarse shouting coming from the first-floor landing, so she said to Detective Scanlan, 'Come on,' and started to climb the stairs. She was only halfway up, however, when Bobby Quilty appeared at the top, with armed gardaí on either side of him. He had already been handcuffed. He was wearing a sweaty pink T-shirt and a pair of droopy grey boxer shorts, and his bloated face was florid and patchy with rage.

'Ach, it's *you*, DS Maguire! I might have fecking known it! What in the name of *feck* is going on here? A man can't get even snatch a decent night's sleep in his own house without a bunch of polls busting his door down and pulling him out of the scratcher like a bag of dirty washing! You'd better have a fecking good reason for this, I can tell you now, a fecking *amazing* reason, because I'm calling my brief right here and now and he won't be any more delighted than I am to be woken up at half past fecking four in the fecking morning!'

One of the armed gardaí said, 'We've been through all rooms up here, ma'am. There's nobody else here but him.'

'Nobody? Not even Margot Beeney?'

'No, ma'am. We've even checked the presses. He has the place to himself, like.'

Katie carried on climbing the stairs. When she reached the landing she stood in front of Bobby Quilty and stared up at him for a few seconds without saying anything. His huge belly rose and fell as he breathed, and he reeked of stale alcohol and Lynx Fever Body Spray, and some other oily smell that Katie couldn't identify, but which put her in mind of tinned sardine oil. She also noticed for the first time that the wings of his bulbous nose were peppered with blackheads.

She took a deep breath and then she said, 'Robert Boland Quilty, I am arresting you for incitement to murder Detective Gerald Barry. I am also arresting you for the false imprisonment of John Patrick Meagher. You are not obliged to say anything unless you wish to do so, but anything you do say will be taken down in writing and may be given in evidence.'

Bobby frowned at Katie for a moment as if he hadn't caught on, but then his face gradually cracked apart in a grin like a Hallowe'en turnip. 'Is this some kind of a geg, doll?'

'Do you want me to repeat myself? You're under arrest. Now, get yourself dressed and we'll take you into custody.'

'You're having a laugh, aren't you? I told you before that I had nothing at all to do with thon detective getting himself run over. Just because you can't think of anybody else to pin that on. And who in the name of God is John Patrick Meagher? I never heard of anybody of that name in my life. Your head's full of wee sweetie mice, DS Maguire, so it is.'

'Let's talk it over at the station, shall we?' said Katie.

'I want to ring my brief first, so that he can meet us there. I'm not saying a word to you without my brief.'

'You can do that once we've taken you in and formally charged you.'

Bobby Quilty said something back to her. It sounded caustic, but Katie didn't hear it because it was blotted out by an urgent voice in her earphone. It was Inspector O'Rourke, calling her from Parklands.

'DS Maguire? Hallo? We've just found Darragh Murphy.'

'What do you mean "found"? Haven't you lifted him?'

'He's dead, ma'am. He was sitting in front of his telly when somebody shot him in the back of the head.'

'*What?* Serious?'

'Oh, yes. Blew half his head off. I reckon they used a silencer because the surveillance team didn't hear anything.'

'Okay,' Katie told him, trying not to show any reaction in front of Bobby Quilty. 'We've just detained Mister Quilty here so I can be with you in twenty minutes or so. Have you contacted Bill Phinner?'

'Detective Markey's doing that now, ma'am. It's a touch too early to go knocking on doors asking for witnesses, but we'll be starting that as soon as it's reasonable.'

'Don't disturb anything yet, and if the Technical Bureau turn up before I do, tell *them* not to disturb anything either – this is something I need to see for myself. Was there anybody else in the house?'

'No, ma'am. Some women's clothing in the bedroom. Underwear and such. A second toothbrush, too, in the bathroom, but that's all. We'll be searching the premises thoroughly of course, when you give us the say-so, but I thought you needed to know that Darragh Murphy's out of the picture.'

'Yes, thank you, Francis. Just give me a couple of minutes and I'll get back to you so.'

'Problems?' asked Bobby Quilty, with that same hideous grin.

'Nothing that concerns you,' said Katie. Then, 'Get yourself dressed, will you? These officers will go with you. Wouldn't want you jumping out of the window or harming yourself so.'

'None of them are gay, are they?' said Bobby Quilty. 'Wouldn't like a gay garda to see me without my gunks!'

As the armed gardaí escorted him back to his bedroom, Detective O'Donovan came up the stairs with Garda O'Leary behind him. He was holding up a sparkly pink iPhone in his latex-gloved hand. 'We found this in the kitchen waste bin, ma'am. No SIM card in it.'

'There's no sign of "Sheelagh"?' she asked, looking round to make sure that Bobby Quilty was back in his bedroom and out of earshot.

Detective O'Donovan shook his head. 'Nowhere downstairs, no. We took a sconce out in the garden and the fellers in the back are searching through the woods. It might be kind of previous to say so, like, but I get the feeling that she isn't here at all.'

Katie was beginning to feel a cold sinking sensation in her stomach. Her father had always said that when an operation started to go wrong it was like standing on the deck of the *Lusitania* – you know that it's going down under your feet and there's nothing you can do about it. She had planned for Operation Trident to be successfully completed in minutes, but already it seemed to be foundering. If Darragh Murphy was dead, she had lost the only witness who could testify that Bobby Quilty was guilty of incitement to murder. And where was Kyna? If she wasn't here, why hadn't she got in touch? And what about John?

She was about to contact Detective Sergeant Begley at Leitrim Street when he called her.

'We've just this minute finished searching the building, ma'am. Top to bottom. Basement, attic, back yard, everywhere. Not a trace of your John.'

'Nothing at all? How can that be? I was told that his feet were fastened to a bed. *Bolted*, in fact, though I'm not sure what that meant.'

'No beds in the building at all, ma'am, except for some bogging old mattress that the two people who live here use to sleep on. Their names are Charles Rearden, unemployed, and Sorcia MacKenna, part-time hairdresser. Well, that's what she calls herself, any road.'

'And they know nothing about John?'

'They both deny that there's been anybody else in the building since they moved in there five months ago.'

'Who's their landlord?'

'They're squatting, so they say. They found the building empty so they decided to move in. It's actually owned by a property company in Dublin called Watergrass Holdings.'

Katie could have asked him a hundred more questions, but this wasn't the time for it.

'I'll get back to you in a couple of minutes,' she said, and then she turned to Detective O'Donovan. 'Send a car round to Detective Sergeant Ni Nuallán's flat, will you, just to make sure that she isn't at home. I've rung her a few times without getting any answer, but you never know.'

Katie didn't say so, but it was remotely possible that Kyna had become so stressed that she had decided to quit this assignment and go back to Dublin, and that she hadn't had the courage to tell Katie that she couldn't take the pressure any more. After all, she had not only had Bobby Quilty to contend with, she was still recuperating from a serious bullet wound and she was suffering from painful emotional problems.

Katie couldn't believe that Kyna would do that, but even if she had, she could forgive her. What she needed to know more than anything else was that Kyna was safe.

'Padragain, would you contact Detective Sergeant Ni Nuallán's parents and ask them if they've heard from her?' she asked Detective Scanlan. 'Try not to alarm them. Just say that we've lost contact with her – like, maybe her mobile battery's dead or something, or maybe she's staying overnight with a friend – but it's important that we get in touch with her.'

Bobby Quilty reappeared, wearing the same creased green linen suit he had been wearing when he first told Katie that he had abducted John, as well as a lime-green shirt.

'I'll see you at the station, then sweetheart?' He grinned at her, as the armed gardaí escorted him down the stairs. 'I'll be writing out my invoice for having my front door repaired.'

Katie didn't answer. She was aching to ask him where Kyna was – but of course she wasn't supposed to know about the existence of 'Sheelagh Danehy', and until she heard that Kyna was somewhere safe she couldn't risk revealing her real identity. With Darragh Murphy dead it was likely that Bobby Quilty would have to be released from custody within a few hours.

Inspector O'Rourke called her again. He had cordoned off the street in Parklands outside Darragh Murphy's bungalow and had put in a call to the coroner.

'But still no trace of John?'

'Nothing at all, ma'am. I'm sorry.'

Katie took a look around the house and then went back outside. It had started to rain now, a soft drifting rain that had soaked her hair even before she was halfway back to the car. Now that Bobby Quilty had been arrested, all the Garda vehicles had switched on their flashing blue lights. They made the rain sparkle, so that it looked to Katie as if the darkness was swarming with bright blue fireflies.

Twenty-two

At that time of the morning there was scarcely any traffic, so it took them only fifteen minutes to drive north-west across the city to Parklands. Katie left Detective O'Donovan behind at Bobby Quilty's house to supervise an intensive search and, most importantly, to see if there was any evidence, apart from her mobile phone, that Kyna had been there, or where she might be now.

She took Detective Scanlan with her. She knew that Padragain had never attended a homicide scene before, even though she had seen dead bodies in the morgue, and mangled families in traffic accidents, and bloated teenagers hauled grey-faced and dripping from the River Lee. Homicide scenes, though, were something different altogether. They were a silent tableau of the very instant when, for some reason, a person's life had been taken by somebody else. 'Storybooks left open, halfway through,' that's what Katie's father had always called them.

As they made their way through the wet, deserted streets, Detective Scanlan managed to get an answer from the Ó Nuallán number in Dublin.

'Oh, hi there, I'm so sorry to ring you so early, but this is Detective Padragain Scanlan from the Cork Garda. Who am I talking to?'

She covered her phone with her hand and said to Katie, 'Detective Ni Nuallán's sister Bridget.' Then, 'No, no, it's not bad news. Nothing like that. It's just that we need some information about a case that your sister was working on and we haven't been able to contact her. We were wondering if maybe she'd gone back home for a bit of a rest, like. No? Then have you heard from her at all? No? All right. I see. No bother at all. I'm very sorry to have woken you. Yes, I will, of course. Yes. Goodbye.'

Almost immediately Katie had a call from the gardaí that Detective O'Donovan had sent round to Kyna's flat on Wellington Road.

'She's not there, ma'am, no. We talked to her flatmate and she said she hadn't seen her in two days now. She had no idea where she was, no. She didn't usually ask her, like, as a rule, because most of the time Detective Ni Nuallán wasn't at liberty to tell her.'

'Thanks,' said Katie. She sat saying nothing for a while, biting her thumbnail. She was desperately worried now because Kyna's disappearance and Darragh Murphy's shooting led her to one inescapable conclusion: Bobby Quilty had been tipped off about Operation Trident.

Bobby Quilty's nonchalance had made her suspect from the moment she had arrested him that he must have been forewarned – that, and the absence of anybody else in the house. She couldn't believe that he didn't habitually sleep with his mistress and keep at least one bodyguard on the premises to protect him in case of an invasion. He had too many enemies in Cork, and in the North, too – both criminal and political. The Ulster Volunteer Force had twice attempted to ambush his car when he was in Armagh, and his youngest nephew had been shot dead by Red Hand Defenders as he was stepping out of Loughgall Road Spar in Portadown.

By the time they arrived at Darragh Murphy's bungalow the sky was beginning to grow lighter, although the street lamps hadn't yet switched themselves off. The whole street had been cordoned off with blue-and-white tape and there were three Garda patrol cars parked there, as well two vans from the Technical Bureau and an ambulance. In spite of it being so early, and raining, a crowd of about thirty or forty people had gathered on the corner and Katie recognized at least two cars belonging to local reporters parked further up the road.

Inspector O'Rourke was waiting for her in the shelter of the bungalow's porch. He looked tired and bored, shifting from one foot to the other like a hotel commissionaire. The interior of the bungalow was already brightly lit with halogen lamps, although the three technical experts who had arrived to inspect the crime scene were all crowded into the kitchen in their bulky Tyvek suits, along with five gardaí, three in uniform and the other two in plain clothes, all of them waiting for Katie to take a look at Darragh Murphy's body in the exact position where it had been found.

Inspector O'Rourke looked at Detective Scanlan and said, 'Had your breakfast yet, detective? If not, good, because this isn't pretty.'

Katie said, 'Don't worry, Padragain. You can step outside for a breath of fresh air whenever you want to.'

Inspector O'Rourke led them in single file along the hallway. The bungalow was cramped, with threadbare carpets and badly chipped paintwork, and Katie noticed that it had all the telltale signs of a house in which domestic abuse had regularly taken place. One of the living-room door panels was missing and there was a darker rectangle on the wallpaper in the hallway where a picture had once hung. On the windowsill at the end of the hallway stood a single porcelain dog which had probably been one of a matching pair. In spite of the damage, the bungalow was scrupulously clean, which told Katie that Neala had tried her very best to keep Darragh happy, right up until the very last beating.

The living room was papered with a pale green diamond pattern, with darker green velveteen curtains hanging at the windows, although one curtain was sagging where half of its nylon hooks had been pulled down. On a low cabinet in the far corner of the room stood a flat-screen 42-inch television, still switched on to the 5 a.m. *Euronews*, but with the volume muted.

Close behind Katie, Detective Scanlan said, 'Holy St Joseph.'

Darragh Murphy was sitting upright in a large armchair covered with orange stretch nylon. He was wearing light grey trousers with a partially dried damp stain in the crotch, and a grubby yellow polo shirt. On the floor beside his chair there were three cans of

Murphy's. A fourth can had dropped between his grey-stockinged feet and spilled dark beer across the carpet. He had obviously been drinking from it when he was shot.

In the centre of the room stood a three-legged plywood coffee table in the shape of an artist's palette. An untidy copy of yesterday's *Racing Post* lay on top of it, as well as a glass pub ashtray that was heaped with crushed-out cigarette butts, and a fifth can of Murphy's, also with its ring-pull open.

'Looks like he treated his murderer to a swallow before he died,' said Katie.

'It does, too,' said Inspector O'Rourke. 'Some people have no gratitude at all, do they?'

Katie could see that Detective Scanlan was trying not to look at Darragh Murphy's body directly, but that she couldn't stop herself from glancing at it every few seconds, as if she needed to keep checking that what she was looking at was real, not a prop created by the special effects department for some grisly horror film.

Darragh Murphy had been shot directly from behind into the nape of his neck. Katie guessed that his assailant had been kneeling behind his armchair when he fired, although she could only guess what reason he had given for doing so, if he had given any at all. Maybe he had pretended that he had dropped something on the floor and was kneeling down to pick it up. Darragh Murphy must have known his assailant, or at least not felt threatened by him, or he wouldn't have given him a can of stout. Then again, his assailant could have helped himself after he had killed him, as a small reward, or to steady his nerves.

'Padragain, take a close sconce at this entrance wound,' Katie told her. 'You can see by the width of the abrasion collar that the bullet entered just beneath the base of his skull at a slight upward angle. You can also see that the collar has gunpowder stipple marks around it, and that there's this sooty starburst effect directly under the skin. That tells us that it was fired at very close range, even if the muzzle wasn't actually touching him. The starburst was caused by the smoke and the explosive gases dissecting between the skin and the skull.'

'Yes, I have you,' said Detective Scanlan, nodding much more emphatically than she really needed to. She would have seen dozens of photographs of various gunshot wounds during her forensic training, but photographs could never convey the glistening, bloody reality, or the flat, pervasive reek of gunpowder residue. Without a hint of a smile, Bill Phinner had said that it always smelled as if the victim had let off a breezer when they were shot.

Apart from the entrance wound, the back of Darragh Murphy's skull was intact. The rest of his head, though, looked as if a hand grenade had exploded inside it. His eyeless mask of a face was sloping steeply forward, and his jaw had dropped down so that his stubbled chin was resting on the collar of his polo shirt. The sides of his head had been blown wide apart, like the two flaps of a cardboard box, with an ear still attached to each of them. Between them, his brain had been roughly mashed into glutinous beige lumps, and his sinuses and connective tissues had been torn into tangled scarlet strings.

'Typical of high-velocity bullets,' Katie told Detective Scanlan. 'They don't leave much of an entrance wound but they fragment inside the skull so that they leave multiple and very destructive exit wounds. The technical experts will be able to see all the bits and pieces when they X-ray his head. A "lead snowstorm" is what they usually call it.'

'You'd wonder what was inside that brain, wouldn't you?' said Inspector O'Rourke. 'Think of all of the incriminating information he'd have stored up in there. Still, too late to retrieve it now.'

Detective Scanlan pressed her hand over her mouth and made a retching sound and Katie said, 'Go on, Padragain, Get yourself outside. I'll join you in a second when I've talked to Bill Phinner.'

Bill had come out of the kitchen and was waiting for her in the hallway. He gave her a pinched, resigned smile as Detective Scanlan made her way quickly to the front door, retching again before she got there.

'Well, and the top of the morning to you, DS Maguire.'

'What's the story, Bill? Sorry to drag you out so early.'

'Oh, no bother at all. I could see the whole station was buzzing last night, what with all of those off-duty fellows coming in and the armed response lads getting themselves tooled up. I reckoned I'd be needed sometime during the night, so I made sure I turned in early. I slept like a child. Didn't even wake up when the missus came to bed and she usually bounces up and down like she's riding in the 3.15 at Mallow.'

'There's some glaringly obvious things for you to analyse,' said Katie. 'The beer can on the coffee table there, and the cigarette butts. But – I don't know. I have a feeling that none of this fits together.'

'In what way in particular?'

Katie turned towards the kitchen. 'Garda O'Leahy, isn't it?' she asked one of the plain-clothes officers.

'That's right, ma'am.'

'What time did you see Darragh Murphy driving home, did you say? It was after eleven, wasn't it?'

'Eleven-seventeen, though it was eleven-twenty before he managed to get in through the door. He was so wrecked he could barely stand up.'

'So you couldn't have missed seeing him coming home?'

'He crashed into them garage doors and it was like thunder, I'll tell you. Half the street was twitching their curtains to see if a bomb had gone off. You'd have been deaf as a doorpost not to hear that.'

'And you're sure it was him?'

'Well, it was his car all right, and he was wearing that fawny-coloured windcheater that's hanging up there by the door, and that cap. We were watching the house from the other side of the road, like, and the street lighting's not that grand, but there was no lights on in the house before he came home, so who else could it have been?'

'What's on your mind, ma'am?' asked Inspector O'Rourke. He nodded towards the body in the armchair and said, 'You're not thinking that this isn't Darragh Murphy at all? And maybe he's had his head blown off so that we couldn't tell if he was or he wasn't?'

Katie shook her head. 'No, Francis. I don't have any doubt that it's Darragh Murphy. I'm pretty sure, too, that it was Bobby Quilty who arranged to have him taken out. Murphy was the only person who could testify that Quilty incited him to kill Detective Barry, and he was also a loudmouth. If you're suggesting that Quilty had someone else killed in his place and whisked off the real Darragh Murphy away to somewhere safe, that's not Quilty's style at all. What incentive would he have, like, when at any time in the future Murphy could decide to incriminate him? Besides that, Bobby Quilty may sound as if he needs to take his boots off to count to eleven, but he's very far from stupid. He'll be well aware that we'll test Murphy's DNA and it'll only take us a matter of hours to confirm if it *is* him or not.'

'Well, I agree with all of that,' said Inspector O'Rourke. 'I was just wondering why you think there's something askew here.'

Katie said, 'Just look at this scenario. According to our surveillance team, Darragh Murphy came home so langered that he couldn't even fit his key into the front door. What would *you* do if you came home as drunk as that? I doubt you'd hang up your jacket and your cap neatly by the front door, then go and fetch yourself a six-pack of Murphy's out of the fridge and sit down to watch a couple of hours of late-night telly.'

Inspector O'Rourke said, 'You're right. It's been a brave few years since I came home in that condition. Herself wouldn't allow it. But, yes. He'd have been more likely to drop his coat on the floor, stagger into the bedroom and crash out fully dressed on to the bed. That's if he didn't take a detour to the toilet first for a gawk. That's what I always did.'

'It's far too early yet to start jumping to conclusions,' said Katie. 'I think, though, that one of the possibilities we ought to consider is that Darragh Murphy was shot much earlier in the afternoon. Whoever killed him could then have driven off in his car. Somebody returned in the car several hours later. Maybe it was the killer himself, maybe not. If Murphy was already dead, it wouldn't have mattered. But he made as much of a show of it as possible so that if anybody was watching the house he would be guaranteed to attract their attention and lead them into believing it was Murphy coming home. He could have left immediately through the kitchen and of course at that time we didn't have any officers deployed round the back of the house.'

Bill Phinner said, 'Tyrone! Would you test that kitchen door for me? With your gloves on, please. Tell me if it's locked or not.'

Tyrone tried the door handle and the kitchen door opened. 'Not locked, sir.'

'In that case, can everybody make sure that they don't go trampling out into the garden, even if you feel like a smoke. We'll need to be checking the garden for recent footprints.'

Katie said, 'It might be worth calling the dog team out. They could at least confirm if the last person who was sitting in Darragh Murphy's car went out through the back door and which direction they went in. They won't be able to tell us much more than that because your man would probably have been picked up and driven away. If that was the case, though, there must been another vehicle waiting for them somewhere nearby, and if so, one or more of our local residents might have spotted it. There's not much that you can get away with in Parklands without half the estate goggling at you.'

'Fair play to you, ma'am,' said Inspector O'Rourke. 'But once he was home, maybe Murphy sobered up a bit. Like, you know, maybe he *did* sit down with a few cans to watch some telly. Maybe the offender was already in the house waiting for him, or came in through the back door after he had settled down. Maybe he picked the lock, or Murphy had simply forgotten to lock it. After all, there's nothing in here that's worth anybody stroking.'

Katie turned to Bill Phinner. 'If you can give me an accurate time of death, Bill, that would help us no end.'

Bill Phinner looked at Darragh Murphy's burst-open head. The halogen light that had been set up behind his chair shone through the holes where his eyes had been so that it cast a shadowy, ghost-like face on to the carpet.

'We'll be taking his liver temperature now and checking the degree of rigor. Of course we'll be testing his blood-alcohol level, which will give us a much clearer idea if he really was drunk when he came home – if it *was* him, as you say. His temperature will probably give us the best estimate. It's warmish in here so that may give the impression he hasn't been dead as long as he really has been, if you know what I mean.'

Katie checked her watch. 'In that case, I'll leave you to it,' she said. 'I want to go and check on the house where John Meagher was supposed to have been held.'

Bill Phinner beckoned to his technical team and now they all came rustling into the living room, carrying their shiny metal cases of instruments and test tubes and chemicals. They started work right away, taking flash photographs of Darragh Murphy's body from every angle, as well as the living room itself. They carefully packed up the fourth beer can from the coffee table, as well as the brimful ashtray and the *Racing Post*, and sealed them in polythene boxes.

Katie watched them for a while and then walked to the front door. Detective Scanlan was waiting for her, her face drained of colour so that the two spots of blusher on her cheeks looked like a clown's make-up. She was clutching her lavender-coloured waterproof jacket tightly up to her neck

'How are you feeling, Padragain?' Katie asked her.

'A touch better, thanks,' said Detective Scanlan. 'I'm sorry about that. It won't happen again.'

'Oh, don't promise that. I've seen much worse than that, and so will you.'

Bill Phinner had been following closely behind Katie and as she stepped out into the rain he said, 'You're right about the timing, ma'am, in my opinion. Whenever Murphy was shot, it wasn't when we're supposed to think that it was. That scene of crime in there, I was pure suspicious about it the moment I walked in. It looks *staged*, if you understand what I'm talking about.'

Katie stood in the rain with Detective Scanlan beside her. She could tell that Bill Phinner had something more to say to her, but something he was reluctant to tell her.

'Go on,' she said. 'There can't be any question about it, can there? Bobby Quilty knew everything about this operation hours before we'd even finished setting it up.'

Inspector O'Rourke had joined them now. 'Of course he did,' he said, and he sounded angrier than Katie had ever heard him before. 'He's only done it again, Quilty, hasn't he? He's put us into a position where we don't have the evidence to prosecute him and we can't say too much to the media, either, without making ourselves look like an incompetent bunch of culchies, or corrupt, or both, or laying ourselves wide open to a libel action.'

Katie said, 'You and I need to talk about this later, Francis. Meanwhile I urgently need to find out what's happened to John Meagher and Detective Sergeant Ni Nuallán.'

'Don't lose heart, ma'am, that's all I can say,' said Inspector O'Rourke.

Katie looked down the street and she could see Dan Keane from the *Examiner* waiting for her in his long IRA-style trench coat, smoking, as well as Branna MacSuibhne from the *Echo* and Muireann Bourke from Newstalk.

'I want all of our lips sealed tight on this,' she said. 'If it's someone in the station who's been tipping off Quilty, they'll have guessed that we suspect them, but I don't want us to say openly that we have any suspicions of leaked information at all. I would rather say that I personally made a bags of Operation Trident because I didn't double-check the intelligence I was given, something like that. Let's give our mole the confidence to leak more information to Quilty – except that the next time he does it, let's make sure it entraps him. Or *her*, whoever it is.'

'You know something,' said Inspector O'Rourke. 'The mole could just as easy be me. Then what?'

'Then I'll find you out somehow, Francis, I swear it. And by God, you'll suffer for it, believe me.'

Twenty-three

She received two messages on her way to Leitrim Street, even though it was only a ten-minute drive back down towards the city centre.

A dog team had been dispatched to Parklands to see if the killer had left Darragh Murphy's bungalow by the kitchen door, and if he had, which direction he had taken after that. Seconds later, Chief Superintendent MacCostagáin called her to say that he had just received his morning paper.

'It's all over the front page, Katie, about the Langtry family.'

'Well, that doesn't surprise me. It's a very unusual story.'

'Yes, but it has all of this cat's malogian about Langtry's wife having an affair with a British army officer so that she could wheedle information out of him. They've quoted that Professor Pendle and *he* says that it's highly likely that it was the Brits who executed them by way of punishment. Nobody's happy about this, Katie, believe me. I've had Jimmy O'Reilly on to me already.'

'Pendle, Jesus,' said Katie. Sean Pendle was an emeritus professor of Irish history at Cork University and he was notorious for his extreme republican opinions and the way in which he would distort historical facts to suit his agenda. He had published a controversial book, *Fenian Glory*, which many bookstores in Northern Ireland had refused to carry. He was also a relentless publicity seeker, and Katie didn't doubt that by this evening he would be on the television news to give his own explanation of how and why the Langtrys had been shot and buried under the floorboards.

'I'll talk to you about it when I get back to the station,' Katie told him. 'Meanwhile, sir, just to make your morning even brighter,

Operation Trident has turned out to be an utter disaster, beginning to end.'

As briefly as she could, she updated him on the arrest of Bobby Quilty, the murder of Darragh Murphy and the disappearances of Kyna and John. Chief Superintendent MacCostagáin said nothing while she spoke, but she could almost feel his gradually deepening glumness.

'All right, Katie,' he said, when she had finished. 'It looks like we're in for one of those days that we'd rather forget.'

She arrived at the junction of Leitrim Street and Pine Street, where gardaí were already taking down the tapes that had cordoned off Pine Street and were waving traffic through. Detective Sergeant Begley was standing outside the terracotta-painted house where John was supposed to have been held, talking to a sergeant from the Regional Support Unit from Limerick.

'Good morning to you, ma'am,' said Detective Sergeant Begley. 'This is Sergeant Norden from Henry Street.'

'Yes, we've met before,' said Katie. 'You're the one they call "Buzz", aren't you? I really appreciate your backup on this operation, sergeant. Not that any of it has worked out the way we planned.'

'Well, you know what they say about the best-laid plans, ma'am,' said Sergeant Norden. He was a big man and his protective vest bulked him out even more. That was why his colleagues had given him the nickname Buzz, after Buzz Lightyear in *Toy Story*. His head was shaved shiny blue and his eyes bulged and he breathed very laboriously as if he had just finished weightlifting.

'Do you want to talk to the squatters?' asked Detective Sergeant Begley. 'They're upstairs, smoking their heads off and asking us every two minutes when we're going to eff off and give them some peace.'

'There's absolutely no sign that John was being held here?' asked Katie.

'Like I told you, ma'am, there are no beds here except the mouldy old mattress those two scummers use to sleep on. There's three bedrooms altogether. One of them's filled up with old junk so you can hardly open the door. The other one must have been a kid's bedroom at one time, but there's no bed in it now, although there's impressions on the carpet where a bed must have been.'

'All right, let me go upstairs and take a look for myself,' said Katie. 'And, yes, I'll have a word with our friends.'

'Good luck with that,' said Sergeant Norden. 'I was close to lifting the both of them on a charge of pretending to be human.'

They went inside the front door and Detective Sergeant Begley showed Katie the two ground-floor rooms which had once been the shop premises. Both of them were empty, apart from five or six packing cases and a tipped-over chair.

'No indication that there was ever a bed in either of these rooms,' said Detective Sergeant Begley. 'In fact, when you look at the dust on the floor I'd say that nobody's even stepped in here for years.'

He led her upstairs. The first-floor landing was foggy with cigarette smoke and he pointed to the door on the left-hand side and said, 'They're in there, Punch and Judy. I reckon they've been through fifty fags each since we got here.'

'Let me take a look at the rest of the rooms first,' said Katie. 'I don't have any doubt at all that John Meagher was being held somewhere here – probably right up until yesterday evening.'

'Your informant was sound, then?'

'The best, believe me.'

Detective Sergeant Begley opened the doors to the bathroom, and then to the gloomy room where Chisel and Sorcia slept. The sour smell of sweat-stained bedding was so strong that Katie held the back of her hand against her nose, and there were two wrinkled condoms lying on the carpet under the window.

'Holy Mary, Mother of God,' she said, shaking her head. 'Whoever said that romance was dead?'

The next bedroom was stacked with more packing cases, as well as a banjaxed wooden ironing board and a dented paraffin heater. The third bedroom was long and narrow, wallpapered with spaceships and planets. There was a small window at the very end and, as Detective Sergeant Begley had told her, the purple carpet bore four deep impressions from the square legs of a single bed.

Katie went down on one knee and touched the carpet pile. 'There's a damp patch here, did any of you notice?'

'I can't say that we did, ma'am. We had those two squatters hovering around us cribbing and moaning and puffing out smoke like a couple of volcanoes.'

'Well, this would have been where the end of the bed was. My informant said that John's feet were bolted to the bed. I thought that might have meant that he was chained, or fitted with ankle-cuffs, but his feet were really *were* bolted.'

'So there might have been blood on the carpet and that's why it's damp?'

Katie stood up. 'I'll ask Bill Phinner to send a couple of technicians down here. You can scrub a carpet till doomsday but you'll never get the DNA out of it.'

She went to the window and looked out. Then she took her black forensic gloves out of her jacket pocket, snapped them on, and opened the window wide. It was raining even harder now and the rain made a clattering sound as it fell from a broken gutter somewhere below.

'There's a safety cable on here, but somebody's unscrewed it,' she said. 'Recently, too. Look, they've left one of the screws on the windowsill here.'

She stepped back and peered down at the floor to see if she could find the second screw, and as she did so she saw a red-handled screwdriver lying close to the side of the chest of drawers. She left it where it was, because she wanted to have it photographed and then sealed into an evidence bag, but she beckoned Detective Sergeant Begley to take a look at it.

'Here's a couple of questions,' she said. 'Why would those two squatters bother to take off the safety cable? But if they did, why would they just drop the screwdriver on the floor once they'd done it? I can see how messy they are, but that doesn't seem natural.'

'You mean it might have been done in a hurry, like?'

Katie leaned out of the window. She could see that several of the slates were cracked and that four or five of them had been dislodged. The broken guttering was directly underneath them.

'Let's take a sconce outside,' she said. 'I'll talk to those two after.'

They went back downstairs, through the kitchen, and out of the back door into the cluttered yard. The rabbit started snuffling and scratching at the chicken wire at the front of its cage.

'Jesus, you poor creature, the state of you la,' said Katie, bending down to peer into its cage. 'Sean, give Lisa O'Donovan at the ISPCA a call after, would you? If ever there was a case for cruelty to animals, this poor creature is definitely it. This hutch is a wreck. It looks like—'

She stood up straight and shielded her eyes against the rain, frowning up at the broken gutter. When she looked down again she saw the stack of broken window frames next to the hutch, with some of their panes smashed.

'Borrow your flashlight?' she asked Detective Sergeant Begley.

She shone the flashlight on to the shattered glass of the topmost window and lit up a spatter of translucent amber stains.

'That could be blood,' she said. 'I'll have the technicians check that, too. Do you have something we can cover it with?'

'Oh, sure. I've a roll of plastic sheeting in the car. What are you thinking?'

'I don't know for sure. But there's all the indications here that somebody fell out of that bedroom window and dropped down here. Maybe they fell or maybe they were pushed out.'

'So they might have been unconscious, or dead?'

'It's possible. But why didn't they just carry him down the stairs? They must have taken the bed out that way, so why push somebody out of the window, dead or alive?'

Detective Sergeant Begley shook his head. 'Don't ask me. And I doubt you'll get any sense out of those two squatters. I don't think either of them's going to be appearing on *Mastermind* any time soon.'

* * *

'Can we have the window open?' asked Katie as she entered the room where Chisel and Sorcia were sitting. The smoke was filling the air in lazily curling layers.

Chisel was wearing a black short-sleeved shirt and green-striped boxer shorts, while Sorcia was wrapped up in a yellow towelling dressing gown with threads hanging from the hem. They were both puffy-eyed from smoking and lack of sleep.

The garda who had been standing in the corner keeping an eye on them opened up the window and the smoke gradually eddied out into the rain.

'I'm Detective Superintendent Kathleen Maguire,' said Katie. 'I'm in charge of investigating the whereabouts of a man named John Meagher. I have very good reason to believe that he was unlawfully held in this house against his will, and that you two aided and abetted that detention.'

Chisel and Sorcia looked at each other as if they were utterly baffled.

'Come on,' said Katie. 'He was being held in that back bedroom there, on a bed. You disposed of the bed yesterday evening and you cleaned the carpet underneath it. What I want to know is, where was John Meagher taken, and who by?'

'John Meagher?' said Chisel. 'I don't know nothing about no feller of that name. There's been nobody here, like. Only me and Sorsh.'

'So why did you get rid of the bed?'

'Bed? What bed? I don't know nothing about no bed.'

'Don't play stupid,' said Katie. 'There was a bed in that room and even if you didn't dispose of it yourselves, you must know who did.'

'Can't help you,' said Chisel. 'If there *was* a bed, and I'm not saying that there was, maybe it just took off by itself. They have legs, you know, beds.'

He grinned slyly at his own joke and then began to cough so violently that Sorcia had to slap him on the back.

Katie was still waiting for him to recover when Detective O'Mara knocked at the half-open door.

'DS Maguire?' He was holding up an electric drill, with its plug dangling. 'Just found this in the cupboard under the stairs, in a toolbox.'

'What's that?' said Chisel, still coughing. 'I don't know nothing about that.'

'The toolbox has the name Charles Rearden stencilled on it,' said Detective O'Mara. 'That would be you, wouldn't it, Mr Rearden?'

'Yes, well, that's mine all right,' said Chisel. 'Some scummer hobbled that toolbox from me months ago and I've been wondering where the feck it was. If they've put their own stuff into it, that's nothing to do with me whatsoever. Nothing at all. What's that you have there? A drill? I never had any drill like that, not me.'

'There's what looks like dried blood on it and remnants of skin,' said Detective O'Mara. He passed the drill over so that Katie could examine it more closely. He was right. The chuck had prune-coloured blobs of dried blood on it and there were papery shreds of skin twisted around the thread of the drill bit.

'Never saw that before in my life,' said Chisel.

'Seriously, Mr Rearden, do I really look like I was just washed in with the last tide?' Katie asked him. 'I'm arresting both you and Ms MacKenna here on suspicion of falsely imprisoning John Patrick Meagher. You are not obliged to say anything unless you wish to do so, but anything you do say will be taken down in writing and may be given in evidence. Get yourselves dressed and we'll take you into the station.'

'Jesus, Chisel, what a fecking careless browl you are!' Sorcia snapped at him. 'There's no way they could have known, otherwise.'

'I'm afraid you're wrong there, Ms MacKenna,' said Katie. 'There's plenty of evidence that you and your partner here were helping to keep John Meagher imprisoned. I'd just like you to tell me who ordered you to do it.'

'I'm not saying a single word,' said Sorcia.

'You could save yourself a rake of trouble if you did tell me who it was, I can assure you of that. You might even escape prosecution altogether.'

'*Mmmmm-mmmh*,' said Sorcia, shaking her bleached-blonde hair and keeping her lips tightly closed.

'Was it Bobby Quilty, by any chance?'

'Who?'

'Bobby Quilty. Don't try to pretend that you don't know Bobby Quilty. If it was him, you could nod your head. That's all you'd have to do. Then you wouldn't have had to say anything.'

'For feck's sake,' said Chisel. 'You can't ask nobody to tout on Bobby Quilty. You might just as well ask them to jump into the Lee with their pockets full of bricks.'

Sorcia rolled up her eyes in total exasperation. She dug into the pocket of her dressing gown for her packet of cigarettes, momentarily revealing the depths of her cleavage, with a Celtic cross tattooed into it, complete with a rose and thorns.

'Give me a light, you gom,' she told him. 'The condemned woman might as well have one last fag.'

Twenty-four

Not only had the rain been dredging down all morning but now the wind had risen into fierce blustery gusts. Because of that, the traditional football game that would have been played in the yard at Sunday's Well Boys' School for the last day of Rang a Sé was cancelled. Kevin Doherty picked up his son, Tom, just before noon and took him and his little sister, Sibeal, to McDonald's on St Patrick's Street for lunch.

They sat by the window and watched the shoppers struggling along the pavement as if they were drunk, with their umbrellas flapping inside out.

'So, Tom, do you think you could manage a Big Mac?' said Kevin. 'That's your baby school all behind you now. You're almost a man now. You'll be starting at the Mon after the holliers.'

'Miss Cashman was crying,' said Tom seriously. 'She said we were the best Rang a Sé she'd ever taught and she's going to miss us.'

Kevin reached across the table and patted Tom's hand. Tom was a thin, thoughtful boy, with short brown hair that stuck up at the back and very large brown eyes and protruding ears. His grandmother always said that he was going to grow up to be a poet like W. B. Yeats, but in reality he was more interested in wildlife conservation. He had built a hedgehog house in the garden with a sign saying *Gráinneog* over the entrance, although no hedgehogs had yet decided to nest there. His friend Charlie said that was only because hedgehogs had come from England originally and couldn't read Irish.

Kevin could tell that even if Tom wasn't quite tearful himself, like his teacher, the reality had struck him now that he was never going to go back to Sunday's Well BNS, and that he was no longer a senior in Rang a Sé, the sixth form. Next term he would be a new boy in An Chéad Bliain, the first year at North Monastery School. His infant days were over.

Sibeal said, 'I want chicken, but I don't want pissy-bed leaves.'

She was four years old, with blue eyes and long tangly blonde hair. She looked like a miniature version of her mother, Órla, and was just as strong-willed. She was clutching a red-haired rag doll with only one eye and a crazed expression on its face. 'Pissy-bed leaves' – dandelions – was what she called lettuce.

'What's the magic word?' asked Kevin.

Sibeal frowned and then she blurted out, '*Abracadabra!*' and giggled.

Kevin was a little sad, too, that Tom was growing up, but he was feeling mellow and relaxed. He loved taking the children out, especially when he was under less pressure at work. After two months of wrangling he had closed the sale yesterday on that three-storey commercial building on North Main Street that had once housed a branch of Allied Irish Bank, and the lease of a substantial corner property on Tuckey Street was very close to completion.

Although he had wild wavy hair and rather a large nose, he was an attractive man, slim and smart, with the permanent smile of somebody whose career depends on making people feel welcome. He had turned forty in April and while he had been depressed about it at first, he was now feeling mature and confident and in control of his life. He had woken up one morning and suddenly thought: *I'm happy. Jesus, I'm actually happy. This is what it's like, being happy.*

'One week and three days to go and then we'll be off to Gran Canaria,' he said. 'Sunshine, swimming in the sea. We'll be having the time of our lives.'

'I want to take Blossom,' said Sibeal. Blossom was her rocking horse.

'No, sweetheart, you can't take Blossom. She's way too big to fit on the aeroplane. Daddy will buy you a blow-up horsey when we get there.'

Kevin helped Sibeal to cut up her chicken. She sang as she ate, with her mouth full, while Tom swung his skinny legs as he ate his burger and stared out of the window.

After lunch, it wasn't far for them to drive home. The Dohertys lived in a three-storey red-brick terraced house on Military Road, up the hill from St Luke's Cross, where Katie had met with Kyna. When they arrived, Kevin was irritated to see that a battered green van had parked directly outside his front gate, where he usually parked, and it took him several minutes of wrestling with his steering wheel before he managed to manoeuvre his Audi estate in behind it, so close that it was almost touching.

'Some people, you know? They don't think at all that you might need to park outside your own house. I'll bet it's Mrs Doody has the decorators in again. That woman can't let her house be for more than a month without changing the wallpaper.'

'I *like* Mrs Doody,' said Sibeal. 'She gives me Smiley Face Jellies.'

'Well, she shouldn't,' Kevin told her, as he helped her climb out of her child seat. 'Your mother says that too much sugar makes you hyperactive.'

'What's "practiff"?'

As they walked up the brown-and-white tiled path, Kevin was surprised that Órla wasn't waiting for them with the front door open as she usually did when he brought Tom home from school, especially since today was his very last day at Sunday's Well. Sibeal rang the doorbell repeatedly, but Kevin took out his key anyway.

'Órla!' he called out as they went into the hallway. There was no answer, so he called out, 'Órla, are you at home, love?'

The house was silent. Usually Órla had the television on because she liked a constant background noise, even though she barely paid any attention to the programmes. Most likely she had walked down to the Cross to buy sausages from Sheehan's.

'You can change out of your uniform now, Tom,' said Kevin. 'Fetch it downstairs after because Mummy will have it cleaned and we'll take it to the school for another boy who needs it.'

Sibeal said, 'I want a drink.'

'You've only just had a drink at McDonald's.'

'I want another drink.'

'Well, all right, but you can have only water. You've had enough Tanora for one day. You'll be jumping all over the place like a kangaroo and then what will Mummy say? And what's the magic word?'

Kevin was about to usher Sibeal along the hallway to the kitchen when he became aware of an unusual smell. Órla had been making barmbrack when he left, which was one of the reasons she hadn't come with him to collect Tom from school, but this wasn't the warm, fruity aroma of Órla's baking. This was more like musty second-hand clothes in a charity shop, with an undertone of strong, cheapish aftershave.

'*Órla?*' he said, but quietly this time. The oak-panelled living-room door was only slightly ajar, whereas normally they kept it wide open.

Sibeal looked up at him. 'Do you think Mummy's *hiding*?' she asked him in a conspiratorial whisper.

Kevin didn't answer. He was concentrating too hard on listening. Besides, Órla never played tricks like this: it wasn't in her nature. She would organize proper party games, and face-painting, and singing children's songs like 'The Bog Down in the Valley-O', but she had never been one for practical jokes and pranks. Their marriage had been through some abrasive times because of the constant clash between Órla's seriousness and Kevin's flippancy, and that was one of the reasons why there had been an eight-year gap between their two children. Sibeal, in fact, had been conceived by accident – but a happy accident, as it turned out, because having their little girl had brought Kevin and Órla much closer again.

Kevin reached his hand out towards the living-room door. He was about to push it open when he thought he heard a squeak, and a faint shuffling sound, and he hesitated.

'*Do-you-think-Mummy's-in-there?*' whispered Sibeal.

Kevin pressed his fingertip to his lips to shush her. It was *his* house: he didn't know why he didn't just push the door open and march straight in to see if Órla really was playing hide-and-seek. For some reason that he couldn't fully understand, however, he sensed that something was badly wrong. Either Órla was in there, acting completely out of character, or else there was nobody in there at all – in which case, why did he feel so apprehensive?

Not just apprehensive – actually *frightened*. But why? Órla was probably standing at the counter in Sheehan's even now, buying sausages, and she'd be back in five minutes. Yet why was the door almost closed like that? And what was that smell?

He touched the door cautiously, but as soon as he did so a man's voice called out in a strong Antrim accent, 'Kevin! Why'n't you come on in here, big lad? What are you footering for outside of the door there for? You're not jibbing it, are you?'

Sibeal looked up at Kevin in alarm.

'It's all right, sweetheart,' said Kevin, although he felt as if his heart had stopped. He pushed the door so that it swung wide open, but he didn't immediately step inside.

Órla was standing on the oval rug in the middle of the living room. She was wearing her long brown apron and her hands were still white with flour. Her fine reddish hair looked frayed where she had tied it back in a scarf and her face was even whiter than usual, ivory white, which showed up the tawny freckles across the bridge of her nose, and her pale pink lips.

Two men were standing close to her, on one either side. The man on her right was bald-headed, with the lumpy face of a former boxer, and an S-shaped nose. He was barrel-chested, but his legs were short and his droopy black jacket made him look even shorter, almost like an amputee.

The man on her left was skinnier and taller, with a messy mop of grey hair and a long, indented face. His eyes were glittery and near-together and he had a downward-pointing nose as sharp as a stalactite. He was wearing a cheap bronze nylon windcheater and tight black spindly jeans. He could have been taken for a giant bird of prey rather than a man.

Both men were holding automatic pistols, the short man in his left hand, the tall man in his right. Kevin reached down and gently pushed Sibeal so that she was standing behind him.

'Come along in, Kevin,' said the short man, beckoning him with his gun. 'There's nothing for you to be nervous about. We're only paying you a social call that's long overdue, that's all.'

'Who are you?' asked Kevin. 'Órla, have they hurt you at all? No – Sibeal – stay behind me, sweetheart.'

Órla looked at Kevin with a desperate expression on her face, her floury fists gripped tightly, but said nothing.

'If you've hurt her—' said Kevin, turning to the short man.

'Ach, away on,' the short man replied. 'We've hardly come here to hurt you. This is all going to be painless, I can assure you.'

'Who are you?' Kevin repeated. 'What do you want? I've some cash upstairs if that's what you're looking for, but otherwise there's not much of any value.'

'Oh, I wouldn't agree with that at all, big lad. What you have here is the most valuable commodity that Ireland ever has to offer. Settling old scores.'

'What in the name of Jesus are you talking about? What do you want?'

The tall man spoke in a slow, mournful voice, almost as if he were giving a sermon. He, too, had a distinct Antrim accent, but it sounded more precise and more educated than his companion's. 'I thought you Catholics were very conscientious when it came to admitting your transgressions. For the Lord loveth judgement, and forsaketh not His saints, but the seed of the wicked shall be cut off.'

'What? What are you talking about?'

'Exactly what I said Kevin – cutting off the seed of the wicked. The sins of the fathers shall be visited upon the children, and rightly so. If there's one thing we never do in Ireland, it's forget those who trespass against us. No sinners should ever go unpunished, but if by some rare chance they do, then their descendants should be punished for what they did, no matter how many generations it takes.'

'I still don't follow you. What sinners?'

'All of the sinners. Every one of those bloody-handed IRA murderers, and you can go back as far as you like. How many anti-Treaty men were never captured during the civil war and held to account? Hundreds! You could argue that they're long dead now, but that's no reason why their heirs and descendants shouldn't be justly punished for all their atrocities.'

'Am I hearing you right? You think people should be locked up for what their fathers and their grandfathers did a hundred years ago – even if they never knew about it?'

'I wasn't talking about prison, Kevin. I was talking about justice. An eye for an eye and a bullet for a bullet. Listen, today's weak-kneed politicians may have gone soft on murderers, granting them amnesty and letting them out of the Maze and sending comfort letters to those on the run. But the fact remains that they are murderers still – bloody-handed murderers! They will never be forgiven by the Lord our God – and no matter how many years go by they will never be forgiven by those grieving families whose parents they killed, or whose grandparents, or whose great-grandparents, *ad infinitum*, and so on and so forth. Why should a murderer's children be allowed to live a happy life when the people they murdered were robbed of all the years that were left to them and never had the chance to see their own children grow up?'

Kevin laid his hand on Sibeal's shoulder and said, 'Wait there, sweetheart. Just stay where you are. No, *please*, magic word, darling, stay where you are.'

He walked into the living room and approached Órla until he was standing directly in front of her, so close that he could have reached out and touched her. He heard a cough and a sniff behind him and he turned round to see a third man sitting in the window seat overlooking the garden – a young man with a khaki woolly hat pulled down right to his eyebrows, wearing a denim jacket and jeans. He looked only about eighteen years old and he had angry red spots on his cheeks and a wispy black moustache. He, too, was holding a gun – an AK-47 semi-automatic rifle which he was holding at a slope across his knees.

Kevin had to try hard to keep his voice steady. Without taking his eyes off Órla, he said, 'Maybe I'm very stupid, but if you haven't come here to rob us, I'd very much like you to explain to me exactly what you're doing here and why you're threatening my wife and my family like this. What's all this talk about settling scores and punishing people? All I want you to do is get out of our house and leave us in peace and I swear on my children's lives that I won't breathe a word of this to anyone.'

'Could you believe it – that never entered my mind, do you know that? – your breathing a *word* to anyone!' said the short man in mock surprise. 'Like, if you're not breathing, like, you *can't* breathe a word, can you, big lad?'

Kevin stared at him, hardly able to believe what he had said, but the short man didn't even look up. He was too concerned with ejecting the magazine from his automatic, frowning at it, and then clicking it back into place.

'You've come here to *kill* me?' said Kevin. 'What have I ever done to anybody? What? You're just going to shoot me, in front of my wife and my children? I don't even know who you are!'

'No, you're right there, you don't know who we are,' said the tall man. 'But the whole point of this is, we know who *you* are. Have you not been listening to the news and reading your paper in the past few days?'

Kevin was beginning to hyperventilate. Almost silently, Órla had begun to cry now and tears were running freely down her cheeks. She kept opening and closing her mouth as if she wanted to tell him something important but was too distressed to get the words out. In the hallway, Sibeal had started to whimper, too, clutching her rag doll as tightly as she could.

'If you've been paying attention to the news, Kevin, you'll be aware that the guards discovered some bodies under the floorboards of a cottage in Blarney. A whole family – father, mother, two children and even the family dogs.'

'I heard about that of course,' said Kevin. 'But they'd been dead for nearly ninety years, hadn't they? I think that's what they said on the news. So what does that have to do with me?'

'It has everything to do with you, Kevin. The Langtrys, that family was called, and it was members of your family who shot them.'

'You're *cracked*!' Kevin protested. 'My family never had anything to do with anything like that!'

'Maybe they never told you about it, but they did. The Langtrys came from Dripsey originally, to work at the woollen mills in Blarney. Everybody was told that they had simply done a moonlight flit. But now we know for sure that they were shot by your great-grandfather, Martin Doherty, and your great-uncle, Killian Doherty, amongst several others.'

'Are you out of your *mind*? My great-grandfather was a grocer! Doherty's Grocer's, in Coachford. He was never anything to do with shooting anybody. I don't know what my great-uncle did for a living, but I think it was something to do with shipping.'

The tall man shrugged, 'There were plenty of men in those days who were shopkeepers by day and soldiers by night. Your great-grandfather was one of them. Didn't you know that after the Dripsey ambush in 1921 he was hauled in by the British army and interrogated for nearly a month before they had to let him go?'

Kevin said, 'No, I didn't. All I know about him was that he was a grocer and my grandfather was a grocer, too. In the end, my grandfather sold the shop and ran a pub for a while, the Mills Inn at Ballyvourney.'

The tall man came around and stood closer to Kevin. He had a large brown wart on his chin instead of a dimple. Now that he was standing so near to him, Kevin could tell that he was the one who made the living room smell like a charity shop.

'You can say what you like,' the tall man told him. 'My family had it on the best possible intelligence that Martin Doherty and

Killian Doherty had been sent to do for the Langtrys. We never once believed for a moment that it was the Brits who did it. It was Captain Frank Busteed of the IRA at Kilcullen who ordered it.'

Kevin didn't know what to say. He felt as if he had opened the living-room door and stepped into a world of total madness. He was terrified and he was sure that these men were intent on killing him, but he couldn't even begin to understand why.

The tall man said, 'The only reason that the Brits let your great-grandfather go was because a letter arrived from the Langtry family in America to say that they had taken it upon themselves to emigrate and that they were all alive and well. Under the circumstances, the Brits could hardly charge him with murder, could they? Our family, though, we were never totally convinced that they had actually emigrated – but what else could we do? The Langtrys sent more letters from America, and there was no sign of them anywhere around Blarney, and no graves found – no bodies burned or buried in bogs. We had to assume that they really *were* in New York. No emails in those days. No phones, even.'

He paused and then he said, 'You can understand why we've been so devastated that their bodies had been found, can't you? After all this time, we've found out at last that our suspicions had been right all along and that they *had* been murdered by the IRA.'

'I still don't see how you can blame *me* for what happened,' said Kevin. 'Not in a million years.' He lifted his chin and flared his nostrils, trying to look defiant.

'Are you having a laugh? Of course we can blame you! Your family murdered one of our families – *all* of them, even the bairns. Even the fecking *dogs*, man! It's time you lot paid for it.'

'You're not a Langtry, though, are you?'

'No, of course not. The Crothers, we are. Our family used to keep Leemount House for Mrs Mary Lindsay, back in those days. My great-great-grandfather Payton kept the gardens. My great-great-great-grandmother Aideen did the cooking and their youngest daughter, Radha, helped her and did the house-cleaning.

'I still don't—' Kevin began, but the tall man interrupted him and now his voice was shaking with indignation.

'It was Radha who married Stephen Langtry and ended up buried under those floorboards. She was the flower of the family, that's what they used to call her. I should have brought you a photograph of her so that you could see for yourself what kind of a beauty she was. The loveliest young woman that you could ever imagine. But your great-grandfather – *your* great-grandfather, whose blood is flowing in your veins even now – he forced his way into Radha's house, that beautiful young woman, and he shot her with no hesitation whatsoever.'

To emphasize his outrage, the tall man lifted his own automatic and pressed the muzzle against his forehead. '*Shot* her,' he repeated. 'Killed her.'

Kevin raised both hands, as if to show the tall man that he was sorry for Radha and her family being murdered, but he could think of no way of making up for it, even if his great-grandfather had been responsible for it. If Radha hadn't been shot she would have been dead by now, anyway, no matter how beautiful she was.

None of them spoke for almost half a minute. The rain spattered against the living-room windows and Órla continued her painful, muted sobbing, although Sibeal had stopped whimpering now and stood silent, swallowing and swallowing as if she were close to being sick.

It was then that they heard Tom bounding down the stairs, calling out, 'Dad! I can't find my blue top! Do you know where my blue top is? I didn't put it in the wash!'

Kevin froze for a second. Then he strode to the living-room door and just as Tom came jumping to the bottom of the stairs he shouted, '*Tom! Get out of the house now, quick as you can! Run to Mrs Doody's next door and tell her call for the guards! Go!*'

Tom hesitated, blinking in bewilderment. He was wearing only his black tracksuit bottoms and a white vest, and he was carrying his grey school uniform bunched up close to his chest.

'*Go!*' Kevin told him, and this time he was almost shrieking.

The short man came out of the living-room door behind Kevin and roughly pulled at his sleeve. 'What the feck you playing at, big lad?'

'*Tom! Go and call the guards!*'

Tom dropped his school uniform on to the doormat and reached for the front door latch. As he tugged it down, however, the short man levelled his pistol at him, left-handed, still gripping Kevin's shirt sleeve with his right. The distance between the muzzle of the gun and the back of Tom's head was less than three metres.

In films, guns are fired in slow motion, so Kevin would have had time to twist his sleeve free from the short man's grip, dive towards Tom and rugby-tackle him to the floor, while the bullet would have slammed harmlessly through the door panel.

Instead, Kevin heard a sharp crack and at the same time a splash of bright red blood appeared on the door panel in front of Tom's face. Tom hesitated for a split second, still holding the door latch, but then he dropped sideways on to the staircase. He slid lifelessly down to the bottom, his arms and legs jumbled, his face turning towards Kevin as he did so. His eyes were open, but above his eyebrows his forehead been blown away and the top of his head was filled with bright red lumps like roughly mashed tomatoes.

Sibeal may have screamed. Kevin didn't seem able to hear anything. Even though the pistol was fitted with a silencer the shot had still been loud. He couldn't even hear himself let out a rising groan of grief. He dropped heavily on to his knees beside Tom, and collected him up in his arms, and held him close. He was warm, he was still warm, and when Kevin hugged him tight he let out a breath.

The tall man came out of the doorway to see Kevin hunched over Tom's body, his head nodding up and down in anguish like a religious penitent. He looked with obvious distaste at the blood that was already smothering Kevin's hands and drenching the front of his shirt, and at the fan-shaped spray of blood on the front-door panel.

'Man, dear, would you believe the fecking state of this place? It's going to be a right pain in the arse cleaning all this up.' There was no more emotion in his voice than an interior designer who disapproved of his client's choice of colour.

'The kid was going for the peelers,' the short man explained. 'What else could I do?'

'I don't care *where* the feck he was going, you didn't have to make such a fecking pig's dinner out of it. Oh well, it's not like we'll be trying to keep *this* family hidden for the next ninety years.'

Kevin raised his head. His eyes were almost blinded with tears and his mouth was dragged down in anguish.

'Come on, then, you can kill me, if that's what you came here to do. But don't hurt my wife, don't hurt my daughter. You've taken my son, you evil bastards, isn't that enough?'

The tall man looked back down at him, heavy-lidded. 'I think you've missed the point, big lad. An eye for an eye, that's what I said. A bullet for a bullet. A father and a mother, a boy and a girl. And I saw you have a couple of cats in the kitchen. You have to pay in full.

'Ker-*ching*,' he added, making the noise of a cash register.

Kevin looked down at Tom's staring eyes and the bloody chaos where the top of his head had been. 'This is not real,' he whispered to himself. 'This is a nightmare. None of this is real.'

'I expect our Radha said that, too, or something very like it,' said the tall man, while the short man gripped Kevin's arm and started to pull him up on to his feet.

Twenty-five

Katie drove home before she interviewed Bobby Quilty. She needed a shower and a change of clothes and something to eat, even if she didn't manage to get any sleep.

As soon as she had returned to Anglesea Street she had initiated a nationwide search for Kyna and John by ordering bulletins to be sent out to all six police regions in the Republic, and the same information to all eleven districts of the Police Service of Northern Ireland. After that she had gone to Chief Superintendent MacCostagáin's office to give him an outline briefing on the disaster that had been Operation Trident. She hadn't tried to make excuses for what had happened. She had told him, though, that Bobby Quilty must have been warned of the raids in advance.

'You think it might be coming from inside?' Chief Superintendent MacCostagáin had asked her. 'Is it somebody here at the station?'

Katie could only shrug. 'I don't know yet, sir. I really have no idea. But I *will* find out, you can count on that.'

That morning there had already been several discussions on both TV and radio about the Langtrys. Professor Pendle had repeated his assertion that the British army had shot them, and Oraltih Mac Aindríu of Sinn Fein had said that it was high time the British came clean about some of the atrocities they had committed in the 1920s. So far, however, there had been no response from London. Katie had given a short and non-committal statement to Mathew McElvey in the press office to keep the media at bay until later, but she was anxious not to compromise her arrest of Bobby Quilty in any way.

She had been passing the station's front desk when a call came in for her from Bobby Quilty's solicitors in South Mall. She had flapped her hand and mouthed '*no – not in!*' to the telephone operator and the girl had told them that she was still tied up in a strategy meeting and she would ring them back later. She knew Bobby Quilty's solicitors only too well: Fairley and O'Counihan, especially Terence O'Counihan – a tall, handsome bully with swept-back hair who represented some of the wealthiest businessmen in Cork, and some of the most unsavoury, too.

She arrived at her front door back in Cobh almost at the same time as Jenny Tierney, her neighbour. Jenny had been taking Barney for a walk, in spite of the rain. Jenny was a small, bustling woman who never stopped talking. All bundled up in her pink plastic scarf and yellow vinyl raincoat and bright red rushers she looked as if somebody had brought a rather untidy Russian *matrioshka* doll to life.

'Oh, thanks a million, Jenny, you're a saint,' said Katie, as she took Barney's lead. Barney snuffled up to her and then shook himself violently so that the rain flew off him. 'Barns! You've *soaked* me now, you silly mutt!'

'Were you working all last night, Kathleen, were you?' Jenny asked her as she unlocked her front door. 'Did you get any sleep? I couldn't do without my sleep myself. Sure and I'd be dozing off in the middle of the day if I didn't get my full eight hours, and it doesn't help with himself snoring like Dooley's timber yard.'

Katie switched off her security alarm. 'Did you enjoy your walk, Barns?' she asked him. 'Where did you go?'

'He used to be pure reluctant to go out in the wet now, didn't he?' said Jenny. 'Last week, though, I took him down to the end of Whitepoint Drive for a bit of a change, like – down by the water, you know where I mean, and there's a lady golden Labrador he's taken a fancy to who lives down there, so now he doesn't object to going out at all, even if it's lashing. I have only to say, "Come on, Barney, let's go and see Oona," and if he could clip on his lead himself, he'd be doing it like a shot, I can tell you.'

'Barns!' said Katie. 'You didn't tell me you were in love!'

'Oh, I'd say he's head over paws, but that Oona's awful flirty with him, too. You should see the pair of them together! They'll be voting for dogs to marry next, I shouldn't be surprised, now they've legalized the gays! I expect you're tired, girl, but why don't you come next door to mine for a bit of a sit-down? A cup of tea will crown you.'

'That's very kind, Jenny,' said Katie. 'Right now, though, I have a heap of things on my mind. I don't think I'd be very good company.'

'Well, if you change your mind, like. I have some Guinness gingerbread my sister just sent me and if I don't share it out I'll be finishing it off all by myself, like.'

Jenny kept on talking until Katie had taken off her coat and hung it up and smiled and said thank you again and slowly but firmly closed the door. Then she had gone through to the living room and sat down on the couch to take off her shoes. She felt exhausted. Her head ached and her ankles were swollen and she would have given anything to go to bed and close her eyes and sleep for the rest of the day. All she could think of, though, was Kyna and John. She knew that Bobby Quilty had spirited them away, but she couldn't even begin to imagine what he had done with them – where he might be hiding them, or if he had hurt them, or even if they were still alive. She felt a deep nauseous guilt in the pit of her stomach about both of them, especially Kyna. She should never have sent her to try and infiltrate Bobby Quilty's gang, she should have known that it would end in tragedy. It made no difference that Kyna had agreed to do it: her life was worth a hundred of Bobby Quilty's.

And John – there he was, with his ink-blue eyes and his black curly hair, smiling down at her from his photograph frame on the fireplace. She could almost feel the wind on the day that picture had been taken, on the beach at Dingle Bay, with only the sound of the sea coming in and the thumping of horses' hooves on the sand as five riders galloped by.

She suddenly realized that she was crying.

Barney had been in the kitchen lapping up his water but now he trotted into the living room and stared at her, licking his lips.

'Don't you worry, Barns, I'm grand altogether,' she told him, wiping her eyes with the back of her hand. 'Just tired and emotional, that's all. It's what I get paid for. And what about you? I would have thought you'd had enough of water outside, visiting your fancy-woman in the rain, like.'

She went into the bedroom, unfastened her holster and laid her gun on top of her dressing table. It was her new Smith & Wesson .38 Airweight, which she had only recently changed for her previous revolver. She preferred this because it weighed only 425 grams, lighter than her previous weapon and less than half the weight of the SIG Sauer P226 automatics issued to most of the Regional Response Units. It also had a concealed hammer which guarded against accidental snagging in her clothes. She hadn't yet fired it on duty, and maybe she never would, but she had practised with it every week since she had been issued with it. It had a hard kick to it because it was so light, but she had learned how to handle that, and the grip really suited somebody with small hands like hers.

She undressed and went into the bathroom for a shower. She was surprised to see in the mirror over the basin that she didn't look as tired or as anxious as she felt. In fact, she looked unnaturally calm and composed, and the neat new cut that her hairdresser, Denis, had given her, which tapered into the nape her of her neck, was completely unruffled.

After her shower she wrapped herself in her thick white towelling dressing gown and lay on her back on her bed, crossing her arms over her breasts like a medieval saint on a tomb. She closed her eyes, but after a few seconds she had to open them again. She knew that she wouldn't be able to sleep, so she would have to take two or three caffeine pills if she wanted to be fresh and focused when she faced Bobby Quilty.

She almost felt like asking God why He had created men like Bobby Quilty. Maybe it was just to test the faith and moral courage of people like her.

'All You had to do was *ask* me if I believe in You,' said Katie to the ceiling. Barney heard her talking and let out a gruffing noise, as if he agreed with her.

She was about to get up and get dressed when her iPhone played '*Buile Mo Chroi*'. It was Inspector O'Rourke, sounding as croaky and tired as she was.

'What about you, ma'am? I've just had a call from a retired CID inspector from the PSNI.'

'Oh, yes? What did he want?'

'One of his former colleagues in the Crime Operations Department in Belfast told him about the bulletin you put out regarding DS Ni Nuallán and John Meagher.'

'Okay. And?'

'And if they're still alive he says he has a reasonable suspicion that he knows where they are. Or even if they're not.'

Katie sat up. 'Serious?' she said. 'He must still have some contacts.'

'I think that's the gist of it, ma'am. Any road, he said he'd like to talk to you personal, if he could. I think he remembers you from that time you went up to Belfast to help them to break up that child abuse ring.'

'What's his name?'

'Harte. Alan Harte. He said he's living in Cherryvalley now, in East Belfast.'

'Cherryvalley? He must have been given a golden handshake and a half. I'm not sure I remember him, though.'

'Well, let me give you his number and you can talk to him for yourself.'

'I'll get back to you after, Francis, as soon as I have. Stall it for a second, would you, and let me find a pen?'

Katie jotted down Alan Harte's number and as soon as Inspector O'Rourke had rung off she called him. The phone rang and rang for a long time and she began to think that there was nobody home. Just as she was about to put the phone down, however, it was picked up and a man with a clogged-up voice said, 'Alan

Harte,' then cleared his throat and repeated, softly but much more distinctly, 'Alan Harte.'

'Oh, hallo to you there, Alan. This is Detective Superintendent Kathleen Maguire, from Cork Garda headquarters. I was told you'd been trying to get in touch with me.'

'Well, well, DS Maguire! Thanks a million for calling me back! I don't know if you remember me at all. I met you when you came up to Belfast two years ago and you helped us to scoop those toerags in the Khan–Norris gang.'

Katie said, 'I should have called you on Skype and then I would have been able to see what you look like.' She didn't tell him that she was wearing only her dressing gown, so the Skype conversation would have had to have been one-sided. 'Not to worry. Detective Inspector O'Rourke tells me you might have some information on those two people we're looking for.'

'That's right. One of my old colleagues from Lisnasharragh called me as soon as he saw your message. He's always promised to let me know if a certain name comes up, and there it was, that certain name, big and fat and unmissable.' He quoted from Katie's bulletin: '*These two have been missing since a Garda operation at 0430 hours to detain Robert Boland Quilty on suspicion of keeping them unlawfully imprisoned.*'

'So, you and Bobby Quilty have history, do you?' asked Katie.

'Oh, aye, we have history all right. Why do you think I had to quit the force? We tried to pull a sting on Quilty when he was smuggling drugs in through Larne. To this day I still don't know who he paid off or who he threatened, but nearly seventy-five thousand pounds' worth of heroin was found hidden in my garage roof at home and I could offer no explanation at all as to how it got there. I resigned on grounds of ill health – in inverted commas, if you know what I mean – and it was all hushed up. But of course it was Bobby Quilty who set me up and I swear to God that I will get him one day and fasten his family jewels to the floor with a nail-gun, so I will, if you'll excuse me for saying so.'

'Well, maybe this is your big chance,' Katie told him. 'If we can locate John Meagher and Detective Sergeant Ni Nuallán, and they're still alive, they should be able to give us all the evidence against Bobby Quilty that we could need.'

'Even if they're dead they should be able to,' said Alan.

'I'm trying not to think about that possibility yet,' said Katie.

'No, I can understand that. But I think we have to be realistic about this. Both you and I know what Bobby Quilty is capable of.'

'All right, Alan. Let's concentrate on John Meagher and DS Ni Nuallán. Where do you think we might find them?'

'This is not one hundred per cent, DS Maguire, but it's very much more than just a wild guess.'

'Oh, come on, Alan, call me Katie. You're a civilian now and I'm not in the mood for formalities. I don't mind you knowing that both John Meagher and Kyna Ni Nuallán are personally very close to me.'

'Right you are, then, Katie it is. And like I was telling you, this is more than just a wild guess. Bobby Quilty always used to envy Chunk O'Connell because of the way O'Connell's farmhouse straddles the border, and it was said that all Chunk ever had to do to avoid arrest was cross from one side of his yard the other. About five years ago, Bobby Quilty bought a very similar property in South Armagh. When I say "bought", it was almost a compulsory purchase. He persuaded the owners that it might be better for their general health if they sold up for a derisory sum of money and moved away.'

'Where is it, exactly, this property?' asked Katie.

'It's just off the Shean Road at Forkhill. You can see it clearly enough when you're driving past, even though it's set well back. You won't find it in any official records that it belongs to Bobby Quilty. It belongs to some trust that belongs to proxy that belongs to some holding company. I didn't discover myself that Quilty owned it until two or three weeks before I was forced to resign. But he has the same kind of arrangement as Chunk O'Connell: if the police come to lift him, he simply walks out of the sitting room into the kitchen and they can't touch him. He can stand a foot in front of them eating sausages and there's nothing legally that they can do about it because he's in another country.'

'And you think John Meagher and Kyna Ni Nuallán might be there?'

'Let's just say that when I first joined the CID there's one or two people in South Armagh that I did favours for. Right from the beginning I always considered that it was good policing to turn a blind eye to what the Lesser Bastards were up to, because the Lesser Bastards could help me catch the Bigger Bastards. What would you rather have? A dozen convictions for stealing second-hand cars, or a single conviction for conspiring to plant a three-kilo bomb in the middle of a crowded shopping centre?'

'Yes, I follow you,' said Katie, a little impatiently.

'Anyway, Katie,' Alan went on, 'one of my Lesser Bastards works part-time in the bar now at the Welcome Inn in Forkhill. Every night when he cycles home he passes Bobby Quilty's place and if ever he sees anything unusual going on there, no matter what it is, he sends me a text about it. In return I keep my mouth shut about some of the stunts he got up to with his two brothers after the Good Friday Agreement. They were all three members of the Provos' Second Battalion. This feller never killed anybody himself, but he smuggled the explosives for a bomb that did.'

'So you're telling me that he saw something unusual last night?'

'Aye, he did. I won't read you his text verbatim because you wouldn't be able to make a scrap of sense of it, but he said that just before midnight last night he saw a black or maybe a dark blue van turning into Bobby Quilty's house and parking outside. Two fellers got out of the front and opened the back doors. They lifted out a stretcher with a man lying on it, but then a girl jumped out and started running towards the road.

'One of the two fellers went running after her and caught up with her pretty quick because it looked like her wrists were tied together, which meant she couldn't run so well. He pulled her back to the house and then another three fellers came out of the house and helped to carry the stretcher inside.'

'Did your informant say what the girl looked like?'

'He said she had short blonde hair, that's all. Well, *shoe blind air* is what he actually texted, but I think we can safely assume that's what he meant.'

Katie said, 'I didn't mention it in my bulletin, but I was told that John Meagher had been physically bolted to a bed. If he'd actually had bolts fixed through his ankles or his feet, it would make sense, wouldn't it, for him to have been carried on a stretcher?'

'And Detective Sergeant Ni Nuallán is a blonde?'

'It does all seem to fit together,' said Katie. 'If they were just arriving at Bobby Quilty's house at midnight, that means they would have left Cork around eight, and that makes sense time-wise.'

She didn't say anything to Alan, but by 8 p.m. the preparations for Operation Trident had been fully under way. If Bobby Quilty had been tipped off about Trident immediately after their tactical briefing, he would have had plenty of time to arrange for the bed to removed from the house on Leitrim Street and for John and Kyna to be stowed into in a van and driven north on the M8 to Dublin, and then on to Dundalk presumably, and the border.

'I can't pretend that this is going to be a doddle, by any means,' said Alan. 'The Public Prosecution Service and the top brass at Knock Street are ultra-wary these days of having anything at all to do with Bobby Quilty. Chief Superintendent Shields said herself that it's worse than trying to prosecute a wasps' nest. No witnesses can ever be cajoled into speaking out against him, not even for money and the promise of a lifetime's protection, and you wouldn't believe the number of times he's sued the police service for harassment or wrongful arrest. Successfully, too. The last time he was awarded 15,000 euros.'

Katie knew that Alan was right. In spite of all the incriminating information that the police forces and intelligence services on both sides of the border had gathered against him, neither An Garda Siochána nor the Police Service of Northern Ireland had been able to bring a prosecution against Bobby Quilty that would stand up for five minutes in court.

Not only that, she doubted if Chief Superintendent Mac-Costágain or Chief Superintendent Shields would grant her authority for a raid on Bobby Quilty's house at Forkhill, even though cooperation between An Garda Siochána and the PSNI was mostly excellent these days and they frequently exchanged officers.

How could she justify going after Bobby Quilty yet again? She could imagine the conversation with Chief Superintendent MacCostagáin.

'I strongly believe that Bobby Quilty is holding Detective Sergeant Ni Nuallán and John Meagher imprisoned in his house in South Armagh.'

'Oh, yes, and what evidence do you have for this strong belief?'

'I was told by an ex-detective inspector of the PSNI.'

'*Ex*-detective inspector?'

'He resigned after he was suspected of drug-dealing, but he claims that Bobby Quilty framed him.'

'And where did he get *his* information from?'

'A former Provo who works in a local pub. While he was still in the service, the ex-detective inspector let this fellow off several charges of handling explosives. In exchange for that, the fellow keeps a sneaky eye on Bobby Quilty for him so that one day he can get his revenge.'

'And that's your evidence?'

She knew what this would look like, especially to Acting Commissioner Jimmy O'Reilly, and to several of the more misogynistic senior officers at Anglesea Street. They would think that she felt so humiliated by the fiasco of Operation Trident that she had worked herself up into a hormonal tantrum and now she was trying to bring down Bobby Quilty in any way she could, no matter how flimsy her evidence might be. 'Policing by PMT,' Jimmy O'Reilly had once called it when she had lost her temper with a particularly sarcastic Cork pimp.

But supposing she was given the go-ahead to set up a raid? What if it turned out the same as Operation Trident? What if

Bobby Quilty was again tipped off in advance and when they broke into his house there was no sign that Kyna and John had ever been there? For Katie, that could well lead to serious disciplinary proceedings – probation, suspension, or even demotion. Jimmy O'Reilly wouldn't take kindly to the Garda being made to look like fumbling culchies, especially in front of the PSNI.

She was desperately worried about Kyna and John, but she had to be rational. If she failed to rescue them at the first attempt and was taken off the case, or suspended, or worse, then she would have very little hope of rescuing them at all.

'I know what's running through your mind, Katie,' said Alan. 'I talked to my old pal at Lisnasharragh before I phoned you and he was of the same opinion. With a cute hoor like Quilty you can't just go barging in with all guns blazing without knowing in advance how it's all going to work out. My informant saw the fellow on the stretcher and the girl with the blonde hair, but let's be serious, we don't know for sure if they're the two people we're looking for, and even if they *are* the two people we're looking for, how do we know they're still there now, or if they're likely to be still there if we burst in looking for them?'

'So what are you suggesting? Further surveillance?'

'You have it exactly. I'll go down there myself and have a scout around. I'll see what pictures I can get and if there's any forensic evidence there to be picked up. And – well, you know, it's surprising what you can hear when you keep your ears open.'

'You mean you're going to hack their mobile phones and tap their landlines?'

'Away on with you, Katie! As if I'd do any such thing!'

'Of course not – not as a civilian, and not without a warrant. Who knows what you might overhear?'

'Katie, I'll get back to you as soon as I can,' said Alan. 'I would have trod careful in any case, but now I know that these two mean so much to you personally yourself, I'll tread extremely light indeed, I promise you. A couple of years ago one of our sergeants got on the wrong side of Bobby Quilty and his Authentic IRA and you don't want to know what they did to him, except that it involved his own baton tightly wrapped in razor wire.'

'You're right, I don't want to hear what they did to him,' said Katie. 'It's bad enough trying not to think what they might be doing to Kyna and John.'

Twenty-six

'I'm sorry that I never thought to bring a priest along with us,' said the tall man. 'Very remiss of me, not to think that you Taigs wouldn't be expecting the last rites and all.'

'Let me cover him up at least,' said Kevin. He hauled himself to his feet, gripping the banisters with one bloodied hand to help himself up. His teeth were chattering as if he were freezing cold.

The tall man went over to the coat rack and lifted down Kevin's own long grey raincoat. Kevin took it and gently draped it over Tom's body. From the living room, he could hear both Órla and Sibeal weeping. Their sobs were so anguished that they barely sounded human – more like lonely seals crying on an ice floe after their cubs had been culled.

'Please,' said Kevin. 'You can do anything you like to me, but please don't hurt my wife and my baby girl. I'm begging you. If you have any human mercy at all, please don't hurt them.'

The tall man looked away, as if he were thinking about something else altogether – like, did I remember to book my car in for its NCT?

Kevin waited, swaying slightly with shock. After a few moments the tall man seemed to have collected his thoughts because he said, 'All right, then, let's get you in here all together. Come on now, big lad.'

'I beg you,' said Kevin. His throat was so dry that he could hardly speak.

'What? Like Stephen Langtry begged for Radha, more than likely, and his kids, too? Come on, come in here and let's get this over and done with.'

The short man pressed his hand against Kevin's shoulder and pushed him into the living room. Órla and Sibeal were standing next to the fireplace, clutching each other, their eyes swollen and their faces dripping with tears. The younger man had propped his AK-47 up against the window while he rolled up the large red Ashanti-patterned rug in the middle of the floor. Once he had done that, he left the room and Kevin heard him open the front door. He came back shortly afterwards, carrying a large roll of translucent polythene sheeting almost two metres long.

'You can't do this,' said Kevin. 'This is just barbaric.'

'Ach, there's been a surfeit of barbarity in Ireland down the years,' said the tall man, without looking at him. 'But there's a way to end it, so there is, and that's to punish every act of barbarity with an act of equal barbarity. I know fine rightly that you're innocent yourself, Kevin, and so are you wife and your bairn, but the Langtrys were just as innocent and somebody has to be punished for their murder, and if not you, then who?'

The young man had unrolled the wrinkled polythene sheeting and spread it all across the polished oak floorboards. Kevin had sanded and polished those floorboards himself, soon after they had first moved in.

Kevin knew that he wasn't dreaming, although everything that was happening felt utterly unreal. It was more like being very drunk than dreaming. It felt like those times when he had been quite aware that he was drunk, and hadn't wanted to be drunk, but hadn't been able to speak properly or walk without stumbling down the stairs.

Now that the sheeting had been unrolled across the floor, the tall man touched Kevin very lightly on the back of his head and said, 'Kneel, will you, Kevin.'

Kevin knelt down, his arms by his sides. He couldn't stop himself from crying now even though he wanted to be brave in front of Órla and Sibeal. He didn't want to look at them. He didn't want to witness the distress in their faces, but he couldn't help it. These might be the last few seconds in which he would ever see them.

227

The short man came up and stood right behind him. He was expecting to be shot in the head at any moment and wondered what it was going to feel like. Did you feel anything at all? Or could you feel your brain exploding, the way Tom's had exploded? Were you aware of everything that you had ever thought or learned or experienced bursting apart like a supernova? How much would it hurt?

He was still waiting for the shot when the tall man went across to the fireplace, took Órla's arm and led her over to the middle of the room, next to Kevin. Órla tried to twist her arm away from him, but he was gripping her sleeve too tightly.

'Kneel,' he told her. When she hesitated, he repeated in the same unemphatic monotone, 'Kneel.'

Órla knelt. She was close enough for Kevin to be able to reach out and touch her, but when he lifted his hand towards her the tall man pursed his lips and shook his head.

'*Mummy!*' sobbed Sibeal.

'Don't you worry, wee girl,' said the tall man. He went over and put his arm around her shoulders and gently steered her over to stand next to Órla.

'Now, you kneel, too, darling, just like you do in church when you're saying your prayers to the Holy Mother. "Hail Mary, full of grace, why do you make that self-satisfied face?"'

Sibeal knelt, awkwardly, but at the same time Kevin started to get to his feet again.

'You lay one finger on her! You touch one hair of her head and I'll find you in hell! I'll find you in hell, you bastard, and I'll make sure that you suffer for all eternity!'

The short man grasped both of Kevin's shoulders and forced him back down into a kneeling position, jarring his left kneecap painfully against the floor. The tall man said, 'I may very well end up in hell, Kevin, but you won't be able to find me. You – you'll be in paradise with your family, big lad, strolling happily from cloud to cloud and you'll have forgotten all about me. Or even if you haven't, you'll have forgiven me. That's what you Taigs do, isn't it? Forgive?'

'Don't you dare hurt her!' Kevin warned him.

'Ach, she won't feel a thing,' said the tall man. With that, he lifted his automatic, cocked it, and pointed it directly between Sibeal's eyes.

Kevin didn't have time to speak before he pulled the trigger and shot Sibeal in the centre of her forehead. Blood sprayed over the glass of the china cabinet directly behind her and up the wall, spattering a small framed picture of St Felicity. Sibeal pitched backwards on to the floor, but still kneeling, as if her knees were hinged. Her blue eyes were still open and, like St Felicity, she was staring up at the ceiling, except that there was a powder-black entry wound between her eyebrows. A large triangular segment had been blown from the back of her skull so that her brains were now tangled with her hair.

Órla screamed and tried to stand up. The short man made a grab for her and as she turned herself around to fight him off the tall man shot her in the right eye, at point-blank range. The fragmentation bullet didn't penetrate all the way through her skull, but her head was violently distorted off to the left so that her face now sloped in a surrealistic parody of herself. She dropped sideways on to the floor close to Kevin's knees and blood ran out of her eye socket and across the bridge of her freckled nose. She was wearing the thin silver bracelet that Kevin had given her on her thirtieth birthday, because that was all he had been able to afford.

Kevin closed his eyes tight. He thought, *Kill me, go on, you're going to do it anyway, and there's nothing left for me to live for now*, but he didn't speak.

The tall man was standing very close in front of him. Kevin couldn't smell him with all that gunpowder stench in the air, but he could sense that he was there.

'Strange thing, revenge, isn't it?' the tall man asked him. 'The sweetest morsel in the mouth that was ever cooked in hell. That's what Sir Walter Scott called it.'

Kevin still said nothing. He could hear the rain sprinkling against the windows and in the distance he could faintly hear the rumbling of a plane taking off from Cork airport. *So this is how my life ends*, he thought. *This is where my destiny was always leading me.*

He pictured the first time he had seen Órla, standing behind the counter at Ryan's, the baker's, with the sun making her look so pale and ethereal, like the ghost of a beautiful girl, rather than a real girl.

'Are you getting?' she had asked him.

He opened his eyes. The tall man was staring at him with an expression that he had never seen on anybody's face before, ever. It was closer to helplessness than anything else, as if he had no choice but to do this because Irish history wouldn't have it any other way.

'I am now,' he said – but of course the tall man didn't understand that this was in reply to the very first question that Órla had put to him and had nothing to do with the bloody tragedy in this living room.

The tall man slowly circled around him, his shoes making a rustling sound on the polythene sheeting. He stood behind him for what seemed to Kevin like an hour, but was less than a minute. Then he raised his automatic until the silencer was only a centimetre away from the back of Kevin's head.

'This is for Radha,' he said. He fired, and Kevin's face blew open from the inside out.

* * *

The tall man and the short man wrapped up each of the four bodies tightly in polythene sheeting, sealing them with silver gaffer tape. While they were doing that, the younger man used a crowbar to prise up six floorboards in the middle of the living-room floor.

Between them, they lowered the bodies into the spaces between the joists and then they carefully nailed the floorboards back down. They replaced the rug and positioned two of the armchairs on top of it.

This took them nearly two hours and then they had to spend a further twenty minutes to clean up Tom's blood from the hallway. Fragments of the bullet that had gone through his head had scarred the upper right-hand door panel, but the younger man had the idea of covering these up by pinning over it a list of reminders that Órla had written to herself and stuck to her fridge.

'Let's put it this way, you're not going to walk in here and immediately think, "Ah, she's stuck her to-do list on the front door to hide some bullet holes", now are you?'

They took a last look around. The Doherty house was silent, as silent as the Langtrys' house must have been when their murderers had finished nailing down their bodies and cleaning up the blood. Then they closed the front door behind them, climbed into their van and drove off.

It was still raining, even more heavily now, and the rain drifted across the city as if God were trailing shrouds across the streets.

Twenty-seven

It was past 2.30 p.m. before Katie arrived back at Anglesea Street. A lorryload of live pigs had broken down in Jack's Hole and the traffic had tailed back all the way to the Euro Business Park. Apart from that, it was raining so hard now that she had to set her windscreen wipers to flap at full speed, and visibility was down to less than thirty metres.

As she came out of the lift she almost collided with Detective Ó Doibhilin.

'Oh, there you are, ma'am,' he greeted her. 'I was just coming back from your office because you weren't there, but here you are now yourself.'

'What's the story, Michael?' Katie asked him. She walked briskly down the corridor to her office and Detective Ó Doibhilin came trotting after her. He was waving a green plastic folder as he did so.

'I heard back from a fellow called Bracewaite, who's like an unofficial historian for the Manchester Regiment. All of their regimental records are kept in the Tameside Local Studies and Archive Centre in Ashton-under-Lyne in Manchester.'

'Did he know who this "Gerald" might have been?'

'He's one hundred per cent sure of it. Lieutenant Gerald Seabrook, whose family came from a place near Manchester called Hale Barns. He'd seen service in France during the First World War and in 1919 they posted him to Ballincollig.'

Katie took off her waterproof jacket and hung it up. 'What we really need to know is, is there any record of his having had a relationship with Radha Langtry?'

She sat down and Detective Ó Doibhilin popped open the plastic folder and handed it to her. 'There's no specific record of that, like, but there's a copy of a letter that was sent just before Christmas in 1920 from the regiment's headquarters in Manchester to Lieutenant Seabrook's commanding officer here in Ireland. I'd say that there's at least an implication in it that Lieutenant Seabrook was doing a line with Radha Langtry.'

Katie took out the typewritten letter and quickly read it. It had been sent by Major D. R. Kettering from Ladysmith Barracks, Ashton-under-Lyne, to Lieutenant Colonel F. H. Dorling, commander of the 1st Battalion of the Manchester Regiment in Ballincollig. It was dated 17 December 1920.

> *Sir,*
>
> *I have received an appeal from Mrs J. Seabrook,*
> *the wife of Lt. G. K. Seabrook, urgently requesting*
> *information about his wellbeing and whereabouts.*
> *It appears that she has had no word from him*
> *whatsoever for more than three months, neither has*
> *she received the usual monthly payment from him to*
> *meet her household expenses and the care of their two*
> *young children.*
>
> *She is particularly distressed since Christmas is*
> *almost upon us.*
>
> *I would be grateful if you could have this matter*
> *raised with Lt. Seabrook and inform me of the*
> *position regarding his contact with his wife and*
> *financial contributions to his family.*

'Is this all?' asked Katie, holding up the letter. 'Did this Major Kettering get a reply?'

'I'm afraid that's all, ma'am – all that's in the archive, any road. There's no further word about why Lieutenant Seabrook hadn't been in touch with his missus. But there *is* a record of what happened to him.'

'Oh, yes? And what was that?'

'He went missing in March 1921. They thought at the time that he'd deserted, because four private soldiers failed to show up for duty at the same time. Here they are – Privates Pincher, Mason, Caen and Roughley. A whole rake of British soldiers went AWOL, according to this Bracewaite fellow, because they'd just come back from fighting the Germans in France and suddenly they found themselves up against the IRA. The stress and the totally different circumstances they were fighting under was too much for some of them. That was in the days before post-traumatic stress disorder was thought of, you know. They'd only just invented shell-shock.'

'But he hadn't deserted, this Lieutenant Seabrook?'

'No, ma'am, he hadn't at all, and neither had any of those four privates. If they *had*, like, we wouldn't be able to check up on it. There's a file called "arrests and illegal absences" in the regimental archives, but it's sealed for a hundred years and nobody's allowed to take a sconce at it until 2040 at the earliest. No, in 1923 the Brits and the IRA were doing some further political bargaining, like, and as a concession to the Brits the IRA told them that Lieutenant Seabrook and the four privates had been abducted and shot and their bodies buried underneath a hedge in Muskerry.'

'So it wasn't only Radha and the rest of the Langtry family who were shot. It was "Gerald" as well?'

'That's what it looks like. At first, all five of the soldiers' bodies were squashed into a single coffin and buried in Bandon, but after some more negotiations in 1924 they were dug up, like, and sent to the regimental headquarters in Ashton-under-Lyne. They were separated and all of them were buried with the full military honours in Hurst Cemetery, which is where they still are.'

Katie leafed through the letters and papers that had been emailed to Detective Ó Doibhilin from England. There was even a photograph of Lieutenant Gerald Seabrook, MC. He was standing in a summery garden somewhere, in his uniform, his eyes half closed because of the brightness of the sun. He didn't look to Katie as if he were particularly tall, maybe five foot seven or eight inches, and his shiny dark hair was parted in the middle, but he was handsome in a cheeky Tom Cruise way and he had an engaging smile.

'Strange to think that he's been dead now for over ninety years, isn't it?' said Katie. 'Taken away, shot and buried under a hedge. And look at him, still grinning away like he doesn't have a care.'

She felt that the motive for the Langtrys' murders was gradually becoming more distinct, as if she were cleaning successive layers of dirty varnish from a very old painting. The information that Detective Ó Doibhilin had gleaned from the Manchester Regiment archives hadn't really helped much, but at least it had confirmed who 'Gerald' had probably been. He could have been shot by the IRA for no other reason than he was a British army officer, but Katie thought it increasingly likely that they had killed him out of revenge for the Dripsey ambush, and that they could have shot the Langtrys for the same reason.

All she had at the moment was 'what-ifs', but the 'what-ifs' made sense and it was worth following them up to see if they helped to make the picture any clearer. Stephen Langtry had been a member of the IRA. What if he had told Radha about the imminent ambush? He might have done it for her own safety, or so that she could caution her employer, Mrs Lindsay, to stay away from Godfrey's Cross that day. If anything happened to Mrs Lindsay, Radha would have been out of a job, and secure jobs like that in those days weren't easy to come by – or, indeed, any jobs at all.

But what if Radha had been having an affair with Gerald Seabrook and she had told *him*, too, in case he were killed? What if the British army's informant hadn't been Mrs Lindsay at all, as the IRA had first thought and the history books still suggested – or at least, not the only informant?

Whether it was Mrs Lindsay or Radha or both of them who had warned the British about the ambush, Katie could understand why the IRA might have been set on revenge once it had gone so calamitously wrong. Most of their men had escaped because they knew the countryside so well, but one had been mortally wounded and eight had been captured, and of those eight, five had been sentenced to death and executed.

In retaliation, the IRA had abducted and shot Mrs Lindsay and her chauffeur. But if they had subsequently discovered that Radha was the source of the leak, it was more than likely that they would have made a point of going after Gerald Seabrook, and the Langtrys, too. That was only another 'what-if', of course, and Katie knew that she might never find the evidence to back it up. But unless the Langtrys had been murdered because they were having some kind of bitter personal feud with another family, it seemed like the most logical explanation.

After all, she thought, the killings had been a classic example of an IRA punishment: you were taken, you were shot, you were buried, and nobody ever saw you again or knew exactly what had happened to you. It was infinitely more traumatic than being murdered in the open, in front of witnesses, especially for your family and friends. You had simply been 'disappeared'. They didn't even have a grave on which they could lay flowers.

'This fellow Bracewaite said he's happy to do some more snuffling around for me,' said Detective Ó Doibhilin. 'He said he might be able to trace the Seabrook family, especially if they're still living around the Hale Barns area. From what he told me, you have to be fierce *flathúl* to live around there – it's all big five-bedroom houses and swimming pools, do you know what I mean, like? – so families don't tend to move so often.'

'That's grand, Michael, keep banging away at it,' said Katie. She looked at the clock on her desk. 'Now I have to go and have a word with our friend Bobby Quilty. After that, I'll be holding a general debriefing about Operation Trident.'

'You don't want to know what they're saying in the canteen about Operation Trident,' said Detective Ó Doibhilin.

'Yes, I do,' said Katie.

'Serious?'

'Tell me. I won't get odd with you, I promise.'

'Well, they're saying, "Two wrongs don't make a right. Three prongs weren't worth a shite."'

'I'll ignore that,' said Katie. 'Just warn them that if I overhear anybody saying that myself, I'll be sending them out in the rain to lick my car clean.'

Twenty-eight

Katie took Detective Sergeant Begley and Detective O'Donovan down with her to the interview room. When she walked in Bobby Quilty was deep in murmured conversation with his lawyer, Terence O'Counihan, their heads almost touching, and even though he flicked his eyes towards the door he didn't stop murmuring and showed no other sign that he had seen her come in.

'Mr Begley, Mr O'Counihan,' said Katie, drawing out a chair. Terence O'Counihan turned around as if he were surprised to see her, and stood up. He was so tall that Katie had to tilt her head back to look him in the eye and he made her feel like a child rather than a grown woman. He was wearing an expensive grey shark-skin suit, double-breasted, and a blue silk tie with a repetitive pattern of herons on it. He was very handsome, in a smooth, well-moisturized way, with black hair that was greying at the temples and immaculate eyebrows. Whenever he was amused, or quizzical, one eyebrow would rise like a raven lifting itself off a rooftop. His nose was very straight, his eyes were slightly hooded. His tan had come from somewhere very much more exotic than Santa Ponsa.

'Well, well, Detective Superintendent Maguire. We must stop meeting like this.'

'We would, Mr O'Counihan, if you were more selective in your choice of clients.'

'Ouch!' Terence O'Counihan grinned. 'You still float like a butterfly, sting like a bee! However,' he said, lifting his wrist to look down with those hooded eyes at his gold Patek Philippe watch, 'time is flying by, Detective Superintendent *tempus fugit.*

I must insist either that you release Mr Quilty on station bail or immediately bring him up in front of the District Court on the charges for which you arrested him.'

'I need to ask him a few questions first,' said Katie.

'My client has nothing to say.'

'He does realize the seriousness of the charges against him? Incitement to murder and false imprisonment?'

'He does, of course. But he vehemently denies both. Whatever it is you're accusing him of saying, he didn't say it, and whoever you're accusing him of imprisoning, he doesn't know them and in any event he wasn't there.'

'We have forensic evidence that John Meagher was held in a property on Leitrim Street belonging to Mr Quilty.'

'He knows nothing at all about that and he has no comment to make.'

Katie found it hard to look at Bobby Quilty, but he didn't take his eyes off her. He sat there with his chubby fingers squashed together like sausages, and a porky, self-satisfied twinkle in his eyes. Now and then he gave a catarrhal snort in his left nostril, and swallowed. He didn't yet know that she had discovered where he was holding Kyna and John, and of course she wasn't going to tell him, because he would either have them moved at once to some other safe house or kill them – she had absolutely no doubt that he was capable of it. She was so angry and afraid that she had to stop and take a steadying breath now and again, in case she burst out and told him how vicious and loathsome she thought he was, and how deeply he disgusted her. Detective Dooley always referred to him as 'Bobby the Hutt', after Jabba the Hutt in *Star Wars*.

'Very well,' she said. 'If Mr Quilty doesn't wish to answer any questions, that's his right in law. However – as you know full well yourself, Mr O'Counihan – if he fails to tell me now anything that he later relies on by way of his defence, the judge will be very much less than amused.'

'I'd say the key to these accusations is evidence, wouldn't you?' Terence O'Counihan replied in a warm, smooth voice. 'May I ask who's going to be standing up in the witness box to confess that my client incited them to murder your unfortunate detective? And may I ask who's going to testify that they were party in any way to the false imprisonment of Mr – what was his name?'

'John Meagher,' said Katie. Her mouth was dry, as if she were reading his name from a gravestone.

'Of course, John Meagher,' said Terence O'Counihan. He spread his hands wide and said, 'But Mr Meagher's whereabouts are still unknown, or so I gather, and apart from some forensics which you claim to have recovered, and which we have not yet had the opportunity to examine ourselves and contest, what evidence do you have to prove that he was falsely imprisoned at all? My client is being in no way uncooperative or obstructive by declining to answer your questions. The plain fact is that there is no case for him to answer.'

'Well, we'll see what the district judge has to say about that,' said Katie. 'Meanwhile, I'm extending Mr Quilty's detention here until we've arranged a time for his appearance in court.'

'I must object to that,' said Terence O'Counihan.

'Your objection is noted, Mr O'Counihan.'

Katie was turning to leave when Bobby Quilty let out a sharp whistle between his front teeth, as if he were calling a dog, and beckoned Terence O'Counihan towards him. Terence O'Counihan leaned over while Bobby Quilty muttered something in his ear. Then he stood up straight again and said, 'My client would like a private word with you, Detective Superintendent if that's possible.'

'What does he mean by that – "a private word"?'

'He's asking if there's somewhere in the building where you and he can go to talk confidentially, without anyone overhearing and without any microphones or other recording equipment. That kind of private.'

'Why would he want to do that?' asked Katie, still not looking at Bobby Quilty directly.

'He says it's a personal matter. But it does have some bearing on the charges against him.'

If any other offender had asked to speak to her in confidence, on a 'personal' matter, Katie would have refused outright. But Kyna and John were in Bobby Quilty's house in Forkhill, in South Armagh, and God alone knew what condition they were in and how they were being treated. She had felt a sickness in her stomach ever since she had talked to Alan Harte, and she kept tasting bile in her mouth, and this morning's coffee.

'All right,' she said. 'If it helps us to clear this matter up.'

'You're welcome to talk in my car, in the car park,' said Terence O'Counihan. 'That would be private.'

'No,' Katie told him. 'For all I know you have a recording device inside it.'

'Or a bomb, even,' put in Detective Sergeant Begley, but nobody laughed.

Katie said, 'We can go upstairs to the fourth floor and out on to the balcony. An officer will be able to keep an eye on us then from inside, but nobody will be able to hear what we're saying.'

'Fair play to you, Detective Superintendent' said Terence O'Counihan. 'Floats like a butterfly, stings like a bee. Sharp as a knife, I should have added.'

* * *

Katie and Bobby Quilty went up to the top floor of the station, accompanied only by a single garda, although he was big and muscular and they could barely all fit into the lift together.

'Ach, this is fierce intimate,' said Bobby Quilty, holding in his belly with both hands. 'But look at the bake on you, Detective Superintendent! You look like a wee bag of weasels the day!'

Katie said nothing, but gave a quick, sour smile.

They went out on to the balcony that overlooked Anglesea Street, although they stayed away from the railing because of the rain. The garda remained inside, his arms folded, watching them bored and stony-faced through the window.

Bobby Quilty took a pack of cigarettes out of his shirt pocket stuck one between his lips.

'There's no smoking in the station,' said Katie.

'Not until now, anyway,' said Bobby Quilty, lighting up his cigarette and blowing smoke out into the rain. The garda took a step towards the door, but Katie raised her hand to indicate that he should stay where he was.

'Well?' said Katie. 'What was this private and personal matter you wanted to talk to me about?'

'Ach, sure, you know yourself that you'll never make those charges stick,' said Bobby Quilty. 'Do you think that I came up the Lagan in a bubble? I respect you, Detective Superintendent Maguire, don't make any mistake about that. But I'm a survivor, and I know how to protect my interests, and you need to give me the credit for that.'

'I give you credit for nothing, Mr Quilty, except for being a dangerous scumbag. You were responsible for Detective Barry being killed, and I have every reason to suspect that it was you who ordered Darragh Murphy to be disposed of so that he couldn't give evidence against you. You told me yourself that you were holding John Meagher, so I don't think I need much more proof of that.'

Bobby Quilty blew more smoke and shook his head in amusement. 'Catch yourself on, will you? As if you'll ever get me to admit that to a judge. No – what I'm trying to say to you now, doll, is what I was trying to explain to you before, but it seems like it fell on deaf ears the last time. You and me, we both have to find a way to rub along together without constantly getting up each other's noses.'

'The thought of getting up *your* nose gives me the gawks, if you must know, Mr Quilty.'

Bobby Quilty laughed and gave another cackling sniff. 'I love you, Detective Superintendent Maguire, do you know that? If you weren't a fecking poll I'd ask you to marry me. I know you have to enforce the law, that's what you get paid for, but at the same time I have to scrape a wee living myself. So if you won't agree to a treaty, I have to have some kind of insurance policy so that you won't keep coming after me and disrupting my business. Like I said to you before, I'm only flogging a few fags at economy prices and there's no desperate harm in that.'

'You're still holding John Meagher, is that what you're telling me?'

'Oh, you catch on quick, no question about that. Yes, Mr Meagher is still a guest of mine and that's how he's going to stay until I'm convinced that you're going to live and let live.'

'How is he? Is he still well?'

'As fit as a butcher's dog. In fact, I'd say he's treating his stay with us as something of a holiday.'

'Don't take me for a fool, Mr Quilty. There was blood on the carpet in that house on Leitrim Street.'

'I wouldn't know about that, Detective Superintendent. Your man is still living and breathing and eating cheesy beanos for breakfast – what more do you want than that? And I would never take you for a fool. I've heard that you have to pass all kinds of fierce hard exams to be a guard. Why, some of the guards I've met, they can count from twenty to one, backwards, and walk forwards at the same time.'

'I don't need to remind you what a serious offence it is, false imprisonment. Not to mention trying to influence a senior police officer by means of menaces.'

'I know that fine rightly, of course. But you haven't left me any alternative, have you? Which is why I wanted to talk to you now, in private. I wanted to let you know that in the light of what you did last night, busting into my house like that, I've doubled my insurance policy and Detective Sergeant Ni Nuallán is now a guest of mine, too.'

'Is she safe?' asked Katie. There was no point in acting surprised. 'She's not hurt in any way?'

Bobby Quilty flicked his cigarette butt over the side of the balcony. 'I think her pride is a wee bit dented, but that's all. She played her part amazing, though, I'll give her that. For a while there she had me believing that she really was some slapper from

Gurra. I even sent her out on a fag run and the boys said she was beezer at it.'

'Who tipped you off?' said Katie.

'Nobody tipped me off, doll,' said Bobby Quilty. He tapped the side of his nose and said, 'I can smell peelers a mile off. It's a kind of a *blue* smell, you know, like rotten fish. You can't mistake it.'

'So you're telling me that you have both John Meagher and Kyna Ni Nuallán as hostages?'

'Hostages! That's the exact fecking word I was looking for and couldn't think of it for the life of me. That's it, Detective Superintendent! Hostages!'

'And in return?'

'In return for them being given bed and board and not beaten on a regular basis, you'll be dropping all of the charges against me and on top of that you'll be recompenserating me for my busted front door.'

Katie stared at him for a long time. Behind him, from the south-west, the grey sky was gradually growing brighter, almost silvery.

'What if I say no?' she said.

'Well, I thought you might be asking me that,' said Bobby Quilty. 'That was the whole reason I wanted us to talk in private, with nobody earwigging. If you say no—'

He didn't finish his sentence. Instead, he drew his finger across his throat and opened his eyes wide, and nodded, and nodded again, to make it clear that he meant it.

Twenty-nine

After Bobby Quilty had been escorted back to the interview room Katie went back upstairs to see Chief Superintendent MacCostagáin.

'Katie!' he said. 'What's the craic? What time are you having your post-mortem on Operation Trident? And you're holding a media briefing directly afterwards, is that right?'

'Yes, sir,' she told him. 'But I wanted to tell you that I've decided to drop the charges against Bobby Quilty. It was probably a misjudgement on my part to arrest him in the first place.'

Chief Superintendent MacCostagáin looked down at the papers on his desk and then looked up at Katie again, and his expression was even more miserable than usual.

'This won't be doing our public image a great deal of good, will it? God knows we've been fighting hard enough to prove to the people of Cork that we're competent and efficient, and that we're making serious progress against organized crime. This is going to set us back badly.'

'It might do, yes, temporarily,' said Katie. 'But I'm totally confident that I can build up enough evidence against Bobby Quilty to bring him in again, sooner rather than later, and on charges that will get us a conviction.'

Chief Superintendent MacCostagáin stood up and went across to the window. 'This is strictly between you and me, Katie, but I know you're a realist. One of the main problems here is that you're a woman, and as you're perfectly well aware, there's still a hard core in the force who resent your promotion, even now.

245

They'll take advantage of every opportunity they can get to see you demoted or removed altogether, and of course that won't go down well with Commissioner O'Sullivan. She's been busting a gut to make sure that women gardaí are given equal advancement, but of all people I don't have to tell *you* that in reality that still means that women officers have to perform twice as well as men. This Bobby Quilty business isn't going to help her cause at all. In fact, to be frank with you, it's an expletive deleted disaster.'

'Yes, sir,' said Katie. 'I'm not making any excuses. But I think it would do our reputation even more damage if we tried to take Bobby Quilty to court on the evidence we have at the moment, or rather the lack of it. He'll make a great big media show out of it and it'll make it harder for us to go after him the next time because he'll accuse us of harassment.'

'And?' asked Chief Superintendent MacCostagáin, turning away from the window. All his years of experience had given him a very sensitive ear and Katie could tell that he had picked up something in her voice – an unspoken 'and' which might have betrayed that she had a much more pressing reason for dropping the charges against Bobby Quilty than the possibility of negative headlines in the *Examiner.*

'And – nothing,' she said. 'Even if the blood that we found on the bedroom carpet in Leitrim Street turns out to be John's, we have no way of proving that Bobby Quilty knew he was there, and even if we did, we have no way of proving that he was responsible for kidnapping him. There's no chance that those two squatters will give evidence against him, even if they really *are* squatters, not unless they want to risk having their heads blown off like Darragh Murphy.'

'So what's your plan?' asked Chief Superintendent Mac-Costagáin.

'I've been working closely already with G2, of course, and we've a heap of circumstantial evidence against Bobby Quilty and all of his associates – phone-taps, emails, surveillance photographs. On top of that, though, I'm hoping to get some more background information from the PSNI. Nobody can spend twenty years running the cross-border rackets that he's been running without leaving *some* incriminating evidence behind them.'

'All right, Katie,' said Chief Superintendent MacCostagáin, in his usual sad voice. 'Good luck with the media so.'

* * *

The atmosphere in the conference room was subdued. There was a strong smell of stale cigarettes and damp clothing, and Katie kept the post-mortem on Operation Trident short and direct.

'I want to thank everybody who took part in Operation Trident. You all carried out your assignments in a highly professional manner, and I particularly wish to compliment the restraint and efficiency of the Regional Support Units. I accept complete responsibility for the outcome, which was obviously not what I had been expecting. I can only plead that I misinterpreted the intelligence that I was given.'

She was quite aware that she was doing herself no favours by accepting the blame for the disaster of Operation Trident. However, if there was anybody in the assembled audience who might be passing information on to Bobby Quilty, she wanted to give them no hint that she was even more determined than ever to see him arrested, charged, and locked up for the rest of his life in Portlaoise maximum security prison.

'I will, of course, be making a full report to the assistant commissioner,' she said. 'Meanwhile, I want you to know that I intend to drop the charges against Bobby Quilty at this time. If you happen to come into contact with him during the course of your duties, I expect you to treat him with the same respect that you give to any other citizen of Cork.'

There was a loud derisory raspberry from someone at the back of the room and a few of the gardaí shook their heads in exasperation, but nobody else had anything else to contribute.

As everybody shuffled out of the conference room, Inspector O'Rourke came up to Katie and said, 'You didn't have to take all the blame, you know, ma'am. You could have come up with some almost nearly true story about Quilty getting wind of it somehow.'

'I would have, if things had been different,' said Katie, snapping shut the clasps on her briefcase.

'Different – like, how?'

'I'm sorry, Francis, you don't have the whole picture yet and I'm not in a position to give it to you. When I can, though, you'll understand at once. Let's just say that if I get myself demoted because of this, it won't kill me. On the other hand, if I'd given out even the slightest suggestion that I suspected anybody here in the station of being a tout for Bobby Quilty—'

Inspector O'Rourke looked at her narrowly for a few moments, expecting her to finish her sentence. When she didn't, but simply raised her eyebrows, he understood what she was telling him, even if he could guess only roughly what it was.

She hated this secrecy, especially since she really felt the need for somebody to confide in, and to support her. Just as she was walking out of the door of the conference room, however, her iPhone pinged with a message. A visitor had arrived for her and was waiting for her downstairs. He didn't have an appointment, but he had said that she would know who he was and why he was here. His name was Alan Harte.

When she arrived at the front desk, a short ginger-haired man was just pushing his way out through the front doors and she thought for a moment that it was him, grown tired of waiting for her. Then she looked across to the opposite side of the reception area and there he was, his face in shadow, wearing a long grey raincoat with shoulders that were still sparkling with raindrops.

'Alan?' she said, and he stepped out of the shadow.

'Katie,' he said, in the same soft Belfast brogue that she had heard on the phone, and held out his hand.

He was tallish, just under six foot she would have guessed, and he looked as if he had once been very slim but had filled out with middle age. His hair was steel-grey, cut short and sharp. His eyes were grey, too – Irish-sky grey. He had a broad face, with strong cheekbones and a square chin. Katie would have guessed some Scottish ancestry. He was carrying a black overnight case.

'You could have let me know you were coming,' said Katie.

'I'm sorry. I didn't know myself until this morning.'

'Come up to my office,' she said – then, as soon as she had pressed the button for the lift, 'What about Kyna and John? Have you seen them?'

Alan nodded. 'I have, yes. That's the main reason I'm here. I could have called you or texted you, but you never know who might be hacking your phone and I didn't want to risk it. I drove down to Forkhill at first light this morning, even though it wasn't very light. I parked my car about a half a mile away from the house and walked through the fields so that I could sneak my way into the paddock at the back. It was lashing down so there was nobody outside in the yard, and I doubt they expected anybody else to be out there, either.'

The lift arrived and Katie and Alan stepped in. Close up to him, Katie caught a smell like a combination of black pepper and cinnamon. Maybe it was some aftershave that he was wearing, or maybe just his shower gel.

'How did they look?' said Katie. 'The last time you saw John they were carrying him on a stretcher, weren't they?'

'They were in a large downstairs room at the back. Your friend John was lying propped up with a cushion on a couch and your detective sergeant – what was her name, Kyna? – she was sitting beside him in armchair. So far as I could make out, she was feeding him out of a bowl with a spoon. I don't know what that says about his physical condition. The room was gloomy enough so it wasn't easy to see them too distinctly. They were alive, anyway. I was going to take some pictures but then some wee man came into the room and pulled the curtains across.'

'And you're sure they didn't see you?'

'Not a chance. I was hiding myself beside this tool shed, and like I say it was lashing. I stayed there about ten minutes longer, trying to see if I could pick up a phone signal, although I had no luck with that. Nobody came out, though, so they obviously didn't know I was there.'

'And you're sure it was them? Kyna and John?'

'No question at all. It was fair gloomy in that room, like I say, but I recognized them straightaway from the pictures on your bulletin. They looked tired and kind of nervous, but if they were being fed I'd say that was something to be optimistic about. If you were intending to kill a pig you'd feed it up, but a human being? You wouldn't bother, would you? Why waste good food?'

Katie gave him a quick sideways look. 'That's not very encouraging.'

'I know, I'm sorry. I didn't mean it like that. Too many years being a copper, that's my trouble. I think it's made me impervious to other people's feelings. I'm not even sure I have too many of my own any more.'

'I've dropped the charges against Bobby Quilty,' said Katie, as they entered her office and she switched on the lights. 'I should never have arrested him in the first place. I suppose I was hoping that St Francis would conjure up some miraculous piece of evidence before I had to let him go.'

'So what happened?' asked Alan.

Katie sat down at her desk, but Alan remained standing. She told him as briefly as possible how Operation Trident had gone so disastrously wrong, and how Bobby Quilty had been one step ahead of her and made a mockery of each of the three simultaneous raids. Alan nodded when she told him about Darragh Murphy being shot, and nodded again when she described what they had found at the house on Leitrim Street – or rather, what they had failed to find.

'Tip-off,' he said. 'You have a tout there, no question about it.'

'Oh, no doubt at all,' said Katie. 'The problem is, I have no idea at all who it could be. To begin with, only a handful of people knew that I'd asked Kyna to work undercover for Bobby Quilty, but on the night we had to warn the Regional Support Unit that she might be inside his house, in case it came to a firefight and they shot her by mistake.'

'Believe me, Bobby Quilty was doing the same in Armagh,' said Alan. 'What makes him so hard to scoop is that he has contacts in all walks of life – politicians, business executives, prostitutes, criminals. He knows everybody from Bamba's Crown to Cranfield Point, I can tell you. He knows bank managers, so that he can easily find out if any police officers are having a struggle financially. He knows hotel keepers, who tell him if they're having affairs with any woman that they shouldn't be. He knows club owners and drug-dealers, so he's always aware if they've ended up addicted to the crack that they're supposed to be confiscating. At the very least he always has three or four poor peelers who are going to be passing him inside information, either in exchange for cash, or for keeping his mouth shut, or for not posting pornographic photographs of them on Twitter for their wives to see. He'll have at least one tout here in Anglesea Street, possibly more than one. As you say, though, Katie, the problem is finding out who. It could be anybody at all, from the highest to the lowest.'

'Well, I have some ideas how I can winkle them out,' said Katie. 'In the meantime, though, what do you suggest we do about Kyna and John?'

'I'd recommend absolutely nothing at the moment. Bobby Quilty's going to be confident now that so long as he holds them hostage, you'll be leaving him well enough alone. He's not so stupid that he'll kill the geese that guarantee him the golden eggs. We had a similar situation in Belfast in 1988. The Provos kidnapped the owner of Sheen's department store and said that they would only return him in exchange for two of their own men who had been caught by the RUC the previous week. The poor store owner suffered a heart attack and died, so the Provos no longer had anything to bargain with. That lesson won't have been lost on Bobby Quilty.'

'So, what else are you doing here?' Katie asked him. 'You didn't come all this way just to tell me about Kyna and John, did you?'

'To be honest with you, Katie, I thought I could maybe help you to do for Bobby Quilty once and for all. I'll admit it's personal, but the man's a general menace. If you could let me look through all of the intelligence that you have on him and I can see first-hand for myself what kind of a set-up he's running here in Cork, there's a fair chance I might spot something that you've overlooked without realizing it, do you know what I mean? If I can help you to build up a strong case against him that will stand up in court, and see the bastard sent down, it'll be like five Christmases rolled into one, I'm telling you.'

'You understand that I couldn't allow you to do that officially? I mean, the Garda and the PSNI swap officers all the time, but you're not an officer any more, and all of the intelligence on Bobby Quilty is highly confidential. If I let you look at it, you'll see how we acquired it, and the names of our informants, and that's all confidential, too, of course.'

'I get that, Katie. And I'm not even a former officer. I'm an *ex*-officer. But this is a fierce unusual problem we're up against here and it's going to take some fierce unorthodox measures to solve it.'

'I don't know, Alan,' said Katie. 'I'll have to give this some very serious thought. I can't see Chief Superintendent MacCostagáin agreeing to it. He's a stickler for protocol, and it's not like you retired from the service in a blaze of glory, if you'll forgive me saying so.'

'I understand that, of course. But I was hoping you might take me on as a kind of unofficial adviser. Let's face it, Katie, what are the options? The second you tell anyone here that Kyna and John are being held hostage, and that you want to raid Bobby Quilty's house to rescue them, Quilty will get to hear of it and the best you can hope for is that you find their bodies. It would be exactly the same if I tried to persuade Chief Superintendent Shields in Armagh to do the same.'

'I know,' said Katie. She was about to answer him, but she knew he was right.

Alan stood there watching her for a while, saying nothing. She opened the file on her desk in front of her, which was a lengthy report on the tightening of border controls between the Republic and the United Kingdom because of the number of illegal migrants who were using Ireland as a back door into England. She read the first two paragraphs and then closed it.

'Where are you staying?' she asked.

'Jury's probably, on the Western Road. I brought my toothbrush with me and a change of gunks.'

'Look – I have a media briefing in ten minutes,' Katie told him. 'It shouldn't take long. I'll take you to the canteen if you like and you can have a coffee while you're waiting. We can talk some more afterwards.'

'Aye, grand, that's fine by me. I've all the time in world, so I have.'

* * *

The usual crowd of reporters and freelance journalists had arrived for the media briefing – although Dan Keane from the *Examiner* was in hospital for X-rays on his lungs and Roisin Magorian was standing in for him, a quiet, thin, sharp-looking woman in a dark green linen suit. Her lips were almost always tightly pursed, which had led Detective Sergeant Begley to christen her 'the Pencil Sharpener'.

Fionnuala Sweeney was there, too, as well as Branna Mac-Suibhne from the *Echo* and Muireann Bourke from Newstalk.

Superintendent Pearse joined Katie to give her moral support and explain the logistics of Operation Trident.

'Everything went exactly as planned,' he said, by way of conclusion. 'No firearms were discharged, no gardaí were injured, and there was no risk to the public at any time. It was a textbook operation from beginning to end.'

'Well, one firearm was discharged, wasn't it?' asked Roisin Magorian, holding up her pencil. 'The firearm that killed Darragh Murphy.'

'I'm sorry, but that was done several hours before Operation Trident was actioned,' said Superintendent Pearse. 'And not by us.'

'You say it was a textbook operation, but the man you wanted for killing Detective Barry was murdered before you could arrest him. Not only that, there was no hostage in the house on Leitrim Street where you suspected there was one, and even though you arrested Bobby Quilty you later dropped both of the charges against him and released him. What kind of a textbook operation was that?'

Katie said, 'Our failure to get a satisfactory result from Operation Trident was entirely down to me. I was given intelligence which I interpreted to the best of my ability, but the intelligence turned out to be misleading, to say the least. That's not to say we shouldn't have acted on it, or that there was any mishandling of the operation whatsoever. If the information had in fact been correct and we had failed to act on it, we would have been guilty of gross dereliction of our duty and it could have resulted in injury or even death.'

She paused, and looked at theTV camera, and added, 'I'm not infallible. None of us are. But I would rather be guilty of making an error of judgement than guilty of causing the death of an innocent person by failing to respond to what seemed like genuine information.'

'I spoke to Mr Quilty before I came here,' said Roisin Magorian. 'If you'll forgive me for quoting him more or less verbatim, he says that the Cork Garda have a certain part of their anatomy hanging out of the window while their grannie throws snowballs at it.'

'Mr Quilty is entitled to express his opinion in whatever language he chooses, provided it isn't obscene or slanderous.'

'However, he says that he isn't a vindictive man and that he's satisfied that his future relations with the Garda are going to be cordial. *Warm*, even. Would you agree with that?'

'An Garda Siochána will treat Mr Quilty in the same way that we treat every other citizen of Cork, no matter who they are.'

'No special treatment, then, in case he sues you for wrongful arrest?'

'No comment,' said Katie. 'In fact, that's a question that doesn't deserve an answer.'

'There's no need to get stooky about it, Detective Super-intendent' said Roisin Magorian. 'I was only asking. You can't deny that the Garda have given preferential treatment to certain people in the past, naming no names.'

'Can I ask what progress you're making with the murder of Darragh Murphy?' put in Branna MacSuibhne.

'Nothing dramatic so far,' said Inspector O'Rourke. 'Several Parklands residents saw a yellowy Volvo estate waiting at the end of the alley that runs behind the houses in Darragh Murphy's street. It was there for at least twenty minutes with its motor running, which is one of the reasons it caught their attention. One witness said she saw a skinny feen in a grey hoodie walking out of the alley and climbing into the Volvo and then it immediately drove off.'

He looked down at his notes and then he said, 'She told our officer, "Your man was walking very quick, like he thought the Devil was close behind him but didn't want to turn around to look, and once he'd jumped into it, the car took off with its tyres screaming like all the bats of hell."'

'Could this have been the same Volvo estate you were looking for after the murder of Detective Barry?' asked Branna.

'I won't deny that's a possibility,' said Inspector O'Rourke. 'However, none of the witnesses at Parklands made a note of the vehicle's index marks. We still have a name and address for the owner of the Volvo that may have been involved in the incident in which Detective Barry was fatally injured, but we haven't yet been able to trace him. Charles Daly, of Rathpeacon. The address was real enough, but there's nobody living there who matches the name in which the vehicle was registered. We're still making inquiries of course.'

'You wanted to talk to Darragh Murphy in regard to the death of Detective Barry,' said Muireann Bourke. 'Now that he's dead, does that mean that the case is closed? Or do you have other suspects?'

'The case is still very much open,' said Katie. 'As yet we have no conclusive proof that Darragh Murphy was responsible for fatally injuring Detective Barry, or that other parties weren't involved. That's all I have to say for now.'

After the media conference had ended, Katie was about to go back to the canteen when Roisin Magorian caught up with her.

'What's the story, Roisin? Anything more I can help you with?'

Roisin reached into her bulging green leather tote bag and took out a springbound notebook. 'This is nothing to do with Operation Trident, Detective Superintendent. This is another story I've been working on altogether.'

'Go on.'

Roisin Magorian had a pair of half-glasses hanging around her neck and she perched them on to the end of her nose. 'I have a friend who has a friend who's an accountant for the Diamond Club casino. He told me in confidence that some very influential people in Cork have desperate gambling debts, some of them running into six figures.'

'That doesn't surprise me one bit,' said Katie. 'You remember that case we had only last year, don't you – that manager at AIB? He'd lost a fortune at the roulette table – a fortune! – and so he lent himself nearly a quarter of a million euros from his customers' accounts so that he could save himself from having his legs broken. Well, when I say "lent", he was never going to be able to pay it all back.'

'This is much more serious, in its way,' said Roisin Magorian. 'There are several politicians who have run up enormous gambling debts and they've borrowed money to keep their creditors off their backs. At least three county councillors and a TD, too. Not just politicians, either. A senior manager in Revenue and a buyer of pharmaceuticals for the HSE. *And* – a senior officer in the Cork Garda. Which is why I'm asking you about it.'

'Do you know who it is?' asked Katie.

'No. Your man from the Diamond Club wouldn't name any names because it would be more than his job's worth. In fact, he said it might be even more risky than that. Most of the money has been lent by sources with powerful vested interests, like developers looking for planning permission, or drug companies that want their product bought by the health service at an inflated price. Or, in some cases, by criminals – criminals who wouldn't be too happy if it got out who they'd been lending money to.'

'Do you have any evidence for this at all, apart from what this fellow from the Diamond Club told you?'

'Some. But I'm gathering more day by day. I just wanted to ask you if you had any inkling that it was true, and if you know that at least one of your senior officers is up to his ears in gambling debt.'

'You're taking a chance, aren't you? It might be a "she", not a "he". It might be me, for all you know.'

'No, I may not know his name yet, but it's a "he".'

Katie could see that Inspector O'Rourke was waiting to talk to her. 'I'm sorry, Roisin,' she said. 'You know more about this than I do. Even if I do find out, I'm not at all sure that I'll be telling you.'

'Well, we'll see,' said Roisin Magorian. 'You might be inclined to, in return for some information from me. I may not know who your gambling Garda officer is, but I'm pretty sure who it was that lent him the money.'

Katie waited for her to continue, but Roisin Magorian did nothing more than tuck her notebook back into her tote bag. 'Good luck to you, DS Maguire,' she told her, and turned to go.

Katie was tempted to call her back, but she knew that she wouldn't tell her any more. She went to join Inspector O'Rourke and make her way back to the canteen where Alan was waiting for her.

'How do you reckon that went?' asked Inspector O'Rourke.

'Not quite as bad as I'd expected. But let's wait until we see the *Six One News* and tomorrow morning's papers.'

* * *

Alan looked up from the copy of the *Echo* he had been reading and said, 'How did it go?'

'As well as could be expected,' said Katie, pulling out a chair and sitting opposite him. 'In other words, somewhere between desperate and disastrous.'

'Have you had any word from upstairs yet?'

'Nothing so far, but I'm sure I will. Jimmy O'Reilly isn't going to let me get away with making a hames of an expensive operation like that. It's all budget with him. That man, I'll tell you. He wouldn't spend Christmas.'

She wondered why she was talking to Alan like this. After all, she hardly knew him. She hadn't even checked if he really had been a detective inspector with the PSNI. But she felt exhausted with worry and badly in need of an ally. Apart from that, he was the only other person who knew where John and Kyna were, and what danger they were in, and everything he had said had rung true so far.

'You look tired, if you don't mind my saying so,' Alan told her.

Katie scruffed her hand through her hair. 'I'm fair beat out, if you must know.'

'Then why don't we leave this till tomorrow? If you don't want me seen around here too often, we could always meet for breakfast.'

'No, I won't be able to sleep until we've talked through how we're going to handle this. I probably won't be able to sleep anyway. I keep getting this picture in my head of John lying on a couch and Kyna feeding him, the way you described it. I mean, like, Mother of God, John was a very fit man.'

'We have to take it careful, Katie. If we try to rush this, it's going to end up like your Operation Trident, only worse. We have to nail Bobby Quilty before we do anything else, and nail him securely.'

'Don't worry, I'll make sure you get copies of all the intelligence we have on him,' said Katie. She was becoming aware that other gardaí in the canteen had noticed her talking to Alan and were obviously wondering who he was and why they were having what must have looked like such an intimate conversation. Katie's personal life was even more riveting to her fellow officers at Anglesea Street than their four-times-a-week dose of *Fair City*.

'How did you get here?' she asked Alan. 'Did you drive?'

'Came on the train,' he told her. 'I didn't fancy driving for four and a half hours in weather like this, and besides there's five kilometres of resurfacing works on the E201 at Two-Mile Borris.'

Katie couldn't help thinking to herself: *Even if he never was a detective inspector, he certainly sounds like one.*

'Listen,' she said. 'Instead of going to Jury's, why don't you come back to Cobh with me? I've a spare room and it'll cost you nothing. I have to take my dog for his walk and get myself something to eat. That's if you don't mind reheated lasagne. It's home-made, not Tesco's best.'

'Katie, I didn't come here to impose on you. I can see that you have quite enough on your plate already, so you have.'

'No, it wouldn't be an imposition. I'd be glad of the company right now, to be honest with you. There's not a lot of consolation in talking to yourself, like.'

* * *

They drove to Katie's house on Carrig View in Cobh and it rained harder and harder all the way there. When they climbed out of her car and hurried to the front porch, Katie noticed the living-room curtain in the Tierney's house next door twitching back and Jenny Tierney peering out to see who it was. Oh, there'd be some chinwagging now all right. *C'mere till I tell you, that Detective Maguire brought a feller home with her last night and he didn't leave until the morning so.*

Barney greeted Alan with his usual suspicious snuffling, but when he realized that Katie was quite comfortable with him he relaxed and went into the kitchen to make some loud lapping noises in his water bowl.

'Sorry about the sniffing,' said Katie.

'Oh, don't worry. They say that dogs can sniff if a man has prostate cancer, so I'm relieved that he's given me the all-clear.'

'Would you care for a drop of coffee?' asked Katie, walking into the living room. Her table lamps were on timers but it had grown so dark so early that she switched them on herself.

'No, no thanks. I've been drinking coffee all day. If I have any more caffeine I'll be gibbering like a baboon.'

'A beer, then?'

'All right, twist my arm. It's a little early for me, but the sun's gone down. It's not visible, any road.'

Katie switched on the television. The *Six One News* would be on in five minutes and she wanted to hear Fionnuala Sweeney's report on Operation Trident. She went into the kitchen and came back with a bottle of Murphy's and a glass for Alan, then she poured herself a vodka and topped it up with lemonade.

'So tell me about yourself,' she said, sitting down on the couch next to him and tucking her feet up.

Alan shrugged. 'There's not much to tell. If I'd followed my heart maybe there would have been. I always wanted to be a musician and have my own folk band, The Cuchulains I was going to call them, do you know? But my older brother went off to England to work in insurance, and my younger brother got himself a managerial job with Green Isle Foods, and my sister married this Belgian fellow she met on holiday, a bit of a looper but pleasant enough, and went off to live in Belgian land.'

'What happened to The Cuchulains?'

'Oh, they never came to nothing, sadly. The problem was that our da was a chief inspector in the RUC. There've been Hartes in the Northern Ireland police service since my great-grandfather was a county inspector for the Royal Irish Constabulary in 1912, and my da was dead set on the family name being carried down through the generations.'

Katie shook her head and smiled. 'You don't have to tell me. You were the only one left and you didn't want to let him down. That was exactly what happened to me. Seven Maguire sisters and the only one to join the Garda was muggins.'

'Still, Katie, fair play to you, you've done yourself proud. And your father proud, too. My da's dead and buried now, but he was mortified when I had to leave the service. Mortified!'

'Are you married?' Katie asked him, nodding towards the gold ring on his wedding finger.

'Separated. Coming up for eight years now. Somehow we never got around to divorcing, and somehow I never got around to taking off this ring. I suppose if nothing else it's a great contraceptive.'

They watched the *Six One News*. A major fire had gutted a whiskey distillery in Midleton, with seven workers injured and three still missing. There had also been a critical vote in the Dáil on further cuts to the health service, so the report on Operation Trident had been dropped altogether.

'There you are, Katie,' said Alan. 'There is a God.'

Katie finished her drink and stood up. 'I'm not so sure about that. I still have to take Barney for his evening patrol and it's flogging outside.'

'Hey, I'll come with you, so I will. There's no point in just the one of us getting skited.'

As soon as Barney heard her take his lead down from the hook in the hall he came running out of the kitchen.

'Look at him,' said Katie. 'He thinks I'm going to take him all the way down to Whitepoint Drive to see his girlfriend, Oona. Sorry, Barns, not on a night like this. We're going as far as the ferry and back again, and that's it, and if you don't do your business by then you'll just have to bottle it up till the morning.'

Alan laughed, and Katie turned to him, and suddenly realized for the first time in days that she had something to smile about, no matter how briefly.

Thirty

'Oh, Jesus!' John cried out. He sounded desperate, as if he had been trying to keep silent for the past half-hour but couldn't contain his agony any longer. 'Oh Jesus – oh holy Jesus, my feet!'

Kyna opened her eyes. The clock outside in the hallway had only just struck half past seven and the overhead light was still on, but she had been awkwardly curled up in her armchair trying to sleep. She was exhausted, and there was nothing else to do in this large, dull, brown-wallpapered room – no television, no radio, no books, not even a newspaper, and the only picture on the walls was an autumn landscape of County Fermanagh that was almost as brown as the wallpaper.

When John started moaning, however, Kyna lifted herself out of her armchair and went across to the couch to kneel down beside him. She said, 'Ssh, I'm here, John,' and gently laid her hand on his forehead. He felt chilled and sweaty, and he was trembling uncontrollably from head to foot.

'They'll have to call a doctor for you,' she told him. 'You can't go on like this. You'll get blood poisoning, if you haven't already. Let me look at your feet.'

John shook his head. 'No, no, please don't touch them. Please. It's like they're on fire. It's like they're on fire and my legs are starting to burn, too.'

'John, you have to let me take a look. I might be able to clean them up for you. If you leave them wrapped up like that they're only going to get worse. You could die from septicaemia.'

John was wearing only the dirty blue shirt and boxer shorts

that he had been wearing when he had first been snatched on his way to the Hayfield Manor. His legs were bare, but both of his feet were swaddled in thick white towels – the left towel very much larger than the right, more like a bath towel, so it looked disproportionately huge. Both towels, though, were stained with brown and yellow blotches, and they smelled strongly of dried blood and pus.

Even before she started to unwind them, Kyna was disturbed to see that John's calves were swollen and red, almost up to his knees.

'I'll be as gentle as I can,' she said. John nodded, gripping the edge of the cushion with one hand and pushing the knuckle joint of his other hand into his mouth and biting it.

She lifted up his left leg and carefully began to unwind the towel. John sucked in his breath and bit harder on his hand. Although she hated to hurt him, she knew she couldn't let his feet continue to fester like this.

With every layer she unwound, the brown and yellow stains became wider and wetter and the smell became stronger. She retched, although she tried to suppress it because she didn't want to John to become any more distressed than he was already. All she had eaten since this morning was a ham and tomato sandwich that Ger had bought at a petrol station on the way here, so she had nothing to bring up except saliva.

When she finally dragged off the last corner of the bath towel, she could see how badly John's feet had become infected. His whole foot was swollen and purple and his toes were black. The hole that Chisel had drilled through his foot was now clogged with glistening greenish-beige pus.

She stared at it helplessly. She couldn't bandage up his foot again, not with the same sodden towel, but she had nothing to clean it with. She always had make-up wipes in her bag, but Ger had taken that away from her, and in any case they wouldn't have been enough to clean out John's suppurating wounds. All she had now was the clothes in which she had first met Bobby Quilty, which Margot had washed for her: her pink TROUBLE

T-shirt, sports bra and skinny black jeans. Ger had even taken her shoes.

She turned to John. He was biting his knuckle so hard that blood was sliding down his wrist and his eyes were crammed with tears. He was in so much pain that he couldn't even look at her.

She laid her hand gently on his forehead again and then she said, 'That's it, John. They have to call a doctor for you. You need to be in hospital.'

John took his hand out of his mouth and said, 'Please, Kyna, for the love of God. I can't take this take any more. I don't care if they kill me. Just make it stop.'

Kyna stood up and went to the living-room door. She banged on it with both fists and shouted out, 'Open the door! Open the door! We need a doctor! You have to send for a doctor!'

She stopped, and listened, but all she could hear was the muffled sound of a television in another room.

'*Open this fecking door, you bastards!*' she screamed, and beat at the door panels even harder. '*We need a doctor! This man is dying in here! Open this fecking door!*'

She waited again. This time she could hear the television suddenly become louder as a door was opened, and then footsteps coming along the corridor outside. The key was turned and the door pushed inwards, so that she had to step back two or three paces. Ger was standing there, beaky-nosed, smoking, barefoot, in a crumpled striped shirt with no collar and his usual raspberry chinos. He was still wearing his huge dark glasses, and even indoors he was wearing his stained white hat.

'What the feck is this all this fecking commotion for, girl?' he demanded. 'Jesus, you're making as much noise as ten pigs stuck in a gate!'

'It's John,' said Kyna. 'He needs a doctor, urgently. Look at his foot. I mean, *look* at it, will you, he's going to die of the blood poisoning if we don't get him treated.'

Ger wrinkled up his nose and looked at John over Kyna's shoulder. 'Mother of God, I don't have to look at his fecking foot, I can smell it from here. Worse than a knacker's flange. I don't know how you can stand it. Except you don't have the choice, do you?'

'You need to call for an ambulance,' said Kyna.

'Oh, is that right? So I call for an ambulance and then what happens? The paramedics will want to know what happened to your man's feet and who he is and what he's after doing here, won't they? And I don't suppose you'll be keeping your bake shut either, will you, Sidhe, or whatever your fecking name is?'

Kyna tried to snatch at Ger's sleeve and pull him into the room so that he could see close up how badly infected John's feet were. He wrenched his sleeve free from her and said, 'Away to feck, would you? There's feck all I can do about it. If I call for an ambulance, the next person who'll be needing a fecking ambulance will be myself, don't you have any doubts about that. And you, too, more than likely.'

'At least fetch me a bowl of hot water and something I can bandage his feet with. And maybe you have some disinfectant – iodine, anything will do. And some Nurofen, if you have it, or aspirin. Anything. He's in terrible pain.'

'You have some nerve, you know,' Ger told her. 'Making out you're some skanger and all the time you're an undercover guard. My sense of smell fair let me down then, I should have smelled bacon the minute you walked into the pub. Mind you, it's come back since. The stink in here is pure mank. I'm not codding, I'd feel sorry for you if you weren't a shade.'

Kyna was close to tears. 'Have you no heart in you at all, for God's sake? Look at the state of him. All I'm asking you for is some hot water and some disinfectant, and a few bits of old torn-up sheet or something to bandage his feet with. If he dies, you'll be done for manslaughter at the very least.'

'If he *dies*, darling, nobody will ever find him, or know what became of him, and the same will go for you, too. The Big Feller doesn't like to leave evidence behind him or people to open their yaps and say what he did.'

'*Please*,' Kyna begged him.

After thinking and smoking for a few moments, Ger nodded and said, 'Okay. I'll see what I can do. But, you know,' and as he said this he looked Kyna up and down, 'maybe there's something that you can do for me in return, do you know what I mean, like?'

Kyna said, 'Please, whatever you want. Just fetch me something to clean his feet.'

'That's a promise, like?'

Kyna closed her eyes and nodded. She couldn't imagine that Ger could do anything worse to her than Bobby Quilty.

When Ger had gone, she knelt down beside John again and held his hand. John was still trembling, but he managed to glance at her quickly two or three times and say, 'Katie – does Katie know about this?'

'I'm sure she does. Maybe she doesn't know exactly where we are, but she'll find us. You know she will.'

'Do *you* know where we are?'

'Not exactly. But we must have been driving for at least three hours, and judging by their accents I'd say we're north of the border somewhere. Probably South Armagh, because that's where Bobby Quilty comes from originally.'

'Holy Mary, Mother of God, my feet hurt. Even if they won't call for a doctor at least they must have some painkillers.'

'I've asked him. Whether he brings some or not, I couldn't tell you.'

'I walked out on her,' said John.

'Katie? Yes, I know.'

'Did she tell you why? She was expecting another man's baby and I was jealous. Seems petty, doesn't it, when you look at me now? Hurting so much that I can hardly think and expecting her to come and rescue me.'

'She lost the baby.'

'I know. I heard. I know one of the radiographers at CUH.' He paused and clenched his teeth, his face a mask of a suffering. After a while, though, he relaxed a little and said, 'Comes in waves.

266

One second I feel better, the next I feel like I'm being cremated alive, feet first.'

He clenched his teeth again and groaned in the back of his throat. Then he breathed out and said, 'She didn't – she didn't get rid of the baby because of me, did she?'

Kyna said, 'No. She was going to keep it. We even talked about names. Brendan, she was thinking of, if it was a boy, or Cliona if it was a girl. She liked the idea of naming a little girl after a fairy.'

'I was worried it was my fault.'

'Then you don't know Katie very well, do you? Katie takes total responsibility for everything she does, no matter how bad it is. No – she had a serious scuffle with some scummer while she was trying to make an arrest and got herself kicked. She hasn't got over it, even now.'

John turned his head and looked at Kyna through eyes that were slitted with pain. 'You almost sound as if you know her better than me.'

Kyna squeezed his hand and tried to smile, and said, 'I love her.'

They heard the key in the door again and Kyna stood up. Ger came into the room, followed by one of the men who had helped carry John into the house on a stretcher – an unshaven, narrow-faced man in a dark grey turtleneck sweater, his hair brushed forward in a widow's peak.

Ger was carrying a grubby white flannelette sheet over his arm. He rolled it up and threw it over to Kyna. 'There, that's the best I can do you in the way of bandages.'

'This is filthy,' said Kyna. 'This is only going to make the infection even worse.'

'Well, in case of that, I fetched you some disinfectant,' said Ger. He turned around to the man with the widow's peak, who handed him a blue plastic bottle of Domestos bleach, with the top already taken off. He walked over to the couch where John was lying and held up the bottle as if it were the Olympic torch.

'What are you *doing*?' asked Kyna. John looked up at him in pain and bewilderment.

267

'First aid, that's what they call it, isn't it?' said Ger, and poured undiluted bleach all over John's exposed left foot.

The only scream that Kyna had ever heard that was higher and more agonized than the scream John let out then was when a young woman had thrown herself in front of a train at Heuston station in Dublin. He arched his back and dug his fingers into the seat cushions and kicked his left leg again and again as if he were trying to kick it off. He was incoherent with pain.

Kyna dropped to her knees and twisted the sheet that Ger had given her around John's foot. She tried frantically to dab the bleach out of the blackened, pus-clogged cavity that Chisel's drill hole had now become, but every time she touched it John's whole body went into a spasm and he started to pant as if he had been running to the point of exhaustion. At last he clutched at her arm and said, 'Stop, stop, Kyna, leave it, leave it, don't touch it any more!'

'Oh, Kyna, is it?' said Ger. 'So that's your real name? You're not Sidhe then, after all?'

'Fetch some hot water!' Kyna told him, standing up. 'You could have killed him with shock, doing a stupid thing like that, you gowl!'

'What did you fecking call me?' Ger demanded. He brandished the Domestos bottle in front of Kyna's face and said, 'How would you like a splash of this straight in your eyes, Miss Undercover Shade?'

'Just stop acting the maggot, will you, and fetch me some hot water,' Kyna screamed at him, 'If you don't, I'll go fetch it myself and damn you!'

Ger swung back the bottle. Before he had the chance to throw any bleach at her, however, Kyna spun around and kicked him in the face, her right heel hitting his left cheekbone so hard that his neck jerked sideways. His sunglasses snapped and his dirty white hat flew off. He staggered backwards in a complicated dance, dropping the bottle of bleach so that it emptied down one leg of his chinos. He nearly fell over but the man with the widow's peak made a grab for his upper arm and he managed to regain his balance.

Without his hat, Kyna saw that Ger was almost bald, except for a few stray clumps of wild grey hair. Without his dark glasses, she saw that he was blind in one eye. His right eye was totally white and bulging in its socket, like a hard-boiled quail's egg.

He bent down and picked up his hat, jamming it back on to his head at a rakish angle, as if he had done it for comic effect. The man with the widow's peak found his dark glasses on the floor and handed them to him, but the right lens was missing and Ger slung them across the room in a fury.

He advanced on Kyna, holding up both fists. Kyna stayed where she was, tense but calm, her knees slightly bent and both hands lifted, and it was obvious that she wasn't afraid of him at all – not in a fair fight, anyway.

Ger's chin was tilted upwards and his one good eye was wide open, staring at Kyna without blinking.

'Ger – don't try it, Ger,' Kyna warned him. 'It's not worth it. You won't prove anything except that you're older and slower and blinder and that I can give you a fierce bad beating if I want to.'

Ger thought for a moment. He opened and closed his mouth as if he were about to say something, but then thought better of it. He slowly lowered his fists, stepped back and said, 'No, maybe you're right, girl. Maybe you're right. I wouldn't stand a chance in hell against all that martial arts jiggery-pokery of yours, now, would I? That take-one-door or whatever the feck you call it.'

'*Now* can I have some hot water?' said Kyna.

'Sure, yes. Absolutely. Of course you can. Grady, there's a plastic bowl under the sink in the kitchen. Fill that up with hot water, will you, boy, and bring it back here, quick as you like.'

The man with the widow's peak left the living room. Kyna knelt down beside John again and took hold of his hand. 'John?' she said. 'How are you feeling?'

John's eyelids were fluttering and he was licking his lips as if he were thirsty, but he was only barely conscious and he didn't answer. Very carefully, she unwound the towel that was still wrapped around his right foot, and when she lifted it away she could see that his right foot was even more seriously infected than the left one. It was charcoal-black from his toes to his ankle and glistening with thin liquid pus, as if it had been varnished.

Ger was standing close behind her. He whistled and said, 'Jesus Christ on a fecking wagon wheel! That feller's going to be needing some replacement plates of meat, if you ask me.'

The man with the widow's peak came back with another, younger man, who was carrying a blue plastic washbasin half filled with steaming water. The younger man set it down beside Kyna and grinned at her as he did so. He had fair curly hair thick with dandruff and raging red spots and he was wearing a red baseball cap backwards. He smelled strongly of skunk.

'Thank you,' said Kyna.

'Oh, you're very welcome,' he told her. As he stood up, however, he seized her left arm, gripping it very tight, and at the same time the man with the widow's peak took hold of her right arm.

'You – *bastards*! Let – *go* of me! *Let go!*' she shrilled at them, trying to wrench herself free, but the two of them were far too strong for her and they hauled her up on to her feet. She bent her knees so that they would have to drop down to the floor, but she weighed less than fifty kilos and they easily held her up between them, even with her feet in the air. They turned her around to face Ger and she could see by the look on his face that he hadn't forgiven her for kicking him and breaking his dark glasses, not one bit. His left cheekbone was crimson and swollen now, and his one good eye was beginning to close up.

'Do you know what happened to the last old doll who tried to hit me?' he said, and gave her a grin. 'I have to say *tried*, because you're the only old doll who's ever succeeded. But even though she only tried, she got herself beat up so bad that her own mother couldn't recognize her when we dropped her off home, and I'm not shitting you, I promise.'

Kyna lowered her feet to the floor and took a deep breath. 'Let me tell you this, Ger. I was shot in the stomach less than six months ago. I'm still recovering. Look here, if you don't believe me.'

Even though the man with the widow's peak was holding her arm, she was able to lift up her TROUBLE T-shirt to show him the swastika-shaped scar next to her navel. Ger stared at it and then said, 'All right, doll, I believe you. What the feck does that have to do with the grass and the goose on the side of a mountain?'

'If you beat me, I'll start to bleed again internally and you won't be able to stop it and I'll die. You probably won't give a damn yourself, but Bobby Quilty will. Why do you think he's gone to all of the trouble to keep me and John here as hostages? In fact, if you kill me, he'll probably kill *you*, and if he doesn't they'll find my body whatever you say and you'll be done for murder.'

Ger couldn't stop himself from grinning. 'Fair play to you, girl, I think that's the best fecking excuse for not getting beat up that I ever heard anybody come out with.'

'You can call it an excuse but you know it's true,' Kyna told him. She was trying to sound brave, but her heart was beating so hard against her ribcage that it hurt, and she had wet herself a little.

Ger came up very close to her so that she was almost suffocated by the smell of stale tobacco and alcohol. She had always dreamed that she would die in some loving woman's arms, with the sun going down and filling the bedroom with its last tangerine light – not beaten to death in a shabby living room by a one-eyed criminal with poisonous breath.

'No beating, then,' said Ger. But then he grasped both of her shoulders and tilted his head back. For a split second she wondered if he were going to give her some kind of mock-benediction, but then he butted her hard in the face with his forehead. Her nasal bone snapped and blood gushed out of her nostrils, and her knees gave way from under her. The two men let her collapse on to the floor, concussed, both of her eyes rolled up like Ger's one blind eye.

John was still unconscious, too. Ger looked over at him and then down at Kyna, and said, 'There. Let that be a fecking lesson to the both of them. Don't try messing with Ger Daley because that's what you'll get. Grady – find my glimmers for me, would you, boy, and the lens that dropped out of them? See if you can't stick them back together for me.'

He left the room. Grady and the spotty young man scouted around the floor for his sunglasses and the missing lens, giggling to each other like children, and once they had found them they left the room, too, and locked the door behind them.

More than twenty minutes passed before Kyna became aware of her surroundings again. She was seeing double and her head was banging so hard that she could barely think. She was struggling to breathe, too, and when she put her hand up to her face she found that the blood had dried hard around her mouth and chin like a Hannibal Lecter mask. With extreme caution she touched the bridge of her nose, and sucked in her breath when she felt the broken bone crunch inside it.

'Mother of God,' she whispered to herself, and awkwardly sat up. John was still lying on the couch with his eyes closed, his face an asbestos grey, although she could hear him softly snoring.

She wanted to sob, but she bit her lower lip hard to stop herself because it would have hurt too much. She had never felt so hopeless and abandoned in the whole of her life.

Thirty-one

The rain began to ease off as they took Barney for his walk up to the Carrigaloe Rushbrooke pier. On the way back the wind was blowing dry and cool and the ferry terminal lights glittered on the river. Katie began to feel calmer and more composed than she had for days.

In the back of her mind she was still fretting about Kyna and John, but she knew that Alan was right. So long as they remained alive, Bobby Quilty had a guarantee that the Garda would turn a blind eye to his cigarette-smuggling business and that they wouldn't try to implicate him in the murder of Detective Barry or the shooting of Darragh Murphy.

When they reached Katie's house she saw the next-door curtain twitching again, and Jenny Tierney peering out, and she gave her a little finger-wave.

'Nosey neighbour,' she told Alan, as she opened the door. 'She's sound out, pure helpful, I'll give her that. She feeds Barney and takes him for walks when I'm late back from work. But she does like to keep herself abreast of everything that's going on, like.'

They went inside. Katie had left the oven on low while they were out and there was a herby smell of lasagne in the hallway.

'I'm starved,' said Alan, following her into the kitchen. 'I've eaten nothing at all since breakfast and that was only toast.'

'Would you like another beer?' she asked him. 'Then I can show you where you'll be sleeping.'

She refilled his glass with Murphy's and poured herself another vodka, and then she took him into the spare room, which had once been the nursery. She had redecorated it less than three months ago, so it no longer looked like the room in which her little Seamus had died in his cot. There was a new double bed and the walls had been painted cream, with four framed samplers hanging on them.

Alan read one of the samplers and said, 'Here, I like this, *Three things there are that can never come back . . . the arrow shot forth on its destined track . . . the appointed hour that could not wait . . . and the warning word that was spoken too late.* How true is that.'

In spite of herself, in spite of the room looking so different now, Katie couldn't help thinking of the morning she had walked in and found Seamus lying chilly and wet-lipped and as white as wax, with his small blue teddy bear lying close to him, smiling.

Alan frowned at her. 'Have I said something I shouldn't?'

'No, not at all,' she told him. She opened the fitted wardrobe and said, 'Here, look, there's a dressing gown here you can use.'

It was John's black silk Japanese dressing gown with a picture of a flying crane on the back, a *tsuru*. She had bought it for him because cranes always mate for life and the Japanese regard them as a symbol of fidelity. Alan said, 'Thanks,' and laid it on the bed. It was rather James Bond-ish, and Katie could see that he was tempted to make a comment, maybe even a joke, but he resisted the temptation.

* * *

They ate lasagne and salad at the kitchen table and talked more about Bobby Quilty and how they could incriminate him. Even if they couldn't find anybody who was brave enough to stand up and testify against him in open court, Alan thought that he might be able to bribe one of his gang to pass him enough material evidence to sustain a charge against him.

'I doubt if we'll ever be able to get him for incitement to murder, but false imprisonment . . . I think we might have a reasonable chance there. He's holding Kyna and John in his own house, after all.'

'So long as we can prove that it's his house.'

'Well, yes, there's that. But I know some solicitors in Belfast who may be able to help us untangle who the deeds really belong to. Wellings and McCormack, on Victoria Street. They used to be some of my Lesser Bastards and I have quite a lot of background on them, so I'm pretty sure they'll oblige.'

After they had eaten they went into the living room for a night-cap and talked about their families and their different lives in law enforcement. Barney came and sat close to Katie and put his head in her lap so that she could stroke his ears for him. Katie found Alan very easy company, much easier than her late husband, Paul, had been. As economic times in Ireland had grown harder, Paul had frequently been involved in less than legitimate dealings in the building trade and he had never felt he could tell her the whole truth about what he was up to. Alan was easier than John, too. John had always been so jealous – not just of other men who found Katie attractive and came on to her, but of her career. She had made it clear to him that An Garda Siochána was her vocation and she couldn't give it up to follow him to America, or anywhere, and that had made him deeply resentful.

'Have I misunderstood something here?' John had shouted at her once, in the middle of an argument. 'You belong to me, don't you? Or don't you?'

'Apart from Jesus, there's only one other person I belong to,' Katie had retorted. 'That's myself.'

What made Alan so relaxing to talk to was that he had served as a police inspector, so she didn't have to explain to him the stresses of the job, nor the antagonism she had faced from so many of her male colleagues when she was promoted over their heads. Alan understood police procedure and what they could do in the name of the law and what they couldn't. He also knew what corners were cut, and what rules were bent, and what evidence was fabricated, and how, and why. After talking to him for nearly four hours, and asking him scores of questions, Katie felt confident that if anybody could help her to put Bobby

Quilty out of business, and rescue Kyna and John, then Alan could.

Maybe he was telling the truth about why he had been forced to resign from the PSNI and Bobby Quilty had set him up. On the other hand, maybe he *had* been involved in the drug-dealing. She had no way of knowing for certain, but whatever he had done in the past, she needed him now.

Just after midnight, Alan went to take a shower while Katie watched television with the sound turned down. He came into the living room, his grey hair still wet and sticking up, wrapped in John's dressing gown.

'I'll say goodnight, then,' he told her. 'And thanks a million for putting me up.'

Katie stood up and he came over and gave her a kiss on the cheek. He no longer smelled of black pepper and cinnamon but her own peach shower gel.

'We'll save your John and your Kyna,' he added, and gave her a reassuring smile. 'Sleep well and I'll see you in the morning. I'll make you my famous Ulster egg-in-a-cup if you fancy that for breakfast. Do you have breadcrumbs?'

* * *

It took her a long time to fall off to sleep. The wind had risen even more and she could hear her rotary clothes line rattling in the yard outside. She couldn't stop herself from thinking about John, and what Kyna had meant about his feet being bolted to the bed, and about Kyna, too, because she still hadn't fully recovered from her gunshot wound. It had badly torn her small intestine and she had needed more than seventy centimetres cut out of it.

Three things there are that can never come back, she thought, but the words on that sampler didn't make her feel any less responsible for what had happened. John and Kyna were being held because of her, and she couldn't turn back the clock.

When she slept, she dreamed that she was in her father's house in Monkstown, across the river. It was a large, green-painted

Victorian house with a garden that had long since become tangled
and choked with weeds. Inside the house it was gloomy and cold
and empty, and there was no sign of her father anywhere. The fire
had died in the grate and was nothing but a heap of ashes.

She had opened the front door and was about to leave when
she heard whispering upstairs, like someone saying a novena. She
went to the bottom of the staircase and looked up. The first-floor
landing was in darkness and she was filled with dread at what
she might find if she went up there. But the whispering went on
and on and she knew that she couldn't go until she found out who
was praying.

'Da?' she called out. 'Da, is that you?'

There was no answer, only the whispering, so reluctantly she
began to climb the stairs. For every step she went up, it seemed as if
two more appeared ahead of her in its place, so it felt as if it took her
hours to reach the landing. The doors to all of the bedrooms were
closed, except for one, and she thought she glimpsed somebody
in white moving around inside. The whispering had stopped and
now she could hear only rattling, faint but persistent.

'*Da?*' she said, although she wasn't sure that she had said it
out loud.

She seemed to glide across the landing and through the open
bedroom door. The bedroom was dimly lit with a silvery lumines-
cence, as if everything in it were radioactive. Beside the window stood
a nun, dressed in white, her face hidden by her cowl. She was praying,
and it was her rosary beads that were making the rattling sound.

In the middle of the room were two single beds, side by side,
and on each bed a body was lying, covered with a white sheet.
Katie didn't have to go over and lift up the sheets to know who
they were. Her chest tightened in panic and she tried to turn round
and leave the room. Every time she turned round, however, she
found that she was still facing the same way and that she couldn't
find the door.

She circled round and round, but the door was always behind
her and the two bodies were always there in front of her. The nun

came sliding towards her, her rosary still rattling, and Katie knew that she was going to take away the sheets and show her who was lying underneath. She didn't want to see them. She didn't want proof that they were dead.

'*Three things there are that can never come back*,' the nun whispered and reached out to tug the first sheet away.

Katie screamed, and turned around again, and this time the open door appeared in front of her. Before she could reach it, however, the nun caught her around the ankles and wound her scapular around them, over and over, so that she was powerless to move her legs.

'*Let me go!*' she screamed. '*Let me go!*' – so loudly that she woke herself up.

She wasn't in her father's house at all. She was in her own bed, hot and tearful, and all twisted up in her duvet. Her pillow had dropped on to the floor and her patchwork bedcover had slipped halfway off. The rattling of rosary beads was her clothes line, rattling in the wind.

She heard a tentative knocking at her bedroom door.

Alan said, 'Katie? Katie, what's wrong? Are you all right in there?'

'I'm fine,' she called back. 'I had a bad dream, that's all. You can come in, if you like.'

She reached over and switched on the bedside lamp. Alan came in, wearing John's dressing gown, tightly belted at the waist.

'Boys a dear! The way you were screaming there, that must have been one bad dream and a half. I thought some intruder had broken into the house and you were being murdered – serious.'

Katie dried her tears on the duvet cover and then picked up her pillow and straightened the bedcover. 'I had a dream about John and Kyna. Both of them were dead.'

Alan sat down on the side of the bed and took hold of her hand between both of his. 'I can understand you feeling guilty, Katie – but them being taken like that, it's Bobby Quilty's doing, not yours.'

'But he wouldn't have taken them, would he, if it hadn't been for me?'

'Oh, so you're blaming yourself for being some kind of a jinx, are you?'

'Why shouldn't I? It's true.'

Alan shook his head. 'From what you've told me, you and John only got together in the first place because you saved him from having his throat cut. And whatever you say, Kyna's a cop, and cops know the risks of what they've chosen to do. If anything, Katie, it's you who're keeping them alive right now.'

Katie said nothing. Alan lifted one hand and brushed her damp red hair away from her forehead.

'Come on,' he said. 'It was a nightmare, that's all. I've had worse ones myself, especially during the Troubles. One night I dreamed that the Provos had planted a bomb in my car and my legs were blown off. Can I fetch you anything? Maybe a drop of tea?'

'No thanks, Alan. I'm grand altogether. I just need some sleep.'

He stood up and said, 'Okay, then. But if you have any more dreams like that, just scream before you wake up and I'll chase them away for you, so I will.'

He was halfway to the door when Katie said, 'Stay.'

He stopped, but he didn't turn around. Katie pulled back the duvet and said, 'Stay. Alan. Please. I really need somebody to hug me.'

Now Alan turned. It was difficult to read the expression on his face. It was questioning, but interested, his eyebrows slightly lifted, and there was a sparkle in his eyes, too.

'Do you think it's a good idea?' he asked her.

'I don't need to apply to the District Court for a warrant, do I?' said Katie. 'I just want you to hold me and help me get to sleep.'

She had no idea what this might lead to. Nothing at all, probably. But she simply didn't want to switch off the light and lie there alone for the rest of the night, afraid to go to sleep.

Alan hesitated a split second longer and she was almost tempted to tell him to forget it. But then he came back, and she shifted herself over to give him more room, and he climbed into bed with her. They lay there, face to face, looking into each other's eyes.

'This wasn't what I expected, when I got on the train this morning,' said Alan.

'Me neither,' said Katie. She touched his cheek, where silver prickles of stubble were beginning to grow. There was something about him that made her feel secure and protected. He hadn't spent all evening challenging her or teasing her, like so many men did. He hadn't even flirted with her. He was handsome, too, but in a mature, confident way, as if he didn't need to keep checking himself in the nearest reflective surface to make sure that he still looked the berries.

'I have to tell you that I find you very attractive, Katie,' he told her. 'A fellow could put to sea in those green eyes of yours, and sail away, and never come back.'

'I thought you were a peeler, not a poet,' she teased him.

Alan jostled himself into a more comfortable position and then put his arms around her.

'I'm sorry, I'm a bit sweaty,' she said.

'Jesus.' He smiled. 'Have I had that effect on you already?'

They stared at each other, so close that the tips of their noses were almost touching, and then he kissed her forehead, and her eyelids, and her cheeks, and then her lips. She kissed him back – little friendly pecks at first, with her eyes only half closed, but then deeper, and longer.

As she did so, she felt his penis rising under the thin silk of John's dressing gown. That was when she stopped kissing him and touched his lips with her fingertip and said, 'Now I must get some sleep. It's going to be a long difficult day tomorrow and I don't want to look beat out.'

She gave him one more kiss and then turned herself over, with her back to him, although she reached around and took hold of his wrist and placed his hand against her stomach, so that he was holding her very close. His erection was pressing hard against her bottom, but he made no move to lift her nightdress, and somehow she felt that there was an understanding between them. She took his stiffness as a compliment, that he was doing nothing to hide the fact that she aroused him, but was prepared to wait until she was ready. She was highly stressed, and exhausted, and she had asked him for comfort, and that was what he was giving her, comfort.

She fell asleep after only a few minutes, but she had no more nightmares. She was woken just after five by the hooting of a ship in the estuary and for a moment she thought that John was lying next to her. When she turned her head and saw that it was Alan, however, she felt a sense of both grief and relief. His eyes were closed, but she could see that his pupils were darting from side to side under his eyelids in REM sleep, so he must have been dreaming. Maybe he was dreaming of her, she thought. She snuggled herself in closer to him and took his left hand and cupped it over her breast.

Thirty-two

Celia rang the doorbell three times but nobody answered. The last time, she pressed it and kept it pressed for more than fifteen seconds. Still no answer.

She stood on tiptoe so that she could peer into the living-room windows, but there was no sign of Órla Doherty or either of the children.

That was very queer, because the children were on their summer holidays now, and it was only 8 a.m., which was very early for Órla to take them out anywhere. Even if she *had* taken them out, she would have been sure to have told Celia last week what her plans were. After Celia had finished cleaning the house they always sat down together for a cup of tea and an intimate chat.

What was even queerer, both of the Dohertys' cars were still parked in front of the house – Kevin's Audi estate and Órla's pale blue Ford Focus. Kevin always took his car to work, and if Órla had gone anywhere with the children she must have walked, unless a friend had picked them up.

Still, Celia had her own key so if the Dohertys were out she could at least make a start with the hoovering. Over five years she had been cleaning for them now, so she was almost part of the family.

She let herself in. The house was silent and Celia was immediately struck by the smell. It was only faint, but it was acrid, like the smell of spent fireworks, and the house had never smelled like that before. Maybe Kevin had been setting off some indoor fireworks to celebrate the beginning of the holidays.

She opened the cupboard under the stairs and reached inside for her floral housecoat. As she was lifting out the vacuum cleaner, though, she stopped and listened, and sniffed again, and looked around her. She wasn't used to the house being so quiet because Órla always had the television on, regardless of whether it was *Shortland Street* or *The Doctors* or the RTÉ news. She had the strangest feeling, too, that something wasn't quite right.

It was then that she saw the list pinned to the back of the front door. She went up to it and stared at it. It was Órla's list of things to do – dry-cleaning to collect and birthday cards to buy and bills to be paid. But it was usually stuck on to the fridge, this list. It had *always* been stuck on the fridge. Why had she suddenly decided to pin it up here in the hallway?

She went into the living room. There was something strange in there, too. Two of the armchairs were side by side, on top of the rug, at an awkward angle so that people sitting in them would have been facing away from each other. Órla was always meticulous in the way she arranged the furniture, and she never placed the armchairs on top of the Ashanti rug.

Celia could see herself in the mirror over the fireplace, biting her thumbnail and thinking. She could carry on with her cleaning and leave when she had finished, but where had the Dohertys disappeared to? Órla hadn't even left her a note to say when they might be back.

She went back into the hallway and took down the list. It was then that she saw the jagged splintering in the door panel, and even though she had no idea what might have caused it she knew at once that the Dohertys must be in some kind of trouble. Maybe they had argued and their argument had turned into a fight. She knew from what Órla had told her over tea and biscuits that the Dohertys' marriage hadn't always been the smoothest. Maybe she had left and taken the children with her and Kevin had simply gone off to work.

But why had neither of them taken their cars?

Celia went next door and knocked at Mrs Doody's. It took a long time for Mrs Doody to answer and for a while Celia was worried that she might have disappeared, too. At length, however, she opened the door, cradling a black-and-white miniature schnauzer in her arms. The instant it saw Celia, the schnauzer started barking.

'Corky, will you whisht awhile!' Mrs Doody snapped at him. She had her hair pinned up in a tight grey bun and was wearing a splashy summer dress with huge yellow chrysanthemums all over it. She had an oddly tiny head and a pinched, shrivelled-up face, with black-rimmed spectacles that looked enormous by comparison.

'Sorry to be bothering you, Mrs Doody,' said Celia. 'But have you seen any sign of Kevin and Órla today by any chance?'

Mrs Doody thought about it and then shook her head. 'No, girl, not today. Órla I haven't seen since yesterday morning. She came around to borrow some brown sugar for her barmbrack. Yesterday afternoon I saw Kevin out the window bringing the kids home, but that was all. They were very quiet last night, I have to tell you, and I haven't heard a squeak from them today. Usually I can hear their telly, like, and the kids running up and down the stairs.'

'They're not at home this morning, but look, their cars are still there. And the house . . . I don't know, come and see it for yourself. There's something desperate quare gone on there, I'm sure of it.'

'Let me find my slippers and I'll be with you.'

She disappeared for a few moments and then returned, still carrying her miniature schnauzer, which barked at Celia when it saw her again.

'*Whisht*, Corky, will you? Oh, they tell you when you buy them that they're affectionate, these little fellows, and they are, but they don't tell you that they've more bark than Gougane Barra forest.'

The two of them went next door to the Dohertys' house. Both Mrs Doody and Corky started to sniff suspiciously as soon as they stepped into the hallway. Corky barked once and then started to make an extraordinary squeaking noise in the back of his throat. He wriggled and twisted in Mrs Doody's arms so that she had to drop him on to the floor. He trotted without hesitation into the living room.

'Well, you're right, this is desperate quare,' said Mrs Doody. 'I can't think what that smell puts me in mind of, but it's not the way this house usually smells, and that's for sure. Órla's always squirting that flowery room spray around.'

Celia showed her the splintered door panel. She lifted her huge glasses a little so that she could focus better and then she said, 'Now, then. A bullet's done that, no mistake about it.'

'A bullet? Serious?'

'My uncle used to run Hickey's Bar in Bandon and in the back room there was panelling which the Brits had shot at during the war. The marks you could see on the wall there were the identical spit of these, I'll tell you.'

'Mother of God,' said Celia. 'I know that Kevin and Órla have their fights all right, but I can't see them *shooting* each other. You didn't hear a gun going off, did you?'

'No, I didn't,' said Mrs Doody. 'By the looks of it, though, by the *smell* of it, I'd say that nothing good's happened here.' She reached up to touch the splintered front door, and then she turned around and snapped out, '*Corky!* For the love of all that's holy, will you hold your whisht!'

Corky had started barking again, a high-pitched monotonous yapping, and they could hear him scratching at the floor, too.

'What's that little pesht up to now? *Corky!*'

They went into the living room and saw that Corky had managed to scrabble the red patterned rug to one side and was clawing furiously at the floorboards. Mrs Doody picked him up and tried to stop him barking by holding his jaws together, but he struggled and kicked and jumped down out of her arms again.

Celia went down on one knee and ran the palm of her hand over the floorboards. 'Look here,' she said. 'There's marks here like somebody's pulled the floor up – see, there's holes where the nails were taken out and they've been knocked back in different places.'

There was nothing that either of them could do to stop Corky from barking and scratching, and every now and then he pressed his snout against the cracks in between the floorboards and gave a deep, quivering sniff.

'There's something under there,' said Mrs Doody. 'He can smell it, like. He's not exactly a bloodhound, but he can always tell when I fetch home tripe in my shopping bag.'

'Oh, God,' said Celia. 'You don't think—? Did you see that programme they had on the telly a couple of days back, about that family in Blarney that was found buried under the floorboards? Father and mother and children, too. And dogs.'

'I saw that, yes. There was a piece about it in the *Echo*, too. But that occurred back in the 1920s. Jesus, that was before even *I* was born!'

'I know. But where are the Dohertys?'

'Like you say, they could have had an argument,' said Mrs Doody, although she sounded more than a little apprehensive. 'What's under here, though – it's more likely to be a pigeon that's got itself stuck, don't you think? Or a cat maybe, or a rat.'

Celia hesitated, but then she crouched forward and sniffed at the floorboards herself. Immediately she sat up straight, cupping her hand over her face.

'I can smell something all right. Something *sweet*, like. Sweet but bad, do you know what I mean? Like when you buy a chicken and it's off.'

'Do you have Órla's mobile phone number?' Mrs Doody asked her. 'Why don't you try ringing her? Maybe she and Kevin had a fight, but it's the first day of the holliers, isn't it? Maybe she's just taken the kids out shopping for some summer clothes.'

Celia went out to the hallway to find her purse and came back with her mobile phone. She pressed Órla's number and waited.

After a short while they heard a ringtone. It was muffled, but there was no question where it was coming from – underneath the floorboards. Even Corky stopped barking and listened.

'Call the guards,' said Mrs Doody. Then she stepped back so that she was no longer standing in the centre of the living room, where the rug had been, and crossed herself.

Thirty-three

When she opened her eyes again and reached across the bed, Alan had gone.

She lay there for a while, looking towards the window. The wind that had been blowing most of the night had died down now and it appeared to be quite bright outside, even though it wasn't sunny. She couldn't hear rain, anyway, and that was a blessing.

She thought about Alan. She wasn't sorry that she had invited him into her bed, especially since he had given her all the emotional comfort she had needed, and at the same time had been so restrained. They weren't yet lovers – maybe they never would be, but they were as close now as two acquaintances could be.

She lifted her head from the pillow to check the time. It was nearly ten past eight – later than she had slept in for months – and she felt all the better for it. She wasn't due in to Anglesea Street until lunchtime, when she was supposed to be having a meeting with Assistant Commissioner O'Reilly and Chief Superintendent MacCostagáin about their future strategy for dealing with Bobby Quilty and other cigarette-smugglers.

She hadn't yet thought how she was going to explain to them why her investigations into the killings of Detective Barry and Darragh Murphy were making such slow progress. She would probably tell them that after the fiasco of Operation Trident she was insisting that every piece of evidence against Bobby Quilty was triple-checked – fingerprints, DNA matches, witness reports, phone-taps, everything.

She closed her eyes again for a few seconds, but then she heard the bedroom door click and she opened them again. Alan came in, still wearing John's black silk dressing gown. He was carrying two mugs, one with a picture of Pope John Paul on it, the other with the badge of An Garda Siochána.

'Ah grand, you're awake!' He smiled. 'I made us some coffee. I guessed that you like yours black, no sugar.'

'You don't know me that well, then,' said Katie, sitting up. 'One level spoonful of demerara. You'll find it in the brown glass jar next to the microwave.'

'Your wish is my command, o Detective Superintendent. You outrank me, after all.'

He set down one mug on the bedside table and went back to the kitchen. He returned, stirring her coffee, and sat down on the side of the bed.

'You've given yourself the pope mug,' said Katie.

'You don't have one with the archbishop of Armagh on it, that's why. But I don't think God will strike me down for drinking out of a Catholic vessel. Careful, it's very hot still.'

'I wasn't going to drink it straightaway,' Katie told him. 'I didn't want to have coffee breath when you kissed me.'

Alan looked at her very steadily. This was the moment when he could have said no, this will get far too complicated. But Katie was telling him that she needed him, for the time being at least, or somebody like him. Somebody she could come home to at the end of each increasingly disastrous day. Somebody who would understand what stress she was suffering and support her, and hold her close in the middle of the night.

He leaned forward and kissed her. Then he kissed her again and she kissed him back. She shifted herself further across the bed to make more room for him and turned down the duvet cover. Then she crossed her arms and pulled off her white short-sleeved nightdress. She was large-breasted for a small woman and her breasts swung a little when she lifted it over her head.

Alan stood up and unfastened the tie-belt, letting his dressing gown slide to the floor. He was broad-shouldered and muscular for a man in his early fifties, although his stomach was slightly rounded. The hair on his chest was as grey as the hair on his head and formed a V-shaped pattern, like grey cirrus clouds. His pubic hair was grey, too, and wiry.

He eased himself into the bed next to her. His penis was already stiff and his testicles were wrinkled tight. Katie took hold of the shaft and pressed the ball of her sharp-nailed thumb up against the opening. He was very big, and very hard, and she squeezed him tighter and tighter until his purple glans turned a dark plum colour.

He cleared his throat. 'Have you condoms?' he asked her.

'I'm on the pill,' she told him.

'Better to be safe, you know. Don't want to be sending another one to school.'

Katie had been taking the pill ever since she had accidentally become pregnant to her former neighbour, who had sworn on his life that he had had a vasectomy. She hadn't thought she was likely to have another sexual encounter quite so soon, but she was terrified that she might have another unplanned pregnancy, and she would never consider an abortion. Her mother had died after giving birth to the last of her sisters. She had been warned that there were complications and she should terminate the pregnancy early, but she had refused. *Only God gives life, and only God can take it away.*

Alan kissed her again, on her lips, and then her neck, and took hold of her breast and caressed it, tugging gently at her nipple and rolling it between his fingers until it stiffened. She felt his glans becoming slippery, so she learned back on the pillow and opened her thighs. With a faint, moist click, like the quietest of kisses, the lips of her smooth waxed vulva opened up to reveal how wet she was.

'Oh, Katie, you're such a beautiful, beautiful woman,' Alan breathed. He ran his fingers lightly down her side, all the way to her hip, which made her shiver. Then he slid his finger between her lips and stroked her clitoris so gently that she could barely feel it.

She kept her grip on his penis and guided it between her legs. He was arousing her with his finger-play and it was almost making her delirious, but she wanted him inside her, as deep as he could go.

He entered her and she let out a moan of pleasure that was almost a laugh. He felt enormous, as if he were far too big for her, and she opened her legs as wide as she could so that he could bury himself inside her, right up to that grey wiry hair, and his testicles bobbed against her. The tip of his glans touched the neck of her womb and she jumped, and laughed again.

He felt so different from John. Most of the time John had been sensual and slow, almost dreamy, although he had sometimes been forceful, when he was drunk or he hadn't made love to her for several weeks. Alan was strong and blunt and deliberate and heavy, pushing himself into her again and again, harder and harder each time, as if he were trying to drive her into the mattress. His skin had the smooth dry texture of unpolished marble, so that Katie almost felt as if she were being penetrated by a life-size statue of a man. He made her feel physically helpless, but at work she was always in charge and in a way she found it exciting to be dominated like this.

He was panting now, as if he had been running a half-marathon. Without warning he levered his penis out of her and ejaculated all over her stomach. She was close to reaching a climax herself and she smeared his warm semen around and around, and over her breasts, so that her nipples were stiff and slippery.

Alan lifted himself off her and lay close beside her, quickly and lightly flicking her clitoris with his finger. It was as hard now as a little bird's beak. She felt that tight, dark, shrinking sensation between her legs, tighter and tighter. Then she was shaking and jerking and gasping and she could see stars.

They lay side by side for over twenty minutes, while Katie felt him drying on her stomach. She looked at him closely and he smiled back at her, but she realized that she was searching for some telltale clue in his expression – like a detective rather than a lover. At the moment he had climaxed all over her she had found it erotic, but now she wondered why he had done it. Surely a man's strongest sexual urge was to climax as deeply as he could inside the woman he was making love to – especially since this was their very first time.

Had he wanted to degrade her in some way, maybe without fully realizing it himself? She was a serving detective Superintendent after all, while he was an ex-detective inspector who had been forced to resign under a cloud of suspicion. As he had said, '*You outrank me.*'

Or maybe there was another reason. Maybe he hadn't believed her when she had assured him that she was on the pill. She was only in her late thirties, after all, still young enough to have a baby, and when they were talking the previous evening she had described how she had lost little Seamus and how much she still missed him.

'Your coffee's probably gone cold by now,' Alan told her.

'Ah well, you can make me some fresh, can't you? And what about that Ulster egg-in-a-cup? I need to take a shower.'

'Katie,' said Alan.

She touched his lips with the tip of her finger. 'You don't have to say anything, Alan. Let's just wait and see where this goes. *Three things there are that can never come back*, and that was a fourth.'

* * *

Katie showered and dressed in her light grey suit. By the time she had blown her hair dry and put on her make-up, Alan had showered and dressed, too, in a tattersall country shirt and dark brown chinos.

Katie sat at the kitchen table with her laptop while Alan brewed some fresh coffee and boiled four eggs for their breakfast.

He had shelled the eggs and was mashing them up with butter, salt, pepper and breadcrumbs when Katie's iPhone rang. It was Detective Sergeant Begley.

'What's the craic, Sean?'

'You're not going to believe this, ma'am, but it's Blarney all over again.'

'Blarney? What do you mean?'

'There's a family of four's been discovered murdered in a house on Military Road. The father, the mother, and two kids, a boy and a girl. Shot dead, by the look of it, all four of them, and nailed down underneath the floorboards.'

'Holy Mother of God. How long do you think they've been there?'

'Oh, these aren't historic bodies, like. The technical experts have only just taken up the floor and they haven't touched them yet. They're all wrapped up in plastic sheeting. The woman who lives next door saw them yesterday afternoon at about three o'clock, so they must have been killed sometime after that.'

'All right, Sean. I'll be with you directly.'

'The reason I said it's Blarney all over again, ma'am, there's a note with them.'

'Do you have it there with you? Read it to me.'

'It says, "This is to show you that we never forget our own. It was the IRA killed the Langtrys and these are the blood relations of those murderers. The score is settled now at long last. *Quis separabit?*"'

'UDA,' said Katie. 'I can't believe it, after all these years. That's all it says?'

'That's all. And it's been printed on a computer and there's no signature or nothing.'

'*Quis separabit?* That's signature enough, isn't it?'

Quis separabit? – Who Will Separate Us? – that was the motto of the Ulster Defence Association, the Protestant paramilitaries that had fought against the Provisional IRA during the Troubles. They were known to have killed at least 260 people, but they were supposed to have ceased their armed campaign in November 2007. It was common knowledge, though, that some of them still harboured grudges – not only against the Provisional IRA but against others in their own organization.

Alan was standing by the table with a mug of mashed-up eggs in each hand. 'Don't tell me – you have to go.'

'I'm sorry,' said Katie. 'They've found a family murdered, just like the Langtrys were murdered. Shot and buried under the floorboards.'

'Jesus Christ.'

'Well, I don't think He had anything to do with it. More like the UDA.'

'I heard you. You want your breakfast?'

Katie shook her head. 'I haven't much appetite now. Sorry. Maybe you can make them for me some other time.'

'All right. But I'll come into the city with you and start poking around to see what I can find out about Bobby Quilty. That's unless you want me to stay here and take Barney for his walk.'

'No, Jenny will do that for me. I think I've given her enough gossip by way of compensation.'

Alan scraped the eggs into the waste-disposal unit, rinsed out the mugs and put them into the dishwasher. Katie could tell that he wanted to say something to her, but he stayed silent. As she had told him, what had happened that morning could never come back.

Thirty-four

She dropped Alan off at the corner of Merchant's Quay and St Patrick's Street. He leaned across the car to give her a kiss, but two uniformed gardaí were strolling towards them and she placed her hand on his shoulder to keep him away.

'I think we've caused enough of a stir already.' She smiled. 'But call me later and don't get yourself into any trouble. You know yourself what Quilty's people are like.'

'I will, and I won't,' he promised, as he climbed out of the car. Once the gardaí had passed them by, however, he turned around and blew her a kiss.

Katie drove across St Patrick's Bridge and up Summerhill to Military Road. She wasn't at all sure what she felt about Alan. She found him comforting and reassuring and very masculine, but at the same time she wasn't entirely convinced that he was everything that he seemed to be. She wondered if he regarded her as more of a conquest than a companion. Or maybe she was just being hypersensitive, and feeling guilty about John.

Military Road was crowded with vehicles when she arrived. Two vans from the Technical Bureau, four patrol cars, two ambulances and six or seven other cars. She was relieved to see that RTÉ's outside broadcast van hadn't arrived yet.

Detective Sergeant Begley met her at the Dohertys' front gate, along with Detective Dooley. When she went inside the house she saw that Detective Scanlan was in the kitchen, talking to Celia, the Dohertys' cleaner, and Mrs Doody from next door. Clearly she wasn't finding it easy because Mrs Doody was still holding

Corky and for all the *whishts awhile, will you,* he wouldn't stop barking.

Katie went into the living room. Bill Phinner was in there, as well as Eithne O'Neill and Tyrone Daley and two other technical experts, all wearing white Tyvek suits and masks. Seven of the oak floorboards in the centre of the room had been prised up and stacked against the wall by the fireplace. In the space under the floor, Katie could see the four bodies, all tightly wrapped up in vinyl sheeting and bound around with silver gaffer tape. The vinyl was transparent enough for her to be able to make out their pale faces and the colour of their clothes, and also the rusty bloodstains around their heads. Not only that, but she could smell the distinctive faecal odour of recent death.

'What's the story, Bill?' she asked him.

'Two adults, a man and a woman, and two children, a boy and a girl. Without taking that plastic off it looks pretty clear they've all been shot in the head. There's bullet fragments in the front-door panel, so that would confirm that a gun was involved.'

'Do we know their names?'

'We won't be able to tell for sure if they're all from the same family until they've been formally identified, but we're assuming for the moment that they are. The Dohertys – Kevin and his wife Órla, Tom and Sibeal. Kevin's an estate agent for Thomas Mahoney's down on South Mall.'

Detective Sergeant Begley said, 'Their cleaning woman found them. Well, actually it was that dog from next door that sniffed them out.'

'Clever dog,' said Katie. 'He should come and work for our canine support unit.'

'I don't think they could stand the noise,' said Detective Sergeant Begley. 'He's been yapping ever since I got here. He's worse than her I married, I'll tell you.'

'We've taken all the pictures we need, ma'am,' said Bill. 'It was washed off, but we've also found blood spatter on the wall here with the infra-red, and some in the hallway, too, by the stairs.

We'll be lifting the bodies out now, but we'll be keeping them parcelled up like this until we get them to the mortuary. You'll be calling the pathologist.'

'Of course, yes. The woman next door – did she not see anybody unusual visiting the house? Didn't she hear anything?'

'She said that the Dohertys were very quiet last night, that's all. She can usually hear their telly. But of course she didn't imagine there was anything wrong. Nothing like this, any road.'

'Come and take a sconce at the door,' said Bill. 'I'd say that it was hit by fragments from a soft-nosed bullet, but only fragments, which could mean that it had passed through something else first – like a human skull, for instance. The blood spatter we found by the stairs would verify that. According to the cleaning woman, there was a shopping list pinned over the door to hide the damage.'

'How often does the cleaner come?'

'Once a week.'

'So if it hadn't been for our doggy friend, the Dohertys may not have been found for days?'

Katie took a close look at the splinters in the front door and then went back into the kitchen to introduce herself to Celia and Mrs Doody. Celia was red-eyed and tearful, and twisting a handkerchief in her hands.

'They were such a lovely family. I'll tell you, Kevin and Órla, they had their arguments sometimes, but they were lovely people. Why would anybody want to do such a terrible thing to them?'

'They had arguments?' asked Katie. 'What about?'

'Oh, nothing serious, like. Maybe they couldn't agree on what colour they were going to paint the bedroom. Or Kevin was getting on her nerves because he was never ready in time for Mass. Or he kept giving Tom those orangey sweeties even though they made the little fellow go stone-hatchet mad.'

'So, Órla used to confide in you?'

'Well, yes, we always had a bit of a chat when I was done

with my cleaning. Only about women's stuff, you know, and family gossip.'

'Thank you, Celia. We'll probably want to talk to you again later. You too, Mrs Doody. In the meantime, I think you can go. We have the sad business of taking out the bodies and I don't think you'll want to witness that.'

Katie went back into the living room. 'Do you have that note?' she asked Detective Dooley.

He handed her a plastic evidence envelope. She read and re-read the message that had been left with the bodies, and as she did so an idea began to form in her mind.

'If the offenders really were UDA, they must have come down from the North especially to do this.'

'They could have been local, though, ma'am, and only signed it *Quis separabit?* to put us off the scent, like.'

'Well, you could be right,' said Katie. 'It just seems a bit too clever for that, that's all. If they were trying to make out that they were UDA, or UFF, but they weren't, I wonder if they wouldn't have simply signed it that way, UDA, or UFF. Like, if I was a murderer and I was trying to make out the Garda had done it, I'd sign it "Garda", not "To Achieve the Highest Level of Personal Protection, Community Commitment and State Security".'

'I'm glad you can remember all that, because that's more than I can,' said Detective Sergeant Begley. 'Mind you, I can't even remember what I had for breakfast.'

It's all right for you, thought Katie. *At least you had some.*

'We'll start knocking on doors along the road, then,' said Detective Sergeant Begley. 'If the old doll next door didn't see or hear nothing, though, I doubt if anybody else did. They keep themselves to themselves around here.'

Katie looked down at the vinyl-wrapped bodies and crossed herself. She just hoped they hadn't suffered. As she turned to leave the room, Tyrone said, 'Oh! By the way, ma'am. We should have had the DNA results back by now on those bloodstains we found in that bedroom on Leitrim Street. I'll call you later so, as soon as I get back to the lab.'

Katie close her eyes for a moment. *John*, she thought. *I haven't abandoned you, don't worry.*

'Thanks a million, Tyrone,' she told him, and stepped outside.

* * *

She had very little to say to the media waiting in the road – only to tell them that four bodies had been found in the house and that they had almost certainly been murdered. She declined to confirm that they were the Doherty family and she didn't mention that they had probably been shot. Neither did she say that a note had been found with the bodies.

'Was this some kind of domestic tragedy?' asked Fionnuala Sweeney from RTÉ. 'I mean, like, the father killing the family and then himself? Or are you looking for somebody else?'

'It wasn't domestic, no. We're looking for a person or persons who might have visited the house sometime yesterday afternoon after three o'clock or later in the evening. If anybody in the locality saw anything suspicious or unusual, or has any other information, obviously we'd be very grateful to hear from them.'

'Who found the bodies?' asked Roisin Magorian from the *Examiner*. 'And can you tell us where exactly in the house they were located?'

'I can't answer that for you just yet, Roisin. I'll be asking the press office to get in touch with you as soon as I can give you more information.'

'Any further thoughts on the other matter we talked about?'

'No, Roisin. Not yet. But I haven't forgotten what you told me.'

Thirty-five

Driving back down to Anglesea Street she kept thinking: *Quis separabit?* The killers hadn't been able to resist taking the credit for what they done and they had made it clear that their revenge had been not only personal but political.

The more Katie thought about the wording of that note and the way it was signed, the clearer her next plan of action took shape in her mind. It wasn't an orthodox plan by any means, but hadn't Alan said that they were faced with a fierce unusual problem – a problem that called for some fierce unorthodox measures?

She was fully aware that she might be placing her entire career in jeopardy, but on the other hand it could be the making of her. Noirin O'Sullivan hadn't been promoted to Garda commissioner by being cautious or indecisive.

The first person she met as she walked along the corridor to her office was Chief Superintendent Denis MacCostagáin, looking even glummer and more preoccupied than usual.

'Ah, Katie. You've been up to Military Road, then? Any ideas?'

'It's a little early to say yet, sir. But believe it or not, there was a note left with the bodies claiming that they were killed in revenge for the Langtry family. It said that the Dohertys were blood relations to the members of the IRA who shot the Langtrys, and that "we never forget". It was signed with the motto of the UDA. *Quis separabit?*'

'Jesus, it's unbelievable. After all these years? Were there any witnesses at all?'

Katie shook her head. 'Not that we've found so far. But I'll be putting out a media statement later. Look, I'll have to postpone our meeting with Jimmy O'Reilly. Maybe we can rearrange it for tomorrow morning.'

'Well, that suits me,' said Chief Superintendent MacCostagáin. 'I'm up the walls right now, to tell you the truth. It's like I'm personally taking the bang for all these attacks on elderly folks out in the rural community that we've been having lately. For God's sake, it's not my fault we've had to close so many local Garda stations! Then there's these ridiculous water meter protests, and on top of that, how are we going to cope with all these migrants? Bobby Quilty and his cut-price Lucky Strikes are about the last thing on my mind. Do you want to fix up another time with Jimmy or shall I?'

'Don't bother, sir,' said Katie. 'There's a couple of other things I want to talk to him about, so I'll do it myself.'

'Thanks a million. I'll talk to you later so.'

Katie continued to walk along the corridor towards Assistant Commissioner Jimmy O'Reilly's office. As she approached it she saw that the door was already a few centimetres ajar and she could hear voices – quite loud, too, as if they were arguing. She was about to knock when she caught what they were saying and hesitated, and listened.

'You'll be the ruin of me, you know that.' That was definitely Jimmy O'Reilly talking.

'But *Jesus*, Jimmy, you know full well what they'll do to me if I don't—' The rest of that sentence was unclear, but it was a young man's voice. Katie thought that she recognized him, but she couldn't be absolutely sure.

A long pause, and then Jimmy O'Reilly said, 'You know it can't go on like this. You'll have to find a way to stop yourself.'

The young man was almost whining now. 'I *can't*, Jimmy! That's the whole trouble! It's not like giving up the fags or coming off coke. At least with coke it's a physical thing, do you know what I mean, like? You can just stop snorting it. But this is . . .' The voice became indistinct. 'This is like it's inside my brain. No, it's more than that. It's *me*. It's what I live for. Without it, do you know, I might as well be fecking dead and buried.'

Another long pause. Katie was ready to knock when Jimmy O'Reilly walked across the room and she saw his reflection appear in the glass-fronted bookcase that stood against the left-hand wall of his office, quite close to the window. It was a very dark reflection, like a reflection in a pond, because the shelves inside the bookcase were lined with leather-bound volumes of Clarus Press case law. Nonetheless, there was no mistaking him – the curved new-moon shine on the top of his head, and his glasses.

She lifted her hand yet again, but then she saw the young man's reflection appear in the bookcase, too. He crossed the room and stood close beside Jimmy O'Reilly, and from his brushed-up hair and his height she realized now who it was – James Elvin, his senior personal assistant.

'So, come on, tell me,' snapped Jimmy O'Reilly. 'How much?'

'Only three thousand this time. Well, three thousand seven hundred. Three thousand seven hundred and thirty-two.'

Very long silence this time. Katie could see Jimmy O'Reilly turn his back on James Elvin and stare out of the window.

'All right, then,' at long last. 'I'll have it for you by tomorrow morning.'

'No chance of tonight? I can't go back there till I pony up. Can't even put my foot through the door.'

'It wouldn't do you any harm at all to take a night off. It might do you some good.'

'Oh, please, Jimmy. Please!'

'I don't know. I'll see what I can do.'

'Oh, thank you, Jimmy. Thanks a million million. You're my gold-plated angel.'

'Angel? You think? More like your gold-plated handpump.'

It was then that Katie saw Jimmy O'Reilly turn back from the window so that he and James Elvin were facing each other. To her disbelief, they put their arms around each other and embraced. At first it seemed like nothing more than a manly hug, but they remained holding each other closely for almost twenty seconds. Katie couldn't see from their reflections if they were actually kissing, but neither of them spoke. Even after they had eventually parted, they said nothing further, and both of them walked back across the room, so that their reflections disappeared from Katie's sight.

Only two or three times in her career had Katie come across critical evidence by accident. Once she had been investigating the embezzlement of public funds from City Hall and a taxi driver had handed in to the Garda station a briefcase that had been left in the back of his cab. It had contained all the duplicate accounts books of the official against whom she had been trying unsuccessfully to gather evidence for months.

Another time she had been drinking with her husband, Paul, in the Old Oak in Oliver Plunkett Street when a man sitting close behind her had boasted to his companion that he was responsible for beating up a car dealer from Togher who had almost died and would have to spend the rest of his life in a wheelchair.

She could hardly believe what she had just seen and heard in Jimmy O'Reilly's office. If she had arrived a split second earlier she would have heard nothing at all, knocked and walked in. *Perhaps God has been watching me today*, she thought, *and forgiven me for putting John and Kyna in such jeopardy. Or at least granted me the means I've been looking for to set them free.*

She tiptoed hurriedly back about twenty metres down the corridor, then bustled back to Jimmy O'Reilly's door, rapping sharply on it with the gold Claddagh ring on her right ring finger.

'Who is it?' called out Jimmy O'Reilly.

Katie stepped into his office and he said, 'Oh, it's you, Katie,' with all the enthusiasm of a man who has just seen the prospect of hours of tedious deskwork walk in through the door.

James Elvin was gathering up papers on Jimmy O'Reilly's desk and sliding them into a green manila folder. He looked up and grinned boyishly at Katie, as if he were flirting with her, and said, 'DS Maguire! What's the craic with those murders up at St Luke's?'

'We'll know more when Dr Kelley has had the chance to examine the bodies,' Katie told him in a dismissive tone of voice. Then she turned to Jimmy O'Reilly and said, 'I'm sorry, sir, I'll have to call off our meeting about Bobby Quilty. Perhaps we can reschedule it for tomorrow sometime.'

'That's fine by me,' said Jimmy O'Reilly. 'James, what's my diary like for tomorrow?'

'You're in Limerick at eleven o'clock tomorrow morning, sir,' said James. 'Garda Sergeant Mulligan's funeral. Then you have a meeting at two-thirty in the afternoon with Kieran Fitzgerald from the Garda Ombudsman. Then at six-thirty there's that reception for the Cope Foundation.'

'Oh, yes, the slow people.' Jimmy O'Reilly pursed his lips and made a thoughtful sucking sound. 'Sorry, Katie. Looks like we'll have to make it the day after tomorrow. You'll have your hands full anyway, won't you? And I don't think that Bobby Quilty's duty-dodging is exactly a priority, do you?'

'No, sir, you're right,' said Katie. 'We're tight enough as it is for time and money. And that's another thing I need to discuss with you, apart from Operation Trident – my budget.'

Jimmy O'Reilly glanced across at James Elvin and Katie saw the younger man frown, as if to say, *Come on, Jimmy, beat on, will you, the clock's ticking and I need my cash.*

Jimmy O'Reilly squinted at his watch. 'Katie,' he said, 'I'd love to go over your budget with you. Unfortunately some unexpected business has just come up and I have to shoot out to deal with it. Besides, it's going to take us a fair bit of time for you to tell me how much you need, isn't it, and what you can justify?'

'Again, yes, sir, you're absolutely right,' said Katie. All she wanted to do now was to let him go. She wanted to give him no hint at all that she knew the real reason for him needing to leave so urgently – or at least that she had a very strong suspicion.

She even managed to give James Elvin a smile as she left Assistant Commissioner Jimmy O'Reilly's office. Not only did he smile back at her, she could have sworn that he winked.

You just wait, you cheeky young steamer, she thought, still smiling at him. *I'll be giving you something to make you both your eyes blink.*

* * *

As soon as she got back to her own office she closed the door behind her and called Detective O'Mara.

'Bryan – listen to me! Assistant Commissioner O'Reilly is about to leave the station. I want you to follow him for me and see where he goes. That's all. You can take pictures of any address he visits, but be very careful and don't let him see you.'

'Assistant Commissioner O'Reilly? Am I allowed to know the reason for this, ma'am?'

'Let's just say it's security.'

'Security?'

'All right – security and health and safety. And time-and-motion study. And anything else you can think of. Just do it, Bryan, and let me know as soon as you're back.'

'Yes, ma'am.'

Next she called Alan. It took him a long time to answer and when he did it sounded as if he was walking along the pavement by a busy road.

'Alan? How's it going with Bobby Quilty?'

'Fair to middling, I'd say, but I've made some progress. I was just about to ring you and tell you. I kicked off by looking for one of Quilty's fag-sellers and I found one just inside the gate to the Bishop Lucey Park. Skinny wee rat, so he was, only about fourteen years old. He was doing a roaring trade with the lunchtime crowd from that takeaway coffee bar.'

'Can you speak up a bit?' Katie asked him. 'You sound like you're down the bottom of a well.'

'I don't exactly want to be shouting this out in the middle of the street!' said Alan. 'Here – hold on, there's an office doorway I can go into. That's better. So, anyway, I found this skinny kid and I bought two hundred fags off him myself so that I could get chatting with him. I wanted to make sure he was one of Quilty's minions. I don't think he meant to tell me anything much, Quilty had probably warned him not to. But I made out that Bobby and me were best pals from way back, and the next thing I knew the kid was even boasting to me how much money he'd made that morning, and how he'd have to go back to Bobby to get some more stock.'

'So of course you went with him?'

'Well, no, because the last thing I wanted to do was bump into Bobby. Bobby never forgets a face and he never forgets a grudge. But I followed the kid at a distance, all the way to this parking lot on Keeffe Street.'

'I know it, yes. Demolition site, more like.'

'There was a black Nissan Navara parked there, with some hard-looking fellow keeping guard on it. He filled up the kid's bag with cartons of Marlboros and the kid went off again.'

'A black Nissan Navara? That's Bobby Quilty's car all right. Did you make a note of its index number?'

'I did, yes. But it wasn't really necessary. I hung around for about half an hour and then Bobby himself came out of the building opposite with two other thugs and some blowsy-looking woman. Quilty had a few words with the fellow who'd been keeping guard and then they all went back in again.'

'Quilty doesn't own or rent any property on Keeffe Street, so far as I know. But with him you can never be sure. He probably owns half of Cork by now, under different names.'

'I managed to take a couple of pictures, so I'll show you when I see you.'

'Where are you now, Alan?'

'Only a couple of minutes away from you now. Copley Street. I thought I'd drop into that pub opposite and treat myself to a cold one.'

'The Market Tavern. All right. But try not to treat yourself to too many cold ones. I've found out something today purely by chance and I may need you do to a bit more following for me later. Let me know when you get there and I'll come across and tell you all about it.'

'Katie—'

'What?'

'Nothing. It can wait. I'll see you after, okay!'

* * *

Katie put down the phone, although she stood looking at it for a few seconds afterwards, as if she expected it to ring again and God to tell her what to do next. From out of the blue, He had given her some highly compromising information about Assistant Commissioner Jimmy O'Reilly. Could He not reassure her that what she was intending to do with that information wouldn't turn out to be madness – or, worse than that, pointless and ineffective? She didn't think her career could stand another Operation Trident.

She realized that she might have misunderstood completely what Jimmy O'Reilly and James Elvin had been arguing about, and that she might have misinterpreted the shadowy reflections in the bookcase. Yet what she had seen and heard made sense of what Roisin Magorian had suggested to her. More than that, it had given her a key to unlock one of the most difficult and dangerous investigations that she had ever had to deal with.

She went into her toilet to brush her hair and fix her make-up. Her eyes were puffy and she hoped she didn't look as slutty as she felt. At home she always kept two teaspoons in the freezer to pat around her eyes if they were swollen.

No, come on, Green Eyes, she told herself. *You're going to win this. And you're not a slut. Everybody needs comfort sometimes, especially when they have the world on their shoulders, like you do, and the lives of two people they really care for depend on them being confident, and brave.*

When she came out, Tyrone was waiting for her. He was staring out of the window at the bright, grey day like a young man in a dream.

'Tyrone!' said Katie, and he gave a little start and turned round.

'Sorry, ma'am. I was miles away there. It's that family this morning, the Dohertys. I can't get them out of my mind, like, do you know what I mean?'

'Yes. It's terrible. It's worse than terrible. Mother of God, it's hard enough when one person in a family dies or gets killed. A whole family gets murdered together, I don't know, it's like some kind of Greek tragedy.'

'Well, yeah,' said Tyrone, although she suspected that he didn't know exactly what a Greek tragedy was.

He held up a printout. 'I have the DNA results from Leitrim Street. The stain on the carpet was blood and it also contains traces of flunitrazepam. The DNA matches the hairs you gave us from John Meagher's comb. So he was there, all right. I suppose the question you're asking yourself is where is he now?'

Katie nodded and said, 'Thanks, Tyrone. Much appreciated. I don't think I tell you technical experts often enough how much we rely on you. If it weren't for you, do you know, we'd be still be crawling around the floor with magnifying glasses, like Sherlock Holmes.'

Tyrone's cheeks went pink. 'It's our job, ma'am. But Bill Phinner told me that John Meagher was a friend of yours, like, and so this meant a lot to you, this test.'

'Yes,' said Katie. 'A very close friend. Well – let's hope that he still is.'

After Tyrone had left Katie called Detective Sergeant Begley. 'Sean, that couple of so-called squatters at Leitrim Street. The fellow that called himself Chisel and that mouthy moth of his. Will you bring them in for questioning, the both of them? Take Scanlan with you. Not tonight – very early tomorrow morning will do it. Tyrone's just confirmed that the blood on the bedroom carpet was John Meagher's.'

'I doubt you'll get them to say anything, to be honest with you.'

'I doubt it, too, Sean. In fact, I'm sure of it. But the DNA test is positive evidence that John Meagher was there and I can't just ignore it.'

'Leave it with me, ma'am. I'll have somebody around there fonya-haun and we'll bring them in for breakfast.'

Katie was absolutely sure that neither Chisel nor his girlfriend would answer any questions, which is why she was willing to take the risk of bringing them in. Now that the technicians had come up with a positive DNA result she had to show Chief Superintendent MacCostagáin, and the media, too, that she was taking steps to find out who had abducted John and where he was now. It was the first investigation about which she had pretended to know less than she actually did, rather than more.

Thirty-six

Alan was waiting for her in the Market Tavern across the street. The tavern's walls were bare yellow brick decorated with brewery mirrors and GAA scarves, and the furniture was rustic-style pine. The bar was often packed out, mostly with a young crowd of students, but this was the middle of the afternoon and it was almost empty except for a young couple having a whispered but intense argument in one corner and Alan sitting under a picture of Muhammad Ali knocking out Joe Frazier, with a bottle of Satz in front of him, reading the *Echo*.

He folded up his paper, stood up and kissed her on each cheek. 'What about you?' he said. 'You look like you lost a cent and found a hundred euros.'

'You could say that I'm the victim of a happy accident,' she told him, sitting down. 'Oh – I'll just have an orange juice, thanks.'

She quickly told him what she had seen and overheard outside Jimmy O'Reilly's office. He listened without interrupting her, but then he said, 'Were you ever aware before that this Jimmy O'Reilly might be gay?'

Katie shook her head. 'He was married before, but his wife left him for some store manager from Dunne's, I think. I never really thought about it. I always assumed it was because he was such a misery-guts.'

'Well, he might well be dancing at both ends of the ballroom, you never know. It certainly sounds like this young man is cadging money off him for some reason. Blackmail would seem the most likely. Maybe he's found out that Jimmy O'Reilly is the father he never knew, or that he's been fiddling the Southern Region's performance records. But there could be any number of reasons.'

'Of course,' said Katie, 'and I'm not counting eggs before they're laid. I have O'Mara following him right now to see where he goes to get the money. It may be the bank, in which case I'll have to think again. But Roisin Magorian definitely gave me the impression that he was being funded by somebody shady and that maybe that somebody shady was demanding more from him than compound interest.'

'I never had you for such a theorist.' Alan smiled.

'I'm not, Alan. Not as a rule. But I'm looking for any way at all to rescue John and Kyna, and so long as there's still a mole in the station I daren't do anything official. I don't want to set up a raid on Quilty's house only to find they've been spirited away, the two of them, or that they're dead already.'

Alan nodded. He traced a pattern on the tabletop with his finger for a moment, like a butterfly, around and around. Then he said, 'I'm going to ask you a favour. I'm thinking of taking a look at that premises on Keeffe Street.'

'What do you mean by "taking a look"? You mean "breaking in and snooping around"?'

'I mean paying a visit after dark without the owner's knowledge or permission, yes. I'm personally interested in anything that might connect Quilty to drug-trafficking, or to his financing of the Authentic IRA, but of course if I can find anything else incriminating – anything relating to John and Kyna – I'll let you know at once.'

'And if you're caught at it?'

'That's the reason I'm asking you a favour. If I'm caught at it, and arrested, you can make sure that it's filed and quietly forgotten.'

'What if it's Bobby Quilty or one of his scumbags who catches you?'

'Katie – I won't be caught. I'll go in there, I'll search the place, I'll leave. That's all. It shouldn't take me longer than a half-hour or so. Nobody will ever know that I've been there. But if I can find evidence that will help us to bring down Bobby Quilty for good and all—'

'No, Alan,' said Katie. 'I can't let you do it. It's way, way too dangerous. Not just for you, but for John and Kyna, too. Don't think that plenty of people haven't seen us together, you and me. If Quilty catches you there, or finds afterwards out that you've been poking around there, he's going to blame me for it.'

Alan puffed out his cheeks and made a soft popping noise in resignation. 'Very well. This is your manor, after all, which is why I needed to ask your permission in the first place.'

'It's not that I don't want you to do it,' said Katie, reaching across the table and taking hold of his hand. 'But at the moment it's still too risky. Let's take it one step at a time. Softly softly, catchee whatever.'

'Not a bother,' said Alan, taking his hand away. 'I understand exactly where you're coming from.' He turned sideways in his chair and crossed his legs and looked towards the bar, making no secret of the fact that he was put out.

'Alan—' Katie began, but then she thought: *Don't say it, don't go there. You may be wrong and you need Alan right now. If you tell him what you really think – that he's far more interested in clearing his own name than he is in saving John and Kyna – you could well be utterly unjust and he may refuse to work with you any more.*

'Apart from that,' she said, trying to sound conciliatory, 'I want you to follow James Elvin when he leaves the station tonight. See where he heads off to. If I understood their conversation correctly, he's going to go somewhere and gamble. He might even come in here. They have Texas Hold 'Em nights every Wednesday. My guess, though, is The Bank at Clarke's Bridge, or the Diamond Club on Father Mathew Street.'

'Okay, I'll do that,' said Alan. 'What time does this James Elvin usually finish?'

'Five-thirty, give or take, unless Jimmy O'Reilly wants him to stay on for anything special. If you wait in reception you'll be able to see him leave the station and follow him from there.'

'Does he have a car? Supposing he drives off? What then?'

'I don't think that's likely, because it's a pig to park near either of those gaming clubs and they're only a five-minute walk away.'

'Okay. Grand. I'll keep in touch with you and let you know if and when he goes into any gaming clubs. I'll tell you what I'll do, though. I'll stay here in the city tonight.'

'You left your bag at my house. What will you do for a change of clothes? And your razor and toothbrush?'

'Marks and Spencer's. I'll manage.'

'Is it something I said? We don't have to sleep together if you don't want to. You're welcome to use the spare bedroom.'

'No, no, Katie. It's nothing like that. I just think you may be right. Let's take one step at a time. Softly, softly and all that.'

'I've upset you.'

'No, you haven't. We're grown-ups, aren't we? Not only that, we're police officers. At least you are.'

There was a long uncomfortable silence between them.

'Would you be wanting any more drinks there?' the barman called over.

'No, we're grand, thanks,' said Alan. 'I'm on duty tonight, any road.'

* * *

She had only been back at her desk for five minutes before Detective O'Mara knocked at her door.

'He didn't see me,' he said, a little out of breath. 'I don't think he saw *nobody*, to tell you the God's honest truth, the way he was pushing people off the pavements.'

'So where did he go?'

'I was hard put to keep up with him, I can tell you. And he was wearing this maroony jacket which I never saw him wear before, and a grey hat pulled down over his eyes. If I hadn't have known it was him I wouldn't have known it was him.'

'So . . . where did he go?'

'Over the Trinity Bridge and then up Morrison's Quay.'

'Don't tell me. He went up to Keeffe Street.'

Detective O'Mara looked decidedly peeved, as if to say why the feck did you send me chasing out after Jimmy O'Reilly on a humid afternoon like this when you already knew where was going?

'That's right,' he said. 'Keeffe Street. Like there's a tatty old office building on the left-hand side opposite the car park and he went inside. I didn't follow him in, but I saw him at one of the upstairs windows for a moment, with his hat still on. He came out again – ooh, no more than ten minutes later – and then he came straight back here.'

'Was he carrying anything? A bag, or a briefcase?'

'A plastic shopping bag in his jacket pocket when he was on his way there, but he was carrying it on the way back like it had something in it, though I couldn't see what it was.'

'Thanks, Bryan. That was really good work.'

Detective O'Mara hesitated for a moment, then he said, 'Aren't you going to tell me what this is all about? Assistant Commissioner O'Reilly walks to Keeffe Street dressed up like some busker and comes back again carrying a bag full of something.'

Katie smiled at him. 'I'll tell you as soon as I can, Bryan. But it's like you've come running into the room with another piece of the jigsaw that I've been missing. Only two or three more pieces to go and it'll be finished.'

'Okay, ma'am, if you say so.'

* * *

It was nearly 6 p.m. before Alan rang her.

'I nearly missed him. I had to go to the jakes and when I came out he was just going out through the front door. But I'm after him now. He's on foot all right. He stopped by the car park and I thought he was going to go in, but he was only chatting to somebody there. Now he's on the move again.'

'Thanks, Alan. Ring me as soon as he gets to wherever he's going.'

'No problem.'

She closed the folder on the desk in front of her and stood up. It would be a good idea if she went to the canteen for a coffee and a sandwich because she had a feeling she would be working late tonight. She had nearly made it to the door when her phone warbled again.

'DS Maguire? It's Dr Kelley.'

'Oh – Dr Kelley. How are you? How's it going?'

'Slow. We've removed the plastic sheeting from all four victims now. I just wanted to tell you that one of Kevin Doherty's brothers has come in to identify them. It's the whole Doherty family all right – Kevin and his wife Órla, née Cronin, and their two children Thomas and Sibeal. All four of them died from massive gunshot trauma to the head.'

'Dear God in heaven,' said Katie.

'I have two technical experts working with me now. We won't have any clear results for several days, I shouldn't think, but they're trying to recreate the crime scene from the angle of the bullet wounds and the blood spatter on their clothes. It looks as if they were very close to each other when they were shot and that they were probably kneeling. That's all I can really tell you at the moment, except that they were all shot with .38 calibre hollow-cavity bullets.'

'That fits in with the damage on the front door,' said Katie.

'Exactly. And as soon as the technicians can check the striations on the bullets, what's left of them, we'll know for sure how many weapons were involved.'

'I'll try to come by tomorrow morning and take a look for myself,' Katie told her. 'Meanwhile, thanks a million.'

She went to the canteen and bought herself a latte and a chicken salad sandwich. She had taken only two bites before Alan rang her again.

'Katie? You were dead on. The Diamond Club on Father Mathew Street, only two doors up from the Gospel Hall. I tried to follow him inside but there was a doorman who wouldn't let me in unless I became a member. Well – when I say "doorman", I mean muscle-bound Neanderthal in a dinner jacket. He was more than willing to sign me up on the spot, but I thought I'd better ring you first. Your wee man James might have seen us together at the station, so I didn't want to go inside there and have him recognize me, in case it messed up whatever it is you're up to.'

'That's fantastic, Alan, thank you. He probably wouldn't know who you were, but it's better to be safe. Listen – do you think you can just keep an eye on the place for me, maybe for half an hour or so, just to check if he leaves? I'm going to go in after him myself.'

'You're codding me, aren't you? He's going to know you the moment you walk in through the door.'

'Trust me, he won't.'

'Okay, then, if you say so. There's a bus shelter right opposite Father Mathew Street. I'll sit there and read my paper and look as if I'm waiting for a bus.'

'Alan,' said Katie. She was conscious that she was treating him like one of her own team of detectives and she didn't want him to feel that she was demeaning him. 'Thanks a million for this. I mean it. It's just that I can't trust anybody else but you. Not at the moment.'

'Katie, don't bother yourself. Anything that helps us nail the Big Feller.'

Katie called for a taxi and then finished her coffee in a series of gulps even though it was still too hot. She left the rest of her sandwich. She had intended to eat it only as a precaution in case she felt hungry later.

Normally she would have asked a garda to drive her, but she didn't want anybody in the station to know where she was going – not that it would have given them any indication of what her plans were. God or Fate had given her a precious lead in saving John and Kyna, and she wasn't going to compromise it in any way.

A red taxi from Sun Cabs was waiting for her outside as she left the station. She could have walked to St Patrick's Street in less than the ten minutes it took drive there, but the early evening was still humid and she didn't want to end up flustered and hot.

315

The taxi dropped her off outside the Brown Thomas department store. Inside it was all bright lights and the smell of perfume. She went up the escalator to the first floor, to women's designer fashions. A thin middle-aged sales assistant came gliding out to meet her with a beatific smile and her hands clasped together and said, 'Madam? Is there anything in particular you're looking for?'

The sales assistant looked so saintly that Katie almost felt she could have said 'redemption'. Instead, she frowned at the rails of designer dresses all around her and said, 'Something that's eye-catching, do you know what I mean? And sexy, and a little too young for me.'

'Eye-catching?' said the sales assistant. 'I see. Did you have any preference as to style or colour?'

'Red, I think. Red would be perfect. And short. And maybe off-the-shoulder. Something that shouts out at you. Something that says "Look at me, I'm out for a bit of fun."'

The sales assistant blinked at her, but Katie said, 'Don't worry about it. It's only for a laugh. We're having a bit of a hen party, that's all.'

'I see. Well, why don't you come and take a look at some of the Carven dresses? Some of them are very eye-catching. And, ah, *fun*.'

It took Katie less than five minutes to choose a scarlet taffeta mini-dress. It was very short and swirly, and cut on a diagonal so that the left shoulder was bare.

'It certainly shouts out, doesn't it?' said the sales assistant when Katie came out of the changing room and did a twirl in front of the mirror. 'Not too young for you, though. In fact, I'd say it makes you look even younger.'

The dress was priced at 390 euros, but Katie intended to bring it back for a refund the next day, when she had finished with it. Once she had paid the sales assistant, she went back down to the shoe department on the ground floor and bought herself a pair of red Kurt Geiger stilettos to match. They were tagged at 120 euros, but she thought she might keep them afterwards because they would go with her own red velvet dress. She could always put them down to expenses: 'specialist footwear for undercover operation'.

She checked her watch. She had taken twenty-five minutes already and she didn't want to keep Alan waiting at that bus stop for too much longer. She bought a blonde urchin-style wig for 45 euros and then carried all of her bags into the ladies' toilet, locked herself into a cubicle, and changed. In the next cubicle she could hear a woman quietly crying and normally she would have asked her what was wrong, but she had no time.

She had entered the store a businesslike woman with dark red hair and a pale grey suit. By the time she emerged on to St Patrick's Street, she was an exhibitionist blonde in a provocative scarlet dress who looked ready to party. She hadn't yet changed her shoes, though. It would be quicker to walk to South Mall where Alan was waiting for her, rather than take a taxi, and she wasn't going to try to teeter there on six-inch stilettos. On her way down Winthrop Street several young men turned round to look at her and she was given two or three appreciative whistles. One even called out, 'Hey, darling! Fancy coming to the Voodoo Rooms with me, do you?'

Oh, yes, she thought. *I can imagine what your friends would say if you brought a detective superintendent into one of Cork's ravingest night clubs.*

As she turned into South Mall, Katie could see Alan sitting in the glass bus shelter He was holding up his folded copy of the *Echo* with a pen in his hand, as if he were trying to do the crossword, but she could see that he had his eye on Father Mathew Street across the road.

She put on her gold-framed, pink-lensed sunglasses and sat down right next to him. He glanced at up at her, but then went back to his crossword.

'What's the craic, sweetheart?' she asked him, in a throaty voice.

He looked up and stared at her, and then he said, 'Jesus! Katie! I thought I was being accosted there! I was just about to tell you that I couldn't afford you!'

He couldn't stop staring at her, shaking his head. 'Well, you're a fine beour now, no question about it! If you hadn't opened your mouth I could have sat here beside you for the rest of the evening and I wouldn't have recognized you.'

'That's the point,' said Katie. 'I'm going to go into that Diamond Club now and see what I can pick up about young James Elvin. This must be the first undercover job I've done in seven years.'

'So, what can I do?'

'There's nothing much more you can do, Alan, not until tomorrow. Then we'll see how this all starts to come together. *If* it comes together. I have my fingers crossed that certain people will act to type, but as you know yourself, they don't always do that.'

'Oh, I know that fine rightly, I can tell you. I'll go and book myself a room at Jury's, then. Do you want me to take all those messages for you?'

'You can still stay the night at home with me, Alan. We don't have to – you know.'

Alan shoved his newspaper into his jacket pocket and bent over to pick up Katie's Brown Thomas shopping bags. 'No, I think it's better if I don't. Not that I don't think you're stunning, not at all. You know I do. And not that I don't want to. But sometimes I think two people can meet and be attracted to each other, strongly attracted, but they're not right for each other. All they'll ever do is end up hurting each other for no real reason at all.'

Katie was taking off her flat work shoes. She dropped them into one of the shopping bags and said, 'Is that what happened with you and your wife – what was her name?'

'Alison, yes. More or less. We nearly tore each other to shreds. I wouldn't want to go through anything like that again, Katie.'

'Is that what you think? That we'd tear each other to shreds?'

'No, not really. I'm just being wary, that's all. Once bitten.'

Katie said nothing. She hadn't been expecting to have a long-term relationship with Alan, but she thought it might have turned out to be more than just a one-night stand. It was clear, though, that he was afraid of committing himself. Perhaps that accounted for his last-second withdrawal when they had made love.

She had a suspicion, though, that there was more to it than that. Maybe he wouldn't fully feel like a real man again until he had harpooned his Moby-Dick. Bobby Quilty had destroyed him and he needed to destroy Bobby Quilty in return, more than anything else.

'I'll ring you after, anyway,' she told him. 'Maybe I'll drop into Jury's, if it's not too late, and we can have a drink in the bar.'

They stood up and he kissed her. She touched his prickly cheek with her fingertips and looked into his eyes to see if she could read what he was really thinking, but they seemed clouded, like one of those grey misty days over the estuary when she could never be sure which was the land and which was the sea.

* * *

Katie crossed the road. Father Mathew Street was narrow and dark and damp-smelling, with high buildings on either side. The Diamond Club was a few doors short of halfway down it, with a purple neon diamond sign over the entrance, flickering intermittently. Inside the front door there was a small purple-carpeted foyer, with a reception desk and a potted palm, where the dinner-jacketed Neanderthal was waiting with his hands cupped over his genitals. He smelled strongly of Aramis aftershave.

'Your boss in?' Katie asked him.

'Might be. Who wants to know?'

'I'm looking for a job, like, that's all.'

'A job is it? What as?'

'Blackjack dealer. I used to work at the Gold Rush on MacCurtain Street, but I don't know, I was fair fried there after a while.'

The doorman looked up and down the street and then said, 'Okay,' and picked up the phone on his desk. 'Mister Kerrigan? I have a girl down here says she's a blackjack dealer looking for a job. Yeah. No. Yeah. Well, put it like this, you wouldn't kick her out of bed for eating Taytos. Okay, then. Yeah.'

He put down the phone and said, 'You can go on up. Mister Kerrigan's tied up with a bit of business at the moment, like, but he shouldn't keep you longer than ten or fifteen minutes, so he says. He says that you can have a drink on the house while you're waiting.'

'What, and some Taytos to go with it?'

'He didn't say nothing about that. Just a drink.'

Katie decided that it wasn't worth trying to explain that she had only been joking. She climbed the narrow staircase at the back of the reception area. At the top there was a small landing and a doorway covered with a curtain of purple and green glass beads. She rattled her way through them and found herself in a long, low, purple-carpeted room with purple Tiffany lamps hanging from the ceiling. All down the right-hand side there were card tables with purple baize tops, and gilt-painted chairs, and in the centre there were two blackjack tables, with a roulette table at the very far end.

On the left-hand side there was a bar with a short fat barman in a white dinner jacket standing behind it. He was throwing dry-roasted peanuts up in the air and trying to catch them in his mouth, ducking his head from side to side like a performing seal.

It was early yet, so the club was almost empty. Four men were playing poker, while another six or seven were gathered around the roulette table, along with three bored-looking girls in low-cut purple dresses. The female dealer had piled-up black hair, Amy Winehouse style, and was wearing a tight purple satin blouse. Standing between two of the girls, his face in profile, was James Elvin. He had loosened his tie and his forehead was shiny with sweat. One or two of the other men looked around when Katie walked into the club, but James Elvin's attention remained fixed on the roulette layout.

The ball clattered to a stop and the dealer announced, 'Red, twelve.'

James Elvin said nothing, but raised his fist to his mouth and bit at his knuckles. One of the other men let out a little whoop.

Kaie went up to the bar. As she did so, the barman missed the last peanut he had been trying to catch and it bounced across the bar.

'*Shite*,' he said, then, 'Sorry about that, girl. How's it going there?' He had a cast in his eye so that it was difficult for Katie to tell if he was looking at her directly or not. On his upper lip he had a thin black moustache of the type that Katie's husband, Paul, used to call a 'thirsty eyebrow'. His elasticated purple bow tie was so greasy it was almost black.

'What can I be getting for you?'

'Vodka tonic, if you don't mind, boy,' said Katie, in a high Mayfield whine. She knew that, like several other casinos in Cork, the Diamond Club didn't have a liquor licence, but the barman took a large bottle of Smirnoff from the neon-lit shelf behind him and poured out a large glass for her, topping it up with Tesco tonic water and a tired slice of lime.

'This your first time?' he asked her, as she climbed up on to a barstool, crossed her legs and tugged up the hem of her dress. 'Haven't seen you in here before, have I?'

'I thought I'd try it out, like,' she told him, perching her sunglasses on top of her wig. 'I was fair bored out of my mind at The Bank and the Gold Rush, do you know what I mean? Same old faces every night.'

'Well, you have your regulars here, of course,' said the barman. 'But there's a lively crowd in later most nights, and at weekends.'

Katie looked around. 'Yes, I like it. It has what-do-you-call-it, you know? Atmosphere.'

'Just as well, right, or we couldn't fecking breathe, could we?' said the barman.

God spare me, thought Katie, *a comedian*. 'What's your name?' she asked him.

'Bertie, that's my real name. Bertie. But everybody calls me Tache. On account of my 'tache, like.'

'Good to know you, Bertie. My name's Nessa.'

'Good to know you, too, Nessa. What do you do, then, Nessa, or are you a woman of leisure?'

'I wish. I'm working at the Clarion at the moment. Receptionist, like. Well, I have to make ends meet, do you know what I mean?

My husband and I split up about six months ago and he's not exactly forthcoming with the maintenance.'

'Sorry to hear that, Nessa,' said Tache. 'Suppose you're looking to supplement your income, then, playing the tables?'

'That – and looking for some rich and handsome feller to take care of me for the rest of my life.'

Tache swivelled his eyes around the club and then shook his head. 'Nobody of that description in yet, girl. You'll have to wait for the late, late crowd. There's a car dealer comes in around eleven most nights, Paddy McGuigan. You might take a fancy to him.'

I doubt it, thought Katie. *When I was a detective sergeant, I arrested Paddy McGuigan for cutting and shutting insurance write-offs.*

She nodded in the direction of the roulette table. 'That fair-haired feen there, between them two girls. He's a good-looking feller.'

Tache let out a raspberry-blurt of amusement. Then he beckoned Katie to lean closer to the bar so that he could speak to her confidentially.

'There's two reasons why he wouldn't suit you, pet. One is, he *always* loses, big-time. He comes in every night, but when he leaves he's hundreds of yoyos down – thousands, sometimes. I'll say this for him, though, he's always back next day with all the grade he needs to settle up. I can't tell you where he gets it from, but he doesn't get it from playing roulette, I know that much.'

'Well, he must have money, then,' said Katie. 'I don't mind a loser so long as he's a rich loser.'

'Yeah, but the second reason he wouldn't suit you is because he's gay as Bogley.'

'You're codding me, aren't you? Him? He doesn't look it.'

'Oh, take my word for it,' said Tache. 'He's a corned-beef inspector, him, no question about it. Comes in here with some twinks some nights and they can't keep their hands off of each other. I've even caught him shifting some feller in the jacks.'

'What a waste.'

'You're not the first girl who's said that and you probably won't be the last. I'm surprised Mr Kerrigan tolerates him sometimes, especially after he's had a few drinks, like, and starts acting like a right batty boy. I don't know what he does for a living but he has friends in high places, I'd say, and that's why Mr Kerrigan never complains to him, not ever.'

'Oh, well,' said Katie. 'The Lord works in mysterious ways.'

'How's your drink?' Tache asked her. 'Like a top-up, would you?'

'No, you're all right,' Katie told him, although a second drink probably wouldn't have affected her. Apart from the tonic being flat, she could tell that the vodka was watered down.

'Now that auld feller right opposite your man, he's minted,' Tache was saying, although Katie was watching James Elvin so intently that she was hardly listening to him. The roulette ball had clattered again and the dealer had called the winning number, and again he was gnawing at his knuckles.

'. . . not only that, he's always on a winning streak. Talk about rubbing fat into a fat pig's arse. I asked him once why he comes here every night, because he doesn't need the money. He said he tries to stay away from the club but his feet always bring him here. Like he has club feet. Do you get it? Like he has—'

'Sorry?' said Katie.

Tache was about to start telling her again when a door opened next to the roulette table and cigarette smoke billowed out. Two men appeared, both of them smoking, but they put their cigarettes into their mouths to shake hands.

One of the men was tall and skinny, with a high shock of wavy red hair that was turning white at the sides. He was wearing a cream suit with wide padded shoulders which must have been at least fifteen years old. She assumed that this was Fintan Kerrigan, who owned the Diamond Club – or managed it, anyway. The other man, in his familiar pale green linen jacket, was Bobby Quilty.

Katie stayed on her barstool, but lowered her pink-lensed sunglasses.

'How about some peanuts?' Tache suggested. 'I have the dry-roasted or the chilli-flavoured.'

'No, you're all right,' she told him. She could see Bobby Quilty having a last few words with Fintan Kerrigan. When they had finished Bobby Quilty raised one hand in salute and walked away, past the roulette table. He stopped, though, when he reached James Elvin. He said something, and James Elvin said something back, and Katie wished desperately that she could lip-read.

Before he walked on, though, Bobby Quilty put his arm around James Elvin's shoulders and gave him a squeeze, like a proud father with his bar-of-gold, or a GAA football manager with his favourite player.

He crossed over to the bar and said loudly, 'What about you, Tache? How's your belly off for wrinkles?'

'Oh, I'm grand altogether, thanks, Big Feller,' said Tache. 'Do you fancy a scoop before you go?'

Bobby Quilty was standing next to Katie now, so close that she could smell him. Cigarette smoke was still curling out of his nostrils as if he were a dragon.

'Well, now, here's an improvement on your usual floozies,' he said, grinning at her, and more smoke leaked out from between his teeth.

Katie said nothing, but Tache said, 'Bobby, this is Nessa. She's bored of The Bank so she's dropped in here to give us a try-out. It's dead right now of course, but I told her we're always buzzing later on.'

'Fierce pity I can't stay,' said Bobby Quilty, angling his head to one side and making no attempt to hide the fact that he was trying to look up Katie's dress. 'Otherwise I'd say you're pulled.'

Still Katie didn't speak. Bobby Quilty continued to stare at her as if he was beginning to suspect that he might have met her before, but couldn't put his finger on where exactly, or when.

'Cat got your tongue, Nessa?' he asked her. 'It's not every day I pay a woman a compliment like that.'

Katie felt her chest tighten. She had her gun in her purse, along with her make-up bag, but she still felt threatened. It was Bobby

Quilty's sheer physical grossness that was so intimidating, as well as his obvious belief that he could say and do whatever he liked to anybody. She was reminded of what she had read in school about the Roman emperor Caligula, who had told his dinner guests that he could have any of them killed at a moment's notice for no reason except that he felt like it.

'So, what do you want me to say?' she replied, exaggerating the Mayfield whine that she had adopted when she first started talking to Tache.

He narrowed his eyes. 'Are you *sure* we don't know each other?' he asked her.

'I think I'd remember you, boy,' said Katie. 'You're not exactly Mister Missable, are you?'

Long pause, then, 'Take off them shades,' said Bobby Quilty.

'Oh, I will, yeah.'

'Take them off. Let's take a look at you proper-like.'

He reached out as if he were going to take them off himself, but Katie was quicker. She seized his wrist and gripped it very tight, digging the ball of her thumb deep into his tendons.

There was a moment of high tension between them. Bobby Quilty tried to force his hand nearer to her face but she wouldn't let him. He didn't speak, but she could almost hear him thinking: *How come this floozy's so quick to react, and so fecking strong?*

He half lifted his left hand and for a split second Katie was afraid that he was going to try to slap her. Just then, however, the bead curtain rattled and a grey-haired man in a brown jacket came through.

'Boss?' he said. 'I have the car outside, but I'm blocking up the street and the guards have just told me to move it.'

'All right, coming,' said Bobby Quilty. He stopped pushing and Katie released her grip on his wrist. He continued to stare at her, though, as if he could penetrate her sunglasses with X-ray vision to see what she looked like without them.

'I'm sure I fecking know you,' he said.

'Maybe you do and maybe you don't,' said Katie.

Bobby Quilty stared at her a moment longer and then went stamping off, crashing his way through the bead curtain to follow his driver downstairs.

'Good luck to you so, Big Feller!' called Tache. Then he turned to Katie and said, 'What in the name of Jesus was all *that* about? I hope you don't have that effect on *all* the fellers who come in here!'

It was then that Fintan Kerrigan came over to the bar and said, 'You're the young lady who's looking for a job, right?'

Tache looked baffled, but Katie slipped off her barstool and said, 'Thanks for the drink, Tache, and for all the gossip,' and followed Fintan Kerrigan into his office.

Thirty-seven

Her interview for the job of blackjack dealer lasted less than five minutes, as she had known it would, because whatever Fintan Kerrigan was going to offer her as a salary, she was going to tell him it wasn't enough.

'You'll have all your tips, too, though,' said Fintan Kerrigan, lighting up another cigarette and leaning back in his black leather chair. 'Good-looking girl like you, Nessa, you should make at least double what I'll be paying you. On a good night, a whole heap more.'

'Supposing it's a real quiet night, like tonight? Then what?'

'It's early yet. The place will be black later on.'

'That's what Tache said. But I don't know. And you say that I'll have to wear purple? I've never been keen on purple.'

'All my girls wear purple, It's the Diamond Club colour.'

'I'll have to think about it,' said Katie. 'Purple, you know. It doesn't suit me at all. Reminds me of funerals, like, do you know what I mean?'

Fintan Kerrigan sat back with the smoke fiddling upwards from his cigarette. After a while he said, 'You don't really want this job, do you?'

'What do you mean?'

'It's that Denny from The Bank, isn'it? He sent you here to find out how much I'm paying my dealers these days.'

'No, he didn't.'

'Oh yes he fecking did. What kind of a gom do you think I am? Go on, away with you. And I'll have ten euros off of you for the drink.'

Katie stood up, opened her purse, and tossed two five-euro notes on to his desk. 'Desperate the price of water these days, isn't it?' she said.

* * *

She met Alan afterwards in the bar of Jury's hotel. She thought that he was looking jaded, but she didn't feel tired at all. Maybe it was the stimulating effect of the dress she was wearing, and her new stilettos, and her swept-forward blonde wig. In the past three hours she had received more compliments and appreciative looks than she had in the past three months. Maybe blondes really did have more fun, especially if they wore very short red dresses.

'I'm not at all surprised that Bobby Quilty didn't recognize you,' Alan told her, pouring a Satz into his glass. 'I can hardly recognize you myself, for God's sake.'

'I'm fierce glad that he didn't,' said Katie. 'That could have wrecked everything. I might be adding two and two together and making five and a half, but I think I have more than enough evidence now that either James Elvin or Jimmy O'Reilly himself has been tipping off Bobby Quilty. It could be the both of them.'

'It looks that way, I agree with you,' said Alan. 'But even if they have, what do you plan to do about it? If you blow the whistle on them now, they'll just deny it. And don't tell me that Quilty has been lending O'Reilly cash that you can trace. If you hadn't seen and overheard O'Reilly and Elvin the way you did, you never would have guessed what was going on, would you? And like you said yourself, it's still possible that you might have misinterpreted what they were talking about and what they looked like they were doing.'

'I know,' said Katie. 'But I'm sure I didn't, and I'm sure that I can prove it. Jimmy O'Reilly's days are numbered, you mark my words. Not only that, I think I can nail Bobby Quilty at the same time.'

'So what do you have in mind?' Alan asked her. 'I know how worried you are about John and Kyna, but you're not rushing things here, are you? If you're going to pull in Bobby Quilty, your evidence has to be watertight, one hundred and ninety per cent, or else his lawyers will make mincemeat out of you – and I'm speaking from bitter experience.'

'You told me yourself that Bobby Quilty knows almost everybody in the North. I assume that includes almost all of the IRA and all of the the loyalist paramilitaries, too.'

'Of course he does. As you rightly know yourself, he was a Provo until they laid down their guns – or laid them down officially, anyway. Then he got himself involved with the Real IRA but he fell out with them about who was in charge of what, particularly the finances. That's when he suddenly discovered that he could carry on the cause but make a heap of money for himself while he was doing it. Hence the Authentic IRA.'

Alan took a sip of his lager and then he said, 'Believe me, Katie, I wouldn't say he knows *almost* all of the paramilitaries. He knows every single man jack of them, full stop. Not only the men who carry the guns but the sons and the daughters of the men who carry the guns, and the grannies and grandpas of the men who carry the guns, and the names of their goldfish. On both sides, too – republican and Orange and all shades in between. If by any remote chance he doesn't personally know somebody, then one of his minions will.'

'That's what I've been counting on,' said Katie. 'If he knows that many loyalists, he'll probably know who it was who shot the Doherty family.'

'Oh, for sure, he's bound to. The killers boasted about who they were on the end of their note, didn't they, with that *Quis separabit?*, even if they didn't actually put their names to it. Take it from me, they'll be boasting about it even louder on the Falls Road or Sandy Row, or wherever it is they come from. Quilty will soon get to hear who did it, if he doesn't know already. Not that he would ever tell *you*, or the PSNI. Not that he would give a damn, either.'

'What if I fixed it so that he *did* give a damn?'

'Sorry? I don't follow you. How could you make a heartless shitehawk like Bobby Quilty care about anything at all that doesn't affect him in the slightest?'

Katie said, 'You're right, you couldn't. Not normally, anyway. But supposing the Dohertys' murders *did* affect him – and I mean personally? Supposing the Dohertys were actually related to him, cousins of his, only two or three generations removed? What's the Big Feller going to look like if he allows some loyalist gang to shoot four of his close relations in cold blood and get away with it unpunished?'

'No question about it,' said Alan. 'He'd track them down and blow their brains out. The slight snag is, they *weren't* related to him, were they?' He paused, and then he said, 'They weren't, were they?'

'It won't make any difference if they were or they weren't,' said Katie. 'Not so long as Bobby Quilty *believes* that they were.'

'And how are you going to make him believe that? You can't tell the media that they were, can you? Apart from that, the Doherty family could easily check with the General Register Office and prove that you were telling a porky. That wouldn't do your reputation a whole lot of good, would it?'

'Just remember that most of Ireland's public records were destroyed when they burned the Four Courts in 1922, so it wouldn't be all that difficult to be a little creative when it came to the Doherty family tree. Besides, I'm not thinking of telling the media. I'm thinking of telling Assistant Commissioner Jimmy O'Reilly. Nobody else. Just him.'

'Jesus. And I thought my Alison was devious,' said Alan. 'But what if O'Reilly *isn't* your tout?'

'Then I'll just have to make sure that Quilty finds out some other way.'

'And then what?'

'He'll go after the killers himself if he behaves true to type, which is what I'm counting on. He'll make sure that he gives them one of his pontificating lectures before he has them executed. He doesn't only want to be the big cheese, he wants the whole of Ireland to *know* that he's the big cheese.'

'Am I understanding you right here, Katie? You're going to feed false information to Bobby Quilty in the expectation that he's going to lead you to the shooters who murdered the Dohertys?'

'You have it exactly. You should have been a cop, do you know that?'

Alan ignored Katie's light-hearted sarcasm. He was open-mouthed with disbelief. 'He'll *kill* them. He'll kill them and you'll be responsible. You won't just be destroying your career, Katie. You could end up in the slammer.'

'I'm not going to let him kill them. *We're* not going to let him kill them, you and me. We can track him and stop him before it's too late. If we do that, we'll know who shot the Dohertys, and have them arrested, and also have Quilty arrested for aiding and abetting attempted murder.'

'For the love of God,' said Alan. 'What if Jimmy O'Reilly or James Elvin aren't your touts at all? What if they are but they smell a rat and they don't tell Quilty that he's related to the Dohertys? What if they don't tell him anyway? What if they tell him but he doesn't give a shite?'

'In that case, I'll just have to carry on my investigation into the Dohertys' murder in the usual humdrum way. But it's going to be well-nigh impossible to find out who did it, especially if they came from the North. I'll need the full cooperation of the PSNI, if they'll give it to me, but I don't think they'll be too devastated that some Catholics got shot in Cork. And I *still* won't be able to touch Bobby Quilty.'

'There are so many "what-ifs", Katie, that's what worries me,' said Alan. 'What if Quilty doesn't go after the Dohertys' killers in person? What if he simply gets in touch with one of his minions in Belfast and tells them do the dirty deed for him? What if the Dohertys' killers are shot and buried under the floorboards like the Langtrys and the Dohertys and nobody finds them for another ninety years?'

'Alan, I have to do *something*. I can't just plod on with nothing but forensic evidence and witness reports and hope that I might get lucky. I've already got lucky, overhearing Jimmy O'Reilly and James Elvin together. Like, what were the odds against that? I have to try and take advantage of it, even if it doesn't work out. If anything happens to John and Kyna and I didn't at least *try*—'

Alan reached across the table and laid his hand on her arm. 'All right, Katie. I'm with you. I think it's a mad idea altogether – totally insane – and it could be very dangerous. I'm prepared to give it a go with you, though, just to watch your back for you if nothing else, and see you stay safe. So, when do you plan on telling O'Reilly that the Quiltys and the Dohertys are related?'

'I'm going to the mortuary tomorrow morning to talk to Dr Kelley – she's the pathologist. I'll tell him when I go back to the station after that. He's in Limerick anyway for a garda's funeral until two o'clock at least.'

'I must say I'm beginning to regret staying here tonight and not coming home with you,' said Alan. She thought he looked dejected as well as tired, and older than when she had first seen him standing in the reception area at Anglesea Street in his sparkling wet raincoat.

She could almost hear her grandmother Aileen, who always used to say, 'It's *life*, that's what it is. It grinds you down like a millstone, life – day after day, week after week, year after year – until one day you're ground down to dust. Then the wind blows you away, *piff!* and that's you gone for good!'

'Here,' said Alan, passing Katie the Brown Thomas shopping bags which were resting against the chair beside him. 'You'd better have your real identity back.'

Thirty-eight

On her way home that evening Katie stopped off at her father's house in Monkstown to see how he was recovering from his recent bunion operation. As she arrived outside she was surprised to see her sister Moirin's green Hyundai blocking the driveway, so that she had to park in the street.

When she rang the bell, it was her younger sister Siobhán who answered. Siobhán was taller than Katie, and plumper, with masses of curly red hair. This evening she was wearing a pink short-sleeved blouse and jeans, and her hair was tied back, and Katie hadn't seen her look so pretty in a long time.

'*Katie!*' she squealed and gave her a hug and wouldn't let go. After a while Katie had to gasp for breath and say, 'I love you, too, Siobhán, really I do, but you're spifflicating me here and I'd like to get inside and see Da.'

'I have a kitten now,' said Siobhán, taking hold of Katie's hand as they walked through the hallway into the living room. 'The Finnegans next door had five kittens – well, six, but one of them died. They gave me one for free.'

Katie could tell that her father's cleaner, Bláithín, had been today because the house smelled of lavender furniture polish and there was a vase of fresh orange-tipped gladioli on the windowsill. Her father was sitting in the kitchen while her sister Moirin was noisily washing saucepans in the sink.

'Don't get up, Da,' Katie told her father. She was pleased to see that there was a tinge of colour in his cheeks and he had filled out a little since the last time she had seen him. He was even showing the first signs of a small pot-belly underneath his pale grey cardigan. She put that down to Bláithín feeding him. Bláithín cooked for the Roaring Donkey pub, not far from Katie's, and she brought him back any unsold meat pies or bread-and-butter puddings.

'How's your bunion?' she asked him, and he heaved up his right leg to show her his hugely bandaged foot.

'I don't *have* a bunion any more, thanks to Dr Murphy. I'll be able to wear slippers of the same size as soon I'm all healed up. Lately, I've always had to buy two pairs, so that I could walk around with an eight on one foot and a ten on the other.'

'Did I tell you that I've got a kltten?' said Siobhán.

'Yes, darling, you did,' said Katie. 'What's the kitten's name?'

'Zebby the Giraffe.'

'That's a pure strange name for a kitten. What colour is it?'

'It's a she. She has grey and black and white stripes, and a pink nose. And a pink bottom hole, too.'

'*Siobhán,*' Moirin admonished her.

Siobhán had turned thirty now but while she was staying with Katie she had been attacked and hit violently on the head with a hammer by her lover's jealous wife. She had suffered irreversible brain damage and now had a mental age of six or seven. Moirin and her husband, Kevin, had been taking care of her ever since.

'Hi, Moirin, what's the story?' said Katie.

Moirin dried up the last copper saucepan and hung it up, so that all the other copper saucepans jingled and clanked against each other. She took off her apron and said, 'You've missed supper, Kathleen. It was chicken pot roast.'

'I didn't come for supper, Moirin. I just came by to see how Da was.'

'That's just as well, then. There wouldn't have been enough for all of us.'

'Where's Kevin?' asked Katie. 'Has he got over that terrible rash yet? What was causing it, red peppers?'

'He's better for now, but don't you worry, he'll be allergic to something else soon. Gluten, or ivy, or beef hand pies. Kevin's

never happy unless he's itching and scratching. He's in Waterford
at the moment, at some estate agents' conference. Three days of
peace. Well, apart from Siobhán.'

'I know a joke,' said Siobhán.

'That's good,' said Katie. 'Why don't you tell us?'

'Mother of God,' said Moirin. 'It's enough to make me wish
I still smoked.'

'Go on, Siobhán,' Katie smiled at her. 'Tell us your joke.'

Siobhán stood up like a child standing up to give a recital at
school. 'There was this old feller and he was standing by a puddle
outside a pub. He had a stick with a bit of string tied to the end of
it and he was jiggling the stick up and down, like this.'

'All right,' said Katie. 'Then what?'

'Another man said, "What are you doing?" and he said, "Fish-
ing." So your man felt sorry for him and took him into the pub
and bought him a drink. And when they were having the drink
your man said, "How many have you caught today?" And the old
feller said, "You're number eight."'

Katie laughed and said, 'That's a good joke, Siobhán. Who
told you that?'

'A man I met in the Garden of Time. Moirin takes me there a
lot. There's fountains.'

Moirin pursed her lips in disapproval. 'Between you and me,
I think he was after a whole lot more than making her laugh.
Nothing more tempting than somebody with the body of a woman
and the mind of a child.'

'It didn't make me laugh,' said Siobhán. 'I don't understand it.'

'Then why in the name of God do you keep repeating it to
everybody you meet?' Moirin snapped at her.

'Because it makes *them* laugh.'

Now that Moirin had finished clearing up they went into the
living room. Katie poured a whiskey for her father and a vodka
and Coke for herself and sat down on the couch next to him.
Moirin busied herself with her crochet – a baby's bobble-hat that
she was making for a friend – while Siobhán sat on the floor and

played with two dolls from *Frozen*, Elsa and Anna, making them talk to each other in squeaky voices.

Katie's father took hold of her hand and said, 'What's wrong, darling? You didn't drop by just to ask about my bunion, now, did you?'

'You make me sound as if I don't care about you.'

'I know you care about me, Katie. You're the first person here when I need anything. But something's bothering you, isn't it? Something serious.'

Katie leaned towards him a little and very quietly told him all about John and Kyna and how Bobby Quilty was holding them in his house in South Armagh – and how she was planning to rescue them.

'What frightens me is, that everything depends on this one snatch of conversation that I overheard outside Jimmy O'Reilly's door and what I saw reflected in his bookcase. They might not have been hugging each other at all – maybe they were close together but from my angle it looked like they were.'

'But Jimmy went to see Quilty after, didn't he, and came back with a bagful of money?'

'I don't know for sure that it was money.'

'Well, I doubt if it was drisheen. Come on, Katie, darling, sometimes you have to trust your own instincts and in this case I think your instincts are sound.'

'Dear God, I hope so. It could all so easily go wrong and I dread to think what Quilty would do to John and Kyna if it does. The bags I made of Operation Trident doesn't fill me with a whole lot of confidence.'

'You know full well yourself that Operation Trident would have gone like clockwork if somebody hadn't tipped off Quilty beforehand. It was decisive, it was bold. You put it all together in only a few hours. It was good police work, Katie, don't you have any doubt about it.'

'Thanks for the compliment, Da, but police work gets judged on results and in this case the result was total disaster. I really don't know if I ought to be taking even more of a risk by trying to lift Bobby Quilty and whoever murdered the Dohertys *and* expose Jimmy O'Reilly, all at the same time. I'm worried that it's going to turn out to be Operation Trident the Sequel.'

Katie's father glanced across at Moirin, who still appeared to be concentrating on her crochet, although she had her head slightly inclined towards them, as if she were trying to catch what they were saying. Siobhán was singing 'Let It Go' in a penetrating off-key falsetto, so it was clearly hard for Moirin to hear them. Katie knew that her father trusted Moirin, like he trusted all of his seven daughters, but she would only have to say a careless word within earshot of the wrong person and Katie's plan could be seriously jeopardized.

'You're right about Jimmy O'Reilly,' he said, not even looking at her, and speaking with his lips nearly closed, like a ventriloquist. 'He was only a sergeant, of course, when I knew him, but there were always rumours about him. You never saw him with a girl, and he was a scouter in his spare time. Sorry to be offensive, but some of the fellows in the station used to call him "Jimmy O'Piley".'

'Just because he was a scouter, that didn't mean that he was gay – or if he was, that he was sexually active,' said Katie. 'Scouting Ireland have the strictest child protection policy you could imagine. Like, all scouters have to be screened by the Garda Central Vetting Unit, don't they? They're not even allowed to put on a pair of shorts until they can produce two references.'

'Jimmy O'Reilly slipped through the net somehow,' Katie's father told her, still in that ventriloquist's mutter. 'There was an incident at the Fota summer camp one year. I'm not sure exactly what he was accused of, but he was forced to give up scouting and he was posted to Limerick. The whole thing was hushed up because he was a garda sergeant, but it was common knowledge around the station.'

'He was married, though, wasn't he?' asked Katie.

'Yes, to a woman who worked in the Dooradoyle library. Beibhinn, her name was. She was a fair few years older than

Jimmy and I think she'd given up hope of ever getting wed. I remember one of the girls saying that she would rather have taken holy orders than marry the most miserable gay in Ireland.'

Katie said, 'So we're fairly sure that Jimmy O'Reilly is gay. But that still doesn't prove that I'm right about him feeding information to Bobby Quilty.'

Katie's father turned to her and looked her steadily in the eye. 'Katie, if you're wrong, you're wrong, and you'll soon find out if Bobby Quilty *doesn't* go after whoever it was who murdred the Doherty family. In which case you'll have to come up with a plan B. My only advice to you is to play this very, very close to your chest. This PSNI fellow who's helping you out, what's his name?'

'Alan – ex-Detective Inspector Alan Harte.'

'Are you sure you can trust him? From what you've said, it seems like he's pursuing some vendetta of his own against Quilty. If that's all that matters to him, maybe he won't be so worried about John and DS Ni Nuallán. So if I was you, I'd be doggy wide with him. After all, if he was slung out of the police service, for whatever reason—'

He paused for a moment and then he said, 'You like him, don't you?'

Katie flapped her hand at him. 'Who'd have a former garda inspector for a father? Mother of God, Da, you can read me like a Book of Evidence. Yes, I like him. But, yes, you're right, I'm not completely sure of him.'

'I have some old RUC contacts who might know him, or who might be able to find out more.'

'I don't know, Da. If he thinks that I've been checking up on him behind his back—'

'*Let it go!*' sang Siobhán, higher and higher, almost screaming. '*I am one with the wind and the sky! You'll never see me cry!*'

Moirin said, 'I don't suppose you can take care of her for a day or two, can you, Katie? This song's breaking my melt!'

'I'd love to,' said Katie. 'Let me wrap up this investigation I'm working on right now and then I'll give you a ring. Maybe I'll take her down to Kerry and stay at Parknasilla. Sometimes you get seals coming right up on to the shore for a sunbathe, close by the hotel. You'd like that, Siobhán, wouldn't you?'

'*Let it go!*' sang Siobhán, oblivious, holding up Elsa and Anna so that they danced in the air. '*The cold never bothered me anyway!*'

Thirty-nine

'I'm starved!' said Chisel. He was lying on his back on the couch with a copy of the *Racing Post* spread over his middle and his big toes sticking out of the holes in his sock, with toenails that needed cutting. 'I could eat the decorations off of a hearse, I tell you!'

'Does that mean you want me to cook you something?' asked Sorcia from the armchair in front of the television. She was sitting with her feet up on a vinyl-covered pouffe, her yellow towelling dressing gown gaping open. An unlit cigarette waggled between her lips as she spoke.

'Of course not,' Chisel retorted. 'It means I want you to dance round the room in the nip whistling "The Broad Black Brimmer" out of your ganny. What do you think?'

'I couldn't do that any road, not while I'm in me flowers. Apart from that, I don't feel like cooking and we don't have anything in to cook unless you count a tin of tuna and a beetroot that looks like my grandmother's arse.'

'Jesus, you're fecking lazy, you are, Sorsh. If there was work in the bed, you'd sleep on the floor. You can ring for a takeaway, can't you? What's the time? The Golden Wok'll still be open.'

'It's either that or Murphy's chipper.'

'Nah, I don't fancy fish. Jesus, I've been smelling you all day.'

Sorcia switched the television to mute and reached down to the floor for her mobile phone. 'I'll say this for you, Chiz. You're the most fecking romantic man I ever met in the whole of my life.'

'I'll have the chow mein and the chicken spring rolls and them chilli spare ribs. And don't go forgetting the eggy rice like you did the last time.'

Sorcia rang the Golden Wok while Chisel went into the kitchenette and took two more cans of Murphy's out of the fridge. He popped the tops on both and handed one to Sorcia before he lay down on the couch again and lit himself another cigarette.

'What's this shite you're watching?' he asked her.

'I don't know. Some fillum about some feller whose brother's a bit on the slow side, like.'

'Why don't you turn the sound back on?'

'Because I don't understand what the feck they're talking about, that's why.'

'That's because you've a wee want yourself, Sorsh.'

'Oh go away and eff yourself.'

'That's more than you ever do for me, you dirty clart.'

Sorcia was just about to snap back at him when they heard the front door downstairs being opened. Opened – pause – and then closed.

'Who's that?' said Chisel, sitting up.

'How should I know?' asked Sorcia. 'You didn't leave the door unlocked, did you?'

'I never go out the front, do I? I always go out the back.'

'That doesn't mean you didn't leave it unlocked. I know you. You'd forget your scunders if they wasn't stuck to your arse.'

Now they heard heavy footsteps drumming up the stairs – at least two people, maybe three. Chisel stood up and said, 'Christ, I hope it's not the guards again. I left my gun on top of the toilet.'

'Typical,' said Sorcia, sitting up straight and wrapping her dressing gown around herself more tightly.

'Who's that?' Chisel called out in a strangled voice. 'This is like private property, like! You're trespassing!'

The living-room door opened and Bobby Quilty came in. Unusually for him, he was wearing a wide-shouldered black suit, and a white shirt with one tail untucked, and a mottled red tie.

He reeked of David Beckham aftershave.

'I know it's private property, Chisel,' he said, with a grin. 'That's because it's *my* private property. You can't trespass on your own private property, now, can you?'

'Oh, it's you, Bobby! What about you, big man? I wasn't expecting to see you the day.'

Bobby Quilty nodded at Sorcia and said, 'All right, Sorsh? Gave you a quare gunk, did I?'

Sorcia pulled her dressing gown even tighter across her breasts. 'You could have given a body a moment's notice, Bobby. I'd have dressed up for you.'

'Don't bother yourself, doll. You'd scare rats out of a stone ditch no matter what you wore.'

Normally, Sorcia would have lashed back at him, but she clearly sensed that this unexpected visit wasn't simply social because she carefully placed her can of Murphy's on the floor and stood up, smoking in quick, nervous puffs and blowing the smoke out sideways.

Chisel was trying to see who Bobby Quilty had brought with him. The two men were waiting on the landing, both shaven-headed, one wearing a black T-shirt with a demonic face on it, the other in a loose-fitting denim shirt that looked two sizes too big for him. Neither of them came into the living room and neither of them spoke. Although it was dark out on the landing, and their faces were in shadow, Chisel was sure that he had never seen either of them before.

'Who's that you've fetched along with you, Bobby?' he asked, tilting his head to one side, trying to see them more clearly behind Bobby Quilty's bulk.

'Business associates,' said Bobby Quilty. 'That's because you and me, Chiz, we have a little business to be sorting out.'

'What sort of business would that be, then? I thought we were all squared up, you and me.'

Bobby Quilty stepped forward and rested one hand on Chisel's bony shoulder. Chisel glanced down at it uneasily, as if a fat predatory bird had just perched there.

'I asked you to do something, didn't I, when we took away that John Meagher fellow? I asked you to clean up the place, didn't I, so that the polls couldn't tell that we'd been keeping him here?'

'We did, Bobby. We scrubbed the whole place thorough, I swear to God. We scrubbed the whole place thorough, didn't we, Sorsh?'

Sorcia puffed at her cigarette and nodded. She was beginning to look seriously frightened now.

'The problem is, Chiz, you didn't scrub hard enough. See, there was a bloodstain left on the bedroom carpet.'

'I know that, Bobby. I saw it, and we scrubbed it. That bloodstain, we even scrubbed it with the bleach. You never would have known it was a bloodstain by the time we finished with it.'

Bobby Quilty pulled a face. 'Maybe *you* wouldn't have known that it looked like a bloodstain, but the polls knew. They took a sample and they checked the DNA and now they have all the evidence they need that John Meagher *was* here, no matter how much you swore that he wasn't.'

'I couldn't help that, Bobby! Me and Sorsh, we did everything we could to make sure that the place was spotless. I don't even know what D and A look like, otherwise we would have scrubbed them off, too.'

'It's DNA and it doesn't fecking look like anything, you tube! It's micro-fecking-scopic! You should have lifted up the whole fecking carpet and taken it down to the dump!'

'I didn't realize that, Bobby. Honest to God, cross my heart, if I'd have known that there was anything microscopic there at all, I would have taken the carpet down along with the bed. I would have thrown away the whole fecking bedroom if I could have.'

'Do you know something, Chiz? You astound me sometimes,' said Bobby Quilty. 'If you didn't exist, I think they'd have to invent you, just to prove how fecking stupid it's possible for one man to be.'

'Away on, big man,' said Chisel, with a sheepish smile. He was beginning to think that Bobby Quilty had come around simply to give him a telling-off and that was all. But Bobby Quilty kept his hand resting on Chisel's shoulder and abruptly his expression turned very grave, as if he had been keeping the bad news until last.

'The reason that this is a problem, Chiz, is that the polls will be knocking on your door here tomorrow morning bright and early and they'll be pulling you in for questioning.'

'I won't tell them anything, Bobby! You know that! I won't say a word! Jesus, I've never been a tout and never will be!'

'Yes, Chiz, I know that. But they have this DNA, see, and whatever you say they can prove to a court that John Meagher was here, and they can call on witnesses to prove that you and Sorsh were here at the very same time that he was.'

'What witnesses? Who can prove that we were here? All we have to do is say that we weren't!'

'So if you weren't here, where the feck were you? And what are you going to say when they put the delivery lads from half the takeaways in Blackpool on to the stand and ask them who it was who answered the door when they came around here with two meat feast pizzas or a chicken kebab?'

'We don't have to say nothing at all, Bobby. That's the law. The polls can't make you discriminate yourself.'

'But what if they say to you that you and Sorsh are both guilty of keeping John Meagher here against his will, and even if you say nothing you're still going down for it, the both of you. And then what if they say to you, "Chisel, wee man, if you *confess* that you kept him here, if you admit it, and if you tell us who asked you to do it, then you won't face any charges at all, and you can both skip off free?" What if they say *that* to you, Chiz? Do you think you'll be able to keep your bake shut, even then?'

'Of course, Bobby. What do you think? You wouldn't squeal, would you, Sorsh? And neither would I. You can count on us, big man, I can tell you that.'

'You've spent some time up on Rathmore Road, haven't you, Chiz? Like it up there, did you? Food was *cordon bleu*, was it? And how about your cell-mates? All decent spuds, were they? None of them wanted to stick it up the old chocolate speedway? And how about you, Sorsh? How do you think you'll enjoy the women's wing in Limerick? There's some desperate rugmunchers in there, from what I'm told.'

Chisel tried to lift Bobby Quilty's hand off his shoulder, but Bobby Quilty gripped him even tighter, so that he winced.

'What more can I say to you, Bobby?' Chisel appealed to him. 'If the polls are coming in the morning, maybe you could find us somewhere to hide out for a while – you know, until this all blows over.'

'This is *never* going to blow over, Chiz. Wherever you go, the polls are going to find you, especially with that mankin' tattoo round your throat.'

Sorcia crushed out her cigarette in an ashtray that was already heaped with crushed-out cigarettes. 'So what are you going to do, Bobby?' she demanded, with a catch in her throat. 'Chuck us in the river, or what?'

'Ach, come on, you two have been brave good when times were good, and you've been brave good, too, when times were bad. The bogging state of that river, I wouldn't do a thing like that to you. I'll make it quick and easy, you won't feel a thing.'

'You're going to kill us?'

'Sorsh, doll, I didn't come round here for a cup of tea. If I had my druthers, I'd give you both tickets for the Maldives, or Lanzarote at least, but money's tighter than a duck's arse these days. I can't risk you being questioned by the polls and that's all there is to it. I have to think of my business, and all the people who depend on me.'

'Do you know what you are, Bobby Quilty?' said Sorcia. 'You're the Devil himself, that's who you are. The Devil Incarnate. I know you're going to hell when you die because that's where you came from. You'll be going off home, that's all.'

With that, she took two steps forward and spat in his face. A lump of tobacco-stained phlegm slid down his cheek and dripped on to his shirt collar.

He wiped his cheek with the back of his hand, then wiped his hand on his sleeve. He made no move to retaliate, but kept his eyes riveted on Sorcia as if he could kill her just by staring at her.

'Bryan, Feilim,' he said, over his shoulder. 'Come here, would you, lads, and take hold of these two for me? Go easy, though. They're good and loyal friends of mine, aren't you, Chiz?'

'Bobby, you don't have to do this, you truly don't,' said Chisel. 'Me and Sorsh could be down to Ringaskiddy and off on the first ferry before it even gets light. We'd be off and away and you'd never see us again ever so long as you live.'

'And what do you think running away is going to prove? Running away is the same as admitting you're guilty. And you don't think the polls have discovered the electrified telephone yet? They only have to call the British cops and tell them to watch out for a feller with a pair of hands tattooed around his neck and a fag-smoking floozy and you'll be back here and banged up before you can say that shite is thicker than water, and that you two are thicker than shite.'

'Bobby, I'm pleading with you now. Don't do this. I thought that you and me were like brothers.'

'I did have a brother once,' said Bobby Quilty. 'In fact, if you must know, I was twins. My brother was stillborn, and my mam never forgave me, ever, not until the day she died herself, as if I'd strangled him in the womb to make sure that I always got the best of everything.'

'Bobby—'

'Shut your teeth, Chiz,' Sorcia snapped at him. 'You're sounding like you sit down to pee. You know that the Big Feller's come here to do us, no matter what you say, so why don't we just get it over with?'

She turned to Bobby Quilty and said, 'Come on, then, wee man. Do what you came here for. Or would you rather we went outside and stepped under a bus, so it wouldn't look like you who'd done us?'

'You have a quare ticket on you, Sorsh, I'll say that,' said Bobby Quilty, shaking his head. 'Come on, lads, let's take them through to the bedroom.'

The two shaven-headed men came into the living room. In the light, they looked surprisingly young and not nearly as hard as they had first appeared when they were standing on the landing in the shadows. The man in the black demonic T-shirt was missing his upper front teeth and wore gold hoop earrings, while the man in the denim shirt had a livid harelip scar.

'Where in the name of Jesus did you find these two scobes?' said Sorcia. 'Did the circus leave them behind?'

'The bedroom,' Bobby Quilty repeated, still staring at Sorcia as if he could happily kill her there and then.

'Don't you fecking touch me,' said Sorcia as the man in the black demonic T-shirt came towards her. 'I'll go there under my own steam, thanks very much.'

She pushed her way past Bobby Quilty and across the landing to the open bedroom door. The man in the denim shirt approached Chisel, but Chisel waved him away and followed Sorcia. His mouth was puckered tight and he had tears in his eyes. He looked up appealingly at Bobby Quilty as he passed him, but Bobby Quilty simply patted him on the back and said, 'You'll be grand, Chiz, don't you worry. It comes to all of us, you know, sooner or later. Think of my brother. He never even got to see the sun for one day.'

The five of them crowded into the untidy bedroom and stood around the mattress with its stained, twisted sheets. The only light in the room came from a pink china lamp on the floor beside the mattress, with no shade on it.

'Okay, let's have you taking your clothes off,' said Bobby Quilty.

'What?' said Sorcia.

'I want you in the nip , the both of you.'

'Oh, I see, you want me scundered, as well as dead. Forget it, wee man. There's no fecking way.'

'*Feilim!*' said Bobby Quilty, and the man in the denim shirt bounded across the mattress in his boots. Sorcia was clutching her dressing gown around her as tightly as she could, but he grasped the lapels in both hands and wrenched it wide open. Then he roughly turned her around, pulling the collar down at the back and dragging her arms out of the sleeves. Within a few seconds she was standing there naked and pale and freckled. Her rounded stomach was decorated with a multicoloured tattoo of a parrot, its wings spread wide, rising from her pubic hair as if it were launching itself out of its nest and its tail was the string of her tampon. Her legs were bruised and marbled with blue varicose veins.

She made no attempt to cover herself, but stood there defiantly with her hands resting on her hips, as if to say, *You can do what you like to me, you Devil, but I refuse to be ashamed.*

Without being prompted, Chisel crossed his arms and lifted off his sweat-stained orange polo shirt and then unbuckled his belt and stepped out of his faded blue jeans. He left his holey socks on, but he was wearing no underpants. Apart from the tattoos around his neck of the two hands throttling him, the rest of his body was covered with snakes, and lions, and naked women, and on his sunken breastbone the face of Jesus, with His crown of thorns, but looking more like Bob Geldof than Jesus..

'Lie down on the bed,' said Bobby Quilty.

'Bobby,' said Chisel. 'I'm begging you, man. Look at me here, bollock-naked, and Sorcia, too, no threat you at all. If we can do this on your say-so, do you really think we'd squeal to the polls about you?'

'Lie down,' Bobby Quilty told him.

Awkwardly, Chisel and Sorcia lay down next to each other, their arms by their sides, but their eyes darting around them – from Bobby Quilty to the man in the black demonic T-shirt, to the man in denim. Chisel tried to hold Sorcia's hand, but she snatched it away.

'Now, turn back to back,' said Bobby Quilty.

'What? What do you mean?'

'I mean, lie with your backs to each other, and real close, so that your heads are touching.'

They did as they were told, although as he turned over Chisel suddenly let out a high, girlish laugh. He was beginning to think that this was all an elaborate joke, just to frighten them. He couldn't see any weapons. He knew for a fact that Bobby Quilty never carried a gun in case he was stopped and searched by the guards, and neither of the two men appeared to be armed, unless the man in the denim shirt had a gun tucked into his belt.

'That's it, Chiz, good man yourself,' said Bobby Quilty. 'Heads together. That's cracker.'

He went to the bedroom door, opened it wider and stepped out on to the landing. There was silence for a while, except for Sorcia occasionally coughing and the man in the black demonic T-shirt monotonously sniffing. That, and the muffled sound of the traffic outside.

Chisel was tempted to call out to Bobby and ask him how much longer they were going to have to lie here, as naked as the day they were born, with the backs of their heads pressed uncomfortably hard together and Sorcia's sweaty buttocks sticking to his.

He had already taken a breath when he heard footsteps coming up the stairs, light and businesslike and quick. He heard Bobby Quilty saying something like, 'Ready for you, Sandy.'

Sandy? he thought. *Who for feck's sake is Sandy?*

The bedroom door was flung wide open now, so hard that it banged against the wall. A thin man dressed in a black sweater and grey trousers stalked in, like the long-legged scissorman, his head completely covered in a black balaclava. He dropped to his knees beside the mattress and before either Chisel or Sorcia could react he gripped Chisel's tufty hair by the roots. Chisel said, '*Ow!*' but without any hesitation, the man pressed the muzzle of a silenced automatic hard against Chisel's forehead and fired.

Chisel's head swelled up and blood and brains squirted out of his ear. Sorcia's head ballooned, too, and her face exploded all over the pillow.

The man in the black demonic T-shirt retched and covered his mouth with his hand and said, '*Jesus Christ!*' The man in the denim shirt stared at the bloody hollows that had once been Sorcia's face, his hand held up to his forehead as if he were stunned. Her jawbone was hanging wide open so that she looked as stunned as him. One of her brown eyes was hanging off the edge of the pillow on the end of its stringy pink optic nerve, peering anxiously down at the floor.

Bobby Quilty came back into the bedroom and looked down at the two naked bodies lying on the mattress, with their mangled heads. There was no emotion in his face, but his tongue was roaming around inside his mouth as if he were trying to dislodge shreds of his lunch that might still be stuck between his teeth.

'Grand job, Sandy,' he said at last. 'Nothing like a suicide pact to sort out a feller's problems, especially mine.'

Sandy quickly unscrewed the silencer and dropped it into his pocket. Then he lifted Chisel's right hand and bent his fingers one by one around the butt of the automatic, leaving his trigger-finger until last. Finally, he angled Chisel's arm and bent back his wrist so that it would appear that he had shot himself in the forehead, killing Sorcia at the same time.

'Nice piece, that SIG Sauer,' he said. 'Fierce pity to leave it.'

'Don't you worry,' Bobby Quilty told him. 'With what I'm paying you for this, you'll be able to buy yourself another five like it. Now, away with you.'

Sandy got up and left, and after Bobby Quilty had taken a quick look around he and his two 'business associates' left, too. They clattered down the stairs, but as they were letting themselves out of the front door a noisy moped pulled into the kerb outside. A young man climbed off it and started to unbuckle a large red food-delivery bag on the back.

'What you got there, wee man?' Bobby Quilty asked him.

'Takeaway order from the Golden Wok, for Chisel.'

Bobby Quilty stuck out his lower lip and shook his head. 'Nobody called Chisel living here. Not any more, any road.'

Forty

By the time Katie arrived at the mortuary Dr Kelley was already at work. She was closing the gaping Y-shaped incision she had made into Órla Doherty's chest, using quick, tiny sutures that were almost as neat as a dressmaker's stitches.

'Good morning to you, DS Maguire,' she said, looking up from her suturing and standing back. She was a tall, willowy woman in her mid-forties, with a long, exotic face. Her eyes were very dark, even without make-up, and her eyebrows were finely arched. Even in her long white lab coat, Katie thought that she looked like a figure from an ancient Egyptian frieze.

'A pure tragedy, this one,' she added. 'I thought I'd grown impervious over the years, do you know? But to see the little ones murdered like this, for some historical grudge—'

Katie nodded. The bodies of the other members of the Doherty family were lying side by side against the far wall, all three of them draped in dark green sheets. They were lit up by the shafts of sunshine that fell from the clerestory windows high above them, as if they were lying in a chapel.

'Any other injuries, apart from the gunshot trauma to the head?'

'A few fresh bruises on the father's and mother's arms, as if they were manhandled. Your technical experts took pictures and they thought it might be possible to make a match from one of the bruises on the father's left biceps because his assailant was wearing two rings.'

Katie went up to the side of the stainless-steel autopsy table. She knocked accidentally against the analogue scale that was used to weigh dissected organs, such as livers and brains, and its metal pot dolefully clanked like a funeral bell.

Órla's eyes were closed and the way in which her face had been distorted by the fragmentation bullet made her look as if she were dreaming some surrealistic dream.

'You would have to check her medical records to find out whether she knew it, but she was showing early signs of systolic heart failure,' said Dr Kelley. 'If it had been left untreated, she may have had only a few years left before she suffered a serious or even fatal heart attack.'

'She doesn't have to worry about that now,' said Katie sadly. Like Dr Kelley, she had seen scores of dead bodies, including children, but there was something about this whole family lying here that was particularly poignant. If they had really been killed in retaliation for the Langtrys, it made her feel sorry for Ireland, too. Could there still be people in this country with such long memories and such a lack of forgiveness?

'Once I've closed Mrs Doherty here, I'll be finished,' said Dr Kelley. 'I'll send you my full report as soon as I've written it up, but the long and the short of it is that all four of them were killed by a single devastating gunshot wound to the head. The boy was hit in the back of the head and not at point-blank range like the others, so it's possible that he may have been trying to escape when he was shot. Your technical experts had some theories about that, and about the sequence in which they were killed.'

'I'll be talking to them later,' said Katie. 'Meanwhile, thanks for all the work you've done on this. Let's pray that we don't get any more like it.'

* * *

As Katie was climbing into her car to drive to Anglesea Street her iPhone pinged. It was a text from Alan, saying: *BQ's pickup @ Keeffe St. CU l8er.*

She texted him back, telling him that she would arrive at the station in less than fifteen minutes.

Almost immediately, before she could start the engine, Detective Sergeant Begley called her.

'I'm at Leitrim Street, ma'am, but we're getting no response at all. We've been shouting and hammering fit to wake the dead, but not a squeak. We called around at five-thirty, but they didn't answer and we thought that maybe they were wrecked, the way they smoke and drink, those two, and we just couldn't stir them out of their scratcher. But we came back twenty minutes ago to try again and we're still getting nothing. I didn't want to go barging in without a warrant, though, especially after all the trouble we had with Operation Trident.'

'No, good man yourself, Sean. You're wise to hold off. The courts have been taking a very dim view lately of raids without warrants – and apart from that, I don't want to be ruffling Bobby Quilty's feathers again, not so soon, anyway. Post a uniform there to keep an eye on the place, will you, just in case the two of them make an appearance, and find yourself a District Court judge for a warrant. I'm on my way back to the station from Wilton so I'll see you after.'

As she drove east along the South Link Road, Katie began to feel increasingly apprehensive. She wasn't particularly worried that Chisel and Sorcia couldn't be roused. It wouldn't surprise her if Bobby Quilty had kicked them out of the house on Leitrim Street, or maybe Detective Sergeant Begley was right and they were too hung over to be woken up. But it was time now to put her plan into action and she was losing confidence that it was going to work out. There was so much that could go wrong, right from the very start, or simply not happen at all. What if she had completely misjudged Assistant Commissioner O'Reilly and James Elvin? Even if she hadn't, what if Bobby Quilty didn't react the way she expected him to? It was like one of those elaborate games in which a ball rolls down a slide and drops on to a hammer which activates a catapult which knocks over a row of dominoes.

She turned into the Garda station car park. The trouble was, she still couldn't think of any other way to try to rescue

John and Kyna that wouldn't risk them being moved to another location where they couldn't be found, or even killed. Bobby Quilty had to be put out of action quickly and effectively, and if possible, legally – although she had decided that she would worry about the legality of what she was planning if and when it had worked.

She was pleased and relieved to see Alan waiting for her in the reception area. He was wearing a light fawn Gentleman's Quarters jacket which was obviously new and he looked as though he had slept well last night. Before she went over to him, though, she approached the garda sergeant at the front desk and said, 'Has Assistant Commissioner O'Reilly come back yet?'

'About ten minutes ago, ma'am.'

'Thanks,' said Katie, and walked across to where Alan was sitting.

'You're looking worried,' he said. He stood up and half raised his arms as if he wanted to hold her close, and kiss her, and reassure her that everything was going to be all right – but of course he couldn't, not in front of the desk sergeant and all the other gardaí and visitors who were coming and going.

'Let's go up to my office,' she said. 'I have the tracker ready for you, and the briefcase.'

'Good. I walked past Keeffe Street on my way here and Quilty's pickup is parked exactly where it was before, with the same shamfeen guarding it.'

'I'll give you fifteen minutes and then I'll go and see Jimmy O'Reilly. That should light the blue touch-paper.'

'You're still sure you want to go ahead with it?'

'I don't have any choice, Alan. If it doesn't work, it doesn't work. But I have to try.'

They went up to Katie's office in the lift. She smelled that black pepper and cinnamon fragrance on him again, but they still didn't touch or exchange any kind of intimate look. There was CCTV in the lift and more cameras along the corridors.

Once they had reached her office Katie went straight over to

354

her desk, unlocked her top drawer and took out a black GPS tracker, about the size and shape of a small mobile phone.

'Here,' she said. 'MicroMagnetic Four, one of the newest available. I "borrowed" it yesterday from my drugs team. You can stick it under a wheel arch or anywhere you like. I've already set up the mapping panel for it on my laptop and a mapping app on my phone. The second Quilty moves off we'll be able to see where he's headed, and it'll show his position every five seconds after that.'

She handed it to Alan, as well as a cheap brown briefcase packed with thirty or forty sheets of A4 paper. 'Don't worry if you lose any of the documents. They're only last year's council minutes on flood defences.'

'Okay,' he said. 'Give me fifteen minutes or so, that should be easy enough. In any case I'll text you as soon as it's done.'

There was no CCTV inside her office and Katie was tempted to give him a kiss. Even if his true motive was revenge, he was being brave and he was helping her. Instead, though, she touched her fingers to her lips and smiled at him and said, 'Be careful, that's all.'

'Careful? Do you know what they called me in the service? "The Underwriter." Before we went out on a shout I always insisted that we ran through every conceivable risk. I might have been mocked for it, but it saved some lives, I can tell you.'

'Just make sure you take care of your own life,' said Katie.

Alan touched his fingers to his lips in the same way that she had, and left.

* * *

It was a bright, warm afternoon, with a gusty breeze blowing so that the grey surface of the River Lee's south channel was ruffled. It took Alan less than five minutes to walk along Copley Street, cross the river on to Morrison's Quay, and walk up towards Keeffe Street. He walked quickly because he was keeping his fingers crossed that Bobby Quilty hadn't finished his business for the day and driven off home.

When he reached Keeffe Street, though, he saw that the black Nissan Navara pickup was still parked on the demolition site, and that the hard-looking guard was still leaning against it, with his arms folded, looking almost terminally bored.

Alan entered the demolition site, walking slowly between the double line of parked cars. He stopped when he was less than twenty metres away from Bobby Quilty's pickup and took out his mobile phone, as if he were answering a call. Loudly, he said, 'Yes, yes! Of course, Bill! No, man, I have it with me! Hold on, I'll find it for you!'

With deliberate awkwardness, he wedged the mobile phone between his ear and his upraised shoulder, lifted the briefcase and opened it. He took out the sheets of paper and started to shuffle through them.

'I have it here somewhere, Bill! Yes, just hold on a moment, would you?'

Bobby Quilty's guard showed no interest in him, but yawned ostentatiously.

Alan shuffled through more papers, and just as another gust of wind rose up, he dropped them all. They flew everywhere, flapping and dancing across the demolition site. Some of them caught against the wheels of Bobby Quilty's pickup and some of them disappeared underneath it altogether. Some of them wrapped themselves around the guard's ankles and he irritably kicked them off.

'Sorry! Sorry! My fault! Sorry!' said Alan, bending down repeatedly like a penitent monk and making futile attempts to snatch at the papers as they skipped away. The guard started picking them up, too, particularly those that were trapped up against the pickup's wheels.

Alan circled round to the opposite side of the pickup and went down on his hands and knees so that he could reach for some of the papers that had blown underneath it. At the same time, he took the magnetic tracker out of his pocket and clamped it in a small rectangular space next to the exhaust pipe. Even if the underside of the vehicle was inspected with a mirror, it would be very difficult to detect it.

Eventually, he and the guard had gathered up all of the papers except for three of them that were tumbling away towards Fitton Street.

'Thanks a million,' said Alan, as the guard handed him two handfuls of crumpled-up papers. 'I'm like a pig in reverse, me. Always dropping stuff. Dropped a scalding hot cup of coffee right on me foot only yesterday. Thanks.'

'You'd best be getting after them,' said the guard, pointing towards the papers that were blowing out of sight.

'Yes, thanks! Thanks again!' said Alan, and went off at a jog, stuffing the papers back into the briefcase as he went. Before he turned the corner, he glanced back and saw that the guard was leaning against the pickup again, with his arms folded exactly as before, oblivious to what had really happened.

Alan took out his mobile phone and texted Katie: *Stuck!*

* * *

Assistant Commissioner O'Reilly was on the phone when Katie knocked at his door, but he called out *'Come!'* and when she stepped into his office he indicated that she should sit down opposite his desk.

'Oh yes, it was pure moving,' he was saying. 'A fitting tribute to a very fine officer. Yes. So I'll see you next week when I come up to Phoenix Park. That's right, Thursday. All right, Diarmuid. Good luck to you so.'

He hung up the phone and then looked at Katie inquiringly, with his hands steepled and his head cocked slightly to one side.

'Can I help you at all, Katie?'

'Not really, sir, but there's something you need to be aware of – just in case there are any repercussions, you know, like Operation Trident.'

'Yes, well, I have some news for *you* on Operation Trident. It seems as if Bobby Quilty is prepared to withdraw his complaints about his home being broken into, and his unjustified arrest, so long as we compensate him financially for the damage caused to his property. He has also asked that we issue a media statement to the effect that we were acting on misleading information and that he is not under suspicion for any offence or misdemeanour.'

'Holy Mary, what else does he want? A civic reception and a year's free subscription to *Ireland's Own*?'

'There's no need for cynicism, Katie. I understand that you feel defensive about Operation Trident, but if Bobby Quilty is prepared to overlook it then so am I – and so, too, is the deputy commissioner in charge of operations.'

'You've discussed it with her?'

'Of course. I have to say that she's prepared to be much more lenient than I would have been if I had been in her position, but then it's all girls together these days, isn't it, from Frances Fitzgerald downwards. So long as you've learned a lesson from this, and we don't have any more debacles like Operation Trident.'

He pronounced 'debacles' with a long 'a' like 'di-*bahh*-kulls'.

'I can't guarantee it,' said Katie. 'In this job, you can never tell what misleading information you're going to be fed, can you?'

'All I can say is, Katie, don't let anything like it ever happen again. Now, what was this something that I need to be aware of?'

'It's the Doherty family, sir.'

'Oh, yes. What about them? Very sad case, that.'

'It said in the message that was found with their bodies that they were shot in revenge for the Langtrys back in 1921. Because of that, we checked up on their genealogy. You know, just to see if they really *were* related to any known IRA soldiers at the time. Apart from anything else, we were hoping that it might solve the question of who shot them, and why.'

'So did it?' asked Jimmy O'Reilly. He started to open and close his desk drawers as if he were looking for something, or wanted to show Katie that he wasn't really very interested.

'No, it didn't, unfortunately. But the big surprise was that the Dohertys were direct descendants of Niall Quilty, who was one of Captain Frank Busteed's men – you know, the IRA contingent who set up the ambush at Dripsey.'

Jimmy O'Reilly stopped opening and shutting drawers and looked up. 'Niall *Quilty*, did you say? You're not telling me that he was related in any way to *Bobby* Quilty?'

Katie held up a torn-off sheet from her notebook. 'I have it all here, sir. According to the Quilty family tree, Niall Quilty was a cousin of Bobby Quilty's grandfather. One of his daughters married a Doherty and *their* youngest son was Kevin Doherty's grandfather, so the family connection to Bobby Quilty is very close. Essentially, the Dohertys were Bobby Quilty's cousins, only three generations removed.'

'Oh, I see. That *is* a surprise. So how's your investigation into the Doherty murders coming along? Do you have any idea yet who might be responsible?'

'Apart from that message, and the suggestion that the killers might have been UDA or UFF, nothing at all so far. Dr Kelley has only just completed her autopsy and the technicians are working on the ballistics, but there was scarcely any forensic evidence and no eyewitnesses.'

'So how do you rate your chances of catching them?'

'At the moment, zero to nought per cent,' said Katie. 'But it's very early days yet. I'll be in touch with the PSNI and they may be able to give us a lead.'

'Fat chance of that, if they really were UDA.'

Katie nearly said, *There's no need for cynicism*, but she kept her mouth shut. Jimmy O'Reilly stood up, walked over to the window, and then came back and sat down again. Katie could tell that he was deeply agitated by what she had just told him. He drummed his fingers on his desk as if he were trying to make up his mind about what to do next, and Katie could easily guess why. *Should I tell Bobby Quilty that the Dohertys were related to him, or should I say nothing at all? What if I don't tell him but it comes out later?* At least, that's what she imagined he was thinking. She could be wrong.

After a long silence, Jimmy O'Reilly said, 'What do you have there? The family tree, is it?'

'That's right. Of course, most of the family records before 1922 were lost in the Four Courts fire, but we found the connection between the Quiltys and the Dohertys in the parish register in Inniscarra.'

'Can you make me a copy of that?'

'Have this one,' said Katie and handed him the sheet of note-paper. 'I thought you ought to know about it, that's all, in case Bobby Quilty was accused of something else that he hadn't done.'

'It's not a joke, Katie,' said Jimmy O'Reilly. 'We know perfectly well what Bobby Quilty gets up to, but it all comes down to man-power and budget. Let Revenue deal with him. He's much more their problem than ours.'

Katie stood up and said, 'I'll let you get on, then, sir. Thank you for the update on Operation Trident. I appreciate it.'

Jimmy O'Reilly was frowning at the family tree that she had given him. 'Hmm,' was all he said, and raised his hand to acknowledge that she was going.

Forty-one

Half an hour later, when she was sorting through all the paperwork that had piled up on her desk, she heard a *click* from her laptop and saw that Bobby Quilty's pickup was leaving the car park on Keeffe Street. She kept her eye on the little blue vehicle symbol as it flashed up every five seconds on the MicroMagnetic mapping plan. She watched it crossing over the Michael Collins Bridge and then turning north up Ship Street and she wondered if it would continue heading north. It stopped at the end of Ship Street, but then it turned eastwards on the Lower Glanmire Road, towards Tivoli, in the direction of Bobby Quilty's house.

Alan had only had coffee for breakfast so he had gone across to the Market Tavern for a drink and a beefburger. He, too, was following Bobby Quilty's progress with his mobile phone app, and he texted Katie: *The Big Fellers on the move. Going home by the looks of it.*

Katie thought: *Maybe Jimmy O'Reilly hasn't been in touch with Bobby Quilty yet. Or maybe he has been in touch with him, but Bobby Quilty isn't interested in historical vendettas. Or maybe he is interested, and he's raging about it, but he's going to arrange for somebody else to do the dirty deed for him. On the other hand, maybe I'm dead wrong about Jimmy O'Reilly and he would never pass confidential information to anybody, especially a scummer like Bobby Quilty, no matter what personal pressure he was under.*

She almost felt guilty for suspecting him. So what if he was homosexual and James Elvin was blackmailing him for money?

361

That didn't necessarily mean that he would breach Garda security, just to protect his own reputation. He had a very impressive record of service, even if he was old-school and intolerant of women being promoted any higher than tea-makers and crossing-patrol officers.

Bobby Quilty's pickup turned into Tivoli Park and stopped. There was nothing that Katie could do now except wait and see if he suddenly drove off somewhere else. Alan texted her: *Dont panic. He may not have heard yet. Or hes making some calls to find out who did it.*

Glad UR so confident! Katie texted back.

There was a pause, then Alan replied: *It wont be over till the fat man gets scooped.*

Katie went back to her paperwork. She was having to deal with complaints from victims of crime in rural areas that detectives were either late in responding to robberies and assaults or not turning up at all. In some villages the closure of Garda barracks was leading to crime waves, with hundreds of thousands of euros of farm machinery being stolen and elderly people assaulted and robbed in their own homes.

'I never answer the front door now after dark,' one complainant had written. 'I never know who it might be – a neighbour come for a chat, a priest come to pray, or a knacker come to rob me.'

Katie jotted down some notes. She was trying to think of ways in which she could improve response times without incurring extra costs, and it wasn't easy. If Bobby Quilty had been guilty of nothing more than cigarette-smuggling, she would have been inclined to agree with Jimmy O'Reilly that present budget restrictions made it uneconomical to go after him. As Detective Dooley had said just yesterday, 'It's only money, after all, and the nation's health, and when did we ever care about either of those before now? What about the Godfather fry-up at Tony's Bistro? Eight sausages and six rashers and four slices of black pudding! I know it's in aid of charity, but how healthy is that?'

As Katie worked, she continually flicked her eyes across to the mapping plan on her laptop, but Bobby Quilty's pickup remained stationary outside his house.

She had almost finished her report on response times when Detective Sergeant Begley rang her. She could tell immediately from the sound of his voice that something was badly wrong.

'Sean! Did you get the warrant all right?'

'Oh, sure, I got the warrant,' he told her. 'Judge Coughlan was kind of uppity about it at first, but when I told her that we were looking to build a case against Bobby Quilty she issued it straight off. I got the feeling that she's allergic to the Big Feller.'

'I know that. She had to let him off twice last year on charges of extortion because we couldn't find any witnesses with enough nerve to give evidence against him. So, what have you found? Anything? Have the lovebirds flown the nest?'

'No, they're still here, the both of them.'

'And? Are you bringing them in?'

'They're both dead, ma'am. Shot in the head. Looks like a suicide pact, but if Bobby Quilty's involved, you never can tell, can you?'

'*Dead?* Mother of God! Where did you find them?'

'In bed, lying with their backs to each other, but head to head. Chisel blew his brains out and hers, too, with just the one bullet. It's a pig's dinner, I can tell you. Here – hold on – I'll go back into the bedroom so that you can see for yourself.'

After a moment's hesitation a view of the bedroom at Leitrim Street appeared on Katie's desktop computer, tilting sideways as Detective Sergeant Begley approached the mattress and slowly scanned the two naked bodies lying back to back. Then he held his camera close to Chisel's hand, so that she could see the gun that he was holding.

'How long do you think they've been dead?' asked Katie.

'They're both in full rigor, so they were probably lying here dead when we first came around this morning. We've called the technicians, so they should be able to give us a more accurate time once they've taken their temperature and all that.'

'Any sign of a suicide note?'

'No, nothing. Mind you, I doubt if either of those two could read or write.'

'No witnesses? Nobody heard anything, or saw anything?'

'Nobody that we've talked to so far. This is a fierce noisy junction between Leitrim Street and Pine Street, especially first thing in the morning, so that's hardly surprising.'

'All the same, Sean, that's a SIG Sauer 2022. Nice gun, but not the quietest weapon in the world.'

Detective Sergeant Begley slowly walked around the mattress, giving Katie a panoramic view of the two white bodies, and then a close-up of Sorcia's devastated face. When Katie saw the beef-red sinus cavities and the flapped-down letterbox jaw she was glad that she hadn't eaten anything since she had come back from CUH.

She glanced again at the mapping plan. Bobby Quilty's pickup still hadn't moved.

'All right, Sean,' she said. 'I'll come straight up there. You have Detective Scanlan with you, don't you?'

'Scanlan and two uniforms. They've already called Super-intendent Pearse for backup.'

'Is Scanlan okay?'

'Scanlan? She's grand altogether. To tell you the truth, I think her stomach's stronger than mine. I was craw sick when I first walked into that bedroom and found those two squatters lying there with their heads blown off. Jesus, they smelled bad enough when they were alive.'

'I'll bring Dooley with me,' said Katie. 'He has a cast-iron stomach, too.'

Katie rang Alan and told him what had happened and where she was going.

'Rather you than me,' he told her. He paused, and hiccupped. 'I've only just finished an eight-ounce beefburger and I think I wolfed it down too quick.'

'Keep a watch on Quilty for me, won't you, and ring me or text me as soon as you see any sign of movement.'

'Don't you worry, Katie,' he said, and hiccupped again. 'He'll only have to budge an inch and I'll know about it.'

'Hold your breath and count to a hundred,' Katie told him. 'I'll ring you later so.'

* * *

She stood by the door and watched while three of Bill Phinner's technical experts examined the bodies and the bedroom. One of them was taking photographs of Chisel and Sorcia, while the other two were down on their hands and knees with SPEX Forensics HandScopes. Centimetre by centimetre they were systematically shining infra-red and ultra-violet light on to the carpet and the skirting boards and walls, searching for shoe prints and any other kind of indentations, as well as hairs and fibres and fluids.

Bill Phinner stood close beside Katie, with his brow furrowed, and he kept making little sucking noises, as if this was the very last place he wanted to be. Katie had sprayed perfume on to her handkerchief and was holding it over her nose and mouth. The bedroom smelled overwhelmingly of stale cigarette smoke and excrement and dead fish, and with their pallid skin and all their tattoos Chisel and Sorcia reminded her of the common goby that her father used to catch in the River Lee estuary. He never ate them, because they were the bottom of the food chain. *Rather like Chisel and Sorcia*, thought Katie, even though she knew that was less than Christian.

'So what time did they die, do you think?' she asked Bill. 'They were in rigor already when Detective Sergeant Begley broke in, so he reckoned that they must have been dead before he came round at half past five this morning.'

'From their rigor and their body temperatures, I'd say at least eighteen hours ago. We've taken some blood samples so we can narrow it down more exactly than that, but a fairly good estimate is ten or eleven last night.'

Detective Sergeant Begley came into the room behind Katie.

'That bedside lamp was lit when we first entered the room, so I think it's fair to assume that it was night-time.'

Katie took her handkerchief away from her face, but tried not to breathe in too deeply. 'Let's face it, we see a fair number of double suicides don't we? But they're mostly old couples, when one or both of them is terminally ill, and in practically every case they take an overdose.'

'Oh, we've had one or two exceptions,' Bill Phinner put in. 'You remember that poor old couple who jumped in front of a train at Kent station last year, hand in hand?'

'Of course. And those two who drove their car into Lough Mahon and just sat in it while it sank? But double suicides like that are very rare, like. And whenever guns are involved, it's almost always the man who shoots the woman and then shoots himself. I've never seen a double suicide like this, with only one shot. How did he know that she wasn't going to sit up at the very last moment and he'd only end up killing himself and not her?'

Detective Scanlan appeared behind Detective Sergeant Begley. Katie thought she was looking a little pale, and there were dark circles under her eyes. 'Do you want to come and take a sconce at the living room, ma'am? I think it poses more questions than it answers, do you know what I mean?'

'Yes, I'll come now,' said Katie. 'I think I need a breather, anyway.'

'Don't entirely blame you,' said Bill Phinner. 'There's some whiff in here, isn't there? Would you believe that before I decided to take up forensics I was going to go and work for Topps in Ballincollig making lollipops and Life Savers? It might not have been so meaningful, the work, but by God it would have smelled sweeter.'

Katie went across to the living room where Detective Dooley was taking notes and another of Bill Phinner's technical experts was taking photographs.

'So what are the questions?' asked Katie, although she could see for herself that the TV was still on, even though the sound was muted, and there were open cans of Murphy's on the floor, as well as packets of cigarettes, two over-full ashtrays and a copy of the *Racing Post*. She was reminded of the scene of Darragh Murphy's murder – an ordinary evening that had been suddenly and violently interrupted.

'It strikes me as fierce quare that they should have been sitting here drinking and smoking and watching the telly but then they decide to get up and go into the bedroom and take off all of their clothes and kill themselves. Those two cans of stout are still nearly full, like they had only just been opened.'

'That's right,' said Detective Dooley. 'If it really was a suicide pact, you'd have thought they would have sat here and finished their drinks. A last toast to life, do you know what I mean? And if they didn't finish their drinks because they had a blazing argument, they wouldn't have gone to bed and laid down that way back to back and shot themselves together. One of them would have shot the other, or vice versa, and then himself, or herself, as the case may be.'

'I spoke to the woman who lives in the flat next door,' said Detective Scanlan. 'She said they were always at each other's throats and some of the rows they had were, like, epic. Always effing and blinding. The language they used would have a made a knacker blush, that's what she said. But she didn't hear them argue last night, or this morning.'

'And she didn't hear any gunshot, either,' added Detective Dooley. 'If she could hear them swearing at each other, surely she could have heard a SIG Sauer blowing their heads off – that would have been more than 140 decibels. On the other hand, they were always slamming doors and throwing furniture at each other, so she might not have realized that it was a gunshot and not a chair.'

'So your thinking is . . .?' Katie asked them, looking around. The smell of cigarettes was so strong in here that it made her eyes water. It permeated everything, the curtains, the carpet, the furniture. The ceiling was stained brown with nicotine, the way that pub ceilings used to be.

'Well, like you're always telling us, ma'am, don't jump to any premature conclusions,' said Detective Scanlan. 'In this case, though, both Dooley and I believe that they were murdered by a third party – or *parties*, most likely. And they were taken by surprise, like, because we found a Browning Hi-Power automatic on top of the toilet cistern, which was probably Chisel's. It's an old one, with gaffer tape around the butt, but it was loaded and made ready. So he would have been able to defend himself against an intruder if he had been given enough warning.'

'The downstairs doors were both locked, front and back,' said Detective Dooley. 'They hadn't been forced, either. If it *wasn't* suicide, which we don't believe it was, then there's four possibilities. The first is that one of the doors was originally unlocked, so that the intruders could just walk in. The second is that Chisel or Sorcia opened the door for them because they knew them. The third is that they opened the door for them even though they *didn't* know them but they were immediately forced to let them in. The fourth is that the intruders had a key.'

'I think you're right,' said Katie. 'And since this building is owned by Bobby Quilty, even though it's only through a holding company, I think your fourth possibility is by far the most likely.'

'Wouldn't Bobby Quilty have done more to cover his tracks?' asked Detective Dooley. 'I mean, leaving the telly on like that, and these half-empty cans of stout. That's pure amateur.'

Katie shrugged. 'Maybe Bobby Quilty wasn't involved in person, although the way these two were murdered, that has all the hallmarks of a Bobby Quilty punishment – like Darragh Murphy's. Well – maybe not punishment so much as insurance, to make sure they couldn't give evidence against him and to frighten off anybody else who might be thinking of informing on him.'

She thought for a moment and then she said, 'I believe it *was* him, and I have the feeling that he *was* here, but I don't think he gave a tinker's damn about the details, like the telly and everything. All he needed was an alibi in case we lift him on suspicion – "It was suicide, your honour, I didn't have nothing to do with it." Nobody else is going to be brave enough to say different.'

Bill Phinner came into the living room, still frowning – always sour and serious, with a permanent air of professional disappointment about him.

'I heard what you said, ma'am, and you're absolutely correct. It wasn't suicide, either double or single. The male victim is holding the gun, but the HandScope showed that he has no gunpowder residue on his fingers whatsoever, so he didn't fire it himself. Firing that particular weapon can sometimes leave redness on the web between finger and thumb, and there's no sign of that either.

'On top of that, there's a semicircular impression in the skin around the entry wound in the male victim's forehead. It doesn't match the muzzle of the gun, but it's consistent in diameter with the muzzle of a silencer being pressed hard against his forehead. My armaments expert in there is probably showing off, but he thinks it could have been a Griffin Revolution or a Gemtech Tundra, which is a lightweight silencer that's ideal for a SIG Sauer 2022. Personally, I doubt if we'll be able to identify the make of silencer conclusively. Whichever one of those it was, though, it was fitted to the gun when it was fired, and they're eighteen centimetres in length, which would have made the weapon far too long for the male victim to hold it against his own head at that particular angle.'

'So it was murder,' said Katie.

'No question,' said Bill Phinner. 'I'd go further than that myself, even as a man of science, and say that it was an execution.'

He had only just uttered the word 'execution' when Katie's iPhone pinged. 'Excuse me,' she said. It was a text message from Alan.

BQ on the move. On N8 headed east.

Katie said, 'Okay, everybody. I have to go now. A summons from on high. Bill, thank you, as usual. Sean, Michael, Padragain, I'll leave you to finish up here. See you after at the station.'

With that, she hurried down the stairs and out on to Leitrim Street. Two more patrol cars had just arrived and five gardaí had cordoned off the entire pavement in front of the building. She ducked under the blue-and-white tape and crossed over to her car.

If Bobby Quilty was heading east on the N8 it could be that he was simply driving to Fota to play a round of golf. He was a member, after all. But if he turned left at the second roundabout he would be joining the M8, which could take him north to Belfast.

She turned on the engine, but before she drove off she texted Alan: *On my way. 5 mins.*

Forty-two

She was turning into MacCurtain Street when Alan texted her again: *BQs taken M8. Going N.*

She drummed her fingers on the steering wheel as she waited at the lights at the end of the Brian Boru Bridge, where Detective Barry had been crushed. If Bobby Quilty was on his way north, then maybe her plan was going to work out – at least partially. The driver in front of her was slow to move off when the lights turned green and she repeatedly blew her horn at him. He turned around and glared at her as if she had interrupted him saying a novena to St Monica, the patron saint of patience.

Alan was waiting for her outside the Market Tavern. She lifted her laptop off the passenger seat and when he had climbed in and fastened his seat belt she handed it to him.

'There . . . It's already logged in to the mapping plan.'

Alan showed her the app on his phone. 'He's just passed Rathcormac. He'll be going through Fermoy in a couple of minutes. He's really giving it the tittie, if you'll excuse the expression.'

Katie watched as the tiny car symbol flashed up on the screen every five seconds. It looked on the app as if Bobby Quilty was gradually creeping his way north, but in reality he must be driving at over 130 kph, at least 10 kph over the speed limit. Against all of her professional instincts she found herself praying that he would slow down – the last thing she wanted was for him to be pulled over for speeding.

As she drove eastwards alongside the river she put in a call to Detective Inspector O'Rourke. When he answered he sounded as if he had his mouth full.

'What's the story, ma'am?'

'I'm sorry to do this to you at such short notice, Francis, but I've had a bit of a family crisis and I'll be needing to take the rest of the day off, and probably tomorrow as well. Have you heard from DS Begley about that pair found dead at Leitrim Street?'

'I have, yes. Don't worry about it. Do you want me to make a statement to the media about it? I can liaise with Superintendent Pearse if you do.'

'All you need to tell the media at the moment is that we suspect the deaths were murder and that we're investigating further,' Katie told him. 'And of course make the usual appeal for witnesses. How's it going with that water meter protest?'

'They've called it off, thank God. For now, anyway. I never had to deal with such a bunch of raving headbangers in the whole of my career, I'll tell you. The way they talk, you'd think that water meters were invented by Satan.'

'Thanks, Francis. If anything urgent comes up you can contact me at any time. I'll send you a text as soon as I know when I'll be back.'

Alan was keeping his eye on the mapping plan. 'He's passing Fermoy now. He's still heading north on the M8. Just going over the Blackwater River. Still speeding.'

Then he turned to Katie and said, 'You're a consummate liar, you know that, don't you? "Family crisis" – I almost believed you myself when you said that!'

'Well, it's true in a way. John is practically family, and so is Kyna. Take a look in the glovebox.'

'What?'

'Take a look in the glovebox. See what's in there. But be careful.'

Alan opened the glovebox. He put in his hand and took out two black woollen balaclavas, and then a Garda-issue SIG Sauer automatic.

'You're really going to do this, aren't you?' he said.

372

'What did you think? That I was going to chase Bobby Quilty all the way up to Belfast and then do nothing but phone the police?'

'No. Of course not. But you're taking one hell of a risk here. You're an awful scary lady, did anyone ever tell you that? I think I'm more afeard of you than I am of Bobby Quilty.'

'You've used one of these SIG Sauers before, have you?'

'Oh yes. I did all my firearms training with a two-twenty Carry.'

'We'll have to make it snappy, Alan. Really, really snappy. No hesitation at all. There won't be any time for procedure or warrants or calling for backup.'

'I'm with you all the way. You know that, don't you? And I've done a fair few things myself that were off the menu, so to speak. But this – *fewfff* . . .'

'Where he is now?' asked Katie. They were approaching Fermoy themselves now, although she was keeping to the speed limit. There was no need to have Bobby Quilty's pickup in sight when they were tracking him on the mapping plan.

'Oh—' said Alan. 'He's just passed the turn-off to Mitchelstown. He'll have crossed the Cork county border into Limerick in a couple of minutes.'

Katie had guessed for herself how far Bobby Quilty had progressed but she had wanted to change the subject. She had enough doubts about what she was doing without Alan asking her if she wasn't being too reckless.

Ever since they had left Cork City she had seen heavy grey clouds following them in her rear-view mirror, trailing veils of rain, and by the time they crossed over the Blackwater themselves the clouds were on top of them, like a huge grey blanket being dragged over their heads, and large clear droplets were starting to patter on the windscreen. As they reached Limerick it began to lash down, so that Katie had to turn on the windscreen wipers at full speed and the road ahead of them vanished in a fog of spray.

Alan said, 'Weren't you even tempted to go to America with John? I mean, for the love of God, think of the weather, if nothing else.'

Katie shrugged. 'I still wake up in the night thinking that I made a terrible mistake. I could be living in San Francisco right now, happily married, working for Pinkerton's. I might even have a child. Who knows?'

'What was it that decided you? Not only your sense of duty, surely. I have a sense of duty – that's part of what makes you decide to be a police officer in the first place. But I make plenty of selfish decisions, too.'

'You decided you weren't going to sleep with me again. Was that a selfish decision?'

'No. Yes. In a way. Let's just say that it was self-preservation.'

'Meaning what, exactly?'

'Meaning that I find you incredibly attractive, and sexy, and strong, and self-willed, and that I would probably find myself falling in love with you even if I haven't already. And like I said before, having a relationship with you would probably rip us to bits. Well, it would probably rip *me* to bits, anyhow.'

Katie said nothing for nearly half a minute, while the windscreen wipers furiously flapped from side to side and the tiny car symbol on the mapping plan continued to click every five seconds.

At last she said, 'Don't you trust me?'

'Of course I trust you. But I'm not sure that I could handle you. What we're doing now, I don't know how you had the nerve to think about it, let alone actually carry it out. From what you've told me, you fought tooth and nail to get yourself promoted to Superintendent but now you're putting your entire career at risk, not to mention your life. And all for a man you never really loved.'

'I didn't say that I didn't love him.'

'You didn't have to, Katie. If you'd ever really loved him, you'd be in San Francisco right now, sunning yourself, with your new child on your knee, instead of raking through the pissing rain in Limerick chasing after some fat revolting shitehawk like Bobby Quilty.'

Katie was about to answer, but then she didn't. Maybe Alan was right. She had adored John. She could still close her eyes and think of the way that he used to make love to her, strong and slow and rhythmical, so that sometimes it was like being in a boat on a gently swelling tide, rather than a bed. She could still picture him standing naked by the bedroom window in the morning looking out, but then she could also remember that his eyes seemed to be focused far away instead of on the yard outside, and that she had always felt that she was gradually losing him. Once a man has left Ireland, he never finds it easy to return, not for good. But John was in danger now, appalling danger, and she couldn't imagine how devastated she would be if she lost him.

'Crossing into County Tipperary,' said Alan.

* * *

The rain slowed Bobby Quilty's pickup down to 90 kph, but on Katie's laptop it still kept on clicking its way relentlessly northwards. After two hours Katie and Alan reached Kildare, where Katie pulled on to the hard shoulder at the side of the road and they changed places so that Alan could drive for a while. The rain was still hammering down, so they scurried from one side of the car the other as quickly as they could, like two characters in a silent comedy.

'Jesus,' said Alan, as he fastened his seat belt. 'You hardly need a car in this weather. You'd be better off with a fecking speedboat!'

Katie said, 'I'm going to close my eyes for a while. Wake me up if Quilty does anything strange.'

'It has occurred to you that it may not be Quilty himself in his pickup, only a couple of his minions?'

'It's him all right,' Katie told him.

'What makes you so sure?'

'Because he's driving to Belfast to show the whole of the country that he's not to be messed with, either him or his family. And the only way he can do that is by doing it in person. He thinks somebody's challenged him and he's not going to let them get away with it.'

'But what if it's not him? What if Jimmy O'Reilly hasn't even told him and he's just sent one of his little scummers on some errand or other?'

'Then I'll have egg on my lap, won't I?'

'Face.'

'What?'

'It's "egg on my face". Not "lap".'

'If that's not Bobby Quilty in that pickup, then I'll probably have both.'

She didn't think she would be able to sleep, but the monotonous flapping of the windscreen wipers and the continual clicking of the laptop soon began to make her feel drowsy. She dreamed that she was in a car, driving through the rain, and then she dreamed that she was sitting in the kitchen at home, talking to her mother.

She was surprised and pleased that her mother was still alive. She looked very much like Katie, with her coppery red hair tied back in a loose, untidy pleat, and intense green eyes. She was wearing a cream-coloured smock with a broderie anglaise collar, which she had been wearing the day before she was taken to hospital to give birth to Moirin, and died.

'I think you're making a terrible mistake,' said her mother, without looking up from her embroidery.

'Why? I love him.'

'You think you love him, but you've never been in love so you don't know what love is. Not real love. Not the way your da and I love each other. Not only that, he's a desperate chancer. You know he is. It won't do you any favours in the Garda, being married to a man like that.'

'Ma, I don't care what you think. Me and Paul are going to get married and that's an end to it. *Paul!* Come on, we're leaving!'

Alan said, 'Who's Paul?'

Katie jolted and opened her eyes. Her shoulder was stiff from leaning sideways against the passenger door and her mouth felt dry. It was still raining and the windscreen wipers were still furiously throwing themselves from side to side.

'Did I say "Paul"?' she said. 'I was dreaming. I was having an argument with my mother about my first husband. Well, my only husband. He's dead now.'

She peered out of the window and asked, 'How long have I been asleep? I didn't think I would actually sleep! Where are we?'

'You've been out for half an hour at least. We've just passed Rathcoole. We'll be going around the Dublin ring road in a few minutes, God help us. Let's hope the traffic's not too sticky.'

'Where's the—?' Katie began, but Alan lifted up her laptop from where he had tucked it down the side of his seat.

'I've been keeping track on the Big Feller on my mobile,' he said. 'He's still heading north.'

Katie opened her laptop and saw that Bobby Quilty's pickup had now bypassed Dublin city centre on the M50 ring road and was passing through Swords. From here, it would take them about another hour to reach the border with the North and then a further fifty minutes to get to Belfast. She reached behind her to the back seat, where she had left her large maroon leather tote bag, and took out two bottles of Celtic Pure water. She opened one and passed it to Alan.

'Thanks. A cold Satz would have hit the spot, but this'll do.'

The late rush-hour traffic around the M50 was slow, a carnival of red brake lights, but it kept moving and as soon as they had bypassed Dublin Alan was able to speed up. The rain was gradually easing off, too, and as they drove over the twisting River Boyne between County Meath and County Louth the clouds began to break up, so that the sun held up a few last silvery swords of light before it sank behind the distant trees.

At last they reached the southern suburbs of Belfast. Alan stayed in the driving seat because he knew the city so well, while Katie kept the mapping plan open on her lap and gave him directions.

'He's turning off the main road, left, on to the A55,' she told him.

'That's the Monagh bypass, which goes off to the west,' said Alan. 'He won't find many loyalists in that direction.'

Bobby Quilty's pickup had slowed down now and they were less than two kilometres behind it.

'He's heading along Springfield Road.'

'I think I know where he's going,' said Alan. 'His cousin Maxy

O'Mara lives just up here in Dunboyne Park. Maxy was always Bobby's fixer. He'd get guns for him if he needed guns, or a car with a number plate that nobody could trace, or rent him a lock-up where he could store his smuggled fags if he'd shipped in too many. Jesus, Maxy O'Mara. We scooped Maxy more times than I can remember, but we were never able to get him up in front of a court.'

'Not even a Diplock Court?'

Alan shook his head. 'He wasn't strictly a terrorist, that was the trouble. And we could never get enough admissible evidence against him. You remember that poem, "The other day, upon the stair, I met a man who wasn't there"? That's what we used to call Maxy O'Mara when I was in the COD – "the Man Who Wasn't There". No matter where a witness testified that Maxy had been, he could produce two more who would say that he hadn't been there at all.'

Katie watched Bobby Quilty's pickup as it turned off the Springfield Road into Highcairn Drive. It travelled a few metres and then it turned left into a short cul-de-sac called Dunboyne Park, just as Alan had predicted. There it stopped.

Alan pulled into the forecourt of the Mount Alverno petrol station, about a kilometre and a half short of Highcairn Drive. 'Okay then,' he said. 'Now what do we do?'

'We'll have to wait, that's all,' said Katie. 'He might just have stopped for a comfort break. In fact, I'd say that's a certainty, knowing him. But it all depends on what he does next.'

'On balance, I think it's unlikely that he'll try to do anything tonight,' said Alan. 'He might have found out by now who it was who shot the Dohertys. If they were loyalists, though, like they made out they were, then even *he's* going to be cautious about going into a staunchly loyalist area at this time of night. That's if there isn't an interface around it and it's locked for the night.'

'Quite honestly, I could use a comfort break myself,' said Katie. 'Keep an eye on him, would you? I won't be long.'

When she came back from the petrol station toilet, Alan was standing beside the car with her laptop open on the roof.

'Any movement?' she asked him.

'No. He hasn't budged an inch. I reckon I'm right and he's going to stay there till the morning. Listen – we don't want to be sitting in the car all night, do we? What do you say we go back to my place? It's only twenty minutes away and we can take it in turns to keep a watch on him. I can knock us up something to eat, too.'

Katie thought for a moment. It was a very high risk. If Bobby Quilty did decide to go after the Dohertys' murderers tonight, and they lived in one of the nearest loyalist enclaves like Ainsworth Avenue or the Highfield Estate, it would take him only a few minutes to get there and by the time she and Alan arrived it might be too late. On the other hand, the murderers might live further away, and in any case she guessed that Bobby Quilty would want to spend some time relishing his revenge and making sure that his victims knew exactly what a fatal mistake they had made by killing anybody related to the Quilty family.

'I don't know,' she said. 'I'm beginning to think I was out of my mind, doing this.'

'Well, me too,' said Alan. 'But like you said, if it doesn't work, it doesn't work, and we'll have to think of some other way of rescuing John and Kyna.'

He laid his hand on her shoulder and said, 'Listen, if it would make you feel happier to stay close by and keep a watch on Quilty all night, I don't mind doing it. I've done plenty of stake-outs before, albeit when I was a few years younger. The garage sells sandwiches and drinks, and there's a toilet. What more do we need?'

Katie couldn't help smiling even though she felt so tense and confused. 'No . . .' she said. 'Let's go back to your place. So long as we're ready to scramble the second that Quilty makes a move. I have the feeling that you're right and that he won't try anything until tomorrow.'

'You're sure about that? I mean, you're in charge.'

She looked at him and for the first time she could see in his expression that he accepted that she outranked him, even if he was no longer in the service, and that he was prepared to do whatever she told him. She couldn't stop herself from wondering what he would be like if they went to bed now, if he would make love to her any differently than he had the first time.

'Yes, I'm sure,' she said. 'But before we do, let's just cruise past Dunboyne Park and take a look.'

Alan started the engine and they drove further along Springfield Road until they reached Highcairn Drive. On the left-hand side of the road there was a low brick wall and a hedge. On the right-hand side, there was a patch of rough grass, with a spiked steel fence behind it, and beyond the fence two terraces of houses. On the end wall of each terrace were paintings of masked men with guns, and loyalist badges, and the letters UFF, for the Ulster Freedom Fighters.

Katie had visited Belfast many times before, but mostly to the city centre, for meetings with the Crime Operations Department, and she had forgotten how blatant the hostility still was between republicans and loyalists. UFF could almost have stood for Us? Forgive and Forget?

Dunboyne Park was two neat rows of red-brick houses with neatly tended front gardens. About two thirds of the way down Katie could see Bobby Quilty's Nissan Navara, with one of his men leaning against it, smoking. Even as Katie and Alan drove slowly past the entrance to the cul-de-sac she saw the man leave the side of the pickup and disappear into one of the houses.

'All right,' she said. 'Let's hope they're all inside, sitting down to a pasty supper and tapping their feet to the Wolfe Tones' greatest hits.'

'I wish I'd met you years ago,' said Alan.

They turned around and then Alan drove them into the city centre. They crossed over the River Lagan, with the street lights sparkling in the water, and out to King's Road, in the Cherryvalley area, which was lined with large detached 1930s houses – the prosperous Protestant part of the city. They turned into a small mews with modern blocks of flats at the end of it.

'Home,' said Alan.

Katie's attention had been fixed on her laptop, making sure that Bobby Quilty's pickup was still parked outside Maxy O'Mara's house. 'Oh,' she said. 'We're here. That was quick.'

Alan led her in through the communal entrance and upstairs to his third-floor flat. He opened the door and switched on the lights and said, 'Sorry about the mess. I keep meaning to tidy up, but somehow I never get around to it.'

The flat was very small, but very modern, with polished wooden floors and a kitchen with pine cupboards and black faux-marble work surfaces. The living room was bare except for a purple couch, a glass-topped coffee table and a bookcase. The only mess that Katie could see was a heap of crumpled shirts at one end of the couch and a stack of scribble-filled notebooks on the coffee table, along with a half-empty coffee mug and an oat bar wrapper.

'I expect when I said I lived in Cherryvalley you imagined somewhere very grand,' said Alan, picking up the shirts and carrying them through to the bedroom. Katie could see that there was a double bed, unmade, with a pale yellow bedspread, and a fitted wardrobe, but hardly enough space between the bed and the walls to walk around sideways.

He came out of the bedroom and said, 'When I was married, of course, we had a three-bedroomed house and a garden and all. But can you imagine what this place cost me? €129,000! For a flat no bigger than a bus shelter!'

Katie sat down. She was beginning to feel very tired now.

'What can I get you?' he asked her. 'Tea? Coffee? Wine? Beer?'

'Tea would be good. I don't drink on duty.'

When she said that, they both looked at the mapping plan on the laptop. Bobby Quilty's pickup was still in Dunboyne Park. What he was saying, or doing, or planning to do, Katie couldn't even guess.

* * *

She had a shower and dressed again in her black trousers and grey blouse. She always carried clean underwear in her tote bag because she never knew when she would unexpectedly have to stay out overnight.

While she was putting on her make-up in the bathroom mirror she thought that there was nothing more poignant than a single toothbrush, standing in a tumbler.

'What can I fix you to eat?' Alan asked her when she came out of the bathroom. 'I have pizza in the freezer. Or I can beat up some eggs and make you a cheese omelette. I'm renowned throughout Ulster for my cheese omelettes.'

'Pizza would be grand,' said Katie. 'That's what I always have when I'm too tired to cook.'

'Okay,' he said. 'Pizza it is. We can catch some shut-eye then, but we'll have to take it in turns.'

'Well, that solves *that* moral dilemma,' said Katie.

Alan took hold of her shoulders and gave her a kiss. 'More like *im*moral dilemma.' He smiled. Then he pointed at the blue car icon on the mapping plan and said, 'Quilty, you bastard, if you move so much as one inch before I've had something to eat I'll clean your clock when I see you, so I will. Your own father won't know you – not that he ever did.'

* * *

Alan slept first, fully dressed except for his shoes, while Katie kept herself awake by watching television with the volume turned right down and her laptop open on the coffee table right beside her.

After a while she stood up to stretch her legs and look through the books in Alan's bookcase. Most of them were dog-eared paperback thrillers, Clive Cussler and James Patterson, but there were two or three hardbacks on Irish history and even *Hunger Strike* by Danny Morrison. *Hunger Strike* was an anthology by various writers about the dirty protests and hunger strikes by republican prisoners in the Maze prison in the 1970s, which struck Katie as an unusual book for a former PSNI officer to have on his shelves. Perhaps he had wanted to see the Troubles from both points of view.

There was also a photograph of a dark-haired woman in an oval silver frame. She was quite pretty, but wistful. Katie looked at the back of the frame, but there was nothing written there, so there was no indication of who she was. Alan had said that he and his wife, Alison, had nearly torn each other to shreds, so was it likely to be her?

Alan had set his alarm for 3 a.m., and when it buzzed she heard him stir himself and groan. After a few moments he came shuffling into the living room, blinking and scratching the back of his neck.

'Your turn,' he said. 'But I pray to God you don't have anything like the nightmares I've just been having.'

'No, I think I'd rather keep my eyes open,' said Katie. 'It's going to be daylight before we know it and if I go to sleep now I'll be wrecked when I wake up.'

'In that case I'll make us some coffee.'

When he came back with two mugs of espresso, Katie said, 'I see you have Danny Morrison's book on the hunger strikes.'

'I bought it when it first came out. I thought, "know your enemy".'

'You don't think of them as your enemy now, do you?'

'It's still hard not to. Our next-door neighbour, Tommy, was a prison warder and he was shot one day when he went out shopping with his five-year-old daughter.'

'So, what do you think? Are we forgetting or are we just pretending to forget?'

'If you're right about Bobby Quilty, then we're not even pretending. Do you know how many interfaces we have in Belfast?'

'Fifty? Sixty? I know it's quite a few.'

'Ninety-nine, even today. What kind of people in a so-called civilized city need concrete walls and locked gates and barbed wire to keep them apart?'

Katie was on the verge of asking Alan about the woman in the photograph when there was an insect-like click from the mapping plan on her laptop. It was 5.11 a.m. and although the sky was cloudy and overcast it was growing light outside. Bobby Quilty's pickup was moving to the end of Dunboyne Park and turning round. It came out on to Highcairn Drive and then turned into Springfield Road, heading east towards the city centre.

'That's it,' said Alan, reaching under the couch to retrieve his shoes. 'He's on his way!'

Katie slipped on her shoes, too, and then stood up to clip on her holster and tug on her short black jacket. She picked up her laptop and the two of them left the flat and hurried down the stairs.

They ran across to Katie's car and climbed in. As soon as she had fastened her seat belt Katie opened her laptop and said, 'He's just turned right on to Cupar Way. Any idea where he might be headed?'

'Sandy Row, somewhere like that. Hardcore loyalist territory, anyway.'

Mother of God, thought Katie. *Bobby Quilty's actually fallen for it*. She didn't know whether to be elated or terrified.

Forty-three

Bobby Quilty's pickup turned right on Blythe Street and then into Felt Street in the Blackstaff ward. It went a third of the way along Felt Street and stopped.

'He's in Felt Street,' said Katie. She waited for two more five-second clicks and then said, 'He hasn't moved. That looks like his final destination.'

'Felt Street is totally loyalist,' said Alan. 'There's more Union flags hung up there than washing.'

'How long is it going to take us to get there?'

'Ten minutes, if I put my foot down.'

'Okay then, put your foot down. He's still hasn't moved.'

They crossed over the Lagan again. Because it was so early there was hardly any traffic in the city centre apart from a street-sweeper and two or three buses with pasty-faced shift-workers staring listlessly out of their windows. It took them less than eight minutes to reach Felt Street, a long red-brick terrace, and as soon as they turned the corner they saw Bobby Quilty's pickup.

Alan pulled in behind a white builder's van and parked. Katie opened the glovebox and handed him one of the black balaclava helmets and the SIG Sauer automatic.

He checked the gun's magazine and then said, 'Okay. So what's the plan of action?'

'There is no plan of action, except that once we see Quilty, we have to neutralize him before he has a chance to use his phone.'

'"Neutralize" meaning—?'

'Make him drop his phone and any weapon that he might have

385

on him, although in my experience he's not usually armed. It's his minions who carry the firearms.'

'And if he refuses?'

'Alan, I haven't given you that gun for the fun of it.'

'Whatever you say. Let's do it, then, shall we? But for the love of God, Katie, be careful, will you? I've already attended one too many funerals.'

She held out her hand and he squeezed it tight. 'Okay,' she said. 'Showtime.'

They pulled on their black balaclavas. Alan looked at Katie and said, 'Holy cow! I thought I was afeard of you before. You should see yourself now. Hallowe'en Part Two!'

They climbed out of the car and walked side by side along Felt Street. There were Union flags hanging outside almost every house and even from the lamp posts. There was no wind, though, none at all, and they hung down limply under a sky as grey as human ashes.

One of Bobby Quilty's men was standing outside the house where his pickup was parked. He had a shaven head and a tight white T-shirt which emphasized his body-builder's muscles. Katie took out her revolver, but the man had his back to them as they quickly and quietly approached, so he didn't see them until they had almost reached the metal garden gate.

'Hey – what the *feck*—?' he began, but Katie pointed her gun directly at his face and said, 'Shut your bake. Not a sound. Get inside.'

'What?'

'I said get inside. *Go*. But *no* – don't put your hands up. Just walk in normal.'

The maroon-painted front door was already half open and the overhead light in the hallway was on. The shaven-headed man pushed the door open wider and stepped inside. Katie followed him, with Alan close behind. Alan had cocked his automatic and was holding it up in both hands.

The hallway was narrow with a floral carpet and gilt-framed prints of flowers on the walls. On the right-hand side there was a steep staircase, and down at the end of the hallway two open doors, the left-hand door leading to the living room and the right-hand door leading to the kitchen. Katie was about to ask the shaven-headed man where the Big Feller was when she heard Bobby Quilty's distinctive voice coming from the living room. She could also smell cigarette smoke.

'—but *now look* at the three of you, wee men!' Bobby Quilty was saying. 'Not so fecking scary now, are you?'

Katie prodded the shaven-headed man in the back with the muzzle of her revolver. 'Go on. In you go.'

The shaven-headed man glanced over his shoulder at her and it was obvious that for all of his muscular bulk he was frightened – probably more of Bobby Quilty than of her. He had a single gold earring and although his T-shirt was very white he smelled of stale sweat.

'Are you dee-efff, man?' said Alan. 'Get yourself in there before the lady makes a hole in you.'

'Who's that?' called Bobby Quilty. 'Murtagh, is that you? Who's that out there with you? Is that the kids back already?'

The shaven-headed man went reluctantly in through the living-room door. Katie went in after him and then shoved him hard between the shoulder blades with the heel of her left hand. He staggered forward two or three steps and that allowed her to step smartly to one side of him and point her revolver directly at Bobby Quilty. Alan came in close behind her, although he still kept his gun raised, James Bond-style, ready to point it at anybody who looked like a threat.

'What in the name of God—?' said Bobby Quilty. He was standing in front of the brown-tiled fireplace with the back of his cannonball head reflected in the mirror behind him. He was wearing a baggy cream jacket and drooping blue jeans, and a shirt with camels and pyramids and desert sunsets all over it. There was a cigarette stuck to his lower lip, and as he spoke the long ash on the end of it dropped on to the carpet.

A mock-onyx coffee table had been picked up and was now perched on top of the living-room couch, because the space had been needed for the three men who were sitting back to back in the middle of the floor. The first man was bald and beefy-shouldered, with a broken nose. The second was thin, with a wild mess of grey hair and hollow cheeks. The third was spotty and young, with a straggly black moustache. The older man was wearing green-and-white-striped flannelette pyjamas, but the other two had on nothing but underpants – large white Y-fronts for the man with the broken nose, and pink boxer shorts for the spotty boy.

Katie could see that all three men had their hands fastened behind them with nylon wrist restraints, the same kind of PlastiCuffs that the Garda used. In between them, behind their backs, there was a battered black briefcase, standing on its end.

Another of Bobby Quilty's men was sitting in an armchair by the window, with his legs crossed, also smoking. His hair was bright orange and it had been cut short so that it stuck up like a scrubbing brush. His face was rat-like, with icy blue eyes and protruding front teeth.

Bobby Quilty was holding up his mobile phone. Katie said, 'Drop it, Bobby. Drop the phone.'

'Or you'll do *what*, whoever you are, wee doll? Shoot me?'

'I said drop the phone.'

Bobby Quilty looked down at the phone as if he were surprised to see it. 'Ach, there might be a bit of a problem with that.'

'I'll give you till three. Drop it.'

'Just hold your horses and listen,' said Bobby Quilty. 'The problem is that we've paid these three fellers a visit this morning to settle a score. These are the Crothers – Sam Crothers, he's the baldy one, Stephen Crothers, the one who looks like a bomb went off in a scouring-pad factory, and young Kenny MacClery, who's a nephew.'

'I don't care who they are,' Katie repeated. 'Drop the phone.'

Bobby Quilty raised his left hand like the pope giving a benediction. 'I asked you to hold your horses and hear me out. These three fellers have done my family a desperate injustice and because of that they have to be punished for it. An eye for an eye and all that. That case you see in between them happens to contain 450 grams of C4, as well as more than a hundred three-inch nails. The detonator that can set off that C4 is activated by guess what, wee doll?'

He held up his mobile phone and grinned at her. 'If I drop it, then ba-*doom*! These three fellers, as well as the rest of us here in this room – well, we'll all end up as pasty filling.'

'In that case, lay the phone gently down on the floor and step away from it.'

'Or what? You'll shoot me? And what do you think will happen if you shoot me? I might press the key that sets off the bomb, out of spite. Or maybe I'll just drop my phone on the floor. Whichever it is, ba-*doom*!'

Katie guessed that the chances of Bobby Quilty's phone setting off an explosion if he simply dropped it on to the floor were infinitesimal, if not zero. All the same, she didn't know exactly what kind of connection had been set up between his phone and the detonator in the bomb – if it really was a bomb.

'Lay the phone down on the floor, gently,' said Katie.

'Why?' Bobby Quilty retorted. 'What the feck has any of this got to do with you, any road? Who are you? Don't tell me the Sandy Row Women's Wombles are back in business.'

For nearly half a minute, nobody moved and nobody spoke, and with every second that passed the tension in the room racked up higher. Bobby Quilty continued to stare at Katie with contempt, while his three handcuffed victims in the middle of the room looked up at her in desperation. The man with the orange hair sat in the same casual position, with his legs crossed, but now his pose was rigid and although a ribbon of smoke was still rising from his cigarette he made no attempt to smoke it. The shaven-headed man in the white T-shirt moved, but only to take two cautious steps backwards – as if that would make any difference if it was a bomb and it really did explode.

Katie couldn't see Alan because he was standing too close behind her, but she could hear him breathing hard and quick. In fact, he sounded almost like a pole-vaulter hyping himself up for his run towards the bar.

'Meara will be back very soon, with the girls,' said Stephen Crothers in a voice that was little more than a croak. 'You can't harm them. They're innocents. Whatever you do to us, you have to spare Meara and the girls.'

'Oh, like you spared the Doherty children?' said Bobby Quilty.

'That was different. That was a long-standing debt that had to be paid. We thought the account would be settled for good after that.'

'Well, you thought wrong, didn't you, wee man?' Bobby Quilty retorted. 'Those were relatives of mine that you did for, very close relatives, and nobody lays a finger on any member of my family without suffering for it. You – look at the three of you, you miserable friggers. Thought you'd make history, did you? Well, you will, I swear to God, but it won't be in the way you thought you would. There'll six coffins all right, so there will, but they won't know which bit to put in which. They might just as well bury you in soup kettles after what's going to happen to you.'

'Nothing's going to happen to them,' said Katie. 'You're going to put down that phone and I'm going to call the police.'

Bobby Quilty suddenly frowned. He took the cigarette off his lip and looked at Katie with his eyes narrowed.

'It's you, isn't it?' he said. 'It's only fecking you.'

'What are you talking about?'

'It's *you*. Detective Superintendent Maguire. I thought I recognized that Corky whine on you. I'm right, amptnah? What in the name of Jesus do you think you're playing at?'

'Holy shite,' said the orange-haired man in the armchair. 'You're having a laugh, aren't you? She's that peeler you was talking about?'

Katie dragged off her balaclava and stuffed it into her pocket. 'Well done, Mr Quilty. I was going to tell you who I was in just a moment, anyway, before I arrest you for making a threat to kill and possession of explosives with intent to endanger life.'

'This is Belfast, wee doll, in case you hadn't noticed,' said Bobby Quilty. 'This isn't Cork.'

'That makes no difference. I still have the power to arrest you here and I'm sure the PSNI will be delighted to assist me in taking you in and bringing charges against you.'

'I don't fecking believe this,' said Bobby Quilty. 'You've set me up here, haven't you? You've only gone and fecking set me up. And who's that knobhead with you?'

Alan pulled off his balaclava, too. 'Reck me, do you, Bobby? It's been a long time.'

Bobby Quilty slapped his hand against his forehead. 'I don't fecking believe this! This is like some kind of fecking bad dream! Detective Inspector Alan Harte, as was! Harte the Fart, that's what we used to call you! All wind and no action!'

'Alan,' said Katie. 'Call for backup, would you? And tell them we'll need bomb disposal, too.'

'Hey, now then, that's enough of that,' said Bobby Quilty, and now his tone was deadly serious. 'You and I have an understanding, Detective Superintendent Maguire, don't we? If I was you, I'd turn around and walk out of here and say no more about what you've seen here, ever, because if you don't, you know what the consequences will be, don't you?'

He held up his phone again. 'I have only to call my pal Ger and even if I don't say a single word he'll know why I've called him and he'll know exactly what to do.'

'You're not getting away with this any longer, Bobby,' said Katie. 'Alan, make that call, will you, please?'

'I wouldn't do that, Detective Inspector Harte the Fart,' Bobby Quilty warned him. 'I don't know if Detective Superintendent Maguire here has, like, *apprised* you of the arrangement that she and me have between us. But you push just one button on that phone of yours and I'll be pushing one on mine – the one button that tells my pal Ger to do for two good friends of hers.'

Katie said, 'It's okay, Alan. Stall it for a moment.'

'It's beyond me why you've showed up here today, Detective

Superintendent Maguire,' said Bobby Quilty. Still holding up his phone, he took a packet of cigarettes out of his shirt pocket, placed one between his lips and then lit it, all left-handed. 'I thought our arrangement was working very well on both sides.'

'That was because I could never find anyone who was brave enough to give evidence against you,' said Katie. 'But now I believe I have.'

'What, these three friggers here? They're *murderers*, wee doll. They were the ones who shot the Doherty family. They shot the father and the mother and the poor wee children, too. I know that for a fact, because I know the scumbag who sold them their guns and not only that, they've been bragging about it all around Blackstaff. Who's going to believe what *they* have to say, even if they have the guts to say it?'

'Oh, you'd be surprised,' Katie told him. 'A court will believe them, if their story rings true. And I think they'll have the guts to say it if it means a substantial reduction in their sentences for shooting the Dohertys.'

There was another long, tense, uncomfortable silence. Then Bobby Quilty said, 'Why don't you call it a day, Detective Superintendent Maguire? Forget you ever came here, wee doll. That way, your two dear friends will stay safe and we can carry on like nothing ever happened.'

'And if I do that, what will you do? Blow these people up? Them and their children?'

'Retribution, that's all it is. Justice. What they did to us, we're going to do the same to them.'

'The Langtrys and the Dohertys were shot and buried beneath the floorboards. They weren't blown up.'

Bobby Quilty blew out a long stream of smoke. 'There was kind of a snag there. I wanted to do that, so I did, bury them under the floorboards. It would have been historically appropriate, do you know what I mean? But I was told when I got here that all the houses along this street have concrete floors, and we couldn't have spent three days hammering away with pneumatic drills, now could we? – and then mixing up the concrete to pour over them.'

The man with the orange hair suddenly spoke up. He had a thin, rusty voice, as if were making a complaint rather than a comment.

'I'll tell you this, too, Mrs Peeler. If you *really* want to make a point in this city, a bomb's always the best way of doing it. A shooting, they'll forget that after a few weeks. Shootings are ten a penny. But if you blow up half the street, they'll remember that for a brave lot longer.'

Katie ignored him and turned back to Bobby Quilty. 'But what's the point that you're trying to make here, Bobby?'

'I'm making the point that nobody murders members of my family and gets away with it, that's all – no matter what their excuse is.'

'The Dohertys were no relations of yours.'

'They were, too. I have the family tree to prove it.'

'And where did you get that from?'

Bobby Quilty squinted against the smoke from his cigarette. 'A reliable source. A very reliable source.'

'Bobby – I invented that family tree myself, for the specific purpose of getting you here and identifying the men who shot the Dohertys for me.'

'Away on!' said Bobby Quilty. Then, 'You're not serious.'

'I was never more serious in the whole of my life. Now lay the phone down carefully on the floor and step away from it. Robert Boland Quilty, I am arresting you under the Non-Fatal Offences Against the Person Act 1997, for making a threat to kill or cause serious harm to another person without lawful excuse. You are not obliged to say anything unless you wish to do so, but anything you do say will be taken down in writing and may be given in evidence.'

If the atmosphere in the living room had been tense before, it was now so charged that Katie almost expected the front windows to crack from the pressure. The orange-haired man uncrossed his legs and slowly stood up, as if his knees were as rusty as his voice. The three handcuffed men in the middle of the floor kept turning their heads around in bewilderment and panic, looking first at

Katie and then at Bobby Quilty and then at the orange-haired man.

Bobby Quilty said, 'You disappoint me, Detective Superintendent Maguire. You fecking disappoint me. I thought you were a woman of your word, but all the time what were you doing? Deviously plotting, that's what you were doing. But now you're going to find out that I'm the kind of man who keeps his promises.'

'I'm telling you this for the very last time, Bobby,' said Katie. 'Put down the phone.'

Bobby Quilty changed the phone over to his left hand and defiantly raised it even higher, angling it so that Katie could see the screen. Then he held up his right index finger and said, 'This is where you learn a lesson, Detective Superintendent Maguire. This is where you learn not to mess with Bobby Quilty. Execution by telephone. But you'll never find out what happened to your friends or where their bodies might be buried, and you'll never be able to prove a thing against me because I didn't do it and I wasn't there, and you're a witness to that yourself.'

Katie kept her revolver pointed at Bobby Quilty's chest but she knew that she wasn't going to shoot him. He was no immediate threat to *her* life, because he wasn't armed, and it would be almost impossible for her to prove that he was a threat to John and Kyna's lives, either. He was threatening these three members of the Crothers family, and their children, too, when they came home, and that was a serious offence in itself, but whether it justified shooting him and possibly killing him was another matter altogether.

For the first time since she had thought of this plan for stopping Bobby Quilty, she hesitated. It could come down to a choice between saving John and Kyna and saving three alleged murderers. She had been prepared to risk her career setting up Bobby Quilty like this, but she wasn't prepared to kill him and go to jail for it.

She could walk out now and call the PSNI, but Bobby Quilty would only have to get the first hint of a police raid and he would almost certainly give the word for John and Kyna to be done for.

'I tell you what, Bobby,' she said. 'I'll give you a choice. I'll walk out of here if you do, too, and take your briefcase with you. You've led me to the men who shot the Dohertys, as I was hoping you would, and now I can deal with them myself. They won't go unpunished, I can promise you that.'

Bobby Quilty drew deeply on his cigarette, and when he spoke, smoke came leaking out of his mouth and his brown-rimmed nostrils. 'How do I know that you weren't codding me when you said that the Dohertys were no relations of mine?'

'You'll just have take my word for it, that's all.'

'I had the information from a very reliable source, wee doll, and that very reliable source never mentioned you.'

'He wouldn't have done. He's not an enthusiast when it comes to female police officers.'

Bobby Quilty's eyes narrowed when she said that, but he didn't respond. For all he knew, she was only guessing that his 'very reliable source' was a garda officer and she was trying to trick him into saying who it was.

'So what do you say?' said Katie. 'Deal or no deal?'

'I'll tell you what I think,' said Bobby Quilty. 'I think you're trying to pull a fast one here, Detective Superintendent Maguire. If I walk out of here and let these friggers live, then the word's going to go around that any scummer can do for Bobby Quilty's relations and he won't have the balls to hit back. That's what this is all about, isn't it? You want me to look windy. You'll get all of the credit for solving the Doherty murders and I'll end up looking like a sooner.'

'Holy Mother of God, Bobby, how many times do I have to tell you? You're not related to the Dohertys. I made it up.'

'I don't fecking believe you. I've seen the family tree for myself. There was a Quilty served with the IRA at Kilcullen and he married a Doherty.'

'There wasn't, and he didn't. I invented it.'

Bobby Quilty shook his head in disbelief and turned to the orange-haired man. 'What's your opinion, Sandy? I definitely think we're being taken for eejits here, don't you?'

As soon as Bobby Quilty looked the other way, though, Alan seized Katie's left arm and swung her violently round behind him, as if they were dance partners and some furious flamenco had just started up. He caught her completely by surprise and she hit her shoulder hard against the door frame, dropping her revolver, which bounced into the hallway. For a split second she thought: *My God, he's been fooling me – he's on Bobby Quilty's side.*

Dropping down on to her knees to pick up her revolver, however, she heard an ear-splitting bang, and then another, and another. She twisted round to witness what looked like a waxwork tableau in which time had stood still and nobody was moving. Through a gauzy curtain of gun-smoke, she saw Alan holding his automatic in both hands, pointing it directly at Bobby Quilty. She saw Bobby Quilty himself, his mouth open in surprise and his cigarette hanging from his lower lip. The sunset pattern on his shirt was so colourful that it was impossible to tell if he had been shot, but his shoulders were hunched forward and his arms were outspread like a man preparing to jump off a wall. He had dropped his mobile phone and it was bouncing across the floor.

The man with the orange hair had hauled up the left side of his mustard-coloured tank top and was tugging a large pistol out of his belt. The shaven-headed man was reaching out towards Alan, his mouth distorted in a silent shout. In the middle of the room, the three handcuffed men had ducked down, hunching their shoulders and squeezing their eyes tight shut, since Alan had fired only a few inches over their heads.

'*Alan!*' Katie shouted, although she could hardly hear herself because the shots had half-deafened her. The orange-haired man had taken his pistol right out now and was cocking it and aiming it at Alan.

Katie picked up her revolver and scrambled out into the hallway on her hands and knees. She heard another shot, a deeper *boom!* this time, then the sharper crack of Alan's SIG Sauer. She stood up, went back to the open door and leaned cautiously sideways, holding her gun up high, so that she could see inside the room.

The orange-haired man was sitting back in his chair with his arms and legs spreadeagled, and there was a blood on his tank top. The shaven-headed man with the white T-shirt had jumped on to Alan's back and grabbed his right wrist and was trying to wrestle his gun away from him.

'*Get us the fuck out of here!*' Sam Crothers screamed, throwing himself from side to side in an attempt to free himself from his nylon handcuffs. Kenny MacClery was trying to bump himself across the room on his bottom. Stephen Crothers's teeth were gritted in pain and concentration as he, too, tried to wrench his hands out of his cuffs.

Katie was about to step into the room and point her gun directly at the shaven-headed man in the white T-shirt so that he would let Alan go, but then she saw Bobby Quilty. He had collapsed sideways into the fireplace and there was a wide triangular bloodstain on his jacket and blood running out of his nose. His eyes were bulging and his chest was heaving, but he was managing to inch his way out of the hearth and across the carpet, reaching out in front of him with his bloodied right hand.

A second too late, Katie realized that he was trying to reach his mobile phone, which had fallen close to Sam Crothers's bare foot. He jabbed at the phone with his index finger, missing it twice, but then he hauled himself a few inches nearer.

'*Alan!*' Katie screamed at him and tried to get into the room. But Alan and the shaven-headed man were struggling around and around, blocking the doorway, and as she tried to force her way past them they toppled against her, grunting and panting, and pushed her back into the hall.

Even when she thought about it later, she didn't remember hearing the explosion. But the whole house shook as if it had been hit by an earthquake and a blizzard of debris was blasted out of the living-room door – bricks, tiles, bits of furniture, curtains, as well as a shower of glittering nails and large pieces of human bodies. Alan and the shaven-headed man were both lifted up bodily and blown across the hallway into the kitchen where they landed with a double thump, splattering blood up the sides of the green kitchen cabinets.

Katie was knocked over backwards, almost as far as the front door. She made a grab for the coat-stand to try and stop herself from falling over, but the coat-stand fell over, too, and she was buried for a moment in donkey jackets and children's duffel coats. The explosion had split the wallpaper in the hallway and made all the pictures drop off, but it hadn't been powerful enough to bring down the wall itself.

As Katie struggled to her feet, a thick grey cloud of smoke and dust rolled out of the living room, so that she was almost blinded as well as deafened. She stood still for a moment, leaning with one hand against the wall to steady herself, then holstered her revolver and dragged her balaclava out of her pocket so that she could press it over her nose and mouth.

Shaking with shock, she stepped carefully over the broken bricks and lumps of plaster until she reached the kitchen. She didn't have to go inside to see that both Alan and the shaven-headed man were dead. They were lying face to face, both of them soaked in blood, and staring at each other with their eyes wide open, like two boxers challenging each other before a match.

She didn't want to look inside the living room but she knew she had to. Right inside the doorway a headless torso was lying against the wall. Its heart and deflated lungs were still inside it and lacerated strings of bloody beige intestine still connected it to the pelvis and legs, which were sitting in the middle of the room. She couldn't see its head, but she could tell from the white underpants that it was Sam Crothers.

The whole of the front of the living room had been blown out, so that she could see the street outside. Half the ceiling had collapsed and the front garden was heaped with bricks and broken window frames and jagged pieces of plasterboard. Lying on his back on the pavement, still sitting in his chair, was the orange-haired man. His face had been blasted off so that he looked as if he was wearing a piece of raw pig's liver as a mask.

Bobby Quilty's pickup was parked right outside. Its windows were shattered and its doors dented and peppered with holes.

Katie was feeling swimmy and there were tiny stars prickling in front of her eyes. The metallic stench of blood and faeces and exploded C4 made her retch. *Stay steady*, she told herself. *This is your job and it was you who brought this about.*

Like Sam Crothers, Stephen Crothers and Kenny MacClery had been sitting with their backs to the briefcase and they taken the full force of the C4 and the nails that were packed inside it. Apart from their hips and legs, there was hardly anything left of either of them but plaited piles of intestines and a jumble of ribs and stringy rags of red flesh.

Bobby Quilty's body, in contrast, was almost unscathed. He had been lying on his side when he had detonated the bomb and the Crothers had shielded him from the worst of the blast and its devastating hail of nails. His eyes were closed and although his his chin was bearded with blood, and the front of his jacket was blood-soaked, too, he could have been contentedly sleeping.

Katie looked down at him and thought: *You always knew, didn't you, that your life would end like this? And you were never going to die alone, were you? You had to have the satisfaction of taking some other scumbags with you – especially since you believed that I was lying to you, and that they had murdered your relatives.*

Now, however, Katie forced herself to switch into professional mode. She could hear people shouting in the street outside and a woman screaming. The police and the fire brigade would be here in a matter of minutes and she needed to be out of here and gone before anybody started asking who she was and what she was doing. She had been shaken to the core, but she had to think about John and Kyna. How long would it be before Bobby Quilty's minions heard that he was dead and made their own decisions about what to do with them? Without Bobby Quilty holding them as hostages to keep the Garda off his back they would be nothing but a useless liability.

She bent down and lifted Bobby Quilty's hand so that she could pick up his mobile phone. It was like a pig's trotter and his fingers were sticky and still warm. She dropped the phone into her pocket and then she searched around for Alan's SIG Sauer automatic. She couldn't see it among the wreckage in the living room, so she had to go back into the kitchen. She didn't want to look at Alan lying there dead, but she couldn't stop herself. His expression had changed and he appeared to be sad now, rather than angry. She knew that it was only the primary flaccidity that occurs immediately after death, before rigor mortis begins to set in, but ever since their night together she had thought of Alan as being sad about something.

She found his gun halfway underneath the gas cooker, with only the butt visible. Once she had retrieved it she de-cocked it and tucked it into her belt. She had been anxious not to leave without it because she had logged it out of the armoury at Anglesea Street and it could easily be traced through its code number.

'Is there anybody in there?' she heard a man shouting. 'Hallo? Is there anybody in there?'

She heard somebody else call out but she couldn't hear what they said. They were probably warning the first person to stay well clear until the bomb squad had determined that there wasn't a second device intended to catch first responders.

Next to the kitchen there was a small utility room, with a washing machine and a clothes horse. There was also a door leading out to the back yard. As quickly and as quietly as she could, Katie let herself out and closed the door behind her. The yard was cluttered with an old enamel bathtub and a bicycle with no wheels and some broken fencing, and she had to climb over two worn-out car tyres, but there was a gate that gave access to the next street. When she opened it she was relieved to see that the street was deserted, so there wouldn't be any witnesses to say they had seen a red-haired woman in black hurrying away from the house after the explosion.

She walked quickly up to the main road and back into Felt Street, where her car was parked. She dropped the SIG Sauer and her balaclava back into the glovebox, as well as Bobby Quilty's mobile phone. Then she started up the engine, did a quick three-point turn, and drove away. As she turned the corner into Blythe Road a police patrol car came speeding past her with its lights flashing and siren scribbling. It was followed almost immediately by another, and then by a fire tender.

Her hand was still shaking as she set her satnav for Forkhill. In current conditions, it told her, the drive would take her slightly less than an hour. She prayed that, apart from using his mobile phone to set off the briefcase bomb, Bobby Quilty hadn't put in a call to the men who were holding John and Kyna.

As she turned on to the main M1 she glanced in her rear-view mirror and could see clouds of dirty smoke still rising over the rooftops from Felt Street. It gave her a strange feeling, driving away from a crime scene like this, instead of towards it. It went completely against her training and her experience, and her natural instincts.

But her plan had worked out so far, even though it had turned out to be more tragic than she could ever have imagined. She had to see it through to the very end, for John's sake, and Kyna's sake, and as a tribute to Alan.

She was passing Loughbrickland when it began to rain again, not lashing down, but a soft, persistent mizzle. She stayed dry-eyed. The time for crying would be later.

Forty-four

She made slow progress south because of the weather, and a broken-down car transporter at Newry reduced traffic to a single lane, but it was still only ten minutes past eight when Katie arrived in Forkhill.

She passed the Welcome Inn, where Alan's Lesser Bastard worked – the young man who had seen John and Kyna taken into Bobby Quilty's house. It was too early for it to be open and the only person on the village street was a woman in a hooded raincoat walking past McCreesh General Store and Funeral Director, with a miserable-looking mongrel on a string.

Alan had told her exactly where Bobby Quilty's house was, only two and a half kilometres further south, right by the border. She drove past it to see how many cars were parked outside, if any. Behind the trees she could make out only one: a mustard-coloured Volvo. She would have bet 100 euros that it was the same mustard-coloured Volvo that had obstructed the gardaí who had been trying to give Detective Barry backup as he chased the cigarette-seller along MacCurtain Street, and the same 'yellowy' Volvo that had been seen in Parklands after Darragh Murphy had been shot.

Bobby Quilty had said that he would call 'my pal Ger' to have John and Kyna dealt with. Katie had guessed that he meant Ger Carmody, who she knew to be one of his closest henchmen, who kept an eye on his affairs in Cork when he was away in the North.

On the opposite side of the road, a few metres further south, there was a narrow farm track with overgrown hedges on both sides. Katie drove down it until she was out of sight of Bobby Quilty's house. She parked her car close to the verge, in case a tractor needed to get past, although it looked as if the track was no longer in use.

Alan had said that when he had visited the house to check up on John and Kyna he had sneaked round the back, so Katie decided to do the same. She crossed the road and walked about 150 metres past the low stone wall in front of the house until she came to its perimeter fence. She looked around. All she could see were the low hills on either side of the road, and fields. The next house was more than a third of a kilometre away. It was still drizzling and there was nobody else in sight. At that moment, she could almost have believed that she was the only person left in the world.

She climbed over the wall and followed the three-bar wooden fence to the rear of the property, keeping her head down. There were enough bushes around the driveway to hide her from anybody who might be looking out of a downstairs window, and although there was a single upstairs window facing in her direction, it had a blind drawn down over it.

She climbed over the fence into the garden. As soon as she dropped down on to the other side, she froze. The back door of the house opened and a man appeared, wearing a white hat and sunglasses and a sagging black jacket. Ger Carmody – that grubby white hat was his trademark. He sucked at the butt-end of a cigarette and then flicked it out into the garden. Katie crouched low, hoping he wouldn't see her in the long feathery grass. He blew out smoke, then he went back inside and closed the door behind him.

Katie waited for a few moments and then made her way towards the house. There was the shed that Alan had used for cover, and there was the large living-room window through which he had seen John and Kyna. The living room was dark inside, so all she could see was the reflection of the garden, and the hills in the distance.

Please God don't tell me Bobby Quilty managed to make that call and they've been shot, or taken away somewhere else.

She wasn't quite sure what she should do next. Maybe she should risk it and try to enter the house. With any luck, Ger Carmody had left the back door unlocked, or she could kick it open. But what if he hadn't, or she couldn't? Should she go to the front door and knock, and demand entry as a Garda officer? Supposing John and Kyna weren't there any longer, and there was no trace that they had been?

She hunkered down beside the shed. She was feeling shivery now, although the morning wasn't cold, just damp. The shock of the bomb on Felt Street was beginning to get through to her and she knew that what she really needed was a hot drink, and quiet, and a good long sleep.

Now that Bobby Quilty was dead, maybe she should give up trying to rescue John and Kyna single-handed and call for the police, although that could still be a highly dangerous option. There was only one car outside, but she didn't know how many more of Bobby Quilty's men might be inside the house. Apart from that, Ger Carmody had a record of extreme violence and if he were found guilty of unlawful imprisonment he would face going to jail for the rest of his life, so if police cars arrived outside he might feel he had nothing to lose. Bobby Quilty had been prepared to go out in a blast of glory, so it was possible that his Ger Carmody might do the same, and take John and Kyna with him.

Alan had been right, she thought. Her plan had been fraught with too many 'what-ifs', and that was what had killed him. She had to make a conscious effort not to think of him lying on that kitchen floor, looking so sad.

She was still trying to make up her mind what to do when she saw a shadowy movement inside the living room. Somebody was walking towards the window – a woman, by the look of it. When she came close, she saw that it was Kyna. She had a fawn blanket wrapped around her shoulders and her hair was all messed up. It was her face, though, that shocked Katie. Both of her eyes were purple and almost closed up, and her nose was swollen.

There was no sign of John, but Alan had said that his informant had seen him carried into the house on a stretcher, so maybe he was still unable to walk.

Katie made her mind up immediately. She drew her revolver out its holster and ran with her knees bent towards the window. As soon as Kyna saw her she dropped the blanket from her shoulders and flapped her hands wildly, as if to tell her to *Come, and come quickly*. She looked startled and relieved, but she was a Garda officer, too, and Katie knew that she wouldn't panic. She mouthed something that Katie couldn't hear, but she raised one finger, as if to tell her that there was only one man guarding the house. Katie lifted her hand to show her that she understood, then she went to the back door and tried the handle. Ger Carmody had left it unlocked. Bobby Quilty clearly hadn't rung him, and he couldn't have heard yet that he was dead.

Katie opened the door and stepped inside. She found herself in a gloomy kitchen with a pine table in the middle of it. The table was crowded with empty pizza boxes and KFC buckets and dirty paper plates and beer cans and coffee mugs and two ashtrays heaped with so many cigarette butts that they looked like maggots. The terracotta-tiled floor was so sticky that Katie's shoes made a crackling sound as she walked across to the hallway.

The door to the hallway was already half open, but she stopped and listened before she opened it any further. She could hear a television, though she couldn't make out what station it was tuned to.

She waited a little longer, but as she reached out to open the door wider she heard footsteps approaching up the corridor outside. Hurried, squeaky footsteps, as if somebody in crêpe-soled shoes had an urgent message to deliver.

She heard a door being unlocked and even though her ears were still singing from the explosion she could clearly hear voices. She heard Kyna saying, 'What in the name of Jesus do you want now, you bastard?' Kyna sounded very clotted, as if she had a cold.

'Mother of God, that's some bang off your man,' said a deep, harsh voice with a strong Cork accent. She guessed that was Ger.

'He's desperate sick, that's why,' Kyna retorted. 'He's nearly dying and you haven't the human heart to send for a doctor.'

'Well, we don't have to bother about it now. Things have changed. It turns out now that you and your manky friend here are surplus to requirements.'

'What are you talking about?'

'It's over, sweetheart. The Big Feller's bought the farm.'

'You *what*?'

'It's just been on the news, on the telly. There was a bomb set off in Belfast and seven fellers were done for, including the Big Feller.'

'You're not serious.'

'It was on the news on the telly only a couple of minutes ago. How more serious do you want to be than that?'

'I can't believe it. So what happens now?'

'So, like I say, you're surplus to requirements. I'm out the gap, like, but I don't need you and your stinky pal here.'

'You can't—' Kyna began, but Ger must have closed the living-room door then because Katie couldn't hear the rest of what she was saying. Not that she needed to. It was chillingly clear what he intended to do.

She pulled open the kitchen door. The living-room door was next to it, on the right-hand side, and she kicked that open. She stepped into the room with her revolver raised high up in front of her.

Kyna was standing by the window, her shoulders still wrapped in her blanket. Ger had crossed the room to the couch where John was lying and he was jiggling a large Colt automatic in his hand as if he were weighing it. John's legs were draped in a sheet that was stained brown and amber with blood and pus, with several bluebottles crawling over it, and he looked appalling. His face was dead white except for the dark circles around his eyes. His jaw was hanging slack and his arms were crossed over his chest, like an effigy on a medieval tomb. His eyes were open but he was staring at the ceiling, and he didn't acknowledge Katie's appearance with even a flicker. Underneath that stained sheet, his infected feet were rotting and the stench in the living room was thick and sickly.

'Put the gun down, Ger!' Katie shouted at him, and she wished that she hadn't sounded so shrill.

Ger jerked with surprise. 'Christ on a bicycle, it's you! And I thought the only bang I was getting in here was off of this feller's feet.'

'I said, put the gun down, or so help me I'll drop you.'

Ger pointed his Colt at the crown of John's head. 'Oh, no. I think I have the advantage here, sweetheart. If you don't put your little peashooter down, I'm going to blow your friend's head halfway to Dundalk.'

'You were going to do that anyway,' said Katie. 'So put the gun down or, believe me, I'll kill you where you stand.'

Ger said, 'You won't, because you don't want to see your friend here die, too. Which he will, if you shoot me, and you know it.'

Kyna dropped her blanket to the floor and said, 'Listen, Ger. You want to get out of here, don't you? I'll tell you what I'll do. I'll come with you as a hostage until you're well clear of here. Then you won't get killed, and John here won't get killed, and by the grace of God I won't get killed, either.'

Katie said, 'If you agree to that, Ger, I'll put down my gun.'

'Even if you do that, darling, you'll still be chasing after me, won't you, and you'll have these two as witnesses against me?'

'Ger – if I *do* manage to find you and bring you up in front of a court, you'll be better off facing a charge of false imprisonment than two charges of cold-blooded murder.'

Ger continued to point his automatic at John's head, but there was no doubt that he was undecided.

'You can say what you like,' he told her, 'there's no way I'm going back to that fecking Portlaoise prison again. I'd rather die than go back to that fecking hell-hole.'

'If you walk out of here peacefully today, without hurting any of us, then I'll testify on your behalf,' said Katie. 'That's if I ever catch you, which I probably won't. If you have any sense, you'll get out of the country and never come back.'

Almost half a minute passed. Katie's hand was trembling from holding up her gun for so long and she could actually taste the rank smell of John's decaying feet.

At last, Ger shook his head and said, 'Nah . . . no chance. I know you, DS Maguire. You look like butter wouldn't melt in your mouth but you have some fierce sharp teeth in that same mouth, too. No matter where I go, you'll make sure you lift me. Jimmy Malone – he was in Gran Canaria, wasn't he, and you still had him extramadited, and what had *he* done?'

'Jimmy Malone set fire to a house with six children in it.'

'Wasn't his fault they died. He didn't know they was home.'

'Come on, Ger, let's all be reasonable,' said Kyna, coming closer to him, with both hands outspread. 'We can't spend all day discussing this. The rest of the boys are going to be back soon, aren't they, and how much do you trust *them*? You're going to let them witness you shooting us? They'll rat you out as soon as look at you. Much better if they come back and all of us are gone.'

She looked across at Katie and said, 'There's four more of them altogether. They went shopping to Newry early this morning because they'd run out of fags and bacon and booze. You know – the three staples of a civilized life.'

Katie didn't take her eyes off Ger. He was talking tough and she found it almost impossible to read his expression behind those dark glasses. All the same, she was beginning to deduce from his indecision and his body language that he was actually frightened of her – or what she represented, at least. When he looked at her he saw Portlaoise high-security prison and that made him doubly unpredictable. From her experience, he was much more likely to pull the trigger if he was frightened, and if he killed John his adrenaline would start pumping and he would find it easy, if not exhilarating, to kill both Kyna and herself.

She went over to the bookcase and laid her gun down on it.

'There,' she said, although her heart was beating so fast that she was breathless. 'All you have to do now is walk out of here. Kyna's offered to go with you, to make sure that you get clear away. I promise you we won't try to stop you or come after you, and I won't put out any bulletins about you for at least twenty-four hours. You have my word on that, Ger.'

Ger lifted his automatic away from the top of John's head, obviously trying to make up his mind. The instant he did so, however, Kyna spun around on one foot and kicked the gun out of his hand.

He said, '*Shite!*' and staggered backwards, but she went after him and kicked and punched him again and again, so fast that to Katie it was nothing but a blur of arms and legs. She kicked him hard in the crotch, and when he doubled forward she kicked him under his chin so that his jaw cracked and his hat flew off. He tumbled backwards into the space between the end of the couch and the wall, and she used the arm of the couch as a vaulting horse so that she could stamp on his ribs, right over his heart.

Katie circled around her and scooped up Ger's automatic from the floor, then went back to the bookcase and collected her own revolver. Meanwhile, Kyna was kicking Ger repeatedly in the side of his head. Finally she stood on his face, using her full weight, so that his dark glasses and his nose-bone both crunched.

'Kyna! Jesus and Mary! I think that'll do it,' Katie told her.

'The *bastard*!' said Kyna in her clogged-up voice. 'The total, absolute *bastard*! I was begging him to call for a white van for John, but he wouldn't. Instead, he headbutted me and broke my nose.'

Katie looked down at Ger, with his dark glasses smashed on the bridge of his nose and blood running in streams down both sides of his face.

'He won't be doing a whole lot to stop us getting out of here now,' she said. She knelt down next to John and took hold of his ice-cold hands. He stared back at her but he didn't seem to know who she was.

'John, it's Katie. Do you understand me? It's Katie. I've come to take you away from here.'

John continued to stare at her, and he whispered something, but at first she couldn't make out what he was saying.

'It's okay, John. Everything's going to be grand now. We'll take you to the hospital to have your feet patched up and then you'll be fine.'

'Barney,' whispered John. 'Time for Barney's walk.'

Katie's eyes filled up with tears. She squeezed his hands and said, 'Yes. Yes, it is. And soon you'll be able to take him out yourself. Let's just get you up off that couch and out of here. Kyna?

Do you think you could give me a hand here? He won't be able to walk by himself.'

Kyna was crouching next to Ger, who still hadn't stirred. She was pressing her fingertips up against his neck, feeling for his pulse.

'I think he's dead,' she said.

'Serious?'

'I can't feel a pulse and he isn't breathing. I think I've broken his neck.'

'Mother of God, that's all we need.'

'He deserved it. The same as Bobby Quilty. He just told me that Bobby Quilty was dead, blown up by a bomb or something like that. That's why he came in to kill us. We weren't useful any more. Surplus to requirements, that's what he said.'

'I know,' said Katie. 'I heard him telling you about Quilty. It's true. I was there myself when the bomb went off.'

'*What?* You were actually there?'

'I nearly got blown up myself. There were six others killed, too. Listen, I'll tell you all about it after. Are you certain he's dead?'

Kyna leaned over Ger's face to make a final check that he wasn't breathing. After a few seconds she said, 'He's gone, yes. I'll bet you he's in hell already.' She stood up and then she said, 'You're here by yourself? Like, this isn't official? There's no other officers outside?'

'This is a highly unofficial one-woman raid. And we need to get out of here fast, especially if those scummers are coming back from doing their messages in Newry.'

Kyna looked around the living room. 'We can't leave the place like this. There's enough fingerprints and blood and DNA to identify us ten times over. What's going to happen when the cops come in and find Ger's body like this, with my footprints on his face? Or are you going to file an official report and admit to everything?'

'If I do that, I might as well hand in my resignation at the same time. This is not only unofficial, it's probably illegal as well. Well, it *is* illegal. You've just killed a man.'

'Self-defence. I wish I'd been there to kill Bobby Quilty, too.'

Katie saw that there was an old Zibro paraffin heater standing in the corner, probably placed there to mollify the drafts that came through the north-east-facing window in the middle of winter. She went across to it, opened up the front panel, and saw from the dial on the tank that it was over half full.

'You're joking, aren't you?' said Kyna.

'Why not? Bobby Quilty's dead, so he won't have anything to complain about.'

'Holy Saint Joseph.'

Katie lifted the fuel tank out of the paraffin heater and unscrewed the lid. The smell of the paraffin reminded her of her childhood, when her father had kept a paraffin heater on the upstairs landing to keep the bedrooms warm. She knew that what she was doing was madness, but her whole plan to rescue John and Kyna had been madness, right from the beginning, and it was better to see it through to its insane conclusion than to start trying to wrap it up by the book. She had seen too many operations falter and fail because officers had been unwilling to break the rules at a critical moment.

She walked from one end of the living room to the other, sloshing paraffin on to the carpet and the curtains. When she reached the couch, she put down the paraffin tank and gently lifted the stained sheet from John's feet. He whimpered and clutched at her arm, and she could see why. Both of his feet were ink-black and bubbling with pus, and the darkness had spread almost up to his knees.

'Here – help me lift him up,' she told Kyna.

'*I can't*,' whispered John. '*Just leave me here.*'

'You have to,' said Katie. 'We're going to burn the place down.'

'*Well, let me burn with it. I can't.*'

'John, we're going to do it anyway.'

Katie and Kyna put their arms around him, and between them they heaved him up to a standing position. He was panting and shuddering, and he kept closing his eyes tight shut because of the pain, but with Kyna supporting him he managed to stay upright.

As quickly as she could, Katie splashed paraffin on to the couch and the bloodstained sheet. Then she knelt down and rummaged in the sagging pockets of Ger's black jacket, her lips pursed tight with disgust, until she found his plastic cigarette-lighter. After that, she turned the tank upside down and emptied the last of the paraffin all over him. It wouldn't burn his body sufficiently to hide who he was, but it might obliterate any evidence of who had killed him.

'Right,' she said, with her eyes watering from the paraffin fumes. 'Let's get out of here.'

They both wrapped John's arms around their shoulders and half-carried, half-dragged him to the living-room door. Katie worked out in the gym whenever she could, but she was impressed with how strong Kyna was. She could almost have humped John out of the house by herself.

When they had managed to heave John into the hallway, Katie went back into the living room. She flicked Ger's lighter and set fire to the bottom of the curtains. Then she lit the hem of the bloodied sheet on the couch. When she lit the carpet, the flames scurried across the floor and set fire to the curtains at the other end. Finally, coughing from the fumes, she stood over Ger himself.

Although he had been so criminal and vicious, Katie still felt deeply disturbed about burning his body like this. This wasn't the way that people were supposed to end their lives – broken and alone and incinerated like so much rubbish. She also had an irrational feeling that, once he had burst into flames, he might jump up screaming.

'Come on,' Kyna urged her from the doorway. 'We need to go now. Poor John's going to drop at any minute.'

Katie bent down and lit the cuff of Ger's jacket. At once, he was enveloped in blue and green flames. His sparse grey hair shrivelled and the plastic frame of his sunglasses melted and dripped down the sides of his face, as if he were weeping black tears.

The heat in the living room suddenly began to intensify and the hot air made the fire burn even more fiercely. Flames were leaping up the curtains like angry dogs to lick at the ceiling, while the polyester covering of the couch was ablaze and its foam filling was already pouring out dense brown billows of noxious smoke.

Katie went back out into the hallway and lifted John's left arm around her shoulders. He looked as if he were close to losing consciousness, because his head kept dropping forward, but together she and Kyna carried him along the hallway to the front door. They passed the room where Ger had been watching television and seen the news that Bobby Quilty had died. The television was still on, but now it was showing a weather forecast. Persistent rain across Northern Ireland for the rest of the day, and tomorrow.

Kyna opened the front door and they carried John outside, his bare black feet trailing across the shingle.

Blinking against the drizzle, Katie said, 'My car's just across the road there, off to the right.'

She twisted her head around so that she could look behind her. Smoke was rising from the back of the house, thicker and thicker, and then she saw flames in the hallway.

They were only a third of the way up the driveway, however, when a dark blue van appeared from the direction of Forkhill and turned into it.

'Oh God,' said Kyna. 'The boys are back from Newry.'

Katie stopped, breathing hard from the effort of carrying John. She had her right arm around his waist and she was gripping his left hand tightly, so without letting go of him she wasn't able to pull out her gun. Kyna might have been able to keep him upright on her own, but she was panting, too. The only alternative would be to lie him down on the wet shingle driveway.

The dark blue van stopped about thirty metres ahead of them. Katie could see three men staring at them through the windscreen, with the wipers squeaking monotonously as they cleared away the drizzle.

Now the wipers stopped and three men climbed out. Two of them were the men who had held Kyna's arms while Ger head-butted her – the man with the widow's peak and the fair-haired spotty youth. The third was tall, with a chestnut-brown beard.

Katie could see a fourth man in the back of the van, but he stayed where he was.

'Hey! Where do you think you're heading off to?' shouted the thin man with the widow's peak. 'Look at it, Jesus, the whole fecking house is on fire! Where's Ger?'

Katie didn't turn around again to look at the house, but she could smell the smoke now because the drizzly wind was blowing from the south-west, and she could hear crackling and popping and the chiming of breaking windows. The three men started to walk slowly towards them, but she could see that none of them was very confident. She could imagine why they were so uncertain. There was no sign of Ger to tell them what to do, and even though the house was on fire they didn't know whether they ought to call the fire brigade. The fire brigade would call the police and that would mean they would be found out for keeping John and Kyna unlawfully imprisoned – not to mention any other illegal activities they might have been involved in, like tobacco-smuggling or drug-running or storing weapons for the Authentic IRA.

Katie was about to tell Kyna to try and support John for a few seconds while she took out her gun. She had only managed to say, 'Kyna, can you—' when there was a shattering bang from behind her and she felt a shock wave pushing the three of them from behind, like a gust of strong wind. The next thing she knew they were being showered with fragments of brick and tile and sparkling glass.

She looked around, and as she did so there was another explosion, even louder than the first, and half of the roof of the house appeared to jump into the air and then collapse completely into the floor below. A cloud of grey smoke rolled up into the rain, and then there was a third explosion, and a fourth, and then a sound like a hundred firecrackers. Part of the facade of the house fell forward, leaving a single chimney stack, and then that, too, teetered and fell sideways with a rattle of bricks.

What was left of the house was still burning and even some of the trees around the garage were ablaze. A huge ivy-covered oak had been uprooted by the blast and fallen on top of Ger's mustard-coloured Volvo, crushing the roof and shattering the windows.

'God Almighty!' shouted Kyna, because both of them were deafened now. 'Bobby Quilty's arms dump!'

The three men who had been approaching them were already running back to their van. They climbed into it and slammed the doors, and then the van swerved backwards, skidded on the wet road, and sped off, heading north.

There was a series of ten or eleven sharp bangs which Katie recognized as hand grenades. More debris flew up into the air and clattered on to the driveway all around them.

'Let's go!' Katie shouted. 'This time, I think God was on our side!'

Forty-five

Katie had only just returned home and given Barney a pat and a cuddle when Detective Inspector O'Rourke rang her.

'How's your family problem, ma'am?' he asked her.

'All sorted, thank you, Francis. I'll be back at my desk at the crack of dawn tomorrow.'

'That's grand. I've been trying not to bother you, but one or two things have cropped up. You've heard about Bobby Quilty, I suppose?'

'Yes. What a turn-up for the books that was. I'd say it was an act of God.'

'Well, whatever, there must have been be a rake of people on both sides of the border who breathed a sigh of relief when they heard that he'd been topped.'

'I certainly did,' said Katie. 'Any information yet on who did it?'

'That's a bit of a mystery at the moment. Of course, they're still examining the house where it happened, but Detective Inspector Humphreys called me from Knock Road and said that it looked like Quilty had intended to murder the people who lived there, for some inexplicable reason. He had them all tied up and he was going to blow them up with a briefcase full of plastic explosive and nails.'

'So, what went wrong? Or should I say right?'

'They don't know yet, not for sure. They can't work out how the bomb was triggered, although it was probably set off by a signal from a mobile phone. I can give you all the details when you come in tomorrow.'

'Do they know who these people were – the ones that Quilty wanted to kill?'

'A family called the Crothers. They had very strong loyalist connections, apparently, but that's hardly surprising. They lived in the Blackstaff ward, and that's more Orange than a case of Tanora.'

'Do they have any idea *why* he wanted to kill them?'

'Not at the moment. But there was one quare thing. Quilty was *shot*, as well as blown up, although they don't know yet who shot him. One of the seven people killed in the blast was an ex-PSNI police inspector, but he didn't appear to be armed. We'll obviously find out more when their technical experts have completed the forensics and they've finished collecting witness statements, but you know what they're like in Belfast. Very tight-lipped.'

'Thanks, Francis. I'm back home now, so you can ring me at any time.'

She put her iPhone down on the coffee table, while Barney looked at her expectantly, wagging his tail. The hopeful expression in his eyes said: *Walk, walk! Please say the word 'walk'!*

She tugged at Barney's ears, but before she could think about taking him for a walk she needed to know that John and Kyna were being treated, especially John. She rang CUH and spoke to a staff nurse in the Acute Medical Unit.

'John Meagher's extremely unwell, I'm sorry to tell you. His feet and his lower legs are badly infected. He's also seriously dehydrated. Doctor O'Connell has instigated several tests and we should be receiving the results tomorrow afternoon. We'll keep in touch with you, of course.'

Next she rang Kyna. She was at CUH, too, being treated for a skin infection.

'They've booked me in next week to have my nose reconstructed. Don't worry. In two or three weeks I'll be as beautiful as ever.'

'How are you feeling?' Katie asked her.

'You mean how am I feeling about Ger? Very mixed. I loathed him and I wanted to pay him back for hurting me like that, and most of all for not allowing John to be treated. But I honestly didn't mean to kill him. I would have preferred to see him sent to Portlaoise again. Then he would have suffered for the rest of his life and I wouldn't be feeling so guilty.'

'Anyway, take good care of yourself,' said Katie. 'Are you staying in the hospital or are they sending you home?'

'I'm just waiting for some pills and then they're going to discharge me.'

'You could come and stay with me for a while. I could use the company.'

There was a very long pause. Katie could hear hospital noises in the background, and a woman calling, '*Nurse!*' Then Kyna said, 'Thanks, Katie, but no . . . I think we've got each other into enough trouble already.'

'Somehow I don't really care any more.'

'Well, you should. This city would be a much worse place to live in if it wasn't for you.'

'I'll see you tomorrow so,' said Katie. 'Maybe you can meet me for lunch. How about Elbow Lane?'

'I don't know. The more I see you the more I want to stay here in Cork and I'm not so sure that we're very good for each other. Maybe in another life . . . if we were florists, or dress designers. Something girly and harmless. Besides, I don't really want to go out looking like this.'

'You look like you've walked into a door, that's all.'

'Every battered woman uses that excuse. No, Katie, let's leave it for a while. I can't thank you enough for what you did to rescue us – the risk you took. I think you're amazing. But I need to meditate for a while, and get myself back together again, body and spirit.'

'Okay,' said Katie, a little sadly. 'But call me when you're ready, won't you?'

'I promise.'

Katie switched off her iPhone and looked at Barney. He could sense that something was wrong because he cocked his head to one side and made that mewling noise in the back of his throat.

'Come on, Barns,' she told him, standing up. 'Let's go outside and get ourselves soaking wet.'

* * *

She was reading through the files that had been left on her desk when there was a complicated rapping at her office door. She looked up as Assistant Commissioner Jimmy O'Reilly came in.

'Katie,' he said. 'Francis O'Rourke told me that you'd been having some family problems.'

'They're all resolved now, thank you, sir.'

Jimmy O'Reilly stood watching her for a moment, then he cleared his throat and said, 'Fierce dramatic news about Bobby Quilty, wasn't it?'

'Yes, sir.'

'Not that much is going to change, I shouldn't think. Somebody else will take over the cigarette-smuggling, no doubt, and all the other rackets the Big Feller was running.'

'There's a couple of likely contenders,' said Katie. 'Matty Fegan, for one. I'm keeping a close eye on him. Fatty Matty Fegan.'

'It looks as if Bobby Quilty did us one favour, though,' said Jimmy O'Reilly. 'He caught the fellows who shot the Dohertys – even if he did set himself up as judge, jury and executioner, and execute himself in the process. I doubt if we would have found those Crothers in a million years.'

'I just wonder why he went after them,' said Katie.

'Come here to me? He went after them because they'd murdered his relations. To Bobby Quilty, that was a personal challenge. He couldn't let them go unpunished. Come on, Katie, you knew Bobby Quilty as well as any of us. To him, that would be unthinkable.'

'But how did he know it was them?'

'Because he had contacts everywhere in Belfast, didn't he? He knew everyone – republican, loyalist, and everybody in between. The PSNI are doing a thorough test on the Crothers' bodies, of course, and what remains of their house, but I was talking on the phone to Detective Chief Inspector MacReady about it yesterday afternoon and he was convinced that the Crothers shot the Dohertys. According to some of his informers, they were boasting about it in their local pub.'

'What I actually meant was, how did Bobby Quilty find out that he was related to the Dohertys?'

Jimmy O'Reilly frowned. 'How should I know? Perhaps he'd *always* known. Perhaps he looked up his family tree. You can do it online these days, can't you? Look Up Your Granny dot.com, or some such.'

Katie was tapping her pen on her desk like a metronome. She knew what she was going to say next, but she also knew that she would have to phrase it very carefully.

'I made a mistake,' she said.

'I don't understand. What kind of mistake?'

'I made a mistake when I was checking up on the Dohertys' genealogy.'

'And?' said Jimmy O'Reilly. It was obvious that he was beginning to sense that Katie was playing him along and he was growing irritated. 'What exactly are you trying to tell me?'

'Bobby Quilty wasn't related to the Dohertys. There *was* a Niall Quilty who served with Captain Frank Busteed, that's true – but he was shot by the British when he was only seventeen and he never got married and he never had a daughter. I mixed him up with somebody else.'

Jimmy O'Reilly stared at Katie as if she were a doctor who had just told him she had failed to diagnose the lump on his neck and he had less than six weeks to live.

'You mixed him up with somebody else?'

'Yes . . . silly mistake. I was working very late and I was tired. But the only person I told about Bobby Quilty being related to the Dohertys was you.'

'You gave me that family tree,' said Jimmy O'Reilly.

'Yes, I did, but it was erroneous. So I know how *you* came to believe that Bobby Quilty and the Dohertys were related. What I can't understand is how Bobby Quilty came to believe it, too.'

'I have no idea. It must have been a coincidence.'

'A coincidence?'

Jimmy O'Reilly suddenly grew angry. 'I've just told you – I have no idea! Maybe he had some other grievance against the Crothers! What are you trying to say here, Katie? Come on, spit it out! Are you accusing me of passing confidential information to Bobby Quilty?'

'Yes.'

'Give me one reason why I should have done. Go on!'

Katie stood up. 'I can give you several thousand reasons why, Assistant Commissioner, and all of them are euros. You were constantly borrowing money from Bobby Quilty to settle your boyfriend's gambling debts. Bobby Quilty had you in his pocket and so did James Elvin. In fact, James Elvin still does. He would only have to tell the media why you've been going easy on Bobby Quilty's cigarette-smuggling and you'd be finished.'

Jimmy O'Reilly looked at her with his eyes narrowed, then he walked over to the window. He watched the rain trickling down it for a while and then he said, 'What do you expect me to do now?'

'Nothing,' said Katie. 'I'm not the commissioner and I'm not the Garda Ombudsman. Well – there's one thing you *could* do, and that's to refuse to give James Elvin any more money. He might go to the media, but that's a risk you'll just have to take.'

Still watching the raindrops, Jimmy O'Reilly said, 'You're a witch, do you know that, Katie? Right from the beginning I said you were a witch, but nobody would listen. They were all too keen at Phoenix Park to be politically correct and show that the Garda were moving with the times.'

He turned around and said, 'You've *done* something, haven't you? You've pulled some fecking evil trick. I don't know what you've done or how you've done it, but I swear to God that I'll find out one day and I'll see you burned at the stake, like the witch that you are.'

Without saying anything else, he walked out of her office, leaving the door open behind him.

Katie sat down again. She was trembling slightly, but that was mostly from tiredness and the delayed shock from what she had been through the day before. She had dreamed about Ger last night, with his glutinous black plastic tears and the flames dancing out of his face. She had dreamed about Alan, too, and in her dream about Alan he had lifted his head from the kitchen floor in Felt Street and said, 'You don't love me, do you? So why did you make me love *you*?'

As soon as he had uttered those words, he vomited a huge gout of bright red blood and it splashed all over the floor.

* * *

It was almost lunchtime when Detective Ó Doibhilin came in to see her. She had heard nothing more from Assistant Commissioner O'Reilly, and when she had walked along to Chief Superintendent MacCostagáin's office to talk about a new gang of Romanian pimps who had opened up an internet page called Magic Massage, she had looked down into the car park and saw that his car had gone.

Detective Ó Doibhilin was holding up a plastic folder. 'Do you have a moment, ma'am? I've heard this morning from that Bracewaite fellow in Manchester – you know, the historian who was trying to see if he could find out more about Lieutenant Seabrook and Radha Langtry.'

'What's he come up with?' asked Katie.

'A letter. It's only the one letter, but I think it's shattering, do you know what I mean, like?'

He came over to her desk, set the folder down in front of her, and opened it. Inside, there were the scanned copies of two sheets of notepaper. They were handwritten, in a strong, well-formed hand, the kind of copperplate script that was taught in schools in late Victorian times.

It was headed 'Ballincollig Barracks, February 23rd'.

My dearest Jane,
I understand how much pain I have caused you by
my infidelity, and I beg your forgiveness. I can plead
only that the horrors of the Front and the unnatural
stress of fighting against the Fenians led me to seek
solace in another's arms; and for this I have no excuse
whatsoever, except to admit my own weakness.

Now, however, a tragedy has occurred and you are
the sole person to whom I can express my grief – a
grief which is compounded by the way in which I have
betrayed you. I have to tell someone about the terrible
events of the past three weeks or I will surely go mad.
I cannot confide in Lt. Col. Evans for that would
inevitably lead to my being cashiered.

The young woman with whom I was involved
was Mrs Radha Langtry, whose husband Stephen
was a member of the Irish Republican Army. She had
learned from her husband that an ambush of our
regular Friday patrol from Macroom to Cork had
been planned, at a place called Godfrey's Cross. He
had informed her because she daily went to work
that way, to Leemount House, the home of Mrs Mary
Lindsay, and he cautioned her to take another route.

Radha did not want me to be harmed, and that
is why she told me, but of course I had no choice
but to warn Lt. Col. Evans of the intended ambush.
However, she also warned her employer Mrs Lindsay,
because Mrs Lindsay was due to drive through
Godfrey's Cross that day to take her car to the
barracks here in Ballincollig for military inspection. (It
is a new regulation because of the number of cars that
have been commandeered recently by the IRA.)

Mrs Lindsay told the local priest, Father Ned
Shinnick, about the ambush, and he warned the IRA
command that their intended attack was no longer a

secret. Unfortunately he was known to have nationalist sympathies and they refused to believe him.

The consequence of this was disastrous. You may have seen in the newspapers that the IRA party were surprised and outflanked and eight of them were captured. They are being held in Victoria Barracks in Cork, court-martialled, and found guilty, and may very well be shot.

Because she is such a staunch nationalist, the IRA blamed Mrs Lindsay for this catastrophy [sic] and have abducted both her and her chauffeur. I have to assume that under great duress Mrs Lindsay informed her captors that it was Radha who had warned her about the ambush.

I attempted to contact Radha, but without success. Eventually I was informed by the local priest in Blarney, Father Thomas, that the Langtry family had decided on the spur of the moment to emigrate to America. I found this difficult to believe, since Radha had never mentioned that she and her husband had any such intention.

The priest saw that I was greatly distressed and took some pity on me. He told me in the utmost confidence that the Langtrys had not, in fact, emigrated, but that the local IRA commander had ordered that they be punished for informing the British about the ambush. Their friends and relatives would believe that they had gone to America because letters would be regularly sent home here to Ireland by IRA sympathisers in New York.

I tried to persuade Father Thomas to tell me what the Langtrys' punishment might have been, but he refused to say any more. Although of course I am not a Roman Catholic he granted me absolution but of what possible use was that?

*I am trying to cling to the belief that the Langtrys
may have been forced to move to another part of
Ireland, but in my heart of hearts, my dearest Jane, I
know they have not. I know that they have been shot,
and their bodies buried somewhere in the mountains,
or in a peat bog, and that they will never be discovered.
What has become of their two children I cannot guess.*

*You will hate me for this, Jane, but I always loved
you and I love you still, in spite of my treachery. I am
riven with grief, and I have been weeping so bitterly
that I have to pretend to my men that I have an eye
infection.*

*You will probably burn this letter and forget that
you ever knew me, but I had to share my agony with
somebody, and also tell how it really came about that
the IRA ambush was foiled.*

*If I had not had a relationship with Radha, our
own soldiers would have been killed; but since I did,
eight Irishmen will almost certainly be executed, and
Radha is surely dead, too. How can there be a God, if
these were the only alternatives which He gave me?*

*I am crying now, my dearest dearest, as I write this
to you. I am so sorry for what I have done, and the
pain is unbearable. Give my fondest love to Kitty and
James.*

Yours, Gerald.

Katie read the letter again and then sat back. 'Mother of God. Where did this historian of yours find this? I mean, like, it sheds entirely new light on the Dripsey ambush. It looks like poor Mrs Lindsay and her chauffeur, they weren't to blame at all.'

'He found it in the files in the family solicitors' office,' said Detective Ó Doibhilin. 'He says there's some other correspondence from the time that shows that all of the Seabrook family were aware of it, but didn't want to shame Gerald's name, especially since he was killed only a few weeks later. They preferred Jane Seabrook to be the grieving widow of a military hero, rather than the abandoned wife of a love rat who got himself tangled up with the IRA.'

'I'll have to talk to Chief Superintendent MacCostagáin about this,' said Katie. 'Maybe this is something that needs to be filed and forgotten. As if enough innocent people haven't lost their lives because Lieutenant Seabrook "sought solace in another's arms".'

'I'll leave it with you, then,' said Detective Ó Doibhilin.

'Thanks, Michael. You've done some incredible work on this. I'll make sure you get a commendation for it.'

Detective Ó Doibhilin left her office and she picked up the letter and read it yet again. *Love*, she thought, *what disasters it can lead to*. If Lieutenant Seabrook hadn't fallen in love with Radha, the Doherty family would still be alive – and if she hadn't loved both John and Kyna, Bobby Quilty wouldn't have taken them hostage, with all of the fatalities that had followed, especially Alan's.

Her phone warbled. It was Detective O'Donovan.

'Patrick! What's the story?'

'We've just had a message from the PSNI. There was a serious house fire yesterday up at a village called Forkhill, near Newry. Not only a fire, a series of major explosions. They reckon the house contained an arms dump for an IRA splinter group, although they're not naming any names yet, except for one.'

'Go on. Was it somebody we know?'

'Only Ger Carmody, burnt to a cinder. They believe it was, anyway, because his car was outside and they found what was left of his hat.'

'Ger Carmody? What was he doing up in South Armagh?'

'Search me. But what a day, ma'am, wouldn't you say? What a result! Bobby Quilty and Ger Carmody both going off to meet their Maker within hours of each other. You didn't say a prayer to St Bonaventura by any chance?'

'Why St Bonaventura?'

'He's the patron saint of bowel disorders. If you'll excuse my language, my auld feller used to say that he takes care of all the shits.'

Forty-six

The following morning she drove to Cork University Hospital before she went into the station. It had rained heavily during the night but now the clouds had cleared and it was sunny and humid.

She had pressed the button for the lift when her iPhone played '*Buile Mo Chroí*'.

A distant voice said, 'Is that Detective Superintendent Maguire?'

'It is, yes. Who is this?'

'Inspector Wallace from the Crime Operations Unit in Belfast.'

'Oh, yes, inspector? How can I help?'

'I'm a friend of Alan Harte. I was the one who passed him your bulletin about your two missing persons. Have you heard about Alan?'

'What about him?'

'He's dead, I'm sorry to say. You obviously know about that bomb in Belfast, the one that killed Bobby Quilty and six other individuals. Well, Alan was one of those six individuals.'

'Oh, God. That's tragic.'

'I know. I'm sorry to give you such bad news. He told me that he was in contact with you. After I told him about the bulletin and he realized you were after Bobby Quilty – well, he was itching to talk to you. He couldn't wait.'

'Yes, he came down to Cork to see me,' said Katie. 'We exchanged information about Quilty, but that was about all we could do. Quilty was never an easy man to corner, as you know.'

'We're still going over the house where it happened, and we will be for several days yet,' said Inspector Wallace. 'One of the things that has us really puzzled, though, is that Bobby Quilty was shot and fatally wounded before the bomb went off. We thought at first that Alan might have shot him, but there's no sign at all of the gun he might have used. One of the other individuals had a weapon, but it wasn't the same calibre as the gun that killed Quilty, and it had only been fired once, while Quilty was shot three times.'

'Maybe somebody else came into the house and shot him but left before the bomb went off.'

'Well, it's possible. But I'd like to know who had more of a motive for shooting Bobby Quilty than Alan.'

'Yes – he told me about Quilty setting him up with all those drugs,' said Katie.

There was a long pause, and then Inspector Wallace said, 'Drugs? What drugs?'

Katie was confused. 'Alan told me that Quilty planted heroin in his house so that he would be suspected of drug-dealing, and that's why he had to resign from the PSNI.'

'I don't know why he should have told you that,' said Inspector Wallace. 'Maybe he didn't want to tell you the real reason.'

'You mean it wasn't true? He resigned because of something else?'

'He resigned because he simply couldn't handle the job any more. He was right on the verge of having a breakdown. He couldn't think of anything else but killing Bobby Quilty. He probably didn't tell you because you would have thought that he was obsessed and unstable and you wouldn't have cooperated with him.'

'So why was he so determined to kill Quilty?' asked Katie.

'He was building a good case against Quilty for drug-smuggling. Quilty knew that he had some sound evidence, and even a couple of witnesses, and was getting quite close to arresting him. So Quilty sent him a message that if he didn't lay off, his family would all be shot, one by one, starting with his wife.'

'I thought that he and his wife were divorced.'

'Are you joking? They were totally inseparable, those two. He would have run stark-naked down the Falls Road if she had asked him to. But Alan called Quilty's bluff and went on gathering evidence against him, and one day Alison was coming out of Wyse Byse and a fellow walked up to her and shot her in the head.'

Katie didn't know what to say. All of a sudden, everything about Alan and his behaviour made sense. And now she knew who the woman was in the framed picture on Alan's bookshelf.

'Detective Superintendent Maguire?' said Inspector Wallace.

'Oh, sorry. What? That – that just took me by surprise.'

'I wondered if you wanted to attend Alan's funeral. I don't have a date yet, of course, but I can let you know when I do.'

'Yes, please do. And thank you for calling me.'

Another pause, and then he said, 'I haven't upset you, have I?'

* * *

She took the lift up to the Acute Medical Unit. At the nurses' station she was met by Staff Nurse Abara, a small, dark, quietly spoken woman with huge brown eyes. Katie had met her several times before and had always thought that she would have taken holy orders if she hadn't trained as a nurse.

Nurse Abara led her along the corridor to the room where John was being treated.

'He is sleeping now,' she said. 'We have given him a massive dose of antibiotics and in the meantime we are considering the various options for treatment.'

She opened the door and they went inside. John was lying on his back, with his eyes closed. He was wearing an oxygen mask and was attached to two intravenous drips. Underneath the mask his face was so pale that he looked as if he were wearing white foundation. There was a hump under the lower half of his blanket where a cage protected his feet and calves.

Katie approached the bed and stood and watched him breathing. He was so deeply asleep that she could tell he wasn't going to wake up.

'So, what *are* the options?' she asked.

'Dr O'Connell can tell you all about them in greater detail when he comes in later. But John's feet and his legs up to his knees are gangrenous and he will require some very radical treatment. One option is debridement, where all the gangrenous flesh is surgically cut away. There is also maggot therapy, which can be very successful in cases of gangrene.'

'Yes, I've heard of that. I didn't know you did it here.'

'Yes, we breed tiny bacteria-free maggots in the laboratory. We bandage them firmly to the gangrenous flesh and they eat it. The wonderful thing about maggots is that they don't touch the healthy flesh, and they also give off substances that kill bacteria and promote healing.'

'Is there another option?' Katie asked her.

'Well, yes, there is, of course, and I'm afraid that Dr O'Connell is already thinking that he won't have any choice.'

Katie reached out towards John's curly black hair, but didn't touch him. She wondered if he were dreaming, and what about. *Once you leave Ireland, you can never go back. Not for good. Everything you loved here will destroy you, in the end. Your memories, your friends – not to mention the music, and the rain.*

'You're talking about amputation,' said Katie.

Staff Nurse Abara nodded. 'Below the knee, hopefully.'

'Both legs?'

'Yes.'

'And then what? Prosthetic legs?'

'They're marvellous these days. Even if we do have to amputate, which we probably will, he'll still be capable of leading a very full life.'

Katie took a deep breath. 'Does he know this?'

'Dr O'Connell has briefly discussed it with him, yes.'

'And what did he say?'

'He said that he was lucky that he survived, and that he owes his life to you, although he didn't explain how, or why.'

'Is that all?'

'No. He also said that he wasn't afraid of the future, even if he did have to lose his legs. You saved him and he knows now that you're always going to take care of him.'

* * *

Katie didn't wait to talk to Dr O'Connell. She walked quickly back along the corridor and went down in the lift. She was shaking again, even worse than after the bomb. She kept her face turned away from the mirror so that she wouldn't have to look at herself, as if she had been disfigured in a serious accident.

Below the knee, hopefully. He knows now that you're always going to take care of him.

As she crossed the reception area the revolving door flashed with reflected sunlight and Kyna came in, in a loose white sweater and jeans, with a plaster across the bridge of her nose.

Katie didn't say a word but went up to her and put her arms around her and held her tight. Several people stared at the two of them as they passed by, but Katie couldn't see them because she was blinded with tears.